Arthur Fenton Hort

Life and Letters of Fenton John Anthony Hort

Arthur Fenton Hort

Life and Letters of Fenton John Anthony Hort

ISBN/EAN: 9783337016432

Printed in Europe, USA, Canada, Australia, Japan

Cover: Foto ©Raphael Reischuk / pixelio.de

More available books at **www.hansebooks.com**

Life and Letters

of

Fenton John Anthony Hort

D.D., D.C.L., LL.D.

SOMETIME HULSEAN PROFESSOR AND LADY MARGARET'S READER

IN DIVINITY IN THE UNIVERSITY OF CAMBRIDGE

BY HIS SON

ARTHUR FENTON HORT

LATE FELLOW OF TRINITY COLLEGE, CAMBRIDGE

' A life devoted to truth is a life of vanities abased and
ambitions forsworn.'—F. J. A. H.

VOL. I

London

MACMILLAN AND CO. Ltd.

NEW YORK: MACMILLAN & CO.

1896

TO

My Mother

I REVERENTLY OFFER

THIS BOOK

PREFACE

THE subject of this Memoir was little known outside
the world of scholars ; and his published work could
give but a partial view of the man, while in him the
man was more even than the scholar.   A scholar's life
contains little of outward incident, and it has been my
endeavour to tell the story of my father's life so far
as possible in his own words.   In all that he wrote his
real self is shown, and nowhere more than in his letters.
Hence this book may perhaps justify itself, if it enables
the voice of a man who was interested in such a
variety of subjects, and who spoke always with such
' singular sincerity,' to reach beyond the limited circle
of those who were privileged to know him in life.

For the earlier years at least the epistolary material
is enough, I think, to give a very fair portraiture.
In later years his letters became inevitably fewer
and shorter, but in all cases I have not scrupled to
insert letters which, whatever their subjects, help
to show what the writer was, as well as what he
did and thought.   I should add perhaps that in his
letters he was wont to express his opinions with considerable freedom ; he would unburden himself to a

friend with a remarkable absence of the reserve which otherwise characterised his utterances. For this very reason it would not be right to give to the world without a caution views which he never meant for publication ; moreover, his letters, even of undergraduate days, often show a maturity of thought and expression which is apt to make one forget the writer's age.

In the brief narrative which accompanies the selection of correspondence, I have aimed generally at little more than filling up with necessary dates and facts the story presented in the letters. For obvious reasons a critical biography could not be part of my plan, and, if my narrative is more than necessarily jejune, it is because I have tried so far as possible to avoid a tone of eulogy which would have been very unfitting, and which my father would vehemently have deprecated— if indeed he would have approved of his life being written at all. I am conscious, however, that I have not altogether succeeded in keeping the balance ; I could wish that this were the only shortcoming in the execution of a task which has been one of considerable difficulty as well as of extreme delight. I have quoted freely from the words, written or printed, of others, especially in cases where I could claim no special knowledge, or where it was difficult for a son to adopt the necessary ' detachment ' of attitude.

To all such, and to very many others, named or unnamed in these pages, I am deeply indebted ; especially to the Bishop of Durham, for the generous freedom which he has allowed me in the use of his letters ; to Mrs. Ellerton, for invaluable help of the same kind ; to Professor Ryle, who, to his numerous other acts of devotion to my father's name, has added that of reading the proofs and giving me his counsel ; and above all, to one without whose constant aid I could not have attempted this book.

I desire also to thank Miss J. Craig for clerical assistance, given in a manner and in a spirit on which my father himself would have bestowed the praise of 'guileless workmanship.'

A. F. H.

HARROW-ON-THE-HILL, *November* 1895.

CONTENTS

CHAPTER I

PARENTAGE AND CHILDHOOD

1828-1841

FENTON JOHN ANTHONY HORT was born at Dublin the 23rd of April 1828. His father, Fenton Hort, was the grandson of Josiah Hort, who is the earliest of the name of whom any record is preserved. Josiah's father lived at Marshfield, near Bath, but that is the solitary fact in his history handed down to his descendants. His son, of whom an account is given in the *Dictionary of National Biography*, was brought up as a Nonconformist, and was a schoolfellow and lifelong friend of Isaac Watts,[1] who spoke of him as "the first genius in the academy," viz. an academy for Nonconformist ministers to which they both belonged. Hort conformed after a time to the Church of England, and went to Clare College, Cambridge ; in 1709 he crossed to Ireland as chaplain to Earl Wharton, the Lord-Lieutenant. Lord Wharton's chaplain presently obtained a parish, whence he rose, through the deaneries of Cloyne and Ardagh, and two bishoprics, of Ferns and Leighlin, and of Kilmore and Ardagh, to be Archbishop of Tuam. He enjoyed some repute as a preacher, and a volume of his

---

[1] See Milner's *Life of Dr. Watts* (Cambridge, 1834).

sermons "on practical subjects" went through several
editions. He is said to have been the last magnate
who ate his dinner from a wooden trencher. Dean
Swift made a violent attack upon him in a satirical
poem ; the rise of the English clergyman was apparently
unpopular in Ireland, and he had to contend with much
opposition. Swift, however, became afterwards so far
friendly that he procured for Hort (or Horte, as he
sometimes spelt his name) the publication of a satire
on the prevalence of the game of quadrille in society.
He was disabled from preaching by an overstrain of the
voice some years before he became Archbishop. In the
preface to his sermons he uses his own experience to
point a warning to "all young preachers whose organs
of speech are tender." The secret, he says, of public
speaking lies " in finding out the right key." He depre-
cates loudness and vehemence, and concludes with the
remark : "Experience shows that a moderate Degree
of Voice, with a proper and distinct Articulation, is
better understood in all Parts of a Church than a
Thunder of Lungs that is rarely distinct, and never
agreeable to the Audience." The sermons themselves
are expressed in simple and dignified language ; indeed
the English is perhaps better than the divinity. The
author shows an anxiety to interpret the Bible in a
manner "agreeable to the Principles of Philosophy and
Morality," and he displays some ingenuity in the
attempt ; for instance, when he explains the doctrine of
Original Sin by the suggestion that the tree of which
Adam ate contained in its juice a "slow poison which,
being incorporated with the Blood of our first Parents,
might in a natural course be transfused through the
Veins of all their Posterity, and carry with it irregular
Desires and Passions, as well as Diseases and Death."

This somewhat startlingly literal exegesis is illustrated by reference to "a Tree in our American colonies (the Manchineel Tree) that bears a very beautiful apple, which yet has poisoned many." The author is perhaps more fortunate in his practical discourses, one of which is entitled, "Great knowledge no excuse for neglecting to hear sermons," while another contains a rather forcible protest against duelling : " I could therefore wish," he concludes, "that our gallant spirits would consider these Things when Affronts are broiling in their Stomachs, and their Blood is kindling to draw the Sword for an ill-chosen or ill-understood Word."

The Archbishop died in 1751. In his will he exhorted his children to carry out his intentions in their obvious sense, "without having recourse to law and the subtilty of lawyers"; in case of difficulty, he desires them to refer the question to "the decision of persons of known probity and wisdom, this being not only the most Christian, but the most prudent and cheap and summary way of deciding all differences."

He had married the Lady Elizabeth Fitzmaurice, daughter of the Lord of Kerry; their second son, John, married the daughter of Sir Fitzgerald Aylmer, of Donadea, who belonged to a branch of the Butler family; moreover, two of the Archbishop's daughters married into the Caldwell and Coghill families respectively, so that not many years after Josiah's migration the Horts had established a fair claim to be considered Irish.

John Hort was appointed in 1767 Consul-General at Lisbon, and was made a baronet the same year. He was sent out by Lord Lansdowne as a trusted semi-political agent, and it appears that the Government and the English ambassador were often annoyed because earlier information was thus obtained than they could themselves command. Attempts were made to detain him in England, but he spent thirty years in Portugal, and then retired on a pension. An estate in Co. Kildare, called Hortland, came to him on the death of his elder brother. If one may judge of him by a fine portrait, he was a man of considerable power. He is said to have been of peculiar temperament, and something of a martinet.

Sir John had three sons and two daughters. The third son, Fenton, who was the father of the subject of this memoir, was educated at Westminster School and at Trinity College, Cambridge, where he obtained a scholarship. He was one of the original members of the Union Debating Society, which was founded in 1815, and temporarily suppressed by authority in 1817, W. Whewell being at the time president and C. Thirlwall secretary.

In 1830, four years after his marriage to Anne Collett, daughter of a Suffolk clergyman, and descended, I believe, from Dean Colet, Fenton Hort bought a house near Dublin, called Leopardstown ; it was delightfully situated at the foot of the Three Rock Mountain, with a view of Dublin Bay in front. Here, after his father's death, his mother lived with him for part of the year ; the rest he spent at her house in Merrion Square, Dublin.

At this house on St. George's Day, 1828, Fenton, his eldest son, was born. When he was nine years old, his father sold Leopardstown, and migrated to Cheltenham, after a temporary residence at Kelsall Hall, lent him by Mr. Collett, and a short stay at Boulogne, where Fenton at the age of ten was sent to his first school. His master, a Mr. Bird, in December

1838 reported of his pupil as "by far more industrious
and advanced than any of his class-fellows ; in fact, he
renders all the rest lazy since they all depend on him
for 'the construe.'" He was then about to begin
"Homer and Xenophon's Anabasis with Horace or
Virgil and Cicero." At Cheltenham Mr. Fenton Hort
resided in various houses till 1851, his mother living
with him till her death in 1843. The move from
Leopardstown was made rather suddenly, and my
father was never in Ireland again till he went to Dublin
in 1888 to receive an honorary degree from the
University. On this occasion, after the lapse of over
fifty years, he drew overnight from memory a plan of
the house and grounds at Leopardstown, which he the
next day compared with the reality, and found to be
completely accurate. Of his early years there and at
Cheltenham it is unfortunately impossible to recover
more than a fragmentary account. He used to look
back to the Leopardstown home and days with the
most loving recollection, especially when across a time
of grievous troubles that earliest period stood out as
one of peculiar peace and happiness. Many years later,
in describing the Fellows' garden at Trinity, he dwelt
with a special delight on the flowers, the blue Apennine
anemone and the scented *Daphne Cneorum*, which he
associated with favourite nooks in the beautiful old Irish
garden.

School letters show the kind of relation which
existed between Fenton and the rest of the home
circle. Of the father no truer description could be
given than that contained in a touching letter [1] written
by his eldest son to his own children in 1878. His
quiet, unostentatious, unselfish nature comes back to

[1] See vol. ii. pp. 198-201.

those who knew it with almost a regret, as if its beauty, even by reason of its own self-forgetfulness, had been at the time but half realised. He had no profession, but was always a busy man. In the Irish days he was much occupied with the administration of the Poor Law, and with many other kindred things. In Cheltenham he took up the same kind of work, visited a great deal among the poor, and had a considerable share in the establishment of the Cheltenham Proprietary College, of which he became a governor. The same unobtrusive devotion was shown in the direction of his own household, where a strict *régime* prevailed, and all were expected to conform to the rules of the house. Towards his children he was all gentleness and tenderness, though his training of them, like their mother's, was based on implicit obedience. Though not demonstrative in showing affection, he was a man who loved much and felt much ; the past, especially the past of his own family, was constantly with him. He was a most tender son to the mother who shared his home till her death ; the loss of his sister at an early age was a calamity whose effect had not worn off at the very end of his life. He treasured little memorials of those whom he had lost with almost womanly care. One characteristic at least he bequeathed to his son, a fastidious love of order and method. This trait is curiously illustrated by the numerous ingeniously contrived cardboard boxes, still extant, and sometimes of the oddest shapes, which he delighted to make ; his wife called them his 'contraptions.' In a word, he was thoroughly domestic ; home to him was everything, and the home life was a real society. Parents and children spent long evenings together after six-o'clock dinner, and the father frequently read aloud, Scott being perhaps the favourite author. This custom survived long after all the children were grown up.

The mother, who, unconsciously perhaps, was the real controlling force of the household, was a woman of great mental power, which she brought to bear on every detail of daily life. She had been extremely well educated, so far as the opportunities of that day allowed ; in English especially her training had been sound, and she could always express herself easily and gracefully ; both in writing and in speaking she used words in the most exact manner. Her education had given her the thoroughness and scrupulous accuracy which she transmitted to her son. She grasped firmly whatever she took in hand and mastered any book which she read. Her reading was not wide, but she was interested in current literature of the more serious sort, such as biographies and books of travel. Her religious feelings were deep and strong. Circumstances had made her an adherent of the Evangelical school, and she was to a certain degree hampered by it ; the Oxford Movement filled her with dread and anxiety as to its possible effect on her son. She was unable to enter into his theological views, which to her school and generation seemed a desertion of the ancient ways ; thus, pathetically enough, there came to be a barrier between mother and son. The close inter-course on subjects which lay nearest to the hearts of each was broken, to the loss and sorrow of both. His love and veneration for his mother remained unimpaired, and his letters to her show his delicate consideration for her different point of view ; but it is sad that he should have had to recognise that the point of view *was* different. She studied and knew her

Bible well, and her own religious life was most carefully
regulated. She had a fine ear for music, and it was
a rare pleasure to hear her read aloud. Her spirits
were naturally high, and she faced the ordinary ups
and downs of life with cheerful courage ; but ill-health,
brought on probably by the loss, within a few months,
of two of her children, robbed her of her natural
brightness and caused often painful depression. In
bringing up her children she was strong enough to
be able to combine the enforcement of very strict
domestic discipline with close sympathy in all childish
ways and interests. The very keynote of her character
was truthfulness ; untruth in any shape was her ab-
horrence. Almost equally characteristic was her
hatred of all half performance. " I hate mediocrity "
was one of her many favourite sayings. It is easy to
understand how straight, under such guidance, the path
of duty became to her children ; the daily tasks must
be learnt and said, and nothing might stand in the
way. There is a story of her sitting with her eldest
son on a roll of carpet during some ' flitting ' of the
family, and going through the appointed lessons, with
which no temporary discomfort could be allowed to
interfere. Yet she was no Spartan mother ; strength
of will and inflexibility of purpose did not make her,
any more than they made her son, incapable of tenderness. It is difficult to analyse such a character.
This sketch must suffice to indicate the nature of her
influence on her family. To her it is evident that in
a great degree her son owed his absolute truthfulness
of soul, uprightness of character, and overmastering
sense of duty ; and not least, the deep trust in God
which he inherited from her own courageous conviction, and which was strengthened by her careful

religious training. This was based upon a close
study of the Bible, of the children's knowledge of
which in quite early years records remain which might
astonish many older children. The effects of such
training were very deep and lasting, however much
particular theological opinions were modified in later
years ; the simple piety and reverential spirit which
passed from mother to son remained unaffected by
time and experience.

At the time of the move from Ireland there were
four children—two girls and two boys ; the second boy,
Arthur, was three years Fenton's junior ; his sisters,
Margaret and Catharine, were born in 1830 and 1833
respectively. A third daughter, Josephine, was born
at Boulogne in 1838, but died at the age of three.
This was the beginning of trouble. Only five months
later Arthur, a child whose sweetness of disposition
and bright intelligence impress one wonderfully even in
the slight records of his short life, died from the after-
effects of measles. His loss had the profoundest effect
on his brother. The series of diaries which he kept from
1842 to 1892 is broken only once, and that during a
period of two and a half years from Arthur's death.

The family having settled in Cheltenham, Fenton
was sent in the spring of 1839, being then just eleven
years old, to the well-known preparatory school of the
Rev. John Buckland at Laleham, where he stayed till
the end of the following year. Mr. Buckland laid
great stress on accurate grammatical knowledge, and
required rules of syntax to be learnt by heart, but he
mentions in a letter to Mr. Fenton Hort that he does
not any longer insist on the *propria quae maribus* or
the *as in praesenti* being committed to memory. The
learning of large quantities of Latin verse was in

vogue at Laleham, as at Rugby, the first two books of
the odes of Horace, for instance, being set as a 'prize-
task' to boys of twelve or thirteen. Mr. Buckland's
first regular report of Fenton speaks of him as "a very
promising pupil," and says that there is no doubt of
his becoming "a first-rate scholar." A year later he
speaks in even higher terms, and he does not seem to
have been a man who shrank from giving true reports
to the parents. At the age of twelve and a half the
boy had apparently been well grounded in Classics,
Algebra, and the first three books of Euclid. Mr.
Buckland's chief complaint was that he wanted more
taste for games. At the time of his leaving Laleham
he predicts a distinguished future as the certain outcome of his "indefatigable perseverance and foundation
of good scholarship." When asked by Mr. Hort to
point out any flaws in the boy's character, he mentions
that he has heard of him as somewhat overbearing
with other boys, a characteristic which assuredly was
not permanent. Of his home letters from Laleham
unfortunately none have been preserved, but a delightful picture of the relations between the brothers is
given by Arthur's letters of the year 1840, when he
was eight to nine years old ; and the parents' letters
add something to the impression. It is difficult to
make out at this distance of time what they thought of
their eldest son ; it is certain that they recognised his
ability and force of character, and it is equally certain
that they never put him forward or in any way made
a show of him. Separate copies of Fenton's letters
from school and of extracts from his reports were made
by the father for himself and his wife, and preserved in
neat cases made by his own hand.

Fenton seems very early to have established a sort

of ascendancy at home. Probably the characteristic which chiefly impressed those around him was his force. Definiteness of purpose and unswerving, almost stern, rectitude of conduct seem terms hardly applicable to childhood, but it is evident that in some such unusual ways he stood out as a marked child among those of his own age. It is likely that he was not a favourite with other children generally, and it is the more pleasant to observe how entirely he and his brother understood each other; and the scores of playful letters which his sister Kate wrote to him help to show that he was regarded at home with respect, but not with distant respect; yet one gathers that even there he was looked up to with a feeling not far removed from fear, as a being of character somewhat alarmingly strong and unyielding. Yet the sweetness of disposition, which was perhaps the most conspicuous side of his character to those who learnt to know him in his latest years, is discernible in his earliest letters, in which moreover nothing comes out so clearly as his thorough boyishness. On the sunny side of his disposition he had much in common with his brilliant and delightful younger sister (afterwards Mrs. Garnons Williams), who survived him but a month. No picture of him as he was in those days has survived, but he is said to have been singularly beautiful as a little child ; his wonderful blue eyes, which spoke eloquently of the vigorous life within, particularly impressed all those who came across him. One of the very few who can remember him as a child recalls that " he was so fond of reading that he generally buried himself in some nook with a book, and his mother often laughed at his gravity and studious habits. He was reserved and silent, always kind and amiable in manner, and unselfish, but we all were surprised at the way he came out in conversation ; as a young man he could talk on any topic, and his company was a real treat."

FROM HIS BROTHER, ARTHUR JOSIAH HORT (AGED 8½)[1]

FARNLEY LODGE, *Wenesday, February* 19*th*, 1840.
[CHELTENHAM]

Dearest Fenton—I was very glad to hear from you. I want to know what was the name of the room in which you sleep. I have begun Greek with Mr. Kershaw I shall say to-day τιμη I think that the caracters are rather easy and that the funnyist small letter is Xi ξ. I have nearly finished the As in praesenti. I am not going to do any more of it. You have had Arnold's Greek Exercises before havenot you ? but not done them. As to being out of Ellirs I do not wonder because you have been at them a long time ever since you were with the 2d Mr. Smith. I saw on a board that there would be a steeplechase on April 1st. Papa thinks it is an April fool. I forgot to tell you that Mr. Kershaw has begun to give me marks such as Bene, Optime. to-day I had my first one it was Bene.

Was Priestley at all hurt when he knocked his head against the wall ? is he older than the former Priestley ? Madmoiselle Gobet sends her compliments to you and told me not to forget to remember you not to forget her. You have the same for your Prize-task as you thought you would have. I have given up the Elegy written in a Country Churchyard because it is so long and so mournful that I cannot learn it so quick as another thing however I intend learning another thing I have not fixed upon one yet. Do you intend going on with Henry 4th's Soliloquy on sleep. Do you know what Stone will have for his Prize-task or wether it is true that he is going away I have redd most of "Lamb's Tales from Shakspeare." I think Puck was a funny fellow in the Midsummer's night dream.

[1] The boys' letters in this and the next chapter are printed with the original spelling and punctuation.

Grandmamma told us a funny story of old Catty who was a servant of Lady Aylmer. Catty begged to sleep in a little room that was not in the house but near the Garden stove. after a few nights Catty came to Lady Aylmer and begged to be taken back to sleep in the house she said she heard the Fairies go by crying Quis Quis Quis Quis   Miss Sharland Mag Kit Nurse and Lucy all send their love to you Goodbye dear Fenton and Believe me your ever affectionate Brother,   A. J. Hort.

Post-Script.—Excuse Bad writing blots mistakes etc[r.]

From his Brother

Farnley Lodge, *February 25th,* 1840.

Dearest Fenton—I think you asked me in your last letter but one if I ever played cricket with Nurse I never play it now.   We have had several falls of snow since you went to Laleham but the snow has all melted away.   You said you hoped I like Greek I like it very much.   I did not know that you ever had the mark Melius.   I do not wonder that you are surprised at our going on with Mdle. Gobet.   Our quarter is up but we are to have 8 lessons more though only on Wenesdays.   As to Greek I know all the caracters pretty well η and μ sadly puzzle me they are so much akin.   When will you begin learning your Prize-task ?   I have looked at that board since and I am afraid it is not an April fool as it is annual.   I found the tracts you gave me I showed Mr. Kershaw your Musæ Musam eating Rasberry jam and he laughed heartily at it.   If you like that when a magazine comes I should send you the heads of the index I will do so if not tell me in your next letter.   I hope when you say your Prize-task you will say it without a mistake   I have fixed upon Cowper's tithe paying here it is

1 VERSE

Now all unwecome at his gate
the clumsy swains alight
with rueful faces and bald pates
he trembles at the sight

2 VERSE

I will not give you any more of it except one verse because I daresay you know it.   5th verse.

> one wipes his nose upon his
> sleeve one spits upon the floor
> yet not to give offence or grieve
> holds up the cloth before.

I think Cowper must have had some very funny ideas in his head when he wrote it.

FROM HIS BROTHER

FARLEY LODGE, *April 15th*, 1840.

Dearest Fenton—As it is my turn to write to you I must scribble a few lines. We have not been to the royal wells for a week so I cannot tell about the Cockeys our gardens are in pretty good order. We got this morning 4 Sweetwilliams 4 pinks 4 Phyollox and 4 Polyanthuses plants one each and 1 of them for you. Papa and Mamma gave them to us. As to Greek I am learning the Adjectives   I will send you a small plan of our gardens here it is. . . . Here is a little note from Kit. Wednesday   Dear Jim Crow   I have finished " Le premier pas " and learnt " Leiber Augustin " " the Guaracha " and the " national Russian waltz " and a few other tunes. Goodbye.   C. Hort.

My seeds are nasturtium, Mignionette Coronella Secunda Lord Anson's peas Sweet pea and Major Convolvolus. Mag mistook a little about the Zoologicals there were 3 sea eagles instead of 2 no grand show of birds among the stuffed I noticed the following—

Sacred Ibis, Gulls, Stork, White owl, Spoonbill and a couple of stuffed monkeys not in a case   As to living there were few birds there were however some cockeys canarys bul and Chaf-inches parrots and piping crow from New Holland as also a few doves Golden pheasants, common pheasants and foreign and common partridges. The east India people are silent for the present   The Chinese are irruptious as the last accounts said there was a naval engagement.   there are a good many men of war lying about Chili.   I think they ought to say " We will lick you if we can " instead of " We will

lick you "—but they have said neither but I hope, they
will make *peace*. Babsy sends you 60 kisses, and Meg or
rather Peg with a wooden leg Kit Charles Baby's pap mum
and Gander all send their loves to you. Goodbye dearest
Sen and believe me your ever affectionate Brother,

ARTHUR JOSIAH HORT.

To ARTHUR JOSIAH HORT FROM HIS MOTHER

Friday, September 18*th* [1840].

My dearest Arthur—I was very glad to receive a letter
from you, and to hear about your garden, etc.; it makes me
feel not quite so far from you all as I really am; I very often
think of what you are doing. . . . The outside of the house
at Haveningham is so completely altered, I should not have
known it for my dear old home. I have not seen the inside,
for Mrs. Owen is too unwell to admit visitors; I should like
to see it.—We must think often of the many mansions of our
Heavenly Father's House, and, my darling, how happy it will
be if we all meet there; not one missing, of all our household
here; then we shall care no more what home we had in this
world, than we care now what sort of cradle we were rocked
in.—So let us all press forward !

To FENTON J. A. HORT FROM HIS BROTHER ARTHUR
[In late summer 1840]

FARNLEY LODGE, *Friday*, 28*th*.

My dearest Fenton—I took the first opportunity to write
to you. None of the seeds you mentioned are ripe but there
are 3 seeds of Nasturtium ripe that pod of sweet pea of
yours that we thought was nearly ripe is rotten Harry came
to play with me on Sat. in the afternoon and both came in
the even —— came here on thursday 20th he —— is not
a nice boy. he often swears. I am afraid I have lost my
trap bat. —— goes to Mr. Kershaws school. Mr. Kershaw calls him a rum chap I can't say I like him I will give
you what he swore to me the other day " Upon my honour
Upon my soul I swear if the bible was here Id kiss it and

swear " I was quite shocked at all he swore on Saturday—I hope he wont do so again   He does not play cricket by rule He bowled to me overhand when I was not ready without saying play hit my wicket and said I was out I told him I was not but would go out he said he had seen many bigger boys play so. . . . Goodbye dear Fenton and believe me your most affecte^{te} Brother   ARTHUR HORT.

(*P.—S.*—I am in a hurry as Miss Sharland is going to the Royall wellls and I must go after Her I wrote as well as I could.)

FROM THE SAME.   [In Autumn 1840]

FARNLEY LODGE, *Friday.*

Dearest Fenton— . . . —— is a getting a little bit better. He used the other day nevertheless this expression By holy, Go to hell, The Devil take you and an ilnatured expression though it does no harm to me Woe betide you.   I pretended to lick him the other day but did not really strike him but he pretended his nose bled however I knew it was only nonsense for I literally touched his nose with the back of my hand but pray do not say a word about what I tell you of him in your letters.   He generally gets naughty and Miss Sharland says she will give him a dose of castor oil which soon sends him away   All send their love   I have nothing more to say so goodbye dearest Fenton and believe me your most affectionate Brother   ARTHUR HORT.

P.—S.—I have sent you a long letter.

FROM THE SAME.   [In Autumn 1840]

FARNLEY LODGE, *Friday,* 30*th* [*Oct.* (?)].

Dearest Fenton—I have lots to tell you. . . . I begun a Greek Delectus to-day with Mr. Kershaw   There are several great boxes of books come from poor old Leopardstown and also Grandmamma's poor old stools and chairs worked and My china French poodle dog like a lion and lamb, resting on a mound with red flowers, and some little affairs of yours. There are 5 Lectures being delivered at the Philosopic institution by Dr. Cantor.   The first is " The intellectual

faculties. Consciousness. Conception. Memory. Improvement
of Memory. Imagination. Asbstraction. Judgement,—Reason
Lecture 2d Theory of sleep dreaming singular pophetic
dream's. Fallacy of the senses. Apparitions,—Ghosts. Lecture 3d Sleep walking,—sleep talking, Animal magnetism in
Germany France and England various modes of Magnetism
Effects produced Animal Magnetism as a curative Agent.
These three have been delivered already. I will tell you the
rest in my next letter.—Goodbye Dearest Fenton and believe
me your ever affec^te brother   ARTHUR HORT.

P.—S.—Don't think I foraget Christmas.

FROM HIS BROTHER

FARNLEY LODGE, *Friday* [*November* 1840 (?)].

My dearest Fenton.—As it is now again Friday I write to
you. I have got 3 of Aconitum Versicolor which I think is
the same as Eranthis Hyemalis or Golden Ball   I got them
at Jessop's as Megg's had nothing of the sort, for 2d. a piece
I had a good deal of difficulty in making the men understand
what I wanted for they did not know it under the name of
" Eranthis Hyemalis " but from their description I think it is
the same.   I have got ¼ of 100 of snowdrops for 9d. most of
them being double.   they are 3s. a hundred.   You tell me I
said Vous voyera.   then certainly it was a great mistake ! and
I must have been asleep when I wrote it ! and I felt quite
ashamed of myself for it   you are right about your guess about
" Fire-Glass-pictures " it is a rather larger one than yours in
Dublin and has 12 slides.   I will provide materials for " a
Royal salute for the triumph over the air "   I must tell you I
have cut out and dug a bed in this shape. . . . You must
understand that it is larger than this and so also the other
beds that I " Dutchly " drew in the last letter   I am in Page
3 in the Greek delectus it is not Valpy's but a Mr. Priest's.
I intend to edge my bed with lattice work of little switches
mind there is plenty of room between it and your garden.

CHAPTER II

RUGBY

1841-1846.   Age 13-18.

HORT entered Rugby in October 1841 as a member of the Rev. Charles Anstey's house, the house to which Arthur Stanley had belonged.   The names of H. J. S. Smith, W. H. Waddington, and J. B. Mayor are among the entries for the same half-year.   G. G. Bradley's school career had just come to an end, and John Conington was the most distinguished boy in the Sixth Form.   It appears that there was not room for Hort the term after his leaving Laleham, and that fever in the town of Rugby delayed the opening of the second 'half' of the year ; he was therefore at home from January to October 1841, for the last two months of which period he went as a day-boy to Cheltenham College together with his brother.   At Rugby he was placed in the Upper Division of the Middle Fifth, his house-master's own form ; the form next above was taken by the Rev. G. E. L. Cotton, afterwards successively Master of Marlborough College and Bishop of Calcutta ; next came the Twenty under Mr. Bonamy Price, and then the Sixth Form.   Mr. Anstey's first report speaks of Hort as very promising but not strong in composition.   He occupied at first a room with

W. J. and A. H. Bull and another boy, and in his second term moved into a study with his cousin Joscelyn Coghill. His home letters of this time have not been preserved, with the exception of those to his brother, which were doubtless specially treasured by the parents after Arthur's untimely death. The first of the following series is dated ten days after the writer's first arrival at Rugby.

To his Brother

Arturo Hort impudentessimo
Chel. Prop. Colleg. M.
Castigari bene merenti
Cujus nomen sine horrore nunquam vocabo.

RUGBY, *Lawrence Sheriff's Day* [*October* 20, 1841].

Dearest Arthur—You must not think that I have forgotten you, because I have not written to you before, but all my time here is split into so many shreds, here half an hour, there another half hour, that I cannot sit writing long. First, to answer your questions. As to the snowdrops, give me two, and the rest of you two apiece. As to the little round bed, enquire the price of the small spring tulips, which, with a few more winter aconites will, I think, be enough for it, but before you buy any tulips tell me the price of them. It will not be time for two or three weeks to plant either them or those which you have got already, of which you must tell me the number. For the large bed, I think it would be as well to get a chrysanthemum or two, if they are cheap; if not it will do very well as it is. I think you had better take in the clove carnation. I wish you would enquire at Hodge's or any of the gardeners', whether it will be better to cut down the verbenas, and if so, do it, but I never heard of their being cut down when they are taken in, or at all events, when they are quite young plants and have no wood. Divide the remaining aconites and crocuses equally between you three. I wish you would buy about a quarter of a hundred ranunculuses. Well now for *my* affairs. I like Rugby extremely, better even

than the C. P. C.,[1] for it is not so monotonous. Old B——
is something like Judd, only a great deal taller. Young B——
is like young Bubb, only more fat-faced. Poles is the most
extraordinary creature I ever saw, his face is like this. . . .[2]
His nose covers his mouth, but he is full of fun, and is always
making puns. One of the boys told me the other day a riddle,
the solution of which I must leave to you. "Why are you
not at all a donkey's tail?" We are not at all pedantic as you
are for instead of your fine Latin "Adsum," we have our good
old English "Here." My examination Extras (Mamma will
tell you what they are) are Classics, 520 lines of the *Œd.
Tyr.* of Sophocles.

Lines. last 2 odes of 1st and whole of 2nd Book of Horace.
Divinity. 14, 15, 16, and 17 chap. of Gospel of John by
heart.
Mod. Lang. German. 4 pages of Schiller.
Mathemat. 3 books of Euclid.
History. The account of the 2nd Punic War in Keightley's
Rome.

I enclose you the list of our lessons; written very badly,
but I am hurried. Tell Lucy that I put in my own candles,
and sweep my study *myself.* I have enclosed to you in
Gran's letter a view of the school, for your scrap-book.
Goodbye. Give my love to every one not forgetting Miss
Sharland and believe me your ever affectionate brother,

FENTON J. A. HORT.

I should write more, if I had time, but I shall soon write
again. Over the door of the chapel is written εὐφράνθην ἐπὶ
τοῖς εἰρηκόσιν μοι Εἰς οἶκον Κυρίου πορευσόμεθα. I leave it
to you to translate it.

TO HIS BROTHER

RUGBY, *November 3rd*, 1841.

Dearest Arthur—I wish you would write if you have time,
if not dont.   FENTON J. A. HORT.

I am very cruel only to send you this scrap but I have no
time, love to the girls, Miss G. and all.

---

[1] *i.e.* Cheltenham Proprietary College.   [2] Drawing inserted.

To his Brother

RUGBY, *November* 10*th*, 1841.

My dearest Arthur—Most sorry am I to hear all the bad [1] news from Farnley Lodge, especially about poor Meg : you indeed are now in a sad condition but (here goes another quotation) "πέτομαι δ' ἐλπίσιν, οὖτ' ἐνθάδ' ὁρῶν, οὖτ' ὀπίσω." Now if you are able to make that out, you will be able to do two lines of one of Sophocles's Choruses. By the bye, with regard to that other εὐφράνθην I was cheerful ἐπὶ τοῖς at those εἰρηκόσιν saying μοι to me, or as our translation has it, " I was glad when they said unto me," etc. The answer to the riddle is not a very polite one, but I must give it : "because you are *no end* of an ass."

I wish you would answer me the questions that I asked about the prices of roots, etc., in a former letter, as it is now full time to plant them. We have now hard frosts here, but as you may suppose, no ice yet. . . .—I remain your most affectionate brother   FENTON J. A. HORT.

H. Anstey has a little Electrical machine which he made himself, and I intend to make one like it in the Holidays. It is a Cylinder one made with an immense bottle.

To his Brother

RUGBY, *Satdy, November* 13*th*, 1841.

My dearest Brother—I was very glad to get a letter from you, though sorry to hear such a bad account of all at home, but I hope the next account will be better. I amuse myself a good deal with young Anstey's Electrical machine, and I hope with but very little trouble to make one or two, when I get home. I enclose you some wax spun on paper by means of it. If I had the money, I would buy a Galvanic battery, for they are only 2s. 6d., but I have not, but I hope to do so at some future time. . . . Your translation is very fair : more freely " And I am flying on the wings of hope, looking neither close to me nor backwards." It is an expression of hope, that

---

[1] Scarlet fever at home.

one is raised on the air by it, and one does not regard either the past or the present, but only looks forward to the future. About the praepostors you know each boy has his particular place in the form, and by losing two places, I mean that the two boys below him are put above him, which among boys of 17 or 18 is a very great disgrace. I must now give you some account of the way of doing marks in our form. There are 35 boys in the form (in one of the forms there are 58 ! !) and you know it would be impossible to give them all a piece to construe in the same lesson, so Mr. Anstey calls up as many as he can indiscriminately : the highest mark that can be got for a lesson is 40, and those who are not called up get the average 20. Now by these marks I have been called up 33 times and my marks are . . . altogether 1158. This does not include marks for exercises, or ‘vulguses’ for which I generally get much less. The highest mark for *copies* is 100, but the marks for them are not given out yet. I do not think I have anything more to say, except to ask you not to forget to write as often as you can, now that you have plenty of spare time. Give my kindest love to every one in the house, and believe me to be, dearest Arthur, your most affectionate brother,

FENTON J. A. HORT.

P.S.—I should have plenty to tell you, if I knew where to begin, therefore I wish you would ask me some questions.

To his Brother

RUGBY, *Wednesday, November 17th* [1841].

My dearest Arthur—I got your letter yesterday, but did not write, until to-day’s afternoon’s post, in hopes of finding intelligence from Cheltenham, but found none. I wish you would ask Mamma to send me every day a letter on a telegraph Newspaper, and I hope to have better news to hear. I have altogether including composition (for which I have 409) 2657 marks leaving me head of the form, where I now am, safe and sound. ‘Tommy,’ viz. Dr. Arnold, told me and Smith who is second that he would have ‘put us out,’ viz. promoted us to the 5th form, but it is so near the end of the half, and there would be the bother of the double examinations, but if I pass a good examination, which I hope to do, I shall still have a good chance of being put out at the *end* of the half. I have taken up all the extras. I have got notes on the *Œdipus Tyrannus*, and I find them of great use to me. The frost has been very hard for some days, and I suppose there will be skating to-morrow. . . .

To his Brother

RUGBY, *November 22nd*, 1841.

My dearest Arthur—I should have written before, but I had nothing to say, however I do not like to delay any longer; I am delighted to hear that Papa is so much better, and I hope Mamma is so too. . . .

I have bought several things for making the Electrical machine: a bottle for the cylinder, bars of glass, and different drugs required for making it, several of which I should find difficult and dearer to get at Cheltenham.[1] I do not think I have anything more to say, but to give my best love and wishes to all, and believe me your most affectionate brother,

FENTON J. A. HORT.

Write soon, and tell me about the roots and bulbs.

To his Brother

RUGBY, *Saturday, November 27th*, 1841.

My dearest Arthur—As I have not written this week, I did not like to let Saturday night pass without writing you a few lines, though I am rather pressed for time, as I am more backward with my extras than I could wish to be: however I hope to know them all in time: I know three already; Classics, Lines, and History, and I know part of my Divinity and German, but I have not looked at my Mathematics. The Examination began on Wednesday, and I like it very well; most of the questions have been very easy: I write

---

[1] This home-made battery is still extant, and was the delight of a second generation of boys.

down in a book all the questions and my answers to them, as I thought Papa might perhaps like to see them. The Examination for Extras will begin, some say on Wednesday, some on Friday, but I shall be prepared for Wednesday. Stills are now the 'mania' here, and a great many of the boys have them, but very simple ones being merely a retort and receiver mounted on a stand, with a spirit-lamp. Tell Papa that I have taken pains to follow his advice as to writing the answers at the examination. Your snuff-box story I have often heard before. With regard to the roots, I told you about them in a letter about 6 weeks ago, and if you can find it, all well and good, but if not, never mind getting any more, as I do not remember them. . . .

I get confused with your verses so I will answer these of yours, and another time I will tell you at once, and not leave you to correct them, as it creates a great deal of confusion. Give my best love to all, and fervent hopes and prayers that all the invalids may be restored to health and spirits, and believe me your affectionate brother,

FENTON J. A. HORT.

.   .   .   .   .   .

I wish you would *always* write your verses on a long *separate* piece of paper, as you have done now, with the quantities *marked*, as I often have a *great deal* of trouble in deciphering them.

To HIS BROTHER

RUGBY, *Saturday* [*November* 1841 (?)].

My dearest Arthur—I write this to show you a sympathetic ink which Joscelyn and I made. I have bought a couple of pair of quoits, which are a very good amusement. Joscelyn is going to set up his electrotype. Give my love to all and believe me your affectionate brother,

FENTON J. A. HORT.

If you want any Prussian Blue, I will send you some I made myself.

Dissolve the enclosed in a tablespoonful of water, dip a clean paint brush in the solution and pass it over the paper, when the writing will appear.

The above letters and the next series are given almost entire, as they are the only ones which remain to represent the interesting period from 1841 to 1845, when the writer was thirteen to seventeen years old ; the next glimpse we get of him in his own letters after February 1842 is as a Sixth Form boy. In December 1841, near the end of Fenton's first half-year at Rugby, his whole family were down with scarlet fever, and his little sister, Louisa Josephine, the 'Babsy' of the letters, died of it.

TO HIS BROTHER

BATH,[1] January 3rd, 1842.

My dearest Arthur—I cannot open better than by wishing all our dear ones many happy new years. Alas ! there is one less than there was last New Year's Day. How mindful should we be that in the midst of life, we are in death. But I will no longer yield to these painful though profitable reflections. I am very glad to hear that you are all so much better, and I hope you will be able to answer my letter. I am very happy here, though still I wish to be again among you all. We danced in the New Year on Friday night. . . . Bath has not such nice walks as Cheltenham. You may tell Miss Sharland that my opinion of the far-famed Milsom St. is that it is a common short street, with a few plate-glass windows, and that <i>this</i> is the handsomest and most fashionable city in England !! Piccadilly is the model of the real Piccadilly 10,000 times 'Piccaninified.' The Abbey Church and the Royal Crescent, and perhaps Pulteney St. are the only things worth wasting one's stare on in the whole place. I must not grumble at the continual sloppiness of the streets, for it is certainly a fact that there can be no <i>bath</i> without water. It is certainly, Caernarvon excepted, the least (instead of, as it is said, the most) elegant town I ever saw, and its

---

[1] He was at Bath for the Christmas holidays, to be out of the way of infection.

hills are worse than Boulogne a great deal. I am now making my Electrical Machine, and I have nearly finished it, but you may tell Papa that I have not forgotten my lessons. Pray give mine and Miss Curtis's kindest love to all of you in Cheltenham, and elsewhere, and accept the same from your most affectionate brother,   FENTON J. A. HORT.

P.S.—Here is a conundrum for you of my own making. "Why is a man who is conquered like an article of ladies' work ? "

TO HIS BROTHER

BATH, *February* 3*rd*, 1842.

My dearest Arthur—I received your letter on Sunday. Before I say anything more, I must wish Margaret many happy returns of the 2nd. I finished my electrical machine yesterday, but as I was cleaning it, some of the cement broke : to-morrow, however, I shall probably set it to rights. . . . I went the other day to see Wombwell's Menagerie. There is a very clever Elephant. When his Keeper said to him, "Supposing you and I were travelling together in a foreign country, and I were to be imprisoned in a castle, what would you do ? " the elephant put up his trunk and unbarred the top door of his cage. He then said, "Supposing you wanted to pay your addresses to a young lady, what would you do ? " the elephant took off the man's hat. He then begged one of the company to lend him a piece of silver money, the keeper then put it on the top bar, and told the elephant to give it to him, he did so, he told him to lay it on the ground, he did so, he told him to take it up again, and give it to the owner, he did so, he told him to thank the gentleman, who was so kind as to lend it to him, he gave a short grunt. He then told him to show what a nice foot he had for a silk stocking ; he lifted up his great paw, he told him to kneel down and thank the company for looking at him, he did so and gave a grunt. This elephant, whenever he wants more food, or to have his cage cleaned out, rings a bell. The keeper also goes in among two lions, a black tiger or jaguar, and six or seven leopards, plays with them, kisses them, makes them all jump through a hoop, which he holds up in the air, puts his head into the Lion's mouth, and makes the leopards jump up on high shelves. There are also, a Rhinoceros, Arni Bull, a Giraffe, Hyænas, laughing Hyænas, Racoons, Ichneumons, Coatimondis, Owlets, Marmosettes, Monkeys, Lions, Tigers, panthers, Leopards, Wolves, bears, Pelicans, Emus, Parrots, Macaws, Love Birds, Boa Constrictors, an Armadillo, and many other animals which I do not now remember. Aunt has given me *The Boy's Own Book*, which contains a great many games, Legerdemain, Puzzles, Riddles, Chemistry, etc. I will now give you some Riddles. . . .

If you cannot guess them, ask Mamma to try. Give my kindest love to all at Farnley Lodge, and believe me your most affectionate brother,   FENTON J. A. HORT.

The two brothers saw little more of each other. In March 1842 Arthur was taken very ill with measles, and Fenton was fetched home from Rugby; he also fell a victim, but recovered in due course. Arthur was also thought to be recovering, and the two boys had a few last happy days together, till Fenton's quarantine was over and he could go back to school. Three weeks after his return to Rugby he was recalled for his brother's funeral; on 25th May he left home again for school, desolated with a grief which, young as he was, had made a permanent mark on him.

This loss (at the age of ten) of a child of such rare promise and such beauty of character made, in fact, a crisis in the family history; the mother's whole subsequent life was overshadowed by it, and in the brother's memory it remained always a subject almost too sacred to be mentioned. At first he was completely stunned, and it was long before his naturally sunny disposition recovered its brightness. The loss of almost all record of this time is the more to be regretted since in home letters the effects on mind and character of this first great sorrow must certainly have appeared.

On 12th June of this same year Dr. Arnold died. The news of this catastrophe was another staggering blow to the sensitive lad ; he never forgot the feeling as of an altered world with which the wholly unexpected news overwhelmed him during a holiday at the sea-side ; the anniversary is marked in red ink in his diary of five years' later date. He can never have seen much of ' the Doctor,' but his personality profoundly impressed him from the first ; he used to recall long after how he longed as a small boy for the ' fearful joy ' of being noticed or spoken to by Arnold ; and letters still extant from Arnold to Mr. Fenton Hort show the interest which he took in his progress even in his first half-year.

He spent some time in the Twenty, in which boys were obliged to stay till they were of age to be pro-moted into the Sixth. Of Mr. Bonamy Price's teaching my father always spoke with enthusiasm ; he regarded him as the man who, at school at all events, had taught him more than any one else : " To him," he said in 1871, " I owe all scholarship and New Testament criticism." Mr. Bonamy Price in his turn, after an interval of more than forty years, remembered him as the brightest pupil whom he had ever had, and delighted to recall the boy's keen eyes, the thoroughness of all his work, and his eagerness in the pursuit of knowledge. A school contemporary remembers how he sat at the end of a row, and ' snapped up ' all the questions as they came round. He is said to have astonished his schoolfellows by the regularity with which he obtained four ' First Classes ' in different subjects. His letters to his father show the variety of his intellectual interests ; he seems to have never pursued one subject of the school course to the exclusion of others, and in his private reading he was omnivorous. The passion for knowledge, which was noted in the man, had taken hold of the boy. At this age also had begun the close observation of outward circumstances which was to the end so characteristic of him. The diaries which recommence in 1845, after a break of two and a half years, caused perhaps by his brother's death, record the weather for every day, and the texts of all sermons, besides details of school debates, prizes, and the like. This record of weather and texts he never gave up ; in 1846 he began to note plants observed in the course of walks, and in many later diaries botanical notes from the principal part of the entries.

Having risen to a high position in the school when he was young for his place, and still younger, it is said, in appearance, he had considerable difficulty in main- taining his authority in his house ; there was doubtless a rather rough element in it, and his authority was not supported by athletic distinction, a deficiency which he always regretted. In his early struggles, when he first entered the Sixth Form in 1844, he received warm encouragement from the new headmaster, Dr. Tait, who, besides recognising his ability and industry, spoke of him at the age of sixteen as having "a thought- fulness of character from which the best fruit may by God's blessing be expected" ; and a year later he predicts that "he will turn out a thoughtful and very valuable man."

Though never distinguished in athletics, he played football with the same vigour with which he attacked his work, and he not only played but watched the school games with close interest. He took part in drawing up a code of rules for the famous game, the description of whose early stages in *Tom Brown* amazes the modern 'Rugby' football player; and he was very proud of his 'cap,' his one athletic decoration. In school politics he took a courageous and independent line. On one occasion he, along with the head of the school and others, was censured by a majority of Sixth Form 'levee,' on what grounds does not appear, but he was proud of the vote, as the contest was between "public and constitutional spirit and private feeling and love of popularity." The strife seems to have been appeased by Dr. Tait's intervention.

The Rev. North Pinder, one of Hort's few surviving Rugby contemporaries, has kindly contributed the following recollections of school-days :—

I could have wished that I had more reminiscences to supply of Hort's school-days at Rugby; but, owing to my having been in another House, my intimacy with him was comparatively slight, and confined principally to being associated with him in the two Upper Forms of the school.

In his case certainly the 'boy was father of the man.' Across the distance of nearly half a century I can call to mind the somewhat awkward figure and resolute earnest face with the blue eyes, bushy eyebrows, and black straight hair, as he might be seen rushing with rapid impetuous steps across the close just in time to anticipate the shutting of the Big-School doors.

He was nearly always at the top of whatever Form he happened to be in. In the Twenty Bonamy Price would usually refer to Hort for what no one else could answer. His width and thoroughness of knowledge, far beyond the usual level of even clever boys, his indefatigable industry, his quickness and precision of mind—not at the same time without a certain awkwardness of expression — foreshadowed in those early years the powers, which later he was to display in a larger field. He was not a boy of many friends, but those he had felt a deep and admiring attachment toward him. There was a natural heartiness and sincerity, a rugged simplicity and honesty, that could not fail to attract those who were brought

into close relations with him. Hort did not shake your hand ;
he wrung it, throwing into his grasp all the warmth of an
affectionate heart. He was no great hand at games, less
thought of then than now. Yet I seem to remember his wild
rushes at Football (especially in the Sixth Match *v.* the School),
plunging into the thick of the struggle, fearless of danger, eager
for achievement, and bent on doing his best for the honour
of the Praepostors' side. It was the germ of the same pluck
and determination manifesting itself in a Rugby 'scrimmage'
which succeeded later in achieving some of the most difficult
ascents in the Alps. We took our degrees in the same year
(1850)—he at Trinity Cambridge, and myself at Trinity
Oxford ; and for many years we never met. Examining at
Harrow long afterwards brought us once more together in
pleasant intercourse, which made me feel how much of the
freshness, simplicity, and warm-heartedness of the boy remained
side by side with all the learning and experience of the man.

The following letters give evidence of Hort's various
efforts for the good of his house. That of Easter Day
1846, marked 'Dies Mirabilis' in the diary of this
year, reveals the earnest spiritual life with which
incessant intellectual activity seems at no period to
have interfered. His own simplicity and sincerity shine
through phrases which are to some extent those of the
religious school in whose traditions he was brought up,
and in whose language it was then natural for him to
express his deepest thoughts.

To his Father

RUGBY, *September 7th*, 1845.

My dearest Papa—I fear this letter must be very one-sided,
for you have left me nothing to answer or remark on of home
or Cheltenham news. . . . Our football rules are to be out
this week, and if the book is as small as I hear, I will send
you a copy by post. I believe we are the only school who
make it a scientific game with an intricate code of laws.

We have filled up the two vacancies in the editorship of the
Miscellany. Shirley is all that could be wished ; Byrne I am not
so satisfied with, as he is a sad Young Englander, . . . but we
must hope for the best.   Our debating Society goes on most
flourishingly ; we admitted and blackballed yesterday week a
very large number of new applicants, and yesterday we passed
a rule making a small half-yearly and also entrance subscription to defray the expense of printing the Minutes half-yearly.
Yesterday we abolished Botany Bay, Port Jackson, Tasmania,
Norfolk Island *et hoc genus omne ;* and next Saturday we decide as to O. Cromwell's right to a 'statty' in Westminster
Abbey ! How grand we are ! Deny it, who can ! As you may
perhaps like to hear what books we have got for our Library, I
may as well tell you.   (Novels and Tales) D'Israeli's *Sybil*,
Marryatt's *Midshipman Easy, Pickwick, Hawkston*, Fougie's
Seasons.   (Travels, etc.) *Crescent and Cross*, Wolff's *Bokhara*,
Pridden's *Australia.*   (History, etc.) Carlyle's *History of the
French Revolution*, Brougham's *Statesmen of the time of George
III.*, vol. iii. ; Brougham's *Lives of Men of Science and Letters
of the time of George III.*, vol. i.   (Poetry) Spenser's *Poems*,
Taylor's *Plays*, besides Periodicals ; so that we have a pretty
good set for our money.   Our Choir in Chapel has been removed
from the Gallery to the Middle of the Body, and increased to
sixteen, eight on each side, so that we have in effect the old
system of 'Versicles' and 'Responses,' and the effect is much
better.

To his Father

RUGBY, *September* 21*st*, 1845.

I am writing in some of the heaviest rain I ever saw, with
a great stream pouring in front of my window from an overflowing water-pipe, and some of the studies presenting 'Baths
for the Poor (Occupants)' gratis, though fortunately I am not
favored with that honour. . . . I have just finished a most
interesting volume of Brougham's *Lives of Men of Letters and
Science in the time of George III.*, with lives of Voltaire, Rous-
seau, Hume, Robertson ; and 2ndly, Black, Cavendish, Sir
H. Davy, Watt (steam-engine man), Priestley, and Simson,
the mathematician.   As might be expected, he is rather too

partial to Voltaire and Hume, but I have seldom read so delightful a biography, or one that gave so favorable an impression of both author and subject, as that of Dr. Robertson. The accounts too of the discoveries by the Chemists, such as that of the various gases and the composition of the Alkalies, are very interesting. We have had two afternoons of the Sixth Match, Monday and yesterday, but we have maintained the fight so gloriously that neither side have gained any advantage, and another ineffectual day will make it a drawn game, whereas last year we were beaten in two days. The Red Cross Knight has fared well from the perilous encounters, but is rather lame from a rub by his own greaves. *A propos* to Red Cross Knights, I have plunged into the *Faery Queene*, but I am afraid it will be rather wading work, for Clarence found a great difference between drinking, and being drowned in, Malmsey, tho' it was the same liquor in each case.

To HIS FATHER

RUGBY, *February 22nd*, 1846.

. . . I see by the *Journal* that even poor Cheltenham was threatened with all the horrors of a Protection Meeting, or demonstration in favor of the Marquis of Worcester. What a noble sight it must have been the other day at the Dorsetshire Hustings! In consequence of this question I have been more of a politician this last fortnight than I have ever been *here* before, having read the chief speeches in almost every Debate. We have had the question discussed in *our* Debating Society; it was adjourned yesterday week, after three or four (for us) long speeches, to yesterday, when, in a house of about thirty-five, with, I think, only five on the Whig benches, a 'glorious majority of one' was obtained for protection; several who had intended a week ago to speak for protection having been brought to the other side by Sir Robert's powerful speech on Monday. It was very amusing to see how I was *sarcasticated* upon by both sides, because I told them that neither they nor I were capable, from want of experience and study of the questions, to form an individual opinion on the expediency and practical working of a commercial measure.

To his Father and Mother

RUGBY, *Easter Sunday, April 12th*, 1846.

My dearest Father and Mother—This is, I believe, the first time that I have ever addressed either both of you together at all or each of you separately by these names; but the occasion of my present letter is sufficient explanation of my using these expressions, and not writing to either of you exclusively. The time draws near when, if I live so long, I am to quit school for ever, and thus the second period of my existence will soon be over; and so my mind naturally reverts more strongly to what has never been altogether absent from my thoughts for full six years, and what both of you have frequently reminded me of,—I mean the choice of a profession for life. I need scarcely say, I have not thought on the subject without much prayer, especially lately; and my present object is to tell you my decision. I should mention that on Friday last I opened a sealed paper written by me at Tenby five years ago, containing reasons for the choice I then made, not however definitively, and I have ever since considered it as not the less an open question. My decision at that time was the same as now, and my reasons are substantially the same, though my opinions are in some respects modified; and *then* I balanced reason against reason, argument against argument; *now*, while I allow argument its proper place, I trust and believe myself moved by an influence not my own. You will at once perceive that my choice is the Church. You will not, I am persuaded, charge me with any want of love or deference to you because I thus definitively make my choice without consulting you. You have shown your kindness and delicate forbearance (will you allow me to add, good sense?) in leaving me to follow my judgment unbiassed, while at the same time there has been no need for my returning your confidence by asking your opinions, for I have long seen, and given due weight to, what you thought on so important a subject; and while I felt that you would not oppose my wish if I seemed bent on any other calling, I could not but pay attention to what I knew to be the desire of your hearts, to see me in the ministry, if a faithful servant of the Lord. Yet I would not have you suppose that I am influenced merely by your known wishes ; such, I know, would not be your desire. The only other profession that would in the least degree suit me is the Law, and my distaste for it has been growing stronger every year, even when there was no corresponding increase of tendency towards the Church. I feel myself altogether unfit to be a lawyer; I speak now of secular mental capabilities. But do not think that I choose the Church merely as the only practicable alternative ; far otherwise. I cannot but see that the Church wants laborers more and more every year. Again, there is another reason connected with the last. This paper I have mentioned was written when our dear Arthur was alive. He, loving his Saviour as sincerely as he was warm in his affection to us, had already, if I mistake not, devoted himself in promise to His service. The same merciful Saviour thought fit to take him to Himself before he could fulfil his resolution, and I cannot but feel his removal an additional call on me to fill the place he had marked out for himself. O that I had but his fervency of love to Him who has spared me !

I have hitherto studiously confined myself to considerations and arguments. But if these were my only inducements I could not think myself justified in entering on so awful a responsibility ; how, then, could I answer the question, " Do you trust that you are inwardly moved by the Holy Ghost to take upon you this office and ministration ? " Here, then deliberately, yet with reverence I say, that I trust and believe that I *am* moved by the Holy Ghost. Nothing less should satisfy me. I believe that the strong and permanent inclination that I feel is of God. I know how miserably and imperfectly I serve Him. I fall into sin, more especially into coldness, indifference, and forgetfulness of Him through the day, yet in the midst of this repeatedly it seems as if He clutched hard at me, and I would not come ; and I cannot believe but that He is thus drawing me perseveringly towards His service.

I had begun to write on Friday, when I was most annoyingly interrupted, having intended to ask your prayers to-day more especially, but your, I mean Mamma's, letter assures me of what I never indeed could have doubted, and I am not sorry now that I was thus compelled to put off writing till to-day. To-day I have made my final resolution, and entreated God at His table to ratify it, and ever aid me to perform it; and I cannot but think I have had some earnest of gracious assistance.   Till last night I never knew what depression was.   I had no illness; one or two things had happened to grieve me, but still they were comparatively slight; but I never felt so thoroughly downcast about myself and all the world, or so bitter and serious a struggle within me.   It tore me through and through, yet it was a great mercy and a special answer to prayer; for having previously felt my own indifference and want of real sense of danger, I had entreated to be bruised and brought low to feel the burthen, that I might appreciate what deliverance might be, and it was granted; consequently this morning I felt such as I had never felt before at the whole service and communion.   I never till then had an adequate notion of the power and beauty of our Liturgy, and, on the other hand, of its inferiority to the Word of God.   I gained some faint idea of what the Bible was; I *felt* the glorious depth of the declaration, " Now is Christ risen from the dead, and become the first-fruits of them that slept," a passage which I had merely understood before.   You will wonder, yet not more than I wonder myself, how I have been able thus to put on paper my inmost thoughts.   The only explanation I can give myself and you is that I could but record with gratitude what appears to me so signal and gracious a token of encouragement in my resolution of to-day.   O that I be not deluding myself!   One thing I can sincerely say: I wish to be the minister of the Lord; but it makes me tremble to read a verse of St. Paul and St. Peter and then look at myself.

I have now given you my reasons, as far as I can distinguish them, for everything would urge me on except the fear of unfitness.   The fear itself is no harm, but quite the contrary; O that the occasion of it may be removed.   It only remains for me to beg your more particular and earnest prayers, for assuredly I shall need them more . . . pray especially for me that I may be given the spirit of prayer. Indifference is the form that the enemy's opposition generally

takes rather than direct temptation; pray that I may be
enabled to call down unceasingly special aid. I am afraid
to be an hour without prayer, and yet how hardly do I find
it! May this day be the first of harvest to me, of my rising
from a sleep truly called death, even as on this day Christ was
gathered in as the first-fruits, rising from the actual death!
    This letter is sadly incoherent and confused. My only
excuse is that I have written it without previous arrangement;
I have said whatever rose to my mind. Perhaps you will
like it the better for this. With love to the dear girls . . .
I remain, ever your affectionate son,

FENTON J. A. HORT.

TO HIS FATHER

RUGBY, *April* 19*th*, 1846.

I really do not know how to answer Mamma's and your
letters of Monday. I can only say that I thank you both very
deeply and earnestly for them, and that for their own sakes as
well as for the assurances of what scarcely needed assurance.
Yet the more I read them, the more must I entreat you to
pray—and pray that I may myself worthily pray—that you may
not have taken too favourable a view.
    . . . Rugby has been honored to-day with the presence of
three head-masters of great schools: 1st, Dr. Tait of our own;
2nd, Charles Vaughan of Harrow; and 3rd, Conybeare (a
Rugbeian) of the Liverpool Collegiate Institution. Arthur
Stanley (Arnold's biographer) is also here, so that we have
quite a constellation. . . . It is not often that I look at our
newspapers, but whenever I do I am disgusted with them:
always some attack, either on the Established Church, or the
Coercion Bill, or the thanksgivings for the Indian victories;
this last is a very fruitful theme for the declamations of these
sentimentalists on Sir R. Inglis' 'gunpowder Christianity,' as
they call it, or the idea of thanking 'a God of peace for
successful slaughter.' I cannot help thinking it a very fearful
sign of these latter days, that godlessness has taken such a
strange form; it began with persecution open and undisguised,
then came Popery, then (to omit minor forms) in the last
century the philosophy of 'reason,' not one perishing in the

meantime, but each springing up by the side of the other. But now such is the spirit of the age, it is driven to take a new shape, the shape of Christianity and religion itself. For I cannot regard in any better light this widely-spread system of assuming the name of the Gospel to wrong principles. But I am running on about what I know little about.

To his Father

RUGBY, *May 3rd*, 1846.

It appears by your letter that my gentle insinivations were not altogether without foundation, and that Mamma's cunning question about which tour I should prefer, just as if she was setting me a subject for a Latin essay, *Quidnam iter præstantius habendum sit*, etc. etc., was, as I suspected, more practical than she was willing to allow. You shout all the way from Cheltenham to Rugby, to know ' my own views—my own ideas.' Poor I haven't got any ideas ; I am not like a flint or steel to strike out new sparks, but the black old burnt bit of tinder that enlarges and spreads the sparks of others : there's what you may call (you needn't if you don't choose) a fine simile. But the fact is that I should like any so well, that I don't know which I should like best.

So like two feasts, whereat there's nought to pay,

(pity that isn't the case with us),

Fall unpropitious on the self-same day ;
The anxious at each invitation views
And ponders which to take, and which refuse ;
From this or that to part he's sadly loth,
And sighs to think he cannot dine at both.'

So sings the immortal Fusboz, and so sing I. . . . The fact is that Italy, Greece, Egypt, and Palestine (all four considerably too far off) are the only countries where I should feel myself at home and have full enjoyment. But don't suppose that I am disparaging those which may possibly be in reach : I only wish that you would choose as you think best and wisest, resting assured that I shall be perfectly satisfied with your decision, and be sure also that *then* I shall undoubtedly find out reasons why that is the best.

To his Father

RUGBY, *May* 31*st*, 1846.

. . . Yesterday Mr. Fox, who was here at the school ten years ago, and has been for five years a missionary at Masulipatam in the Madras Presidency, addressed as many as chose to come to hear him. What he said was Christian, sensible, and well suited to his audience, and no flummery. He hopes to come again next half-year.

To his Father

RUGBY, *September* 13*th*, 1846.

. . . With reference to Dean Carus's question about Classics and Mathematics, I believe your answer was the best. My own *present* idea (tho' of course subject to subsequent modification) is to make Classics my strong point (following my inclination and powers), and Mathematics as much as practicable. I confess I should like, if I might be so ambitious, to take more than a mere junior op. pass ; but I would rather stick to the lower parts of Mathematics, so as to get a thorough knowledge of all their principles and bearings, etc., than take a higher flight if solidity below were thereby to be sacrificed.

To his Father

RUGBY, *September* 19*th*, 1846.

. . . We are endeavouring to establish in this House Shaksperian Readings ; they answer very well at some of the other Houses and are very popular. I look for great benefit from it to the House, hoping it will be a common bond to the different parts of the House, and likewise improve the literary taste generally in the House, giving them something better than Marryatt, Bulwer, and James.

CHAPTER III

HORT returned to Rugby for part of the second half-year of 1846, and in October went up to Trinity College, Cambridge. His first term was spent in lodgings. In January 1847 he moved into rooms in the New Court, on his tutor the Rev. W. H. Thompson's staircase. He did not become a scholar of the College till April 1849. In 1847 and the two following years he competed unsuccessfully for the University scholarships. In these competitions it is likely that width of reading counted for less than what is sometimes called 'pure scholarship'; that he was a very *accurate* scholar can hardly be doubted, but he was never brilliant in classical composition. The making of Greek and Latin verses, at all events, was never a favourite amusement with him, as it used to be with so many classical scholars. He read classics in his freshman's year with the Rev. F. Rendall (afterwards a master at Harrow), and later with W. G. Clark. Mr. Rendall reported after one term's experience: " His knowledge of the classic authors is certainly far above the average; but to this knowledge he appears to me to superadd much more important advantages in the clearness of thought and refinement of taste which his criticism and composition evince in a degree of maturity beyond his years."

It was not to be expected that he would confine his attention to the regular course of Classics and Mathematics. Subsequent letters reveal not only the width of his interests as an undergraduate, but also how well prepared was his mind by nature and Rugby training to gather all the intellectual advantages of the University. He had undoubtedly learnt how to learn.

A word is perhaps necessary to explain his religious development at this period. So far, as has been shown, he had been brought up in the doctrine of the Evangelical school, which was especially influential at Cheltenham ; the effects of this training were doubtless modified in the atmosphere of Rugby. No school letters survive to tell how he was impressed, as impressed he must have been, by the religious teaching of Arnold, and afterwards of Tait ; but the letter of Easter Day, 1846, is sufficient evidence of the deep natural piety which had been fostered under these successive influences. It was natural that at Cambridge he should seek out first the teachers of the Evangelical school, who then represented what was best in the religious life of the University. Chief of these was Dr. Carus, for whom he always retained a great regard. At a not much later period however he outgrew the Evangelical teaching, which he came to regard as ' sectarian,' but he did not throw himself into any opposite camp. It would be a great mistake to suppose that he in any sense cast off what he had learnt in early years ; all that was best in those first lessons had become part and parcel of himself. Before long he was to come under other influences, especially that

of F. D. Maurice; but, without anticipating, it seems
well to note here two very important facts in the history
of a mind singularly receptive, yet singularly independent: that there was at no time any decided break
in the continuity of his religious convictions (one
hardly likes to call them opinions), and that he was
even from the first

Nullius addictus iurare in verba magistri.

Combined with unbounded gratitude and devotion to
those masters under whose influence he successively
came was an absolute independence of judgment. The
extent of his indebtedness to Arnold was certainly
far greater than it is possible now to estimate precisely.
In undergraduate days, if not before, he came under the
spell of Coleridge.   It is significant that in 1847 he
records in his diary the dates of Coleridge's birth and
death.   Nor was this a passing boyish enthusiasm; the
poet-philosopher's works became the subject of deep
and careful study, the fruit of which appears in the
exhaustive monograph published in the volume of
Cambridge Essays of 1856.   Possibly what first
attracted him to Coleridge was the breadth of intellectual interest which in him went along with spiritual
earnestness.   From Coleridge to Maurice the passage
was natural.   Maurice's teaching was the most powerful
element in his religious development, satisfying many a
want which had hitherto distressed him; yet, as indicated above, it would be a mistake to call him without
qualification a disciple of Maurice.   Before he had made
acquaintance with his writings, he had been inevitably
affected by the forces of the Oxford Movement, though
he was throughout alive to the weaknesses as well as
the strength of its leaders.   In the loyalty of his

churchmanship one can trace perhaps the most certain indications of what he derived from this source. For he was emphatically a churchman; he loved greatly the services of the Church of England, and cared much for a reverent observance of all matters of detail in worship. Such things he regarded as of secondary importance, but never with indifference. For instance, his devotional, no less than his artistic, feeling was outraged by the bare and ugly churches which were far commoner forty years ago than now. In these matters, as in those of higher importance, his fairness and openness of mind were conspicuous even in undergraduate days. Yet—and the reservation is extremely important—he was no dispassionate eclectic, balancing opinions with the cool judgment which comes of deficient enthusiasm. The decision was with him no matter of merely intellectual interest. The main current of his religious thought was, as has been said, continuous; but such changes as came in the course of growth were accompanied by anxious self-questionings which tore his whole being through and through. The intensity of his feeling was at least as remarkable as the balance of his judgment. Nothing was more foreign to him than the complacent judicial attitude commonly ascribed to Goethe, speaking of whom in connection with Coleridge he said : " There are other and better kinds of victory than those which issue in an imperial calm." [1] So again, in one of his maturest writings, he says : " Smooth ways of thought are like smooth ways of action ; truth is never reached or held fast without friction and grappling." [2] In fact,

[1] Essay on S. T. Coleridge in *Cambridge Essays*, 1856, p. 351.
[2] " The Way, the Truth, the Life," *Hulsean Lectures for* 1871 (published 1893), p. 171.

both early and late his object was not opinion, but truth.

The following letters all belong to his first term of residence at Cambridge :—

To his Father

CAMBRIDGE, *October* 31*st*, 1846.

My dearest Father—I ought to have written last night, but the time slipped away as I was sitting at the Union till it was too late for the Post. You will see from this that I have joined the Union, which however, if I may judge by the impression anything you have said about it left on my mind, is very much altered since its *Founder's* time. We have a magnificent room, I am afraid to say how long, for Debates and reading-room ; also a smaller and snugger room, and, I believe, a smoking-room, and a really excellent Library of all subjects, which is a great resource. It is very convenient for me at present, the entrance being from the Hoop Yard, not grand or imposing certainly. Our first Debate for this term is to be on Tuesday. There is one alteration that struck me particularly from your account of the antient[1] feuds, viz. there are no fines for non-attendance at Debates. Romilly asked me to wine on Thursday. Professor Sedgwick was there, besides two or three old pupils of Romilly's who had come down for the day, and three or four undergraduates, chiefly, I think, of other colleges. Romilly talked and laughed and joked incessantly for every one else as well as himself. There was some interesting conversation about the new Planet; but I could not make it out, nor can I remember it clearly. Some observer, I think here, thinks he has discovered a ring. It appears that Mr. Adams of St. John's had made his calculations in the spring, and sent them to Greenwich to Airy, the Astronomer-Royal; but he paid no attention to them, and to his neglect Sedgwick attributed the loss of the honour to England of the discovery. He mentioned that in the summer

---

[1] For an explanation of this and some other peculiarities of spelling, see p. 55.

he and some one else had seen Mr. 'Nep' from the Observatory here, but did not recognise him as the planet that they were looking for.

On Sunday I went to St. Mary's to hear the Hulsean lecturer (Trench). It was the concluding lecture of the series, and therefore scarcely a fair sample. It was of course more intellectual than spiritual, the subject being (of the whole, which is in the press) "Christ the Desire of all Nations, or the Unconscious Prophecies of Heathendom," a noble subject, but most difficult to deal with well. His lecture was a sort of *résumé*, cautioning against three errors—1st, of regarding Heathendom as utterly devoid of all true light; 2nd, of exalting the dim light of Heathendom at the expense of Christianity; and 3rd, of finding no matter for thought in the Heathen writers. He was very earnest, tho' he had a painful delivery; and considering its nature, it was a very beautiful lecture, giving here and there by chance expressions 'windows into the man,' which showed what a beautiful preacher he would be on a less directly intellectual subject. . . . I forgot to mention that at Trinity Church in the morning I was fortunately a quarter of an hour early, and so obtained a seat; plenty who came before the service had none, and a good many who came for the sermon could not get in, there not being even standing room anywhere within the walls or doors. . . . It is since you left that the 'Little Go' has been instituted (officially 'The Previous Examination'). It takes place after a year and a half. . . . Thompson is our Classical Lecturer, and does it exceedingly well, shallowly for the shallow, deeply for the deep, though in the latter respect rather pointing to other resources than entering fully on them himself. . . . I have heard since I came up a noble act of Tait's. Byrne had worked very hard for the Exhibitions, and fully expected one, but came fifth; and there was no 'broken' one. On returning to Rugby we were surprised to see Byrne's name on the board for a broken one. Nobody whom I asked could tell me about it. It now turns out that Tait has given him an Exhibition for two years, *i.e.* £120, out of his own pocket, and had it put up as if he had gained it in the regular way.

To his Father

CAMBRIDGE, *November 4th,* 1846.

. . . I answered your last letter but one in a great hurry supernumerarily, and so did not examine all your questions; among them I see the coats mentioned. I must have misunderstood you on that point, for I got the frockcoat some time ago, and have been keeping my best 'tails' as dress, tho' they are not first-rate for that purpose. Before I do anything more, therefore, I want to know your wish. I should add that at the time I asked Law what he generally made *evening* coats of, and he said that of invisible green more than any other colour; however, if you wish the blue, say so. Say also about the brass buttons, *horresco referens.* . . .

Carus mentioned by the way that the King of Prussia has sent a gold medal to Archdeacon Hare with a letter of thanks for his noble vindication of Luther from the attacks of our own Tractarians, in a long note to his *Mission of the Comforter,* lately publisht, which said book Carus likewise highly recommended. One other book he said every one should make it his business to read, the Homilies. You do not often see or hear anything of them now.

I went on Thursday week to one of Mr. Wilson's Scottish Entertainments (the 'Nicht wi' Burns' man), as I was rather curious to hear him. His prose explanations were miserable, very like the showman at Wombwell's, and you couldn't help fancying that if you were to interrupt him, he would have to begin all over again; and the jokes he was evidently tired of repeating to so many audiences. There was a good deal of affectation also in the way that he sang many of the songs. Most of them were rather poor, but "A Man's a Man for a' that" was magnificent; he almost did it and Burns justice, no easy matter. By the bye you made a mistake when you were here in not going into Trinity library to see Thorwaldsen's statue of Byron. He doesn't look very 'morantic' in his dressing-gown, but, as well as I can judge, it is a fine statue; the likeness is particularly good, tho' rather favourable than otherwise.

To his Father

CAMBRIDGE, *November 12th*, 1846.

To make sure of my letter reaching you in good time, I write the hour after I have received yours. I had a treat on Monday night such as I am not likely often to have, and I am sure you would have given something to have had : I heard from the lips of Prof. Challis and Mr. Adams the account of their discovery of Neptune. —— told me that that night was the first meeting for this term of the Cambridge Philosophical Society, and asked me to go with him. . . . Mr. Adams explained in some degree the difficulties and peculiarities of his calculations, but they were all but wholly unintelligible to me. One curious thing I fished out, that the well-known theory of a certain rule in the relative distances of the planets from the sun as compared with that of the earth, is found false in Neptune's case. The rule was that, supposing the distance of one planet from the sun to be x times as great as that of the earth from the sun, the distance of the next outer planet from the sun would be $2(x-1)$ times that of the earth. For instance, Uranus is 19 times as distant; and so they expected Neptune to be $2(19-1)$, *i.e.* 36, but he turns out to be (I think) only 33. There was then some discussion as to the respective honours of Adams and Leverrier ; Adams said that he gave Leverrier the full credit of the discovery, but, as a matter of calculation, he claimed for himself the credit of prior and independent conjecture. Challis said the same, and merely claimed credit for himself on the score of having laboured most, having taken between 3000 and 4000 observations between the end of July and September. He, it seems, actually saw the planet before its discovery at Berlin, and had suspicions of its being the planet, but did not examine it. On coming home I sat down to write an account of what I had heard, but when I had written a good deal, was obliged to go to bed by the hour ; and unfortunately I totally forgot it till this afternoon ; now on trying to complete it I find my recollections very imperfect. . . .

One word on the Union, etc. You are anxious that I

should not devote to its studies too much time in preference to Classics and Mathematics ; these latter should undoubtedly have the pre-eminence, but I am sure you will allow that alone they would form but poor *pabulum* for the mind.   Philology, cram, science, both natural and of abstract symbols, and Paley (ugh !) are by themselves all but useless ; they are rather instruments, but, if you have nothing to employ your instruments on, why keep them ?   I should be the last in the world to join in the insane cry against them (which happily is now somewhat hushed), so strong a sense have I of their value ; only allow room for somewhat else, and depend upon it they will not suffer.   Compare the edition of a Greek play by a mere philologer, however good, with one by a man who has read and thought something else, and you will see how, for the purposes of mere philology, superior the latter is, even with inferior scholarship. . . .

I quite agree with what you say of Trench, but the blindness of the *Achill Herald* in accusing him of Popery made me say more than I intended.   Trench might have learnt by the lines of one who is now, I fear, an Anglo-Catholic—

> Sovereign masters of all hearts !
> Know ye who hath set your parts ?
> He who gave you breath to sing,
> By whose strength ye sweep the string,
> He hath chosen you to lead
> His Hosannas here below :
> Mount and claim your glorious meed :
> Linger not with sin and woe.[1]

. . . .

Here I have been again at my long quotations, but I don't think you'll cry because you have got it. . . . Last night I went to St. Michael's to hear ——. . . . Somehow I never like stars, least of all planets ($\pi\lambda\alpha\nu\hat{\eta}\tau\alpha\iota$) or *wandering* stars.

To his Father

CAMBRIDGE, *December* 14*th*, 1846.

. . . Poor Dr. Mill has, I grieve to say, verified the accounts of him.   Having disposed the Sunday before of the

---

[1] Then follows a quotation of most of Keble's poem.

rationalistic and semi-rationalistic theories, he yesterday devoted his whole sermon to attacking the Evangelistic ; he
praised the truth of the central doctrine, but blamed its being
taught exclusively, assuming that it is so (true to a certain
extent, but the exception is not the rule). In fact his whole
course lay in misrepresentation, confounding Evangelicalism
with Methodism, which last is worse than Popery, as being
more insidious. At the same time his own doctrines were the
reverse of sound ; he advanced the sacraments in a strange,
inconsistent way, denouncing strongly the *opus operatum*, and
any idea of sacrifice in the Eucharist (quoting Heb. x. 12, 14),
and yet attacking the only other alternative ; in fact, timidly
bringing forward Baptismal Regeneration. He wound up by a
far more justifiable denunciation of the Evangelical Alliance
and Pæan over its defeat. It is fair to add that he used no
hard names, and, tho' his doctrines were abominable, his whole
tone inclined me favorably towards the man.

I am much obliged to you for taking the girls to the
sights without waiting for me, more especially Mad. Tussaud's,
which is to me disgusting. Why do we shrink from an ourang-
outang ? because the rezemblance is too great. Where the un-
likeness of the accompaniments preponderates, we admire the
art, as in a painting or statue ; but a wax figure is like a rosy-
cheekt corpse in the attitude of a living man.

In the Lent term of 1847 there was great excitement in the University over the contested election for
the Chancellorship. Hort's account of it in the following three letters shows that he was by no means a
recluse.

To his Father

CAMBRIDGE, *Tuesday night [February 23rd, 1847]*.

My dearest Father—I open Kate's envelope to tell you
that the affair of the Chancellorship is getting most serious.
St. John's are going to work doubly ; they summon all their
own men as a College question, and raise the cry of the Church.
The *Morning Post* has to-day a leader in behalf of them of a

very strange kind, insinuating that the Government are going to throw their weight into the scale of Prince Albert; in short, high and low, from every hole and corner in the kingdom, Johnians and High Churchmen are being summoned up, and have been being summoned since two hours after the news of our late Chancellor's death arrived. Prince Albert, as you will have seen, gave a sort of refusal, but I hear that it is contrary to etiquette for a royal personage to *contest* an election; and his committee have determined to go to the Poll, so that *he* does not come forward as a candidate, but, if they are successful, they will offer it to him, and *there is reason to believe* he would accept it. This was exactly the course pursued in the case of the Duke of Gloucester. Lord Powis' committee and friends include most of the Law Officers and many leading Churchmen; the Prince's all the heads of houses but the Master of John's, President of Queen's, and Master of Clare Hall, and this last has only withdrawn because of the Prince's refusal. We have also almost, if not quite, all the Professors and leading men of the University, and, the papers say, four Cabinet Ministers, but *who* I don't know. But most of all Carus has publicly declared that the real movers of Lord Powis are the Tractarian party, who hope thereby to effect an entrance into Cambridge; and I understand that he is canvassing and otherwise exerting himself most actively against Lord Powis. Now he is so very sober-minded, free from party spirit both in religious and other matters, and charitable, and unmeddling that it must be something real and considerable that would excite him thus. Under these circumstances every vote is of consequence, and the contest seems generally expected to be neck and neck. The Polling begins on Thursday, and ends at noon on Saturday.—Your affectionate son,   FENTON J. A. HORT.

In great haste.

To his Father

CAMBRIDGE, *February 26th*, 1847.

You will read a full account of what has taken place (as well as what has *not*) in the *Times*, tho' I should observe that the latter ingredient will largely preponderate

over the former, *i.e.* the penny-a-liners have proved themselves penny-a-*liars ;* but I must give you some scraps of
information. The story (I am not sure whether it is in the
Times or some other paper) about the marching in procession
and the banners, etc., is a pure fabrication from beginning
to end. I was at the Senate House yesterday five minutes
before the time, and found the Galleries crowded, but managed
to squeeze myself a place. Punctually at ten the authorities
arrived, and here a fable was dispelled. It is popularly
believed that the Proctors' books, which they carry about
with a chain, are no books at all, but mere wood ; however,
something was read out of one of them. All the ceremony
described in the Papers may possibly have taken place, but I
don't think it did. On the right hand on entering was Lord
Powis' table, on the left the Prince's. Every one of the
A.M.'s went up to one of these, and received a ticket on
which he wrote his name and I don't know what else ; he
then (*i.e.* as soon as he could) went up to the ' Vice's ' table,
where sat the Proctors, Registrary, Scrutators, Bedells, etc.,
and handed his card to the Vice, who read it, showed it to
one man to look out the name in the Calendar and make sure
of all being right, and to two or three others to register, and
then deposited it in one of the two slits in a huge box he
had before him, one slit for each candidate, each time calling
forth cheers and groans according to the slit he put it in.
This was the whole business. Early in the day the body was
crowded with A.M.'s ; one of the Bulldogs admitted a certain
number at a time within the rails which separated the dais,
and the rush each time was tremendous. It took some time
each turn for three or four Bulldogs to shut down the bar ;
they forced it down on the heads and backs of whoever was
there. A.M.'s were sprawling on the floor, having their hats
smashed or holding them above their heads, and you may
imagine the undergraduates were not silent. The bar, which
was four inches thick, soon broke ; they brought in carpenters,
but ultimately they made the passage much narrower, and
crossed batons across it. The ' profound sensation ' at the
arrival of the Ministers is a monstrous fiction ; nobody but
the dons knew anything about it till hours afterwards. The

only persons recognised, as far as I remember, were the
Bishop of Norwich, Lord John Manners, and Lord Fitzwilliam;
this last came in his scarlet robe as D.C.L., and elicited great
shouts of " Lobster ! " I hear his vote was refused (I don't
know why), as was to-day that of the Provost of Eton. At
first Lord Powis had a majority, then the Prince, then Lord
Powis, and his steadily increased up to 84, and then
slowly fell, till at nine last night the Prince had a majority
of 17 ; he had about an hour ago (at four) one of between
50 and 60. The Gallery noises have been tremendous;
first of all the cries of " Cap, cap ! " or " Hat, hat ! " to whoever below retained either of those articles on his head, and
the " Three cheers for Prince Albert "—" for the Queen "—
" for Lord Powis "—" for Lord Powis' Committee "—" for
Lord Powis and Church Principles "—"for the Vice-Chancellor"
—" for the Senior Proctor "—" the Ladies " (of whom three
or four from time to time came in), etc. etc., with, of course,
groans and hisses to match. There were shouts for " Poll,
Poll, state of the Poll ! " and then perhaps some patriotic don
would write down the number and hold it up, and then a
shout to hold it higher, and write it plainer, etc. etc. From
eight to nine last night it was awful ; there were only a few
poor candles on the three tables, so that the Gallery was
almost in darkness. It was not, like the morning, a succession
of shouts, but without break one loud, shrill, piercing screamo-
howlo-whistlo-yell, and occasionally the notes of a bugle. At
nine the Senior Proctor came forward to declare the state of
the Poll, but he could not obtain silence, and was obliged to
pronounce the words without being heard. I should have mentioned among the morning sounds whistles to denote Whewell,
barkings for the Bulldogs (the insinuation of the penny-a-
liar is a lie), grunts for the Johnians, and crowings for I don't
know who. To-day there was a terrible uproar about three
from two-thirds of the body of the house assuming at once
their gowns and caps; this was greeted with the most
tremendous howlings and stampings, but it was no use, and
half the Gallery finally assumed *their* caps. Both days papers
and squibs of various sorts circulated below ; one yesterday,
I hear, described thus the merits of the two candidates :

one had saved a mitre and the other invented a hat (*i.e.* the Albert hat, embalmed in *Punch*). It ended with putting into the mouth of a Johnian the assertion of his determination "to go the whole *hog* for *John*." Another to-day was a tolerable parody of the Witches in Macbeth, a trio of P's forming the dialogue, "Powis, Puseyite, and Punch," which last personage has of course been unable to resist the opportunity of a cut at Royalty in any shape.

To HIS FATHER

CAMBRIDGE, *March 12th*, 1847.

. . . Everything is perfectly quiet here after the Election. One of the best things about it is that yesterday *Punch* had a caricatured version of the Address which Crick as Public Orator had to present to his Highness, which represented Crick as mitre-hunting. Now the best of the joke is that Crick is a Johnian and voted for Lord Powis. . . . Two, however, of *Punch's* jokes this week on the subject are good, tho' most of his observations are abominable. He had before observed that Prince Albert, in consideration of his great knowledge of law, was expected soon to be admitted to Lincoln's Inn ; he now observes that there is no difficulty, for, since the Prince originally refused the Chancellorship from want of unanimity and has nevertheless now accepted it, he has *eaten his terms*. The other is that he is coming up to Trinity to reside, and has already entered the young Princes as *Under-sizars*.

With the possible exception of a few schoolfellows, it does not seem that Hort had friends at Cambridge before he came up. One of his earliest and closest College friendships—one which lasted to the very end of his life—was with Mr. Gerald Blunt (now Rector of Chelsea) of Pembroke College, whose family were already intimate with the Horts at Cheltenham. Another early friend was Henry Mackenzie, who died young. At some time in his first year of residence he must have made the acquaintance of John Ellerton, an acquaintance which ripened into a lifelong intimacy. His name will perhaps be more prominent than any other in the following pages, as nearly all the letters on both sides were preserved ; to him he could always talk without reserve, and to him, whenever they were apart, he poured out on paper his thoughts on every subject grave and gay. Ellerton was President in 1847 of the Addison Society, called at first the Cambridge Attic Society, an essay club of which Hort was a member. He also belonged to a Historical Society, and attended Sunday evening meetings at Dr. Carus' rooms. He began before long to speak at the debates of the Union, of which Mr. H. C. E. Childers was President in the last term of 1847. The day of multifarious athletic amusements had not yet come. Hort's principal exercise was walking with Blunt and other friends ; tradition also tells of nocturnal perambulations in the cloisters of Nevill's Court, pro-longed sometimes far into the night. In vacations the object of the walks was generally botany ; the diaries of this and other years are crowded with notices of plants collected or observed, and of botanising walks with C. C. Babington. In the Christmas vacation of 1847 he took a small pupil at Cheltenham, his only ex-perience of this kind of work.

To his Father

CAMBRIDGE, *April 29th*, 1847.

. . . When my Exhibition comes in I do not know, but I suppose it will be soon. Talking of the Exhibition reminds me that I sent in to-day a couple of Epigrams, more for the sake of having something of the sort to take an interest in, than any good likely to be gained. I made the recent dis-

coveries of the 'perturbations' of Uranus by Neptune, and
Saturn by Uranus the subject, to exemplify the thesis 'ὠθού-
μενός τε καὶ ὠθῶν,' 'Pushed and pushing,' showing what a
mistake it was to suppose that the stars went on quietly and
civilly, each minding his own business.

I am not going to carry on a controversy on the respective
merits of *t* and *ed*. . . . I do not clearly understand whether
you set up Addison individually as an authority and standard
in opposition to Hare and Thirlwall. I hope not. If you
regard them as mere 'learned critics,' you do them great
injustice. Not only in learning, powers of mind, and critical
acumen, but in elegance of diction and style, and sound
practical good sense, is each of them worth a dozen Addisons.
As you say '*familiar* diction,' perhaps you would concede
their superiority in writings of a high didactic character, as
Philosophy, Theology, or History; but I would only refer you
to Hare's *Guesses at Truth* for as elegant 'familiarities' as
are to be found anywhere. . . . I by no means think it
incumbent on all, who consider Hare's orthography best, to
adopt it on that account in opposition to the general fashion,
but simply wish to excuse those who have no objection to so
doing. But if I am not very much mistaken, you will soon
find orthography like everything else, getting reformed *universally*; out of the 50,000 words of which our language consists,
it is said that 50 only are pronounced as they are spelled;
and people are beginning to find out what fools they have
been in sticking to such absurdities so long. . . . As to the
character you give Hare, of that I know nothing; I can only
say that all his theological writings that I have read are more
free from dogmatism than any of the present day, and more
liberally minded. However, it so happens I know why you
abuse him; you let the cat out of the bag once before. *He
admired 'Christabel'! !* That is his crime.

To his Father

CAMBRIDGE, *May* 14*th*, 1847.

. . . Last night at twenty minutes past eight, as I was
going to take my letters to the post, when I got into the New

Court, I saw some dozen or two of men rushing distractedly
about in all directions, but mostly under the arch towards the
river. . . . I met a friend, who told me that the kitchens
were on fire. I then looked and saw a slight smoke in that
direction; going into the Bishop's Hostel, it appeared much
more formidable and very lurid. More men came rushing
out and there was a shout for buckets. I attempted to get
into Nevill's Court by the end of the arches nearest the Hostel,
but the smoke was too strong. I saw there was plenty of
work before us, so, while I had time I rushed upstairs and put
on my old greatcoat; by this time there was a good many
men going about, and buckets carrying to and fro. I went
into Nevill's Court by the nearer end of the arches, observing
as I went through a bright red glare on the opposite windows,
and when I got to the corner near the Library door and looked
back, there was a good deal of flame mixed with the smoke.
. . . There were great shouts to form a 'line,' and I of
course joined in. We had a double line, one side passing up
the buckets filled from the river, the other passing them down
again when emptied. And there were several other lines in
the same way. . . . At the river end of each stood several
men in the water, filling the buckets. It was very hard work
at one time, for they passed along very quick. We were a very
expeditious line, for we were silent; the series of common
buckets, fire-buckets, slop-pails, water-cans, and everything
that would hold water or wouldn't, went on pretty continuously, only broken by some man occasionally seizing a water-
can between his knees to wrench off the lid; knuckles occasionally suffered from the iron handles tumbling on them,
when we caught hold of the bucket itself, for we had no time
to be dainty, but snatched at any part of the utensil. The
fire rapidly increased, and soon bright orange flames shot up
terrifically above the roof, and seemed advancing westward;
but just then the first engine arrived amid 'loud cheering.'
Before long the gear was all ready, and Evans, one of our
scholars, carried the first hose up a ladder placed against the
outside of the butteries, and it told rapidly, the flames instantaneously decreasing. One engine after another arrived, till
we had five. . . . I worked two or three minutes at the

engine, but the labour was tremendous, and I soon left off. . . . I stayed there till near 12, and they were then examining the roof all along, the engines having ceased to play about three-quarters of an hour before. . . . Had the engines been five minutes later, it must have caught the first staircase in Nevill's Court, and from one end to the other, with the exception of the outer walls, is one mass [of] old oak, partitions and all ! ! with those massive broad staircases to pro-duce a full draught and the wind setting that way. The New Court is fireproof, but my rooms abut on Nevill's Court. The Hall also must have caught, and the first beam of the Combina-tion Room was just charred. They got the pictures out of it in a great hurry, and I hear damaged several by the corners of the frames of others.

TO HIS FATHER

CAMBRIDGE, *October 29th*, 1847.

. . . As to 'setting about' Composition, I have some thoughts of writing for the College Prize Poem in Alcaics on the occupation of Ferrara, which will be something of interest. I do a little of routine as well as read some one or two books in Classics, besides the *Phœnissae* for Christmas and the March 'Little-go,' alias 'Smalls,' alias 'Previous Examination of Junior Sophs.' Thus much for Classics, but, as I told you, my chief object during this term must be Mathematics, for I cannot like the plan which many Classical men pursue of almost entirely neglecting their Mathematics till the last few months before their Degree, when they cram up as much as they may want to pass their Junior or Senior Op. degree as the case may be ; but whatever benefit may be derived from Mathematics in the way of disciplining the mind, is thus almost entirely lost. Moreover I must, if I intend to get any more 1st classes, conform in a great measure to the College Examinations ; and the approaching one at Christmas is about half Mathematics, two-sixths Metaphysics, and one-sixth Classics.

Gray, the new Bishop of Cape Town (who, you may re-member, preached a sermon at St. John's Church, Cheltenham,

some weeks ago), is to preach at both Carus' Churches on
Sunday: Carus spoke of him in the highest terms on Sunday
evening.

TO HIS FATHER

CAMBRIDGE, *November* 12*th*, 1847.

I fear I shall not be able to write you a long letter, for I
shall have to be at the Union from after Chapel probably till
ten, as the whole Sunday question is stirred *de novo*, and is
become terribly complicated. . . . The validity of the meeting
last term which closed the Union till three on Sundays is (I fear
justly) impugned; the law is, "No meeting of the Society shall
be competent to make new laws, or to alter or suspend existing
laws, unless the meeting shall consist of Forty Members."
Now at the meeting in question there were confessedly above
forty present during the greater part, if not the whole, of the
discussion. How many were *present* at the division, nobody
knows, but those who voted, as shown by the division return,
were only thirty-seven. No counting out had taken place, and
the question is whether under the circumstances forty *voters*
were necessary; the laws do not say, but I must in honesty
think that common sense and justice require it. . . .

I do not feel quite so sanguine as you do respecting the
Bishop of Cape Town's reception at Cheltenham; I heard
nothing that I could object to, but some of his expressions
would somewhat startle the old walls of St. Mary's.

I suspect from your words that you do not quite understand what I said about my Mathematics. It is not a question
of 'earnestness,' or no earnestness about them, but simply
it seems to me better to work out and well understand the
principles and bearings of the fundamental sciences, than
merely 'get up' a string of 'cram' propositions in the high
subjects, without knowing the why and the wherefore of anything. More generally, there are two extremes here, both
very common, and, I think, equally pernicious: one of casting
aside the Cambridge studies, merely reading enough for a
degree, and indulging wholly in other literary pursuits; the
other, of reading nothing but Classics and Mathematics—in
short, setting up millstones but grinding no corn in them; and

again it seems necessary to preserve the balance of *College* and *University* studies. It is almost Chapel time, so I must conclude. Kind love to all.

To his Father

CAMBRIDGE, *November 26th*, 1847.

. . . What you say about sacrificing a principle to a technicality is all very true, provided there be nothing more than a technicality, a quibble, as in the case you mention ; but it was not so with us. . . . Would it be right to give a false interpretation because we disliked the immediate consequences of the true ? nay, more, should we assert, not as a matter of *rule for the future*, but as a matter of *opinion* on *existing words*, —that we believed the words of the law had meant one thing, while we really believed the opposite,—merely because the consequences of speaking the truth might be dangerous and wrong ? Surely not : surely our opponents might say, " Is not your conduct merely a putting in practice of the maxims of doing evil that good may come, and of not keeping faith with heretics ? you tell us that it is for the sake of *Christianity* you wish to shut the Union on Sundays, and then in order to attain this end you have recourse to principles which are most *opposed to Christianity.* . . .''

—— must be an ingenious man in his heterodoxy. A favourite hymn of C. A.'s I have since discovered to be an accurate parody of a short love song of Byron's, but what the man could find in poor Shelley to transmogrify into a hymn *to anything*, is more than I can guess. That sort of Mahomet-anism-and-water is, I fear, very prevalent.

To Mr. John Ellerton

SEGRAVE VILLA, CHELTENHAM, *December 20th*, 1847.

My dear Ellerton—This may appear very early for me to write after my departure from Cambridge. . . . Verily every circumstance of every day, be it news of crime, or of heresy, or of sectarianism, or of aught else, convinces me more and more that the Church is the only center of all our hopes, that only by clinging fast to her, by submitting to her mild and lawful authority, by shaping our ways according to her indications, and above all by venerating and upholding with gratitude and love, and leading others to venerate, those Holy Sacraments, which no less than His Holy Word her Divine Head has entrusted to her keeping and administration, can we hope with any well-grounded cause for hope either to preserve our own souls and minds from the moral and intellectual seductions which swarm everywhere around, or to maintain among others the authority of God's truth and God's holy law amid the con-flicting whirlpools of modern English society.

What think you of the Jew debate? For my own part, I have seen no really good speeches on our side. Lord John's was most valuable as repudiating the Warburtonian notion of the merely physical ends of a state; I can almost forgive him his measure for that declaration. And then what a noble Christian speech Gladstone's is, fallacious though it be ! . . . I am glad that the attack on the King's supremacy is foiled, but I deeply grieve that it should be considered merely as a defeat and baffling of high Churchmen.

The year 1848 was a stirring time for all thoughtful men. For Hort, as for many other minds, no doubt, it was a very critical period; his letters reflect the excitement within, which was the natural consequence of the excitement all round him. And yet it is evident that he was never carried off his feet. While entering into almost fiery discussions on all the controversies of that seething year, he was also quietly pursuing his course at Cambridge, or walking and botanising in North Wales ; and there is something almost ludicrous about the intrusion of the 'Little-go' in the year of revolutions. Apparently he wrote for the English prize poem on ' Baldur,' and he also competed for the Hulsean prize. In this year too he became a corre-sponding member of the Botanical Society of London, and engaged in a good deal of correspondence on botanical subjects, especially on the differentiation of the species of the genera *Rubi*, *Violæ*, and *Ulices* ; in the pursuit of this hobby he was closely associated now, as always, with C. C. Babington.

It is characteristic of his mind that he viewed all the movements of the time in connection with theology. Theology must be with him a living reality, and he was dissatisfied with all systems which did not seem to have a direct bearing on life. Hence he was led to seek firmer foundations than he could find in the Evangelical position ; with all the earnestness which inspired the teaching of the best of that school, he could not discover the religious philosophy which he desiderated. In this search for a definite *locus standi* he was attracted by the writings of F. D. Maurice. Here he found a religious teacher who seemed to bring the doctrines and sacraments of the Church into relation with the needs of individual and social life. In Maurice, moreover, there was not that distrust of the human reason which, so far as it characterised the ' anti-Liberalism ' of the Oxford Movement, made it impossible for Hort to be in complete sympathy with the leaders of that school. Maurice was still personally unknown to him, as were all the Maurician set of social reformers. The social and political history of this time is familiar enough for the allusions in the following letters to explain themselves ; the history, *e.g.*, of the Hampden case has been fully told in Dean Stanley's Life ; in the biographies of Maurice and Kingsley an account is given of *Politics for the People*, a remarkable venture in journalism, which lived for three months in the summer of 1848. Though the controversies of the period have been described more than once, it has seemed worth while to give Hort's comments on passing events with considerable fulness, since, young as he was at the time, they show what effect was produced by these moving incidents on a mind singularly sane, yet withal enthusiastic. If his enthusiasm makes his language sound occasionally somewhat extravagant, it is to be remembered that this was what he would himself have called the 'yeasty' season of life ; and, if he did not on all questions take the view which seems most in accord with 'liberal' principles, it is only a proof of the detachment from parties as parties which was at all times noticeable in him. Moreover in politics, and especially in ecclesiastical politics, the effect of the reaction from early influences was still powerful.

To Mr. John Ellerton

CAMBRIDGE, *January 6th*, 1848.

. . . On coming up here, I find you levanted, and so I am left in wretched solitude, for there is not a single man up whom I know at all intimately; so pray come hither and read as you intended. Write for 'Baldur,'[1] if you feel so inclined, or do anything of that sort, but do not be guilty of the horrible treachery of leaving me any longer without any other company than the excessively shadowy and 'questionable shapes' of Pindar, Thucydides, and Juvenal; in short, I am vegetating, and, if you do not come to my aid, a vegetable I shall be all my days, without hope of becoming an animal, much less a 'human.'

I am gone clean distracted about this miserable Hampden affair. The only persons who seem to have acted creditably are the Bishop of Oxford and Dean Merewether. What a magnificent letter his last was to Lord John (mistaken as I believe his opinion to be)! and then what a gentlemanly, not to say Christian, answer he got written on Christmas Day! . . . Hare's pamphlet seems to me to be quite a floorer for all those who babbled about Hampden's 'heresy'

[1] The subject for the prize poem.

(though the *Record* does not take notice of this passage, which he afterwards only slightly modifies: ". . . I would have implored the minister, on my knees, if it could have been of any avail, to recall what seemed to me an act of folly almost amounting to madness, of which I have never been able to learn the slightest explanation or defense "). It is delightful to read him after Hampden's wordy Protestantism or his opponents' wordy bigotry of all sorts. I was delighted the other day by our little Evangelical curate telling me with a grin that —— had sent him a petition in favour of Hampden to sign, with his name attached in pencil along with some others. All the rest had put 'Yes' opposite; he put NO in large letters. How he must have astonished their weak minds! I have plenty of things to say, as, for instance, about Tennyson's *Princess*, which seems good, though absurd.

To Mr. John Ellerton

CAMBRIDGE, *January* 10*th*, 1848.

. . . Hampden is to be 'confirmed' to-morrow. I see Whately has been asked by his clergy for his opinion on the subject, which he will, give in a day or two. The *English Churchman* has a vehement attack on Hare's pamphlet, saying they now know some one else to suspect, 'German theology,' etc. etc. Still I feel pretty sure Hare will be the next bishop, from the way that Lord John spoke of him; and there are not many fitter for it.

The Princess is absurd, but I like its absurdity. It is not a high flight, but it is a glorious poem for all that; it is anti-Mrs. —— and all Apostolesses of 'Feminine Regeneration.' It gives an account of an university of women (the Princess being the head), and the moral, an excellent one, shows that the rivalry of the sexes is absurd, that each has its own place, and each is necessary to the other. I will give you one exquisite line as a sample of its delicacy and beauty—

> upon the sward
> She tapt her tiny silken-sandalled foot.

I have no time for more.

To Mr. John Ellerton

CAMBRIDGE, *January* 19*th*, 1848.

I have been anxiously expecting a note every morning to
say that you were coming up at once; but I will delay no
longer to write, having far more to say than I shall have
either memory to recall or time to commit to paper. First
as to books, *Sterling* is out, but I do not feel at present
inclined to spare a guinea for it; it is in two foolscap 8vo
vols., of Daniel-Lambert-obesity, and seems intensely interesting. Macmillan says that it appears from the Life that
Sterling was an ardent admirer of Strauss! so that it is bold
indeed of Hare to publish this Life just at the time when the
English Churchman has been calling himself a Rationalist.
But though I have not got Sterling's *Remains*, I have got his
Poems, but have not yet read much of them. On reperusing
Mirabeau, I have been still more struck than before by its
extraordinary power and beauty, though I do not quite understand it all. *The Saint's Tragedy* with Maurice's preface is
also out. I have read the preface, which is excellent, though
the drift is rather odd, viz. to show what sort of a drama a
clergyman of the present day ought to write. The production
itself is a five-act drama, partly prose, partly verse; its main
object being an attack on some of the later 'Anglo-Catholics'
about celibacy and 'holy virginity.' It is a difficult and
delicate subject to deal with, but the interests of Christianity
and of the nation require that the truth should be spoken out
boldly, and Kingsley seems to have done so nobly (though I
have not read the book itself). Its sum and substance,
according to Maurice, is an exposition of the actual struggles
of man between life and death, such as they really are, apart
from all the 'accidents' of circumstance and opinion. He
has also dealt a manly blow at the central *lie* of Calvinism,
viz. that man's natural state is diabolical; in short, he seems
a man quite after Maurice's own heart, and, it is to be hoped,
will prove a valuable ally to him in the glorious war that he
is waging against shams of all descriptions. Some one has
written to the *Examiner* enclosing copies of a note to Carlyle
requesting to know whether the resurrection of the new

Letters was a mere *jeu d'esprit* or a veritable fact, and a somewhat surly rejoinder from the *Elucidator*, asserting that
whatever he put his name to was fact; which settles the
question. Query: How would this rule apply to Herr
Teufelsdröckh of the *Sartor Resartus?* Macmillan has
already sold nearly a hundred copies of *The Princess*, though
so few men are up!!

And now as to Hampden, where am I to begin, or where
to end? First with a good but singular piece of news: the
Morning Herald has all of a sudden, without explanation,
shifted sides, and came out yesterday with a strong anti-
Hampden article. It stigmatises his appointment as "a most
unprecedented and wicked proceeding"; abuses Lord John
heartily for insulting the Church; accuses Hampden of not
caring for anything but his own aggrandisement; of meanness
and ingratitude in writing such a letter about the Bishop of
Oxford, after his disinterested generosity on his behalf. . . .
It also reminds us that we have to guard the interests "of the
Church, not of Lord John Russell, but of Christ." It is
gratifying to find that the judges have allowed Sir F. Kelly to
take a rule *nisi* for a *mandamus* to His Grace the Archbishop
to show cause why the three clerical objectors should not be
heard in court against the Bishop Elect. His argument
seemed to me peculiarly ingenious and good, that since the
'court of the Archbishop or his deputy' was, as he proved,
in all essential points a *bonâ fide* court, it was subject to the
rules of courts, and consequently both parties had a right to
be heard. I understand that the question comes on in the
Queen's Bench on Saturday. I have not read Whately's
lengthy defence of Lord John and his *protégé*, but the glance
I gave at it did not prepossess me in its favour. I am glad to
see, however, that he is eager for a convocation (of course to
include laymen). I might talk for ever about this unhappy
business, but I will say no more now of it, unless anything
particular should occur to me.

Meanwhile what a sad apathy there is on the subject of
the Jews! The *Chronicle* receives absurd letters in praise
from 'Liberal clergymen,' and the *Herald* receives still more
absurd letters in opposition from 'Christians'; but the drift

of them always is a lamentation of how dreadful a thing it is
that we should have men who blaspheme the holy name of
Christ, and call Him an impostor, sitting in Parliament. But
you might say with quite as much reason, " How dreadful
that men who do this should be allowed to live at all," and
then proceed to exterminate them.   O we are perishing for
want of *thought* /   We give and receive money, eat our dinners,
whiz away at sixty miles an hour on railways, drink in wisdom
from the daily press, go through certain alternations of sitting,
standing, and kneeling for a couple of hours once (or it may
be twice) a week in a particular building commonly called a
church, and perform many functions of the same kind, passively and sometimes quasi - actively with our bodies, but
always merely passively with our minds.   And this state of
things is not merely palliated but praised as good in itself.
I read to-day a most singular article on Gladstone and his
Jew speech in the *Daily News*.   They were by no means
unfriendly to him ; said that he must have some practical
statesmanlike qualities, or he never would have risen to his
present eminence, but that what spoiled him was a singular
habit of his, viz. that he never seemed to do anything from
a mere practical sense of 'political expediency' (*sic*), but
referred all his actions to some 'abstract and general principles'; that a statesman never had time to think about
principles (and if he had, they would only perplex him), but that
his business was to use his sagacity to see what was required
by the present moment.   Would to God we had a few more
such 'unpractical' statesmen as Gladstone ! Empirics we have
in abundance, but that men should deliberately wish that
empiricism should sway the destinies of man—— ! ! !
    Speaking of Gladstone reminds me of one of the *Morning
Herald's* crotchets.   A silly pamphlet by a London clergyman
appeared the other day, recommending the enfranchisement
of the Jews, at the same time rather wishing than otherwise
for the separation of Church and State.   On this the *Herald*
concocted an article, sagely attributing said pamphlet to
Maurice ! the extracts which I saw bearing about as much
rezemblance to Shakespeare's style as to Maurice's ; and to
think of his writing such a pamphlet !

Though I proceed very slowly indeed with the *Kingdom of Christ*, every day seems to bring out more clearly in my mind the truth, beauty, wisdom, scripturality, and above all unity of Maurice's baptismal scheme. It is difficult to comprehend at first, but it seems after a while to rise gradually on the mind in its full and perfect proportions and harmony. I love him more and more every day. I am carefully reading Derwent Coleridge's *Sermons on the Church;* they are truly excellent and beautiful, though the tone is occasionally perhaps rather too ecclesiastical instead of Catholic.

The question of the National Defences is interesting enough since the publication of the Duke's letter ; but it is said that at least 140,000 militia and I forget how many of the line are to be raised. Seriously I shall not be surprized at a war within three months.

To his Father

CAMBRIDGE, *February 26th*, 1848.

. . . Our Town and Gown Rows have long ceased. The magistrates had ordered the police never to interfere ! but luckily it was suddenly discovered or recollected that all Heads of Houses are *ex officio* county magistrates, provided they take the oaths. This the Vice-Chancellor did on Monday, and instantaneously called out all the parish constables, and made preparations for swearing in any number of special constables that should be found necessary at a moment's warning ; and it was agreed at a meeting of the Heads of Houses that, should these measures prove ineffectual, they would memorialize the Home Office on the subject of the magistrates' strange and unwarrantable order. But the constables efficiently kept the peace, no 'cads' venturing into the streets, and I believe there has been no row since. There were a few broken heads, but I do not believe there were any very serious injuries received, though doubtless some would soon have ensued ; for on the Saturday night it was a matter of pokers and life-preservers on the one side and the poles of the market booths on the other. It is well the University have checked the rows in good time, for every

one was talking of the legendary 'Anatomical Rows,' when
the Senate issued orders to the whole University to assemble
and defend the Anatomical Schools from the mob *vi et armis*.
. . . I have written this letter as coolly and quietly as possible, but the excitement both abroad and in my own particular cranium is not small in consequence of this terrific
news from France. How strange that Louis Philippe should
twice have to seek shelter in England, where I suppose he is
by this time. Well, I hope he may meet with a generous
reception in spite of all his double-dealing, provided always
that we do not countenance him in his iniquities and
tyrannies.

To his Father

CAMBRIDGE, *March* 10*th*, 1848.

. . . I am getting well on especially with mathematics,
which I like better the more I read, as of course is natural
when getting into the higher subjects; for instance, it was very
interesting to-day to solve the problem by which Newton discovered the laws of the Solar System, and to feel that though
apparently I had only to deal with a mathematical figure of
lines and A's and B's on paper, still that S did really stand for
*S*un, and that 'body moving in an ellipse' meant our own
little lump of earth. You will be sorry to hear that Tait has
been very ill for some time of rheumatic fever; the last
account (two days ago) was that it had reached his heart
and he was not expected to live. I am most grieved about
it for his own sake, and as for Rugby, I know not what will
be its fate.[1]

To his Father

CAMBRIDGE, *March* 1848.

. . . I find on inquiry that it will be very desirable to
make arrangements respecting reading in the summer term
now, if I am to go with a party. Now at the beginning of the
term Clark begged me to ask Budd whether he thought me

---

[1] These fears were of course not realised.

likely to be a wrangler; it was an awkward question to ask, but I laid it on Clark's shoulders. Budd said that at my present rate, working moderately about half at mathematics, if I took up the Differential Calculus, and would read with any one in the Long Vacation, I was sure of being a wrangler. The Differential I have had in lecture this term, and am now going to do some more with Budd, so thus the case stands. I tell you this that you may know the circumstances clearly. This would seem to point to the expediency of going in the summer with a party and tutor, unless there is some reason against it. . . . It seems to me that it is a mistake to regard this vacational reading merely as an extra-terminal *term*, that it is *vacation;* while at the same time it is utterly absurd to do as many parties do, squander money on a tutor, and then scarcely open a book but amuse themselves with gaiety, never-ceasing excursionising, or anything else they like, the whole time. This arises from various causes ; the habits of the tutor, the character and number of the party, the place of abode, etc. etc. The object then is to get a small (not above five) party of quiet reading men, who are likely to go well together ; a tutor likewise quiet and reading, but cheerful and one who would enjoy a walk not merely as a routine 'constitutional'; and lastly, a desirable locality, the four chief excellencies being freedom from much society (for it often happens that the neighbourhood are hospitable to reading parties), freedom from other reading parties as much as possible, cheapness, and fine scenery.

To his Father

CAMBRIDGE, *Saturday night, April 8th,* 1848.

. . . I have deferred writing till after post hour, that I might be able to give the result of the Little-go. I am 'examined and approved'; whether in the first or second class I shall not know for a week, but I am pretty sure in the first. . . . Very few have been plucked as yet, especially at Trinity. One of those *misfortunates* gave a somewhat singular answer in the O. T. history ; one of the questions, speaking of the plague of locusts in Egypt, asked, What became of the locusts?

he answered, "John the Baptist ate them." . . . I was
rather puzzled, in inserting my name (in Latin) in the scholarship book, to know what to put for my native county; I wrote
at last '*Eblanensis*,' but I do not know whether they will
understand.   A friend of mine, born at Bombay, was still more
puzzled.   A Chartist meeting here did not come off; the
cricket-balls on Parker's Piece were too formidable.

To Mr. Gerald Blunt

Cambridge, April 26th, 1848.

My dear Blunt—Having obtained some further information
respecting the new scheme, I am sure you will like to hear
something about it.   The younger Macmillan has been spending some days in London, and consequently had an opportunity of getting two hours' conversation with Maurice on
Good Friday.   The publication is to be a royal 8vo double
column magazine (size of *Penny Magazine*) weekly, at a penny
per week, to be called *Politics for the People;* the chief writers
to be Maurice, Hare, Kingsley, and Scott, a great friend of
Maurice's, whose writings I do not know, but they are greatly
praised by Macmillan, and Ellerton and Howard confirm the
character given him.   Anybody, however, that likes may
write, subject, of course, to the discretion of the editor (who
the editor is, Macmillan does not know).   The tone of it is
not to be, "Don't make such a row, you poor people; the
Charter and all that sort of thing is humbug; you don't know
anything about yourselves; let us alone, and trust wiser heads
than yours"; but rather to sympathise with all their feelings;
show what are the real, true, and good principles which take
such absurd shapes as Chartism, etc., contradicting themselves
in struggling to express themselves; in short, to speak as
working men—workers with brains, to working men—workers
with hands.   Everything is to be anonymous.

I have been greatly delighted to hear that you approve of
Maurice's chapter on Baptism; I think you will now thoroughly
enjoy his second volume, especially its noble ending.   I
cannot say how deeply grieved I have been by your account
of poor Manning, though I have never read a line of his

writings, but should much wish to do so. I would only hope there may be some misapprehension of facts ; all who know anything of him speak of him in such high and affectionate terms ; he would be a loss indeed. At present Newman is, I think, the only really great captive whom Rome can boast, but Manning would be a second. Doubtless, if a man conscientiously thinks that he ought to go to Rome, he ought, but it by no means follows that he is in no degree morally to blame in the process by which his mind has arrived at such a result ; and I certainly think it a most fearful thing to quit the church of one's baptism, if that church be a church and not a mere sect.

Master Humphrey's Clock is an especial favourite of mine ; *The Old Curiosity Shop* is exquisite, though perhaps more ideal than human ; and *Barnaby Rudge* is the perfection of a tale ; but I do not think either are in the least degree to be compared to *Dombey and Son ;* they are quite unrivalled. I have been reading *Tancred* at breakfast and tea ; it is most eccentric, but on the whole striking and good.

TO HIS FATHER

CAMBRIDGE, *May 5th*, 1848.

. . . The first thing you will wish to know about is the scholarships. I have not got one. Only five of the thirteen have been given to our year, while six were universally expected. The successful candidates are Chance, the best classic of the year, and also an excellent mathematician ; Westlake, the second or at most third best mathematician of the year at Trinity, and a first-class classic also, who read both classics and mathematics with the best 'coaches' *at Cambridge* for three years before he entered the University (these two were always quite certain) ; Watson, who is universally set down as Senior Wrangler ; Beamont, who is certainly among our four best classics, and is further well read in mathematics (*N.B.* He reads eleven hours a day both term and vacations alike, and until this term, when he went to London for three days, he had not taken a single holiday except Sundays and Christmas Day since last June twelvemonth, except that in last Easter vaca-

tion he read eight hours a day instead of eleven); and finally
Bowring, one of our best mathematicians and a very good
classic besides.   I am afraid I have been a little disappointed,
for I did so much better in the examination than I expected
that my hopes were raised, though I did not feel the least
certainty of success, and I certainly have no reason to be discontented when I see who the successfuls are. . . . I should
mention here that in a talk which I had with Thompson
between papers on Saturday morning I asked how I had done
in the Craven; he said that the examiners had not taken particular notice of any, but that they mentioned my name among
twelve or fourteen who had struck them as the best.

To his Father

CAMBRIDGE, *May* 19*th*, 1848.

. . . With respect to ——'s scholarship, I certainly
envy neither that nor any other honour he may obtain by
such suicidal means.   He evidently means to get the Craven
next year, and to be Senior Classic the year after; but I do
not think he is at all certain of either of these distinctions,
which are the highest objects of his wishes, and for the
acquisition of which he now sacrifices everything; but two or
three, and I hope myself among the number, will run him
hard for both without turning ourselves into Classics-sausages.

To Mr. John Ellerton

SEGRAVE VILLA, CHELTENHAM, *June* 20*th*, 1848.

. . . You will have seen my unaccountable good luck.[1]   I
suppose some of my philosophical or St. Mark answers tickled
the fancy of the examiners, for the composition of the first
class shows how completely mathematics ruled the roast. . . .
Maurice on the Lord's Prayer I have just finished, and am
delighted with it beyond measure, especially with "Thy will
be done," etc., and the last sermon.   I am steadily advancing
with *Guesses at Truth*, second series, with, of course, a not

[1] *i.e.* In the College examination.

very unequal pleasure. The essays on Progression I think remarkably wise and Christian, particularly at the end. I am ashamed to say I have not yet ordered last Saturday's number of *Politics*. I sent on Saturday a paper (without my name) in answer to Ludlow's attack on Carlyle, signed T.C.C., but I am doubtful whether they will admit it [1] ; its English is detestable, but possibly Maurice may fancy it, as a general 'Help to the Interpretation of Carlylese.' I wrote it at the time when I ought to be in bed (as I am now doing), and consequently it is very crude and imperfect.

I have written, I believe, three lines of the Hulsean Essay, and read scarcely anything, but my eagerness to try increases daily. I read to-day Simon Ockley's *Introduction ;* it is amusing and sometimes sensible, but his ideas on the subject of history are ludicrous and original.

I went yesterday (Wednesday) to the distribution of the prizes at the College, to see my dear little pupil (whom I remember mentioning to you, and who just missed a scholarship there in February) receive his prize. . . . Dobson, the Principal, spoke for an hour, to my great delight ; no flattery or talkee-talkee, but he abused the parents for giving their boys unauthorized holidays, etc., in the most capital style. He evidently fears neither public nor board of directors, and so goes on well enough ; he then distributed the multitudinous prizes, with a suitable modicum of commendation to each. . . . Dobson gave us not a bad free version of

Cælum non animum mutant, qui trans mare currunt.

viz. Change of school
Won't mend a fool.

I was greatly amused by a story that one of my little pupil's sisters told me of his perfect innocence of theological factions. He came home the other day, telling her that a boy had been recounting the several occupations of his uncles in London ; one uncle was a doctor, another was a ' Puritan.' This puzzled her, and she asked him whether he was sure of the word Puritan. " Either that or something like it ! " " Was it ' Puseyite ' ? " " Oh yes ! that was the word ! "

[1] Apparently it was not inserted.

To Mr. John Ellerton

CLIFTON, *July 6th*, 1848.

As it happens that I have some perfectly vacant time to-night, and a letter to you is likely to be a long one, I commence one which may possibly not be finisht for some days. I quite forgot to mention in my last letter that on my transit through London I was detained by want of train some time, and accordingly took the opportunity of paying the Exhibition a flying visit of about an hour. On the whole I was disappointed. I had scarcely time to look at more than those pictures which I had heard particularly mentioned,—scarcely even those, and therefore you must add a grain of salt to my judgment. E. Landseer's 'Random Shot' is certainly a true work of genius, as much in what is left out as in what is painted; so much is left to be filled up by the imagination. The pale red light on the snow, yet no sun visible, falling on the sides of the lumps only, and therefore before the sun has risen any height; a mere sloping piece of snow without background, a clear, grey, transparent frosty air, etc. The pair from the 'Lyra Innocentium' delighted me most; for, though not works of high genius, there was an indescribable air of Raphaelic soft, gentle, calm beauty about them. If I had had time, I could have gazed at them all day long. Stanfield's landscapes are fine, but their style scarcely admits high art. There is a queer one of Armitage's, some interview between Henry VIII. and Catherine of Aragon. His jovial figure was conceived with much fun, nursing his gouty leg, and well drawn, but it is plain that this piece of waggery was the only thing in the picture really felt by the artist. What surprised me most was the miserable execution of nine-tenths of the pictures; so many were mere daubs. The sculpture is execrable, except 'Una and the Lion,' which is more than tolerable. (Three cheers for Spenser!) I was of course interested in the figures of the young princes. The Prince of Wales has a really fine and intellectual face. . . . The busts are coarsely and badly executed, and you can scarcely get light for any of them. Carlyle's is striking, but the engraving gives you a far more living idea of the Iconoclast. The

Archbishop of Canterbury's is quite ideal. I never saw so kind or so stolid a face.

The day before I left Cheltenham I went to the shop where I had ordered the *Politics*. I gather from something in No. 9 that it contains one of Kingsley's glorious letters [1] to the Chartists. I hope you will have got them by this time ; there are some wonderful things in them, particularly Maurice's address in the last number, which, I deeply grieve to say, announces the cessation of the periodical at the end of this month.

Of the Heresy Test agitation I have seen nothing except the official circular to which you allude, which is one of the most dishonest affairs I ever saw; one not in the secret would suppose, not that they were abolishing a test, but setting up one which had been spurned, viz. that of the Articles. The importance of the question seems to me incalculable. I feel most strongly how thankful we should be that God, in His care for this branch of His Church, restrained the framers of our Articles from introducing into them those Calvinistic errors to which they were themselves so much inclined, as is indicated by several phrases in the Articles ; but the policy of the Evangelicals is to have the Articles interpreted by the other writings of their human framers, and not by the Antient and Catholic Symbola and Liturgies which our Divine Chief Bishop has provided for our safeguard. This reminds me of Hooker, whose preface (and a little more) I have lately read with much delight, and it is wonderful how his description of the Puritans of his day fits on those of ours. . . .

I really do not understand what you mean when you expect me to be ' surprized at many things in your views.' What your peculiar position is, I mean as differenced from mine not in degree only but also in kind, I do not know ; but perhaps you will forgive my saying a few words of the thoughts that every event and book confirms in my mind. For it is impossible to forget how important is every event now happening, every opinion now broached in reference to the part that you and I alike, if God spare us, will have to play in life ; and nothing so frequently engages my attention as thinking what my theo-

---

[1] The letters signed ' Parson Lot.'

logical position must be. Now, looking at the doctrinal
question, I think we shall avoid much disquietude by laying
it down as a preliminary axiom that we must not expect ever
to get to the bottom of the meaning of baptism.   One of the
things, I think, which shows the falsity of the Evangelical
notion of this subject, is that it is so trim and precise, so *totus
teres atque rotundus*, as Simeon would have exprest it. Now no
deep spiritual truths of the Reason are thus logically harmonious
and systematic, hence I never expect to get completely *round*,
to comprehend, the idea of baptism.   But I believe we agree
in thinking that Maurice's view, so far as we enter into it, is
the true one, though I, at least,—and I should be surprized
were it otherwise,—am still rather *in nubibus* about some
points relating to it ; chiefly concerning the relation of the
baptized to the unbaptized.   Is the Holy Spirit given only in
baptism (I mean, of course, *not till* baptism), or given before
but increased in baptism, or lastly, is it given to every human
creature, and is baptism only its seal and assurance ?   This is
a point on which I should much like to have a long talk with
Maurice himself.

But with respect to what is to be our conduct in reference
to this question, which seems likely to split our Church, I
think our duty is plain, viz. to remain neutral as far as possible
—neutral, I mean, as to joining a party ; at the same time
in language stating that we maintain 'Baptismal Regeneration' as the most important of doctrines, claiming for ourselves that title, and letting the Romanisers find out the
difference between their view and ours if they will, but considering that no business of ours ; but on the other hand, should
things come to such a pass that, as in the war between
Charles I. and his Parliament, neutrality is an impossibility,
and we must join one party or the other, I should have no
hesitation in cleaving at all hazards to the Church for several
reasons : 1st, . . . almost all Anglican statements are a mixture
in various proportions of the true and the Romish view ; 2nd,
the pure Romish view seems to me nearer, and more likely to
lead to, the truth than the Evangelical ; 3rd, we should bear
in mind that that hard and unspiritual mediæval crust which
enveloped the doctrine of the sacraments in stormy times,

though in a measure it may have made it unprofitable to many men of that time, yet in God's providence preserved it inviolate and unscattered for future generations ; 4th, whatever may be the inclinations of the so-called 'Anglo-Catholics,' they cannot restore mediævalism ; the nineteenth century renders it impossible ; and further, the Bible then was closed, but now, thanks to Luther, it is open, and no power (unless it be the fanaticism of the bibliolaters, among whom reading so many 'chapters' seems exactly to correspond to the Romish superstition of telling so many dozen beads on a rosary) can close it again ; a curious proof of which is afforded by the absurd manner in which the 'Anglo-Catholics' defend, as they think, the Bible from 'Rationalists' ; 5th, to the Church, her constitution being sacramental, we *must* adhere, if we will follow God's way and not our own ; only in the Church does He promise all the blessings of the New Covenant. We may have to suffer the temporary loss of some goodly branches of Christianity, and much of its genial and spiritual quality may be in part debarred us ; still we *dare* not forsake the Sacraments, or God will forsake us. Holding them, we hold the root and the trunk, shorn for a while of its foliage, perhaps of its branches, but in due time they will sprout forth again ; whereas if we forsake the root and trunk to embrace the foliage, we shall find it wither before long, and we shall be embarked on a stormy sea of opinion without rudder or oar.

. . . I do not feel quite so certain of the truth of Arnold's view of the Sabbath as I did. I do not mean that I am returning to the Judaizing notion, but I am inclined to regard the Sabbath as an universal institution for mankind, of the same kind as and coætaneous with the universal institution of marriage. I do not see clearly whether this is Maurice's view, but I believe it is not far from it ; thus its central idea would be not abstinence from work, but rest, in accordance with the words, " The Sabbath was made for man, and not man for the Sabbath." Sabbath-breaking will then include little else than hindering Sunday from being a day of rest to others.

. . . I do not think there is a book more utterly free from Manichæism than the *Christian Year*, nor can I believe that its author's mind, however narrowed by dogmas, could ever lose its genuine and healthy Christian freshness. Talking of your friend Shields and his carnivora forsaking the butcher for the greengrocer, I am inclined to think that no such state as 'Eden' (I mean the popular notion) ever existed, and that Adam's fall in no degree differed from the fall of each of his descendants, as Coleridge justly argues that in each individual man there must have been a primal apostasy of the will, or else sin would not be guilty, but merely a condition of nature.

I have now finisht the *Guesses;* they are mostly good, but I have faults to find. *He* should not slander 'Heathen virtue,' etc., but the pieces on Idolatry, Obscurantism, Independence, where, however, I think he misunderstands Horace, are delightful. I wrote anonymously to him a week ago, pointing out to him his apparent plagiarism about the nettle.

Hearing that J. H. Newman was about to go over to Rome, ———, a perfect stranger, sent him a copy of some book on the errors of Popery, with a request that he would return it when read, as it was borrowed from a friend ; and also a copy of 'my unanswerable Essay on Romanism' : at the same time assuring Newman that he always maintained that it was only on the ground of 'Anglo-Catholicism' that Popery could be resisted ; and that *he* had stood on that ground in his well-known controversy with some priests in Dublin, at which it was generally allowed that he stumped the priests. Newman sent him a cool, pithy, but proper answer, saying that *as the book was borrowed*, he returned it at once.

I hope ——— has had enough of his friends the Communists by this time. What an awful affair it has been ! The blood shed is a cheap price indeed if it have crushed that devilry ; but the quiet, individual, deliberate assassinations and burnings show that there is no security. The utter ignorance of the subject that I meet with surprizes me. The whole is looked upon as a sort of violent and extreme Radicalism or Republicanism ; they use 'Socialist' and 'Communist' indifferently, and there seems not the smallest insight into the deep and turbid feelings of the age. What disgusts me most is the sneers that qualify every expression of praise of

Lamartine. "Oh! he's a *poet*/ a man of imagination and enthusiasm, a dreamer! with a good deal of the sentiment of religion! how can a *poet* be a statesman?" Bah! the utter ignorance of poetry and art that seems universal! Truth to say, however, I have not quite so high an opinion of Lamartine as I had, though I never can forget the noble stand he took in defence of law at the dangerous and critical moment of the first outbreak.

I am getting on very slowly with my essay. I fancy it will startle the Examiners a little—I mean of course by its novel style and mode of treating the subject, not by its merits. Here I have written a tremendous letter all about myself and my own doings, and I hope you will do the same ; for, though I am afraid I have thought more of what I wisht to say than what you would like to hear, it is just all that you have to say on any or all of these or other subjects, that is what I most want to get from you. Since writing the above I have been down in Bristol looking at some of the churches. The Cathedral is very poor, in the Transition style from Decorated English to Perpendicular, but bad of both. There is, however, a very beautiful Norman gateway in the close.

To Mr. John Ellerton

BRYN HYFRYD, DOLGELLY, *August* 9*th*, 1848.
[Finished *August* 25*th*.]

I am at last endeavouring to begin an answer to your most delightful letter. . . . I had a beautiful passage to Ilfracombe, and the sail from Linton to that place close in shore by moonlight was most enjoyable. I had a very pleasant three weeks at Ilfracombe, and botanised extensively, especially at sea-weeds. It is a curious country ; most of the hills themselves are ugly and tame, but they are intersected by beautiful wooded 'coombes' or vallies. At Ilfracombe itself there is a great contortion of the strata, which makes the hills much broken, especially on the sea-shore, where the rocks are very fine. The Old Red Sandstone is there represented by a sort of soft, very fissile slate.

You will be curious to hear of the church. We went to the parish church. The service was excellently performed (not chorally), the choir consisting of nine girls from the schools in white caps and tippets, who were beautifully trained, but deeper and fuller tones were wanted; the chants were mostly Gregorian, and I got to like them exceedingly. The sermons are a great deal quieter than they were four years ago. One man whose face struck me much, preached twice: . . . He seemed really to feel the Church and the Sacraments to be Divine, and not mere amulets, or things to be talked big about. The last Sunday I was there I heard the Bishop of Fredericton preach for his new Cathedral, and was exceedingly pleased. There was nothing very striking in the sermon, which was, however, sensible, moderate, and good; but his earnest, gentle manner quite won me to love him.

I left Ilfracombe this day week by coach to Barnstaple; thence also by coach to Tiverton, and thence by rail to Taunton, . . . and went up into the town to see the churches. St. Mary's is perfectly magnificent. It is early Perpendicular, and has a grand lofty tower of six or seven stories. It has been lately fully restored, and so I had to pay sixpence admission, much to my disgust at the imitation of St. Paul's. It is very large, but naviform, and has no gallery but a small one at the west end for the organ. The columns are light and exquisite, the capitals being an angel-bust holding a shield; the roof is of the finest wood-carving, and the sittings are a sort of open wide seats. There are some good new stained-glass windows, and a fine font with a most magnificent cover to it. I think it would be perfect in its kind, but for the polychrome which covers almost every place; yet so exquisitely has it been managed that you do not perceive the gaudiness till you examine the parts in detail. . . .

After seeing the churches, I met Chambers by appointment at the station, and again railed to Bristol. Here we ran to give him a peep at St. Mary's Redcliffe. . . . We started by the mail at a quarter past 2 A.M., reached Hereford about 6, after seeing the sun rise beautifully over Malvern, and then ran to peep at the Cathedral. It is neither large nor rich, but a noble, simple Early English building (with some Perpendicular windows), and Dean Merewether seems restoring it in the best possible taste. Thence for a long way over the rich undulating plain of veritable Old Red Sandstone to Kington, where we entered Wales.

Thence we wound up through hills of slate, some pretty, others not, passing one exquisite spot, the vale and inn of Pen-y-bont, to Rhayader. Here the scenery became wilder and more mountainous, and gradually we ascended to a most bleak and dismal region on the shoulder of Plinlimmon, a mere bog-dumpling, whose head did not appear. Thence we drove rapidly down, obtaining most glorious views, to Aberystwith, which we reached at 4 P.M. We strolled on the beach in the evening and picked up pebbles, and then went to bed.

At half-past 7 A.M. we again mounted the coach, and after winding over and among some fine hills, on surmounting one ridge, we came upon a sight which I shall never forget. Below us was a rich hill with a mixture of grassy hollows, woods, and thickets sloping down to the noble estuary of the Dyfi (or Dovey), the tide being fully in ; and on the opposite shore, just where the narrow lake opened into the blue sea, lay the village of Aberdyfi, the scene of the earlier part of the first story of the *Shadows of the Clouds.*[1] It was at the base of high hills soon rising into high mountains, swelling with knolls of all colours, some a rich purple with heath, others a dun yellow with furze, others all tints of green, and, as if to complete the whole, the light white clouds hid the sunshine from innumerable spots on the hills, and their 'shadows' were ever shifting and changing the wondrous beauty of the view. This was at ten on a bright August morning, when everything lookt fresh and joyous. I cannot describe my feelings at the sight, which probably on that very spot suggested the title of that wonderful book—perhaps had no small share in exciting the thoughts which there find expression. I do not think the most bigoted of the orthodox could feel any bitterness against the poor doubter *there.* It seemed as if it were not one Oxford student's questionings that came before me, but the groans and cries of a distracted

[1] By J. A. Froude.

world. All the seething abysses of humanity, growing ever
hotter as centuries flew by, seemed boiling over in a
wild negation, emptying the world of its life yet pleading
for living beings, bursting in its phrensy many heart-threads,
yet checkt and pulled aside by others more fully instinct
with the life of God. And then all this misery and madness
was so real and well grounded. I, 'the heir of all the ages,'
inherited, as part of the awful legacy, the accumulation and
culmination of all they had of dark and horrible, and it ever
went with me, casting its shadow on me, and threatening
itself to crush me. And then the 72nd Psalm rang through
my ears, and the calm sea reflecting the sky and the solid
mountains seemed to confirm its words, and I felt that all the
beauty before me was owing to the sun, and the shadows on
the mountains were cast by their own earthy exhalations,
while *he* kept his steady course unchanging above. I am
afraid all this sounds absurd enough on paper; but the
Shadows of the Clouds made an impression on me of a sort
that no other book ever did, and the scene, so glorious in itself,
and entwined with such associations, might well move me
more than ordinary views.

To continue my narrative: we soon reached Machynlleth,
pretty and no more; and then drove through some beautiful
vallies, till at the end of one of them part of Cader Idris
appeared. We descended into the long straight valley of Tal-
y-Llyn, barren and rugged, which runs along his back; walked
up it, and then rounding the end of Cader, came upon a
beautiful view of the rich valley of Dolgelly, with mountains of
moderate height on the other side. We reacht the town at
half-past one. Mathison, Mackenzie, and Gill came three or
four hours afterwards from Chester by Rhuabon and Bala.
We have a most excellent house just outside the town—on,
in fact, the base of Cader Idris, though he is too near to be
visible.

We have now (August 20th, I am ashamed to say) had
many glorious walks, as to the waterfalls of Rhaiadr Dû, etc.,
and the tops of various mountains, including of course Cader
Idris, which has some noble precipices. We read very tolerably, about five hours a day; I botanise considerably, and we

are seldom less than six hours on a walk. Our costumes are, of course, peculiar. I, for instance, appear in a shooting-jacket with a shepherd's plaid over my shoulders, a wide-awake on my head, a large vasculum on my back, and a stout stick in my hand ; to say nothing of knives, small vasculum, hammers, etc., in pockets ; but I get mighty little time for private reading or writing. We leave this on Thursday week, and we have strong hopes of getting a house at Llanberis for the remaining fortnight, when we shall inspect Snowdon well.

The church here is a singular building; the guides call it "a neat structure in the Greek style of architecture." This sketch will give you an idea of the windows, but at a distance the effect is not bad. The inside is most rough and slovenly : coarse open seats like forms with backs to them, rude gallery with an arch of this shape, etc. The morning service and sermon are in Welsh. We always attend, and in fact can take almost as good a part in the service as in England. It not only made one bless God for an uniform Liturgy in which all might join of different tongues, realising the Romish idea of universal Latin prayers, but seemed to give a substantial reality and meaning to Catholicity ; it was truly the Catholic, the universal Church, offering up united prayers, overleaping the bounds of race and tongue, asserting one Lord, one faith, one baptism.

I send you the *Politics*, for I am sure you must long for them. Maurice's *Confessions of William Milward*[1] contain treasures of practical instruction both for our own hearts and our conduct to others. I know no tale to compare to them for divine unconscious humanity; words cannot express the depth of my obligations to them ; verily God's Laws are mightier than theories. The magnificent *Letters to Land-lords* must be Kingsley's ; no one else could write them. They convey the true ideal of English character. You will see that the last few numbers are almost exclusively addrest to the upper classes. There are some invaluable articles of Maurice's on Education, especially in Nos. 14, 15 ; the former has a most pregnant article on the Colonies. In another year

---

[1] A story published in supplementary numbers of the *Politics*.

men will be compelled to see the gigantic importance of the
question.   I have got the plan of the colony of Canterbury,
but not yet finisht reading it.   Also a singular but pithy
Dialogue by W. S. Landor on Italy. . . .

I quite agree with you that Lord Ashley is a noble fellow
when he rises above his coneyism, but I am very suspicious
of his Ragged School Emigration scheme; surely we have
enough colonies already visited with God's curse for being
composed of the dregs of society.   I can't make out from
Maurice's article what he thinks about it.

There are three most interesting things in yesterday's
paper in the debates.   1st, A short, wise, temperate speech
of Gladstone's on the Education quarrel between Government
and the National Society, in which he by no means rejects
lay management, only complaining of the want of interest
shown by laymen.   Lord John thanked him heartily for his
speech, and said that the quarrel was all but settled.   2nd,
Gladstone made a long speech, universally applauded, on
Lord Grey's mismanagement of Vancouver's Island, which
will soon be among our most important colonies.   3rd, The
money voted for the Professorships at the Universities, which,
of course, involved an attack on both Professorships and
Universities.   Goulburn ably defended both; and Lord John
said, in reference to the petition for the admission of Dissenters to degrees at Cambridge, that his idea was to make
us give them certificates of examination (the three and a
quarter's years course they have now) when they had been
examined as if for our degrees, but make the London University confer the degrees.   Gladstone again made a most
beautiful, short, sensible speech, testifying that at Oxford the
colleges were daily becoming more efficacious, real living
bodies, and thanking Lord John warmly for his wise, practical
views and intentions.

I have not time now to talk of . . . so will pass on.   Nor
indeed of the Sabbath; only observing that in my idea
'Sabbath-neglecting' would be the mischief, and 'Sabbath-
breaking' mean simply nothing.

I have just read through *The Princess* again with the
utmost delight; I do not know whether its wisdom or its

beauty predominates. I am still, however, in the dark as to the meaning of one of the Idyls, that beginning—

Now sleeps the crimson petal, now the white.

I utterly and entirely recant the slanders I formerly uttered against its purity; *The Saint's Tragedy* has taught me truer ideas. By the way, I have also just read *that* book again, and of course likewise with redoubled pleasure and, I hope, more than pleasure; somehow or other much of its manifold meaning must have escaped me on the first perusal. I had been thinking for some weeks on one of the mysterious subjects which it handles gently but resolutely; I scarcely know what suggested it to me—I believe a remarkable passage in the first *Guesses*. I had much inward debating, but at last I came to the conclusion which, to my great delight, I have since found *The Saint's Tragedy* teaches.

But I must now (August 25th) return to your kind comments on my scrap of Essay,[1] which I have long received. I agree in the main with your observations, tho' I am not inclined to adopt all your alterations. . . . To tell the truth, as, whether successful or unsuccessful, I can of course *write* only for the former alternative, I am not without hopes in that case of effecting something in poor Oxford, which, I forgot to tell you, is now, I hear on good authority, overrun with earnest disciples of Froude and George Sand; especially a knot of Rugby men. Tennyson I will think about, but I am loth to leave him out; he explains so well what I mean, and is useful collaterally by showing that I am not transcribing cut-and-dry notions from Maurice or elsewhere, but mean what I say, and am able to recognize the same idea under dissimilar forms. Manichæism is very delicate ground, though possibly I may do as you suggest; but I am afraid not only of seeming Μαυρικίζειν, but of marring all by what must be in fact a general attack on the whole religious world of all parties. I have written very little more, being hard up for time here, but will send when I have a decent scrap. There is no limit to the length, but in my case the difficulty will be to write long enough from want of time; I cannot help my introduction being disproportionate. . . .

[1] For the Hulsean prize.

I saw an extract from the article that you mention; it
spoke of a High Church feeling, even when 'Tractarianism
proper' is on the wane, gaining ground in both Universities.
I believe it is true, and we may well thank God for it; we
need it much.   Politics drive me mad, when I think of them.
Ireland I expect every moment to break out afresh, not perhaps in civil war but in endless skirmishing and bloodshed,
and it seems 'the spirit of the age' will not hang traitors.
The Chartists in London have, I suppose you know, been
found to be solemnly leagued with the French Communists,
and the same confederation extends through Europe.   We
shall have a bloody winter in the provinces, perhaps in
London.   O that Gladstone or even Peel were in!   Italy is
vexatious indeed; I suppose her time is not yet come, but
injustice   and   robbery   shall   not   always   prevail,   however
Disraeli may sneer at 'the sentimental principle of nation-
ality'—that's because the Italians are not Jews.

. . . But it has struck 2 A.M., so good night or morning,
which you please.

To his Father

DOLGELLY, *August* 16th, 1848.

. . . On Sundays we have attended the Welsh service in
the morning, which we could easily follow, and the English in
the afternoon.   As there are four services in the day, the
English sermon generally falls to some clergyman passing
through, and they do not always fare well in consequence;
for instance, ten days ago an old canon of Manchester who
preached recommended us to keep regularly a journal for
entering all our good and all our bad actions, and to take
care to keep the balance on the side of the former, as we
should then feel very comfortable on our death-beds ! !

To Mr. John Ellerton

25 ATHENÆUM STREET,
PLYMOUTH, *September* 24th, 1848.

I presume from your silence that you are waiting for a
fresh instalment of my unhappy Essay. . . .

I spent a very pleasant month at Dolgelly, and a still more pleasant fortnight at Llanberis, right at the foot of Snowdon ; C. C. Babington was there for two or three days, and I had some very enjoyable botanical expeditions with him.   But I have no time to say more than that, after scrambling about crags and precipices to my heart's content, I left Llanberis last Monday, went to Bangor, Menai Bridge, Britannia Bridge, Beaumaris, Bangor, and Conway, and came on by a night train to Plymouth, where my family have been nearly a fortnight.   It is an interesting place, but I cannot stop to talk about it.   I hope to enjoy the neighbourhood of Torquay. . . .

I have just got Henry of Exeter's August Charge, as well as Archdeacon Manning's.   The first I have read with much satisfaction ; probably I should not agree with all he says, but his defence of the Prayer-book and his utter demolition of ―― are truly magnificent.   Manning's I have only glanced at ; it is chiefly on the Hampden case, and seems written in quite the right spirit, and promises to be invaluable.   I never read anything more beautiful than some of the passages.

To Mr. John Ellerton

3 Torwood Mount,
Torquay, *October 2nd*, 1848.

This is a most beautiful spot, and the air (on the hills) far less relaxing than I expected ; the verdure is of the richest green, and the view of Torbay through the wooded *villose* hills is exquisite.   At the back we have within a mile or two noble limestone and marble cliffs, and then the beautiful forms into which the sea wears the New Red Sandstone, with the coast trending away by Teignmouth and Exmouth down to the Bill of Portland, which is visible in very clear weather. Henry of Exeter's villa, Bishopstowe, commands the most beautiful spot of the whole.

I never was in such a state of mental and spiritual lethargy, broken only momentarily by occasional circumstances, as in Wales, and for a fortnight before I went there. I do not mean that I did not think and ponder, doubt and believe, *jactabam et jactabar*—I might as easily live without meat and drink—but all the grand scenery did not move me as it should have done; and the utmost effect was to make me separate once or twice from the party, get close down to a waterfall, and chant some Psalm at the top of my voice into the midst of the roar—a singular employment truly. Nor am I much better now, nor expect to be till I hear Trinity organ again, and am able to open my mouth on the subject of subjects.

I am more and more drinking in Maurice's *Lord's Prayer*. I will go so far as to say that, except the *Kingdom of Christ*, there is not a theological book in English to equal it; but it is very hard to get imbued with it. There are, however, some inestimable sermons in the other volume,[1] particularly a Lent series on our Lord's temptation. It is such a pleasure to dwell on them that I must give you a bit that is mighty indeed against the worst and the most unceasing of temptations, viz. to deny our baptism. . . .

[Then follow two quotations from *Christmas Day and other Sermons*, from Sermon xii. pp. 167, 168, and from Sermon xiii. pp. 181, 182.]

I think the Canterbury scheme admirable, and wish it all success. With regard to what you say about joining it, the thought has more than once flitted across my mind. I am afraid that, at all events, a selfish attachment to home would keep me here, to say nothing of unselfish attachment. I cannot bear the idea of being separated from the fortunes of our own ancestral Church and 'not yet enslaved, not wholly vile' England. But more than this, I am sure Maurice is right in dwelling so strongly on the sin of choosing our own circumstances instead of following God's course: now our whole bent and purpose has been to labour in the English Church, and without some distinct call from God, I do not see what right we have to abandon it.

[1] *Christmas Day and other Sermons*, 1st ed. 1843.

To his Father

CAMBRIDGE, *November 17th*, 1848.

. . . Jenny Lind is, I believe, to be here on the 25th ; at least there is some negotiation pending touching the Union room for her, as they say it will hold eight hundred. A more successful attempt than usual has been made this year to get up a football club, which I have joined, as it will relieve the dull monotony of Cambridge walks. I was last night summoned suddenly to a meeting of delegates from various schools, to draw up a code of laws, effecting a compromise between the Eton and Rugby systems, which are totally different. This kept me till late, and I forgot that it was my day for writing, so that I am sorry to say this is Friday. . . . You ask after my brambles : the few which I felt sure I had named rightly, were so ; those I had guessed at vaguely were mostly wrong. Some gave Babington a good deal of trouble to discriminate, being gathered late in the year, when they were no longer in perfection. I had got hold of several good ones, and he accepted of several (I had dried duplicates of many) as useful additions to his herbarium ; one in particular, which I found the day I walked towards Teignmouth, was the only English specimen he had ever seen answering to the figure and description of a German bramble (at least only very unlike varieties of it had been found in England). I had but the one specimen, but it was of more consequence to him than me. The great long-branched thing was, as I supposed, an odd form of a common sort. Curiously enough, the beautiful bramble which filled the wood at Berry Pomeroy Castle, and which I also found on the way to Anstis Cove, was another form of the plant I mentioned last but one, and was quite strange to Babington, though he said he felt sure that I had done right in referring it to that species. He has asked me, when I have full leisure (for he is most careful and anxious not to interfere with my regular work), to write him out a list of those I found, with their localities. Reckoning up roughly, I find that, including recognised 'varieties,' I obtained this summer ten brambles at Llanberis, and sixteen at Plymouth and Torquay, which, I think, is pretty well for a beginning. I will now conclude, as I am in the midst of a high-flown panegyric on 'our good Edmund,' which has to be given in to-morrow night, and the greater part of which is as yet unwritten.

To Mr. John Ellerton

15 Lansdown Crescent, Cheltenham,
December 19*th*, 1848.

. . . I own I have been much annoyed about the Hulsean : not that I had any right to expect it from the literary, annotatory, and other merit which generally decides such matters in Cambridge University. But I do believe mine had some rough life in it, not altogether useless for the times.

What lots of 'historical' debates at the Union we who remain shall witness next year ! I groan at the thought ; only I promise myself the luxury of endless denuntiation (to be received with the additional luxury of endless groaning) of the wretched impostor,[1] calling himself a historian.

To Mr. John Ellerton

Cheltenham, *December* 29*th*, 1848.

. . . What is to become of Ireland ? Of course you have read the deeply interesting letters of Lords Sligo and Westmeath in the *Times*. A letter has to-day reacht some relations of mine here from one of their family who is married to the clergyman of a parish near Skibbereen, which says that an order has just come down from the Commissioners to say that the land shall support all, and that relief shall be given to all in the parish, whether they will work or not, at the expense of all occupiers in the parish, every one being starved already. From all quarters I hear that the sufferings of the clergy and smaller gentry this winter are likely far to surpass any of the previous sufferings of the poor. I do not know a parallel for the cool perverseness of Lord John. There seems a dead silence in the political atmosphere : we must only trust that Gladstone is preparing for a more terrible onslaught on the

---

[1] Macaulay, see p. 106.

English, Irish, and colonial policy of our miserable government. If he anticipates Disraeli and leads the attack, there
is some hope of his attaining the post of pilot to the world.
Yet Ireland will more than perplex even *him*.

Ellerton took his degree and went down in 1849,
and was for some time tutor to some Scotch boys, to
whose education some of the letters of this year refer.
His friend took a keen interest in his efforts for the
boys' improvement, and also advised and encouraged
him in the difficult and delicate task of instilling
'Catholic' principles into the family.

In the spring of this year Hort obtained his
scholarship at Trinity, and in W. H. Thompson's
opinion, did best of his year in classics in the examination. He had begun to attend the meetings of the
Ray Club, prominent members of which were Paget,
the two Stokes, and Adam Sedgwick, and of which he
himself became a member the next year. There was
by way of recreation much botanising with Babington,
and with parties conducted by Professor Henslow.
Other intimate friends were Henry Mackenzie, C. H.
Chambers, and J. Westlake, and he corresponded freely
with Mr. Gerald Blunt, as well as with Ellerton, his
letters to whom had something of the character of a
journal intime. Another important friendship, acquired
in his first term, was that of Daniel Macmillan, to whom
he had been introduced by his tutor, W. H. Thompson.
He himself has told, in a paragraph contributed to Mr.
T. Hughes' *Memoir* (pp. 213, 214), how pleasant talks
in the larger shop recently opened by Macmillan led to
a warm intimacy.

The Long Vacation was spent mostly at the Lakes;
in the course of his rambles there his mind ran much
on theological difficulties, and his perplexities caused

at times deep depression. The result was that not long after his return to Cambridge he wrote to Maurice a long letter on Eternal Punishment and Redemption, which elicited the answer printed in Maurice's *Life*.[1] This important letter led to a friendship which lasted till Maurice's death.

At the end of the same term he took scarlatina; the attack was apparently not regarded as severe at the time, but it left a permanent mark on his constitution. The immediate consequence was that he was only able to take the first part of the Mathematical Tripos in January 1850, and was therefore placed in the Junior Optimes, whereas it had been hoped that he would be a wrangler. He 'passed for honours' in the first part of the examination, and wished to have *æger* affixed to his name in the final class list, but the application was refused for fear of abuse of the precedent. He had not dared to take an 'ægrotat' degree, with the risk of being thereby excluded from the Classical Tripos; strangely enough, it was not certain whether or no an 'honour ægrotat' would count for this purpose as 'honours.' He had therefore to be content with a place much below his merits, and unredeemed by any official explanation. It was necessary in those days to obtain honours in mathematics in order to go in for classical honours, and candidates for the Chancellor's Classical Medals were required to have obtained at least a second class in mathematics; from this competition he was therefore debarred. He wrote as follows to his mother on this unlucky accident: "I am afraid that you all take my humble place to heart far more than I do myself. I now hardly ever think of it. In fact, if I

[1] Vol. ii. pp. 15, 16.

did, I should be convicting myself of insincerity and inconsistency, having always talked pretty loudly against the folly of making the degree the sole end in reading, and supposing it to be the main object for which we come up to the University. Every one here knows why I am so low. You all know it, and I shall probably take an opportunity of letting Tait know before he leaves Rugby. Almost the only reason for regret, apart from the loss of a good chance of a Chancellor's Medal, is that I shall be exhibited in the Calendar in a position which will make people think that I despised the mathematics of the University, and only read enough of them to allow me to take honours in classics, a proceeding which I have always vehemently condemned."

The effects of scarlatina are doubtless also to be traced in his place in the Classical Tripos, which was a disappointment to his friends. He was bracketed third, E. H. Perowne being first, and C. Schreiber second.

His father and mother left Cheltenham in this year for a house which they rented for a year at the village of Newland, in Monmouthshire, whence they moved in 1851 to Hardwick House, near Chepstow. After a summer spent partly in seeing the new home and partly in visits to friends, including one to Ellerton at his first curacy, during which he "sat up all night talking and packing," he returned to Cambridge to read for the newly-instituted examinations in Moral and in Natural Sciences, and for the Trinity Fellowships. He became a member of the Ray Club and a Fellow of the Cambridge Philosophical Society. In this and the following years his activity seemed to expand even further in all directions, while interests apparently conflicting did not distract him from the pursuit of aims clearly seen and deliberately chosen.

His first letter to Maurice had naturally led to others ; he consulted him again about a course of philosophical reading.   Maurice's answer [1] indicates that one object of the letter was to obtain guidance concerning the light thrown by philosophical theories on contemporary social problems.   His interest in Plato and Aristotle, to say nothing of more modern speculations, was anything but antiquarian ; in particular, the subject of Communism was one which was much in his thoughts.

In May 1850 he for the first time heard Maurice preach.   The following day he breakfasted with him to meet some of the ' Christian Socialists '—Mr. Ludlow, Mr. T. Hughes, and Vansittart Neale.   He again breakfasted with Maurice the next day, this time alone, and thenceforward their meetings were tolerably frequent.   His critical attitude towards ' Christian Socialism ' is illustrated by his letters to Ellerton.

Botanical work went briskly forward ; there was much correspondence with Babington, who got his friend to review botanical books in the *Annals of Botany, e.g.* Arnott's new *Flora* published in this year. He also was frequently called on to advise friends beginning the study of botany.   Many friends, and not a few strangers, both now and in later years, received from him ungrudging and valuable assistance of this kind in the Alps or elsewhere.

On theological and literary subjects he exchanged opinions freely by post with Daniel and Alexander Macmillan.   The former gave him an interesting piece of advice with regard to the writing of prize

[1] See *Life of F. D. Maurice*, vol. ii. p. 37.

essays, telling him that he "must put his thoughts
into the form that people are accustomed to : those
who have important things to say should try to say
them in the dialect of those to whom they speak."
From a letter of Alexander Macmillan's it appears
that Hort did not at this time [1] appreciate Tennyson's
In Memoriam. The ground of objection was theological. For instance, he strongly disapproved of the
notion that 'Universalism is necessary to sustain
love.'

To Mr. John Ellerton

CAMBRIDGE, *March 5th,* 1849.

My dear Ellerton—The Addison, or a part thereof, have
just left my rooms after a most exquisitely amusing semi-
paper from Isaacs on 'Solitude'; and now I am sitting down
to begin to spin a yarn of such brain-stuff as I can command:
and in fact I have enough to say to make the Post-Office's
fortune. . . .

The day you left Hare's pamphlet appeared, with a
magnificent letter of Maurice's appended. The former is
very good, tho' certainly abusive and once or twice unfair;
he speaks excellently on Inspiration. Maurice has thundered
again against all parties, charging upon them the prevalent
Pantheism, etc., and prophesying their downfall, and the crash
when it happens; he manfully asserts the Priesthood, at the
same time showing its especial function to be the *setting free*
of conscience, etc.—Most affectionately yours,

FENTON J. A. HORT.

To Mr. John Ellerton

CAMBRIDGE, *March 10th,* 1849.
FINISHT, *April 1st.*

. . . I continue my letter—and really I am bursting with
matter and explosive gas. I believe the book I had better

[1] See vol. ii. p. 71.

next speak of is Froude's *Nemesis of Faith*, a truly wonderful
book.   Its motto needs no comment to assure us of its truth
now; it is from the end of the *Prometheus*, καὶ μὴν ἔργῳ . . .
σεσάλευται and σκιρτᾷ δ' . . . ἀποδεικνύμενα.[1]
It is briefly the tale of a young man tormented with sceptical
doubts, who enters holy orders, is driven from them by the
exposure of an evangelical, resigns his preferment, and goes to
Italy, where his doubts increase, and he falls into a strange
love-affair with the wife of a boorish English squire.   At last, on
her asking him to run off with her (do not judge her too
harshly till you read the book), he rushes madly away, and is
rescued from suicide by an old seceded Oxford friend, who
easily carries him over to Rome; but he seems to abandon
that, and the last sentence only declares his utter desolation
and ruin.   The moral is the vengeance that a faith takes on
such as lightly desert it; but of course it is chiefly the col-
lateral matter which is meant to tell.   The early part consists
chiefly of letters from the young man, and a sort of autobiography he writes.   I like it, tho', poor fellow, he is fast
falling into atheism; it is beyond measure tearfully earnest
and awakening.   There is a most exquisite scene where the
poor rector tells his sad state of mind to his kind and noble
bishop : I *must* copy a page.

[Then follows a quotation from R. H. Froude's *Nemesis of Faith*.]

. . . They must be strange eyes that can read this passage,
and continue dry.   The bishop says soon after what cannot
(to use a review phrase, slightly altered) be too deeply thought
over.   "There is not one," he says, "not one in all these many
years which I have seen upon the earth, not one man of
more than common power, who has been contented to abide
in the old ways."   I have not time to talk more of the book.
I have the first prize for Latin Declamations. . . . Of course
I shall have to laud some 'distinguisht character' in Latin.
Some want me to take Arnold, but you will easily understand
that there are strong objections to so doing.   If poor old
Wordsworth dies in time, he will do gloriously; if he does not,

[1] Aesch. *Prom.* 1080-1088.

I think I shall take Coleridge; and if I do, I will not mince matters, but speak out : it is only a pity one will have to disguise oneself in Latin. With the result of the Craven I have no right to complain, except as sharing the disgrace of my year, three second years being first. Maine seems to have thought Beamont best of us, but some, if not all, the other examiners place me at the head of my year. . . . Of course I must do my best to get senior classic, if possible. I am now (I don't mean *to-day*, Sunday, April 1st) busy enough getting up mathematics for a scholarship. I put off not only the Porson but 'Titus' till yesterday, when at half-past two I began, and wrote forty hexameters before chapel ; but after that I could not write a line, and of course sent nothing in.

I have glanced at an anonymous volume of poems (*The Strayed Reveller, etc.*, by A.) by Mat. Arnold ; it seemed mild, but a by no means contemptible article in the *Guardian* on it and the *Ambarvalia* speaks well of it. The latter book it commends, Clough's part at least. Maurice has just announced his volume of sermons on the Liturgy, " chiefly considered as a preservation against Romanism " : item J. Hare, a second volume of parish sermons : item Kingsley, his Twenty-five Village Sermons. By the way, you do not mention whether you received the pamphlet of Hare's. I have carried Landor's Works into the Union, and we have a lot of odd books, Miss Martineau *inter alia*.

I do not know whether you recollect at the 1688 debate a nice-looking man opposite making a very sensible speech cutting both parties ; his name was ——. Various things made me wish to know him, and I have made his acquaintance. It occurred to me that if I stayed up here any time, should I get a scholarship and fellowship, I should be grievously neglecting an obvious duty if I did not keep an intimate connexion with my juniors, or such at least as, from their possessing heads or hearts, I might be able to lend a helping hand to ; for though bitter experience daily shows how much I need guidance myself, I cannot think that any excuse for shirking the responsibility of guiding others, where possible. This first experiment is not promising : —— is, I really believe, a fine fellow, but no theologian, and entirely swallowed up by rank Toryism and Byron and Shelley, but has an aversion to Maurice, whom he spoke of as 'the well-known radical,' who in all his lectures talkt of nothing but 'the masses' and their rights, and how 'they began to feel themselves men.' He said that Maurice was a most thorough-going disciple of Macaulay (in philosophy as well as politics), and that the one idea of his mind seemed to be '*vox populi, vox Dei*'!!! I had a long battle with him the other day on a point really involving the materialistic controversy. I dare not despair of him; besides I have great faith in his beautiful face and head; but it is no easy task I have undertaken.

I ought to have told you before that I went three weeks ago to hear Jenny Lind, who gave a concert here. It would be useless to attempt to describe it. Her face is utterly unlike all pictures : she has high cheek-bones and a face by no means buttery, as she is represented; but rather plain than otherwise, except in her most beautiful, calm, living eyes. But, when she begins to sing, all is changed; her features indeed do not themselves become beautiful, but they seem to be transparent, and let you see only the pure, heavenly, sunny, joyous spirit venting itself in the softest, richest waves of music. I am afraid these words will sound affected, but they are the best I can think of, to express the peculiar character of her singing.

I really know little of passing politics, except of the last month, for before that I seldom read the papers; so you must not ask opinions where I have none. Perhaps this is wrong; would it were the only duty I have neglected! Of late I have observed Gladstone ever at his post, quietly exposing abuses, giving up private wishes for public good, being reviled and not reviling, in all things a faithful steward to his Master.

If you have leisure to write, do not be afraid of tiring me, even with the petty incidents of your daily life. I long to know (of course, really) your little pupils, how you fare with them, and with their parents. You would smile if I were to write down the prospect of glorious work I see before you, to which it has been God's blessed will for your and for old Scotland's good to call you; He is indeed shaking not earth only, but also heaven. O that we could always rest sure, as

we ought, that it is He that is shaking it, that it is the glorious
God that maketh the thunder! but our wretched selfishness
and sin makes this hard.   Let us pray, my dear Ellerton, for
each other, and for all our unknown fellow-strugglers, that we
may so live that we may shrink from no trial laid upon us,
but rejoice and triumph in all that befalls, as a fresh unveiling
of His perfect glory!

To Mr. John Ellerton

CAMBRIDGE, *March* 15*th*, 1849.

I cannot but regard it as a wonderfully providential thing
that you have been summoned up under such strange circumstances.   Of course you must display your true colors.   You
are no 'Puseyite,' nor should you appear one.   You are a
Catholic Churchman.   You should show yourself as such,
taking every opportunity of inculcating the idea that Catholicity means not exclusiveness but comprehensiveness, that *all*
bonds of opinion must be exclusive, that the bond of a
common divine life derived in Sacraments is the most comprehensive bond possible.   I think, I more than think, you
should claim leave to attend the Communion, and you may
have opportunities of showing that, whether all the prayers
are orthodox or not, the Sacrament remains unchanged; and
point to the numberless passages in our Prayer-book which
militate against absence from the Communion.   With —— I
would be as frank.   Tell him that on the fundamental part of
the Sacramental doctrines as well as the Succession, you agree
with him, though you may have differences in detail.   Tell
him your first object is to make the —— churchmen, and consistent churchmen ; that indoctrination must be a later and
slower process ; that you must start from the points you have
in common with them, and follow that course which God
shall seem to point out, especially avoiding startling them
needlessly.   The prayers you have to read or rather compose
are, I should think, a very powerful instrument, especially for
winning over ——.   But with the boys I think you should
have very little 'dogmatic' teaching, but make the Catechism
and Bible your text-books—not text—in one sense, but you

can make the Bible a wonderful instrument, simply by not treating it as a bundle of texts. Read Maurice's Queen's College Lecture on Theology. I suppose I could *jaw* you in this manner to all eternity, but I must stop for want of time, and really you know as well as I do, and better, how to act. May God direct and bless you and your efforts in the great and glorious post He has assigned you.

To Mr. John Ellerton

Cambridge, *Easter Day*, 1849 [*April 8th*].

. . . Talking, however, of —— reminds me of the Bishop of London, who—all honour to him for it—has abolisht the annual private and select Confirmation of the children of the nobility at the Chapel Royal. It is a disgrace to the Church that it should have lasted so long.

Do not trouble yourself about writing when you have not plenty of time for it; but I am longing to hear all about your little charges, and do not yet know even their names. If you have time, I should think it would be worth your while, as spring advances and you are living in the country, to work a little at botany. Independently of my love for the science itself, and the principles of universal application which seem insensibly to take hold of one from the pursuit, I find it very advantageous and refreshing to be able to take refuge for a while from the circle of restless human interests of all kinds in something lower and yet with all the impress of perfection in its own kind,—something not spiritual, and yet rewarding research with views of infinite order and beauty. This of course increases with the earnestness and reality of one's study of the subject. Dilettantism here, as everywhere, is barren and fruitless. Further, I fancy you might find it good to interest your pupils in pursuits pure and healthy, while yet not a mere matter of books, without diminishing the manliness and freedom which is only acquired (*teste Platone*, etc. etc.) by plenty of bodily exercise and recreation.

I have got a volume of poems by 'Currer, Ellis, and Acton Bell' (*it is said* τριῶν ὀνομάτων μορφὴ μία, but I do not believe it), *i.e.* the author*ess* (as I now feel quite sure) of *Jane*

Eyre and her—sisters, I suppose. There is scarcely a grain of poetry as far as I have read; but under a somewhat commonplace guise there is so much curious earnestness and feeling that they are highly interesting; but that is all. ' Currer's ' are much the best.

Will you mention when you write whether you finisht *Vanity Fair?* Thackeray was here for a day or two to get up materials for his last number, where, I hear, he introduces his hero to ' Oxbridge,' while he has friends at ' Camford'; he has a massive, rugged face, not stupid but, as far as I saw, which was not well, not remarkable.

Macmillan promises to use his best endeavours to get Maurice and Kingsley up here, and introduce me to them. I need not say I shall in that case do all I decently can to deepen and perpetuate the acquaintance, and, if so, I shall have abundant opportunity of letting Maurice know that *some* at least (I greatly fear, not many) regard their battles as their own. That the strife is deepening, I feel more strongly every day. I really must close, and read mathematics for to-morrow; so good-night, my dear Ellerton.

To Mr. John Ellerton

CAMBRIDGE, *May 22nd*, 1849.

Thank you much for your very interesting account of the boys. Are you sure that you are right in making Phædrus the introduction to Latin, whatever be the conventional First Book? He is easy, but stupid and utterly worthless. I must say I think Maurice is in a great measure right when he speaks of " the wisdom of the old notion, that only the best books, only those which carry a kind of authority with them, should be set before boys; when they have been drilled by them into habits of deference and humility, then they may venture, if their calling requires it, upon the study of the worst, for then they will have acquired the true discerning spirit, that spirit of which the judging spirit is the counterfeit; the one perceiving the real quality of the food which is offered, the other setting up its own partial and immature tastes and aversions as the standard of what is good and evil."

You, of course, are the best judge as to whether he is up to
Cæsar, but I should not call Cæsar a hard author, and his
style is plain and vigorous. Livy (even the narrative) seems
to me much harder, chiefly from the condensed style. What
do you say to the more spirited and easy of Cicero's *Orationes*?
Virgil's *Æneid* seems to me particularly good for boys. I
cannot agree with you as to the bad expediency of teaching
Latin before Greek. The change from a non-inflected language
to one so rich in grammatical differences as the Greek, should,
I think, be made gradually, and the direct, rigid nature of the
Latin makes it probably the best of all languages for the
teaching of the mechanical but most necessary part of grammar.
The recent neglect of Latin in Germany and England is producing miserable results, producing very showy and very
superficial *Greek* scholars. Besides, think of the briars and
thickets that would fence off your boys from the 'streaming
fountains' in reading Homer; to say nothing of constructions,
his philology is as hard as that of all other Greek authors put
together: I think it is generally read a great deal too early.
He labours under another disadvantage in common with
Herodotus : surely it is well to have secured a good footing in
Attic before you perplex a boy with other dialects. In prose
Xenophon and Plato's *Apology* and the narrative parts of the
Crito and *Phædo* would do at first, and then Demosthenes'
Philippics and *Olynthiacs*.

Poetry is harder to select. If Euripides were more than
semivir he would be excellent, and still I think selections
might be made, as well as easy bits of Sophocles (who is quite
vir). I should think one great way of chaining his interest
would be to check the boyish (as well as mannish) custom of
considering that a word in Latin or Greek has a certain
number of words answering to it in English, all equally good,
and *vice versâ ;* and to show as you go along (which is easily
done in a good author, whose language really expresses thought)
that no word would have done equally well in Latin, and that
a corresponding care must be exercised in English—in short,
to teach *language*, the most entrancing of all subjects for a
young and active mind. As for English poetry, I should be
sorry if he pretended to like Tennyson, or even Wordsworth ;

it would seem to me purely mischievous and unnatural to force subjective poetry upon a mind which requires only objective poetry, and would otherwise be either disgusted or forced into an artificial and unreal precocity. I think you have chosen very well in making him read Scott. Spenser would, I suppose, be *the* book, if he were not too 'immoral' and Bible-like for ——'s taste; but —— could not object to Southey, who would suit your purpose well, especially in *Madoc*. *If* there were but a decent rendering of Homer ! ! Pope, I believe, may do good by what of the original he has unwittingly and un-willingly let through, but this would not compensate for the mischief of filling the boy's head with a jingle-jangle of pompous nothings.

I cannot say much for the Rugby teaching of history. Pinnock's *Goldsmith* is (I think) the text-book in the lower forms, then Keightley. In the Twenty, Price used to expect us to amass materials anywhence; and much the same in the Sixth. As far as I recollect, the whole *direct* teaching *in Form* was of English History, Greek and Roman being supposed to be imbibed in small doses in the preparation for historical allusions in classical books, which were always required to be well known. History was also learnt among the 'extras,' or subjects taken up voluntarily at the Christmas examination ; an admirable and elaborate system introduced by Arnold, tho' somewhat marred by Tait, for encouraging the peculiar tastes of each individual. History is, I think, also generally the holiday task in all the forms which have one, viz. all below the Sixth and Twenty ; this is a recent and bad concoc-tion of Tait's and the masters'. But in Form nothing in the world helps a boy on so well as being well acquainted with the best-known periods of Greek and Roman history ; and to be able to answer a question in modern history, asked inci-dentally, prepossesses a master wonderfully.

Recollect that the grand secret of preparation for Rugby is a thorough acquaintance with Latin and Greek grammar. . . .

Pray ask for any other Rugby hints you may wish without scruple. I should think thirteen about the age, if a boy is neither genius nor fool. It is bad to enter in the Lower School, and, on the other hand, it is good to go through several forms and get some fagging. If I rightly take your account of ——, I should say that the tone I would especially cultivate in him would be hatred and impatience of *seeing others* bullied and opprest; he would be too explosive to be submissive, and such a bias would turn his vivacity in a right direction, without his forfeiting the consideration among the rest, which *may* be useful in every way. I need scarcely suggest how history, etc., may be brought to cultivate the same spirit on a wider scale, nor how requisite it will be for all —certainly not least for men of station and property—in the coming time. I am quite convinced that robbing boys of manliness and making them spoonies renders their life wretched at school, and is fully as likely as a different course is to lead them into vicious habits.

W—— (who once read the *Kingdom of Christ*, first edition, and calls it quite unintelligible, even to its own author ! !), a great friend of Harvey Goodwin, told me that at one time Goodwin used to employ all his wit in ridiculing Maurice, but that a lady of his relations who was an admirer of Maurice persuaded Goodwin to read his writings more carefully, and that for the last two years he has had a very high opinion of him.

I do not understand from your letter whether you actually are working at botany, or wishing you could, and managing Master —— at his studies. I do not think you would find your eye for wholes incompatible with an eye for parts; at least I do not think one predominates over the other in me. In fact no one can be a real naturalist who has not in a measure both faculties, and cannot seize the *idea* of a species, independently of technical characters. But you are the best judge in your own case. Macgillivray is perhaps the best for a beginning, and you can easily show the boy that the Linnean system there adopted bears little relation to the actual affinities of plants (which you must be able in a measure to detect), but it is an easy system for reference, and was in fact intended as no more by its great inventor. I protest most strongly against your attack on Gilbert White; his cant and senti-mentalism are those of his age; his proneness for theory sometimes led him astray, but he was in general an accurate observer, wonderfully so for his time and circumstances. Surely Bewick generally gets as much credit as you have given him. He is looked on as the father of modern English engraving, and one of our very highest naturalist artists.

When I read the first third of *Vanity Fair*, I was greatly disgusted ; but, as I advanced, my feeling gradually changed, till I strongly admired it, tho' the end annoyed me. On the whole I think it a work of great power and purpose, though with by no means the dramatic genius (to say nothing · of the sunniness) of Dickens. I thought at first that Dobbin was a mere copy of Tom Pinch, but I now would put it quite on its own ground. One would be inclined to praise the way in which he shows Amelia as drawn out from a mere moping, silly girl into something like character by her love for George Osborne, were it not that he most absurdly calls our attention to her rare and remarkable merits ('humble flowers,' etc. etc.) at a time when he represents her, in fact, with scarcely any attribute that would not belong equally well to a pat of butter in the dog-days ; and some of the latter traits of her character are really wretchedly selfish. *Pendennis* is a vast improvement ; there is a good deal of wholesome truth told, and never in a one-sided manner. Dickens's new serial, No. 1, is very good, as far as it goes ; we shall see by and bye how it turns out.

Maurice is very busy rewriting for separate publication his *History of Philosophy*. The *Warburtonians* are all delivered, and are soon to be published ; they are to be startling. But I am anxiously expecting the *Prayer-book Sermons*, which are chiefly on Inspiration and the idea of punishment as purgation of sin.

Do what you can to get hold of the May *Fraser ;* there are several good articles. First, a glorious one by Ludlow (a secret, mind you) on the *Nemesis*, . . . then a capital homely letter of T. Carlyle on ' Indian Meal.'

I have not read F. Newman's book ; it seems weak ; and I hear Maurice has now no opinion of him. I have read his brother's *Loss and Gain ;* it is very painful in the early part from the sneers at the Prayer-book, etc., but it rises out of that, and is John Henry Newman all over. With all its faults and 'dangerousness,' it is a fine book, and much may be learnt from it.

Sara Coleridge has republisht part of the two first volumes of the *Literary Remains*, with some other scraps, as 'Lectures on the Dramatists,' etc.

Macmillan has lent me a MS. written at Maurice's request some years ago, being a picture of the state of mind of young Scotchmen some sixteen years ago. Accompanying it is a long autograph letter of Maurice's, valuable and beautiful beyond measure; possibly I may copy it, *if possible*, but it is strange that so good a man should write so bad a hand. I hear he has a high idea of J. S. Mill, for his unflinching honesty and fairness. J. W. Parker told Macmillan that Mill had said to him that the only positive addition to philosophy since Kant was Maurice's *History of Philosophy*.

At last I proposed Macaulay at the Union. The terms were "that the two first volumes of Mr. Macaulay's *History of England* are utterly wanting in the most essential characteristics of a great history." I took entirely the ground of his bad principles, and was rapturously cheered, tho' I spoke for an hour and a quarter; at eleven we adjourned. The week after we again had a good debate, but it was not over till eleven, and ―― had cleared the house by speaking; so that the numbers were very small, and it went quite against me. He himself was here from the previous Saturday to Monday, and I was afraid he would stay and come to the debate.

To Mr. John Ellerton

CAMBRIDGE, *July* 15th, 1849.

. . . Before I speak of anything else I know you will be burning to know something of Maurice's sermons. They came out on Friday week, and I immediately secured a copy for you, expecting the edition to be off soon. But I had a vague idea that you would be about this time away from ――, and in the lazy, idle, selfish mood I have been in for some time, did not take the trouble to search for your letter. But now I have found it, and suppose you are back again, and therefore herewith send the book by the same post. They are, in my mind, not in general equal to the *Lord's Prayer.* But that on the 'Songs of the Church' and the last four are wonderful.

I am on the whole not sorry that you use Lilly's and not Kennedy's *Latin Grammar*, for I think the latter has English rules ; and though I know not the former, I am sure that in spite of some mere mechanical rote repetitions, infinite good is conferred by constant use of the rigid Latin rules. Of course you parse unceasingly ; it is irksome work to you both, but infinitely important.

. . . I scarcely know how to answer you about Gilbert White, for I never read him through, and I have not looked at him for a long while. Certainly if he took up his natural history pursuits merely as a selfish amusement to kill time, and if he neglected the parish which he had undertaken, I cannot refuse to condemn him. But I am not sure that I understand the meaning of what you consider his rightful function. It is perhaps not inappropriate to apply the title 'a commissioned expounder of God's name to the world' to an honest and hearty naturalist; but if you mean it that Gilbert White neglected his trust because he wrote only of natural objects as natural objects, and did not seek to draw lessons from them, to make them the mystical oracles of moral principles to others, I differ from you *toto cælo.* Such impressions may be *suggested* to the observer himself, but I doubt whether they can be communicated to others without dishonesty and genuine *mysticism.* A few sentences from the *Kingdom of Christ* will illustrate what I mean.

[Then follows a quotation from Maurice's *Kingdom of Christ*, 2nd ed. vol. ii. part ii. pp. 420, 422.]

Much of this refers to quite a different notion, but I cannot separate it from its condemnation of what I fear may be your meaning. An honest student of nature must, I think, make *physical* principles the object of his search. If he be able besides to apply his researches to moral ends, as in some of Sedgwick's orations, well and good ; but he must not suppose that this is the aim of his science, else he will degrade and falsify both. I often think of a passage in Maurice (I forget where) where he revels in the thought of the advance of *knowledge*, and looks with delight to the time when every object, from the meanest moss or insect to the lordliest work of creation, shall be seen, each after its kind, in its true place and order and in perfect fulness of vision. I take my stand on Bacon's glorious words : *Nos autem non Capitolium aliquod aut pyramidem hominum superbiæ dedicamus aut condimus, sed templum sanctum ad exemplar mundi in intellectu humano fundamus. Itaque exemplar sequimur. Nam quicquid essentia dignum est, id etiam scientia dignum; quæ est essentiæ imago.* Further, even though one were not to add to the sum of existing knowledge of Natural Science by writing, one may, I think, feel that it is not selfish enjoyment merely, if one finds it and uses it as a beneficial agent to one's mind, if that mind be in other subjects and occupations devoted to true *work*. But enough of this sermonising, which after all may have been needless.

The present *Fraser* has the beginning of a delightful article on North Devon by Kingsley. Maurice was married at the beginning of the month, took a brief honey-half-moon at Torquay, and was then obliged to resume his collegiate and other duties in London ; as soon as he is released from them, he goes to take the parish next to Kingsley's (who has now returned to Eversley) for a month. I fear there is but little chance of his coming hither.

The Epigrams cost me very little trouble, having been resolved on, thought out, composed, and written out between evening chapel and a private business meeting at the Union ; still, *inter nos*, they were twice as good as those which got the prize, though no great shakes. Since then I have written for and missed the College English Essay. I scarcely read a word for it, and, as usual, wrote more than half the last day ; and it was not long or minute, but crude and ungrammatical ; still methinks not quite nonsense. Mackenzie got it, as he probably deserved.

I am not so sanguine as you about the new Classical Tripos regulations, except in so far that they are generally looked on as temporary, and I hope we may finally get a thorough searching examination in classics, mathematics, and divinity, which *all* must pass, leaving honours as an unnecessary supplement. But unequal and unfair as are the respective treatments of classics and mathematics, I believe the equalising them by the exemption of classics from a mathematical qualification would be an 'infinite worse' to the University, and especially to its classics.

I have scarcely looked at Ruskin yet. I am afraid of his getting into a mere cant phraseology ; the more to be dreaded that he seems fond of saying things that may produce a great effect, and strike the reader with their unfathomable profundity ; still he is doubtless an admirable man. As far as I see, his great fault is his endeavouring to interpret symbols into intellectual notions. Now this, though at first sight it may seem most completely opposed to the vulgar notion of beauty as something having no real absolute existence except as that which is *pleasing* to the eye, is really an offshoot, springing lower and deeper down from the same root ; for it tacitly assumes that whatever is spiritual, has a substantive existence, and is communicable from spirit to spirit, must be capable of interpretation into intellectual ideas, and therefore into language, which is their exponent ; whereas it seems to me most important to assert that beauty is not merely a phase or (as Sterling calls it) the *body* of truth, but has its own distinct essence and is communicable through its own *media*, independently of those of truth. And hence that forms of beauty are valuable (to use a word which most imperfectly conveys my meaning), not as sensuous exponents of those forms of truth which are emanations from Him who is the Perfect Truth, but as themselves emanations from Him who is the Perfect Beauty. I am afraid this is misty, but I cannot express myself more clearly.

To Mr. John Ellerton

CAMBRIDGE, *August* 19*th*, 1849.

. . . . Your mention of the offertory reminds me that Sedgwick, who has from paucity of dons had often to read the Communion Service on Sundays, has proved the most

rubrical of all, for he always read, " Let your light shine," etc.!
A propos of the brave old fellow, he has just finished his
Preface, and made it tremendously long.   Item he has nearly
finisht a big book on the primary strata, especially of the S.
of Scotland, so that he will escape the inglorious fate of the
greatest of pioneers, and leave something for his name to stick
to when his gigantic, nameless labours have been forgotten.
How it would have done poor Mark's [1] heart good to have
known it,—perhaps he *does* know it !!

I quite feel all you say about Claverhouse ; at least he had
in an eminent degree one virtue,—for it is a God-like virtue,
let the Manchesterians say what they will,—loyalty.   It is fast
disappearing.   When it is gone, may God protect England, for
she will need it as she never has done.

KESWICK, August 30th.

I don't know how ——— got his notion of my missing the
Greek Testament prize from doctrinally annoying the examiners.
It may be so ; but I believe not.   My inability to muster the
requisite *caput, mortuum* of cram was the real reason, I have no
doubt.   The Ecclesiastical History paper was full of doctrine
which I answered unreservedly ; yet I was all but first in that
paper.

You will be amused and perhaps not displeased to hear
that Clough was seen on the walls of Rome fighting in Gari-
baldi's army ; that does not look like stagnation.   And if he
has survived, I trust he may indeed be a living worker in the
coming time.

I was very sorry to hear Manning's opinion of Hare.   It
may, however, be some counterpoise to you to know that a
stranger calling on the Macmillans, told them that he had
travelled per rail with a clergyman (unknown) with whom he
had conversed on theological subjects, and who had recommended him to read Maurice's *Kingdom* as a most valuable
book.   On separating he gave him his card—' Ven. Archdeacon Manning'!!   He sees, what so few do see, the
tremendous chasm of opinion on *Church* matters that separates
Maurice from Hare.

[1] Mark Howard, a friend who had recently died.

I have been here nearly a week, and am of course in a great state of enjoyment. I coached from Windermere station (between Bowness and Troutbeck), and had a most glorious drive. One or two beautiful Early English churches are just built about Kendal and that neighbourhood (the only true style, I think, for a mountainous district of this nature). The Pikes were as grand as ever ; in short, everything about that exquisite view was in perfection. My father has been greatly tempted to fix us permanently in a house beautifully situated at the foot of Skiddaw two and a half miles hence, with, I verily believe, the grandest view in the Lakes, but there are many objections. . . . On Sunday morning we went to St. John's Church (F. Myers'), built by one of the Marshall legion. I was struck at the beginning of the sermon by some beautiful expressions, somewhat Arnoldian, and certainly neither evangelical nor belonging to any other form of ordinary theology. Unfortunately I was very sleepy, but heard much good matter in the most exquisite and felicitous language. Imagine my annoyance in finding that I had been listening without recognition to Arthur Penrhyn Stanley !

I am most anxious to set you right, as I have done myself, on a point on which we have both erred grievously in ignorance, viz. in regard to G. Sand. At Macmillan's persuasion, I at last read *Consuelo* and its sequel, *La Comtesse de Rudolstadt*, and am most truly grateful to him for making me read them. The former is a most exquisite pure tale. It is much like *Wilhelm Meister*, softened and smoothed down and purified, in the strictest sense intellectual, and yet not originating intellectual ideas as the German tale does. Music is in a great measure the theme and the relation of art (represented by music) to human life and affections. Love of course fills a prominent part. Nor can I recall any falsehoods on that score in *Consuelo*, and there is much precious truth. The Communistic idea appears quite in the bud, scarcely separating itself from the true idea of brotherhood which it mimics. There are most strange accounts of mediæval German heretics (for whom G. Sand has a great affection, as a sort of anticipators of Communism), chiefly Hussites, worshippers of 'Satan,' whose chief formula of benediction was, *Que celui à qui l'on a fait tort,*

te salue, meaning thereby that before-mentioned worthy. The
second part was evidently written much later. It shows its
author's mind much confused and agitated, with the strangest
mixture of superstition and scepticism, genuine faith and cold
negation. It is full of strange mysterious incidents, much
connected with the Rosicrucians, Freemasons, and 'In-
visibles,' a sort of secretest society to which the Masons
formed a sort of outer court, Communism being the grand
secret and the object of all. There are near the end some
sublime passages on the subject which underlies every page,
love, full of glorious assertions, but drawing the saddest and
wildest conclusions. There is not the smallest trace of the
notion of a community of women, as I had imagined; but
G. Sand declares marriage to be an unnatural bondage, never
undertaken for love. Nevertheless, Balaam-like, she makes her
facts often assert God's truth above her lies. One thing is
very striking in the aspect of Communism which she presents.
Property as such and political privileges never appear; social life
is the subject; she wishes that each may receive his own culture,
and do his own work for himself and for others unoppressed
and unrestrained by kings and priests. She is most bitter
against Voltaire and the 'common-sense' philosophy of
'Lok' (as she calls him), and all who like him virtually think
faith degrading and mysteries an insult to human reason. But
she is most relentless to 'the Church' for having been the
enemy of humanity, for crushing what it ought to have educated. O that her charges were false! and yet no! — then
we could have little hope for the future. Our task it is to do
what in us lies to make the Church the very truest and fullest
exponent of humanity. By all means read the books, and *in
the original*, if you can get hold of them. There is not a
rag of French frippery, scarcely a trace of French prejudice
about them.

When you are next at a railway station, expend one shilling
upon a volume of the Parlour Library called *Emilia Wyndham.*
It is quiet, unadorned, perhaps somewhat dull; but full of
much high and beautiful principle, and an excellent corrective
and complement to the moral of the end of *The Nemesis of
Faith.* I do trust you have been able, or will be able, to see

Copperfield and *Pendennis.* The former is (excepting the August number, which is dull) exceedingly beautiful, with much extravagance pruned off. Without in the least ceasing to be Dickens, he has learnt much from Thackeray. The latter's tale, though not so pleasant, is invaluable. To me the surest sign of its worth is that I never read anything which so really and completely humbled me, which made conscience so painfully importunate, while at the same time it did not in any great degree encourage churlishness and uncharitableness, as was the tendency of *Vanity Fair.* There are of course imperfections and affectations ; but a more faithful picture of what we, — *we* especially, — would wish to blink, I never saw.

To Mr. John Ellerton

KESWICK, *September* 11*th*, 1849. ˮ

. . . I forgot the other day to ask you whether you had seen some time ago a very curious decision of the French Government, refusing to recognise the French Protestants as having a religion which they could tolerate, on the ground that there could be no religion without a sacrifice.

I look forward with great anxiety to the decision of the Privy Council's committee,[1] though one may expect strange things from a theological judgment of Lord Brougham's. It is said that, if the judgment of the Court below be affirmed, hundreds of clergy meditate secession. I trust this is not the case. It is very sad that things should have come to such a pass that a judicial verdict is inevitable, which must consign one or the other class of opinions to not merely actual but *legal* heterodoxy.

To Mr. Gerald Blunt

AMBLESIDE, *September* 27*th*, 1849.

. . . You will of course have Maurice's wonderful sermons [2] by this time ; if not, you will want to know about them. I could not well give you a tolerable account of them in even a moderately small space ; I will only say at present that they

---

[1] In the Gorham case.   [2] On the Prayer-book.

are invaluable indeed.   The subjects that we before mentioned
are treated of only incidentally, but there are some very pregnant hints.   I only wish there were more.   The two last, on
'The Consecration Prayer' (in the H. Communion) and
'The Eucharist,' are grand beyond expression.   If you have
not been in a position to get the book, pray write by return
of post, and I will do my best to give you some fuller
particulars.

To Mr. John Ellerton

AMBLESIDE, *October 5th,* 1849.

. . . We can talk about English reading for the youthful
Alexander when we meet.   You certainly seem to have
played Aristotle with success hitherto.   I crave your pardon
for accusing you of a wish to moralise everything.   I feel the
temptation so often and so strongly myself, in spite of my
vehement sense of the inherent holiness of every branch of
thought, that I am made suspicious of the same thing in
others.   I fear that in a subtle form it discoloured Arnold's
mind.   Meanwhile, without saying more, I must raise my
voice loudly against Pope's *Homer.*   The possible advantages
are great, but the dangers are incalculably greater.

Dreadful as war is, I cannot say that I shrink from it, if
undertaken in such a cause as that of Turkey.   It seems inevitable now.

Crosthwaite Church is hideous, being a compound of every
century *since* the Debased.   Much expense has been lately incurred in fitting up stalls, putting in excellent painted glass,
but all to no purpose in such a fabric.   I was not much struck
by Southey's monument, but did not see it well.

I forget whether I noticed to you Hook's noble freedom
from party spirit and brave honesty in standing forward alone
among his friends publicly to support the Marriage Bill.   I
find that some years ago Wilberforce (I suppose Samuel W.)
urged on him the evil of party spirit.   Hook contended that
it was absolutely necessary to have a party, and to act as a
member of one.   Maurice, hearing this, publisht a letter to
Wilberforce on the subject.   Hook then wrote to Wilberforce

to say that Maurice's letter had quite convinced him, and since then he has never done a factious action.

To his Mother

CAMBRIDGE, *November 2nd*, 1849.

My dearest Mother—It seems quite as long to me as to you since we separated. . . . On Tuesday all lectures, examinations, and 'coaches' began, and ever since I have been like the donkey in the mill at Carisbrook Castle, grinding on in a perpetual round of mathematics.   When I can keep awake in the evening, I read from seven to eight hours in the day (examinations included), but I always get my walk,—almost always the full two hours' trot.   I have four examinations per week, and towards the end of the month the College adds on another per week.   Meanwhile you will be glad to hear that I have secured Westcott [1] for classics between January 20th and February 17th.

. . . It would of course be impossible for you to dry brambles at Cheltenham, but, if you ever get to the lanes, I should be much obliged if you would notice them.   The most common one there, I know, is *Rubus discolor*, which I did not see in the Lakes.   Its leaves are quite white underneath.

Babington has only turned over, not examined, my Lake brambles as yet.   I had a walk with him to-day, and he tells me that my Buttermere *Potamogeton* is most probably what I supposed, viz. *P. fluitans*, which has not before been found in Britain.   He says it is smaller than the continental plant, but it is certainly not one of the known British species.   I have not missed morning chapel more than four or five times.

To Mr. John Ellerton

CAMBRIDGE, *November 9th*, 1849.

. . . Alford has published the first volume of his Greek Testament.   It seems good, and not superstitious.

[1] *i.e.* as private 'coach.'

To the Rev. F. D. Maurice

TRINITY COLLEGE, CAMBRIDGE [*November* 16*th*, 1849].

My dear Sir—It is with considerable hesitation that I venture to trespass upon your time, already so fully employed. I am not even able to plead acquaintance as a warrant for so doing. Only a most hearty sense of inestimable benefits already received leads me to hope for fresh assistance from the same source. And in this respect I have perhaps some claim upon you. Had it been your aim to make us your disciples, we must have been content to swallow whatever crumbs it might please you to scatter; but since you have chosen rather to guide us in to the old ways which God made, and not you,— surely the aid you have already given is a pledge of your willingness to assist us again and again in discerning the eternal order among all the confusions that beset us, and to bear with the perverseness which, more than anything else, blinds our eyes. I have therefore resolved to ask you to guide me, if you can, to a satisfactory solution of a question which has long been tormenting me, and which seems now to be felt universally to be of very great moment indeed, if we may judge from the warmth and passion which both sides display. I mean, the question whether any man will be hereafter punished with never-ending torments, spiritual or physical.

It would be far too much to say that I do not believe that any man will, for I dare not rashly and hastily discard a conviction entertained by nearly all Christians, and sanctioned, as it appears to me, by such plain language in the Gospels and Apocalypse, as well as in our Liturgy and the Athanasian Creed. There is, moreover, this great difficulty in the rejection of the common opinion: we see men becoming more hardened in impenitence every year of their lives, even till death itself. If there be any further state of probation beyond the grave, it will still be monstrous to suppose the sin removed suddenly from their hearts by an almighty Fiat without a corresponding willingness on their part; such a notion is utterly at variance with the idea of a spirit endowed with a will. But how otherwise can we be *sure* of their becoming purer? There is no more reason why they should repent then than there was when they were on earth; nay, there is less, for the longer they exist the harder they may become; they must retain the power of choosing the evil, or they cease to have wills. Many would say that pain and suffering will purify them; but the notion that this result *must* ensue owes its existence to a false material analogy drawn from the purgation of the *passive* gold from its dross by the action of fire. If we could believe sin, as some virtually do, to be merely the shadowy antecedent of the substantial consequent, pain, and heaven to consist in unlimited selfish enjoyment, not a whit purer than a Mahometan Paradise for the supposed absence of its sensual element, then there might be little difficulty in supposing men after a certain period to be tossed, sins and all, into such a sty of 'bliss.' But, as we believe heaven to be the fullest communion with God in His most immediate presence, and the fullest disposition and power to be always working His Will, none but those who have been separated from their sin can possibly enter into its joys. For others there would *seem* to be only two alternatives—an eternal curse, and annihilation. I have never been able to see the alleged inconsistency in this latter notion; surely what God has originated, God can destroy, be it spirit or matter; yet I cannot get rid of a feeling that men never *are* annihilated.

But, on the other hand, not only are the Epistles almost free (as far as I can recollect) from allusions to everlasting torments, but their whole tone is such that the introduction of such a notion would seem to render it discordant and jarring. And little as I like to rest on isolated texts, I cannot get over the words, " As in Adam all die, even so in Christ shall all be made alive." St. Paul cannot mean merely the universal redemption, for he uses the future tense conformably to the whole tenor of the chapter, and is, moreover, speaking of the resurrection; further, the same universality is given to the one clause as to the other.

Again, where is the answer to the common question, "You say that some go to heaven, some to hell; then you must suppose a line separating the two sets of men, but the gradations are infinite. There can be but little difference between the worst of the former class, and the best of the latter. How can you make their future lots so immeasurably different ? " Paley, I hear [? fear], replies that we have no reason for believing that there *is* much difference between the lowest place in heaven and the highest in hell ! ! This answer only brings out the difficulty in greater distinctness. Say, if we will, that the language here employed indicates a corrupt notion of merit of works done just exceeding or just falling short of the price which God has affixed to His merchandise, 'heaven'; still we are as far as ever from justifying God's ways. Every one is perpetually falling ; the difference is but slight between him who falls at last utterly away, and him who just succeeds in not losing hold of his Lord. And what of those who die while oscillating in the midst?

Nor do I see how to dissent from the equally common Universalist objection, that finite sins cannot deserve an infinite punishment. The language may be technical and savouring of mere abstractions, but, I am sure, the feeling which finds utterance in it is real and conscientious enough. I do not think you would look with much favour on the answer given a few Sundays ago from the pulpit of St. Mary's by a Hulsean lecturer. We were told that the mere inquiry was presumptuous ; that "we know absolutely nothing at all" (I quote as nearly verbatim as I can from memory) "of God's nature, or any of His attributes"; "nor is there any reason for believing that when the Bible speaks of the goodness, justice, and mercy of God, it means anything which bears any rezemblance to what we call justice, goodness, and mercy." So that the way to defend what is presumed to be an essential doctrine of Christianity is by denying the fact of a revelation, in any living sense of the word ! for what is the revelation of a Hell ? I know that the great mass of those against whom the Hulsean lecturer was contending is greatly infected by the disbelief in the existence of retributive justice, which is now so widely spread through nearly all classes of people, especially in regard to social and political questions, which causes even men, whose theology teaches them to look upon God as a vin-dictive, lawless autocrat, to stigmatise as cruel and heathenish the belief that criminal law is bound to contemplate in punish-

ment other ends beside the improvement of the offender himself and the deterring of others. Still the consciousness of
this fact can only make it incumbent on us to examine our
ground carefully,—it cannot require us to surrender a truth,
if it be a truth, merely because it is now the property of
scarcely any but such as have become heretics while re-
volting against the popular creed. One answer has sometimes
suggested itself as more plausible than that mentioned above ;
namely, that the sin is not finite but infinite, in virtue of the
fact of its continued self-reproduction—that is, that the
punishment of past sin is increased sin, deserving in its turn
fresh punishment. And yet surely the heart rebels against
such a theory as a cruel mockery of the very essential spirit of
justice ; only here lies the difficulty—is not this theory
merely the expression of a fact, which, however we may
dispute about it, is a fact still? *does* not God punish sin by
making men sin afresh? And now, having reached this
point, I scarcely know where to go on and where to end, for
hither converge multitudes of distracting questions, pervading
every region of theology, to which I have never been able to
find any answer but this—"God is, and Evil is ; both alike
testify their own reality. If the Christian faith does not
harmonise them, at least it is therein not more unsuccessful
than all human theories ; for those which have seemed to
solve the riddle, have merely denied the facts, and contradicted the testimony of their whole being." Yet I am confident
that there must be some deeper answer than this mere confession of ignorance—some more intelligent way of resisting
the horrible Manichæism which, under both its primary and
its secondary forms, is in a thousand dissimilar ways torturing
and tempting our hearts and consciences every hour of the
day, than the mere ban (potent though that may happily
sometimes be)—

> Receive it not, believe it not,
> Believe it not, O man !

Thus there is the question of Substituted Punishment,
which, as it seems to me, is quite distinct from the Atonement
and reconciliation of the person of sinning man and God. I
can at most times thankfully contemplate the fact of God's

forgiveness (in the strict sense of the word; that is, removal
of estrangement from the offender, irrespective of the non-
enforcement of penalties) and His delight in humanity as
restored through its Head; but surely this has little to do
with the principle that every offence must receive its just
recompense. The Father may forgive the child, and yet
cannot justly exempt him from the punishment of disobedience.
"Amen!" says the evangelical; "the penalty must be paid
somehow by somebody. The penalty is tortures to all eternity
for each man. Christ, in virtue of the infinity which He
derived from His Godhead, was able on earth to suffer
tortures more than equivalent to the sum of the eternal
tortures to be suffered by all mankind; God must have the
tortures to satisfy His justice, but was not particular as to who
was to suffer them,—was quite willing to accept Christ's
sufferings in lieu of mankind's sufferings." O that Coleridge,
while showing how the notion of a fictitious substituted
righteousness, of a transferable stock of good actions, obscured
the truth of man's restoration in the Man who perfectly acted
out the idea of man, had expounded the truth (for such, I am
sure, there must be) that underlies the corresponding heresy
(as it appears to me) of a fictitious substituted *penalty* ! All my
reverence and gratitude to him who first taught me to love light
and to seek after truth, believing that it is God's will that we
should attain them, and that He Himself will guide us into
them, cannot make me see much beside dimness (as far as the
present question is concerned) in the note at p. 239 of the
Aids (fifth edition). Nor, as far as I can recollect, have you
anywhere written explicitly upon this point; even on the
corresponding subject of vicarious righteousness I know only
of two pages (*Kingdom of Christ*, 1st edition, vol. i. pp. 32,
33), and they have not been able to make me feel assured
that the language of *imputation* is strictly true, however
sanctioned by St. Paul's example. The fact is, I *do not see
how* God's justice can be satisfied without *every man's* suffering
in his own person the full penalty for his sins. I *know* that it
can, for if it could not in the case of some at least, the whole
Bible would be a lie; but if in the case *of some*, why not *of all?*
A reconciliation of the person may be dependent, at least in

its realization, upon its acceptance on the part of the will ; but how does this apply to the suffering of penalties ?

Again, how is the notion that God punishes sin by sin consistent with the belief that God is not and cannot be the author of evil ? Is there not something strangely significant in the extraordinary language of Coleridge in the last four lines of p. 194 of the *Literary Remains*, vol. i. ? The texts cited go for little, but surely the superficial meaning which Coleridge seems to put upon them is inconsistent with a sound theology.

The discussion which immediately precedes these four lines naturally leads to another enigma most intimately connected with that of everlasting penalties, namely, that of the personality of the devil. It was Coleridge who some three years ago first raised any doubts in my mind on the subject—doubts which have never yet been at all set at rest, one way or the other. You yourself are very cautious in your language ; much of it is such as a person, who was convinced of the truth of the common opinion, would be unlikely to use. The only positive principle, as far as I can see, that you assert is this, that "evil, though by its nature multiform and contradictory, has nevertheless a central root." This certainly is most important ; it seems as if it must be so in the nature of things, if only we presuppose the existence of things that are evil, as facts compel us to do. But the question still remains—Is this central root personal or not ? Can the power of origination be in strict truth ascribed to anything except a will ? On the other hand, surely the continuity of life (or existence—neither word exactly expresses my meaning) of a *person* depends directly on the operation of the Word, unless with the Manichæans we set up two grounds of being. Now if there be a devil, he cannot merely bear a corrupted and marred image of God ; he must be wholly evil, his name evil, his every energy and act evil. Would it not be a violation of the divine attributes for the Word to be actively the support of such a nature as that ? And so in the present day many avoid the difficulty by the monstrous fiction of a regenerated devil. Thus the author of *Festus* (as I am told, for I have not read the poem) supposes him finally restored through the medium of a genuine human affection! But does not this suggest that no image but God's image is possible for a *person*? May I take this opportunity of asking what you mean (in *Kingdom of Christ*, first edition, vol. i. p. 45) by the phrase, " The satisfaction offered to the *evil spirit*, by giving up to him all that he can rightly claim, while all that is real and precious is redeemed out of his hands"?

There is yet another subject of the utmost importance, which is intimately mixed up with every point to which I have alluded—indeed the Manichæan controversy embraces and combines them all—I mean, the opposition of 'the flesh' and Spirit which the Bible speaks of. This, I suppose, is the truth caricatured in the ascription of Evil to matter; but still I cannot see *where* the truth differs from the most deadly falsehood. Only the expressions used by both you and Coleridge respecting 'nature' as essentially evil, seem to point to a wish for isolation—that is, a hankering after assimilation to mere spiritless creatures, as the most especial characteristic of moral evil. It is easy to see that there is a close relation between this idea and that (whatever it may be) which underlies sacrifice, the prohibition of the eating of the blood, circumcision and its abolition, and finally St. Paul's mysterious words, "Without shedding of blood there is no remission of sins." But I have labored so utterly in vain to apprehend in any measure what this idea is, that I hope you will deepen and widen the hints you have already given.

I am quite conscious that I have given but few distinct objections to the common belief in what I have written, but so indeed it must be; language cannot accurately define the twinge of shrinking horrour which mixes with my thoughts when I hear the popular notion asserted (even without the blasphemous adjuncts which too often accompany it), and it is hard to ascribe all this feeling to sentimental weakness and the prevailing Pantheism which (it must be confessed in humiliation) most dangerously assaults those who pride themselves most on their freedom from it. Certainly in my case it proceeds from no personal dread; when I have been living most godlessly, I have never been able to frighten myself with visions of a distant future, even while I 'held' the doctrine. But hereafter to proclaim it as part of the Good Tidings, this is the paradox ! If it be not part of them, and yet be true, it must belong to the Law. But where do we find it in that Old Testament, which many reject as so cruel ? And that the doctrine was previously unknown is tacitly asserted by those champions of Christianity who think it the very cream of the Gospel. There is also surely something significant in the fact of St. Augustin's never having been able to free himself from quasi-purgatorial notions. It is, to say the least of it, as reasonable to suppose that his early struggles enabled him to be more sensitive than other men to the virus stealing over every region of truth from the fearful heresy which he had escaped, as to slight his feelings as those of one who recoiled violently from one error into the opposite.

I should never have done, were I to enter on all the manifold difficulties which I find rising up daily against me on both sides of these questions. This letter is already quite disorderly and incoherent enough ; but if I attempted to methodise it, it would probably lose whatever genuine connection now subsists between the several topics. I should not have troubled you with them had I not felt that a mere notional answer to *isolated* questions would be useless ; only by writing on such a series of kindred points could I enable you to separate mere speculation from real conviction. I hope I desire not opinions but light. Busy as you are, I hope you will suit your own convenience about writing ; it is quite enough of a tax upon you to trouble you at all, only the infinite importance to myself must be my excuse.—Believe me, my dear sir, most affectionately yours,

FENTON J. A. HORT.

To MR. JOHN ELLERTON

CAMBRIDGE, *November* 30*th*, 1849.

. . . I wrote two or three weeks ago to Maurice a letter asking help on Universalism, Sathanas, blood, and heaven knows what else besides. I have received from him a long and most

magnificent—I need not say, most kind—letter,[1] which you shall
see in a few days.   And what I value most of all, he hopes I
will write to him often, and call on him when I am in London.
For the present *A Dieu*.

TO MR. JOHN ELLERTON

CAMBRIDGE, *Christmas Day*, 1849.

I had fully intended that you should have a line this day
to wish you all the manifold blessings of this ever blessed
season.   But the ceaseless whirl of reading carried me round,
and I forgot it.

It was with the greatest difficulty that I screwed out time
to write to Maurice ; and *that* I should have deferred, but that
the question was daily driving me mad.   His letter shall either
accompany or follow close upon this.   W. Howard has it now ;
and I have promised to lend it to Blunt (who is down for
three or four days) to make one or two extracts from before I
forward it to you.   These two, the two Macmillans, and a
noble-hearted friend of theirs, a Mr. Gotobed, an uneasy
Dissenter, are the only persons who have seen the letter ; and
I have no idea of showing it to any more. . . . I shall send
with it my epistle, not that you may spy out its nakedness, but
because *the* letter is scarcely fully intelligible without it.

January 19*th*, 1850.

Your letter has just found me in a sick room. . . . I worked
on tolerably well up to the examination, and passed the three
days seemingly without fatigue, in spite of two nights nearly
sleepless with reading.   But I felt my throat sore on the
Saturday night, and the next day got up late quite ill, and sent
for Humphry in the evening.   He was puzzled.   My throat
soon got worse and became ulcerated ; and on Tuesday he
pronounced it decided, tho' slight, scarlatina.   My father
and mother came up on Thursday night (and stayed till last
Tuesday), not from there being anything approaching danger

[1] See Maurice's *Life*, vol. ii. pp. 15-23.

(I was up some part of every day) but to relieve my mother's anxiety. Meanwhile I am fast recovering, only 'delicate,' the worst of scarlatina being the extraordinary susceptibility to any disorder which it leaves *behind it.* The cold weather has not given me a chance of getting out ; and here I am domiciled in my sitting-room with a venerable nurse, biding my time, and arranging plants, for I am very little in a reading humour. In the 'three days'[1] I did tolerably, not altogether to my satisfaction, and yet in a satisfactory way, with a large proportion of riders—in short, enough to show me that, if I had not most culpably idled and played with mathematics all my course, I should have taken a high degree. Now tho' the 'three days' had exclusively been my work for the last term, they were by no means my *cheval de bataille ;* and I had counted on the intervening week for refreshing myself in Differential, etc. etc., and looking up a few new calculations; and tho' the 'five days'' papers have been hard, I think I should have shoved into the Wranglers. But *Deo aliter visum.* I much fear my 'three days'' work will not obtain me a Senior Op., which will lose me an all but certain Chancellor's Medal ; still, though disposed enough to murmur, I know it is most wrong. I should be thankful that my illness came on after the 'three days,' so that I am still left the Classical Tripos.

My father is very anxious that I should try for a Fellowship. I don't know what to say, for my chance is very small. Westlake will smash me to atoms in mathematics, even tho' I read them still, as I intend doing; and he is not at all to be despised in the 'Moral' paper. Still the thought pleases me, and I shall probably read 'Moral Philosophy' when the Tripos is over, 'like anything.' I understand from Romilly that a grace will probably be introduced this term to admit our year to the New Triposes[2] of 1851 ; if it passes, I shall probably go in for both, which will involve much reading. I have also had dreams of the Crosse, but I am so ignorant of Hebrew and, what is worse, of the Greek text of the N. T., that I have all but discarded them. Still I have, as you see, so much before me, that I don't know what to say to the Hulsean. The

---

[1] The first, or 'qualifying' part of the Mathematical Tripos.
[2] In Natural and Moral Sciences.

subject is tempting, but it will require a great deal of out-of-the-way reading.

I am very glad you have fixed on a curacy, since I do not pretend to judge what you are best qualified to decide, namely, as to leaving ——.   Your neighbourhood is, I should think, delightful.   But, man alive, what do you mean by supposing I shall think you are embracing 'light duty'?   I should think you will have abundance to do if the parish is to be well worked.   As for huge town populations, they must be *under-taken*, if God puts them before us, but as for doing one's duty to all as one would wish, the thing is simply impossible.   But I am sure you will not think little of the school; it is worth more than a deal of cottage visiting.   One thing more: generalising hastily from a few *Morning Chronicle* letters, I should say the country generally is more wretched and godless than the towns (excepting London and its appurtenances).

. . . I have alluded once or twice to the *Morning Chronicle*. I suppose you know that it is employing able and honest agents to examine thoroughly the state of ' Labour and the Poor' in the manufacturing, rural, and metropolitan districts; reporting from official returns, from ocular inspection, and from the accounts of both masters and men.   They are lavishing large sums on it, and have set apart a department of the office to it. The clerks work at it voluntarily at extra hours, and refuse to receive extra pay for such work.   The early letters not having been noticed, and many persons wishing to possess the whole, they began on December 21st to publish gratis bi-weekly supplements to contain a reprint of all letters that had appeared previously to that date.   Meanwhile there is a fresh letter every day.   I regularly take in a half-price copy, which I mean to bind up. Maurice values the letters so highly that, occupied as his time is, he has the paper regularly sent him and reads the letter every morning.   Kingsley also, I heard, wanted to get a daily copy to keep.   It is on this subject that the article in *Fraser* is, and it is by Ludlow; Macmillan praises it immensely, but I have not read it.   The same number contains a most noble article of Kingsley's on 'Sir E. B. L. Bulwer and Mrs. Grundy,' suggested by Sir E. B. L.'s last, *The Caxtons*, a most delightful and, on the whole, healthy story, which gave me very great pleasure.

There are three or four dull spirts at Coleridge and Coleridgians in the *English Review*, but the article to which you allude is rich in the extreme. It begins with an attack on Maurice's vanity, on his shallow criticism, and weakness. He is, it seems, a clever sort of person whom it tickles to write books, which might be readable, only he *will* write on theology and philosophy ; and unfortunately intellect is just what Mr. Maurice does not possess. We are informed (the $\overline{n+m}^{th}$ theory of Hamlet) that Shakspeare meant Hamlet as a type of vapid 'Germanism,' of the dull 'formless Teutonic mind' ! ! ! Kingsley they greatly like, and think him a fine poet, only the fear is that he will fall into Maurice's clutches and get spoiled. "We have heard that Mr. Kingsley holds extreme democratical opinions, and that he has been even mixed up with the Chartists, but this we cannot possibly believe." The article is clearly the production of a mere boy.

Many thanks for your invitation to Easebourne; I hope some day to take advantage of it. I fancy you will like Manning, but not very much ; his last dedication to Bishop Selwyn (whose letter on colonisation I hope you saw) pleased me much. Maurice says he is too 'circular' a man—you know his phrase, too much of 'an intellectual all-in-all.'

I do trust you will contrive to read *Shirley*. I have not had so rich a feast for so long a time. All the morbidness of *Jane Eyre* gone, and we have the freshest and most glowing pictures and the soundest and most needful principles, saving and except the authoress's unbounded hatred of curates.

The expedition to Iceland seems not to have very favourable auspices,—at least I fancy they don't know much about it, but I hope to hear more of it, as Babington has written to Prof. Daubeny. Babington himself has been there, and knows the difficulties and expenses ; in all probability, if I went at all, I should go alone with him, but I fear the expense is too great. This is quite distinct from the talked-of voyage to the Hebrides, Orkneys, etc.

I am quite ashamed of having forgotten the Football Rules all the winter. Our Club Rules are as bad as bad can be, having a basis of the vile Eton system for making skill useless with merely one or two Rugby modifications. On the other hand, our Rugby rules are very complicated and hard to learn (though excellent), and require much explanation. If I can find them, you shall have a copy, but I will not delay this letter to look for them.

I feel greatly tempted to go off, as you request, on politics, but this is the seventh sheet, and I had better wait a little. As for slavery, Carlyle had a most extraordinary article in the last *Fraser* but one, which has been very much abused. The drift of it is this : the W. Indies are going to rack and ruin, for laborers won't work ; niggers like pumpkin and idleness ; niggers never did any good yet, have no enterprise, no nothing. Man's highest business is work ; if niggers won't work, they must be made to work, of course for pay. There is really something in the article, though put paradoxically. J. S. Mill has answered it fiercely in the last number ; it seems quiet and plausible enough, but in the vital principles of his reply there is more Red Republicanism than in anything I ever read. I do not know Kingsley's precise opinions, but infer from his writings that he is communistically disposed ; I know also that he and Maurice have battles on the subject. There is also significance in the fact that one of his sermons praises the benevolence of a Benefit Society. Whatever you think of me, do not suppose me to wish to rest on any respectabilities or conventions whatever ; thus much at least Carlyle has taught me, I hope for ever. If rank, station, wealth have no deeper foundation, they must fall, and *will* fall. I am glad you like *Consuelo ;* you will scarcely understand Albert, and his position with respect to the moral of the story, till you read the mar- vellous sequel, *La Comtesse de Rudolstadt,* a strange wild chaos of thoughts, but instructive beyond measure.

The following is Hort's first note to Mr. Westcott, then his classical 'coach' :—

To Mr. B. F. Westcott

Trinity College, *Monday* [*January* 1850 (?)].

My dear Sir—Having been laid up by a slight attack of scarlatina ever since the conclusion of the 'three days,' I am still unable to leave my room, and have no chance of being able to do so while this unfavorable weather lasts ; I fear I must therefore defer reading with you for a few days. Meanwhile, however, I shall be much obliged if you will send me two or three pieces for composition, that I may at least make an attempt to do something, as I have not yet begun to work. —Believe me, faithfully yours,   FENTON J. A. HORT.

TO MR. JOHN ELLERTON

CAMBRIDGE, *February 7th*, 1850.

My dear Ellerton—I don't know how it is that your two most kind notes have been so long unanswered, but the time flies fast and unheeded as the Classical Tripos approaches.   I am reading, or rather writing, with Westcott daily, and I hope getting some good.   I hear the betting is equal on Beamont, Schreiber, and myself, and altogether I have enough to encourage me, though I am not working with much spirit.

I don't think I shall go in for the Crosse, or Tyrwhitt either, though I am most culpably ignorant of the really essential 'cram' which belongs to the former.   I still waver at the Hulsean.   If I could not go in for the New Triposes, I should probably try; but it is now all but certain that I can, and both are, I fear, too much.   The Master has just announced the special books for his part of the Examination of '51 : viz. Plato, *Charm.*, *Prot.*, *Rep. I.*; Aristotle, *Nicomachean Ethics*; Cicero *de finibus*; Grotius *de jure belli et pacis*, bk. i.; and Dugald Stewart's *Outlines of Moral Philosophy*; and as a special subject, 'Of Things Allowable,' besides a less accurate knowledge of all moral philosophers of note, a list being given. The set is most wretched; and I have a strong idea of writing to Maurice to ask for a short scheme of philosophical reading. This, some Theology, and Politics with especial reference to Communism, I hope to make my *chief* subjects of study for the next three or four years.

Read *Lady Alice, or the New Una* if you can, and don't be frightened by its apparent (and, in part, real) Morning Postism.   In spite of glaring faults, it is a noble book—most noble, considering the quarter from which it seemingly comes, sentimental, all-but-Romish high aristocracy.   It contains few personages of 'lower' station than Marquises and Duchesses, and their sons and daughters; and yet every character is a genuine man or woman of some stamp or other.

To Mr. John Ellerton

CAMBRIDGE, *February 8th,* 1850.

. . . A letter has to-day reacht the Macmillans from Maurice, the substance of which he wishes to have conveyed to all who feel any interest in him, with the assurance that he is deeply interested in its subject.   He and 'his friends' have set up a journeyman tailor's joint establishment, with shared profits; the same is in progress for needlework.   Item they are going to issue a series of tracts called *Tracts on Christian Socialism,* the first a dialogue by himself.   I need not say I look forward to them with the most intense interest; if they merely advise these sort of things, *i.e.* an extension of the benefit-society principle to particular trades, well and good, provided they don't talk nonsense about people being fraternal and benevolent because they take part in a good investment for their money or labor.   If they assert that Society itself and human relations should rest on the same principle, woe woe to them! so at least I feel.   I have pretty well made up my mind to devote my three or four years up here to the study of this subject of Communism more than any but the kindred topics of Theology and Moral Philosophy.

To the Rev. John Ellerton

29 MARLBRO' BUILDINGS, BATH,
March 6th, 1850.

My dear Ellerton—I fear you will have been wondering what in the world has become of me that I have not written to you to congratulate you.[1] . . . But how to congratulate you

---

[1] On his ordination.

I scarcely know — happily you need no formal assurance how deeply and heartily I 'give you joy.' To receive the commission given to the Apostles, to be the consecrated herald of the One Holy Catholic Church to men torn asunder and set one against the other by wilfulness and slavishness—but I need not go on with what you know as well as I do—all these are blessings for which I may well envy you. But my time is not yet come. . . . I have brought down here single volumes of Fleury, Bingham, Guericke, S. Chrysostom *de Sacerdotio*, Origenis *contra Celsum*, and S. Cyprian's *Epistles*, to begin upon the Hulsean, but have not read or written a word yet. I have also brought a little Moral Philosophy and Modern History to read for the Moral Sciences Tripos. I hope in four or five days to hear the result of the Classical Tripos. I venture to make no prophecies, but will only say that, tho' I made heaps of mistakes, I was on the whole more than satisfied. . . . Of course you have seen No. 1 of the *Tracts on Christian Socialism, i.e.* Maurice's dialogue between Nobody and Somebody. I will try hard to write at length to you on that point very soon.

TO THE REV. JOHN ELLERTON

BATH, *March* 19*th*, 1850.

I write this to-night, intending to send it in the morning in company with a Tripos list which I hope to receive from Blunt by to-morrow's post. Macmillan sent me one to-day. . . . After all, really, culpably, idle as I have been, I certainly have not the least right to complain because I am bracketed 3rd. I am quite ashamed to think how gloomy and discontented I have been this afternoon since receiving the list, in spite of many a gentle monition from "Him, the Giver," that it is still He "who satisfieth my mouth with good things, making me young and lusty as an eagle." Meanwhile He has even now, I venture to think, given me a far more precious gift than a degree. The greatest service you can do for me is to pray that I may not need herein too to have my selfish pride bruised, in order to be fitted for His holy service.

. . . Very many thanks for ——'s most interesting letter, which I return. It is glorious, indeed, to think that Maurice should penetrate even such crusts of antique bigotry, but thirsty souls who long for light will welcome it whencesoever it comes. May God bless you in all your future work, as He seems to have blest you already.

To the Rev. John Ellerton

BATH, *March 15th and April 9th*, 1850.

My dear Ellerton—I believe it will be best for me to write specially in answer to your last. . . . I believe the best mode of introducing some kind of method will be to follow Maurice's example, and try to give you, in the first instance, a rapid sketch of the processes which I have myself traversed. This way will, in fact, be a direct answer to your original question how I have come to diverge from our former common track of politics. But you must not expect me to be certainly accurate in details. I must claim the indulgence which Maurice himself so generously, yet so justly, grants to Newman, for, as he says, in such cases the most rapid changes and rechanges are nothing extraordinary, and chronology must be in a great measure disregarded.

I believe you know that my father being, to use his own phrase, a 'Conservative Whig,' I was originally something of the kind, I didn't exactly know what, only I fancy I had great faith in the 'admirably balanced constitution' of Kings, Lords, and Commons, tho' I always kicked against the maxim, 'The King can do no wrong.' Arnold made me really see the dignity and glory of politics, tho' a certain indefined feeling of Liberalism was, I think, nearly all the positive political creed that I derived originally from him; but under this influence I quite sympathised with Peel on Maynooth and one or two such questions. Accordingly, at the Rugby Debating Society I at first joined the Conservative side, tho' in speaking I was generally intermediate. I then read Arnold more, and became more positively Whig-Radical. When the Corn Laws were repealed I said that Conservatism existed no longer.   I could not be a Tory, and so shifted to the Whig side of the House.   Just before I left I was made quite wild by Carlyle's *Cromwell*, which I swallowed whole, and became a mere worshipper of Cromwell, thinking myself a Radical. Coming up to Cambridge I was much the same, tho' I began somehow to feel how very unliberal and unradical Cromwell was.

Coleridge's influence went for something in abating my furor, but Arnold became my almost sole Doctor in politics. Such or similar was my condition when I began to know you, and indeed nearly all the while we were together.   I am bound to confess that the *Politics for the People* were too readily swallowed.   I did not enough consider what I was about, or remember that professedly the writers in it were at variance with each other.   Hence the only *body* of my Chartism was what Arnold had taught my *conscience*.   All the rest was vague sentiment and theory.

In the following autumn the 3rd vol. of Maurice's *King-dom*, 1st ed., made some impressions upon me, but only vague and disconnected impressions.   Meanwhile I found myself compelled to resolve in good earnest the questions to which in reading the *Politics* I had given a hasty assent, and such as resulted from them.   Political rights in the abstract were the prominent feature.   Ludlow had spoken of Universal Suffrage, and I said ' Aye.'   But why ?   Because every man of full age and *compos mentis* had a right to a vote.   And why had he a right to a vote ?   Because all government that is not self-government is old-world tyranny.   The only question was, What was the best form of government for making it *bonâ fide* self-government ?

But then came the recollection of an argument which at Rugby Bradby, a clever and thoughtful Young Englander, had given (from Coleridge) against universal suffrage, viz. that a limit must be assigned to voters, otherwise why not include women and children ?   I had formerly simply ' pooh-poohed ' the argument.   I now felt no real answer to it, but by admitting the consequences.   Practically children might be excluded, but why exclude women ?   Whether or no they had a different mental constitution from men, at least they were educated, they could form opinions, they were individual human beings; why should they surrender their rights as such? It might be expedient for a while to exclude them, even as they had always been excluded; but this touched not *my* point, whether in a right and normal state of things they would not have equal political rights with men. I do not think I ever absolutely assented, but for a long while I could find no reason for refusing assent. But I became soon more and more sensible that, in the state at which I had arrived in the process of making democracy more and more pure, I had been making individualism the true primal characteristic of humanity, the relations of society but secondary—had, in short, been thinking as if a man could only be right when contemplated apart from his fellows. This conclusion *per se* was not agreeable to my strong disgust (drawn from Coleridge) against the French Encyclopedist theories of man being, in the first instance, savage and then by degrees civilising himself by experience. But, what was stronger, this view of political *rights* plainly set aside the idea of family; such an idea could consistently be but an accidental and non-essential one.

A society, however democratic, yet composed of a number of individual bodies possessing each an unity within itself, did not satisfy the *desiderata* of my primal numerical troop of human beings; but this led to and involved yet deeper considerations. When talking of a nation it is easy to think of all men as on the same level; but when we get into the narrower region of a family, we find its members bearing to each other *de facto* the most various relationships. It is not easy to persuade oneself that father and son possess a merely fraternal relation to each other. But above all, is the authority (or whatever name you choose to give it) of father over son, of husband over wife, a purely factitious and unnatural one?

This is the root of the matter. Leaving out the latter case, we find the former acknowledged virtually by the common consent of mankind to be the type of all authority, regal or otherwise; even were it not so, knock down all political authority, commonly so called, and you will still have this paternal authority obnoxious to all the objections which beset authority generally, and no one will pretend that it merely arises from the consent of the son to be governed. Possibly then *this* authority too must needs go; only, not merely factitious institutions, but every monition of conscience and reason must go with it. That which, however abused, does still seem the main bond of order to society, the channel through which all education must (ideally) flow so long as men have not the power of begetting full-grown men—full-grown in mind and body—*that*, it seemed, must give way to the imperious requirements of our theory, itself founded, as it seemed, on equally deep and universal principles. All this is and was independent of the teaching of the Bible, which I do not think you will be willing to allow to be *quite* beside the point. For my own part, whatever else might be true, I could not and would not give up the divine and permanent rightness of the paternal authority; and so for a while I remained, of course not exactly quiescent, but oscillating in erratic curves; what I tell you, however, was, I believe, my *punctum medium.*

Now in all this theory there was, I think, a vague notion interfused that obedience to authority, however warranted by occasional circumstances, has in it somewhat of an essentially servile nature. But about this time I had constantly in my mind that wonderful reconciliation of half the theological enigmas which ever have arisen, which Maurice points out in one of his sermons on the Temptation, and expounds more fully (tho', I think, not so forcibly) in one of his latter Prayer-book series [1] on the Consecration Prayer. He reminds us how " worldly men in their carnal and proud hearts cannot conceive how the Father commands because the Son obeys, and the Son obeys because the Father commands."

This had for some time given to me a most blessed and practical solution of the question of Free Will. I dared not apply the term 'servile ' to this loving and willing yet eternal obedience of the Son " begotten before all worlds "; yet surely it was the fullest, completest obedience, the perfect type of all imperfect obedience on earth, and likewise was the authority

[1] *Christmas Day, and other Sermons,* Sermon xii. p. 160 (1st ed. 1843).

of the Father the fullest, completest authority, the perfect type
of all imperfect authority on earth. This fundamental doctrine
of the filial subordination of the Son from all eternity (in no
wise interfering with His co-eternity and co-equality with the
Father) is hard to receive, and will always be rejected when
the understanding seeks to exert an universal empire; yet I
fully believe that it is the keystone of theology and humanity,
and that without it men *must* 'confound the Persons.'   It is
very remarkable that Coleridge, in spite of his underlying
tendency to Sabellianism, which (as it seems to me) gives
evident tokens of its presence in his *Literary Remains*, clung
with such determined energy to this doctrine that he rejected
the Athanasian Creed mainly because it seemed to him to be
silent about it, if not to deny it by implication.   Thousands
of persons who do not dream of rejecting St. John's Gospel,
would be horrified at its distinct enunciation, concluding
(correctly enough, according to logic) that it is incompatible
with the belief of the equality of the Three Persons of the
Trinity.   And I am now persuaded that this same scepticism
of the carnal understanding is what makes us confound obedience on earth with slavery, authority with tyranny; and set
down freedom as inconsistent with obedience.   And I am
likewise persuaded that practically men gain this seemingly
impossible reconciliation in and through that same Spirit in
whom the Son and the Father are (I do not *now* say *one*
—that is another question) *equal*.

In conjunction with this idea I found great help in one
somewhat different, at least in form.   Maurice, in the *Politics*,
discusses the fundamental axioms from which Mill deduced
Universal Suffrage.   The first was, "Government was made
for man, and not man for government."   The first half
Maurice allows; the second is, he says, ambiguous: if it
means that man was not made to be governed, it is false.   I
do not recollect Maurice's arguments; the idea was pregnant
enough in itself.   You must have observed that nearly all democratic theorists lose sight of God's government of mankind;
if reminded of it, they say, "Oh yes! we know that,—that of
course superintends everything, but we are thinking of the
government of men by men."   If, however, the analogy of

God's dealings with men in other matters is to be here preserved, we must start from God's government, and make that
the central idea of all our speculations. Men therefore, I say,
are made to be governed by God. They are not, in the first
instance, free from superior controul; this is the essential
point. Whether or not democracy be true, men are ideally,
normally in their right state only when they obey a law not
of their own creation. I appeal to you whether this doctrine
is not really as opposed to the general broad axiom that no
reasonable being can be bound by what he has not consented
to, as any Tory doctrine is ; and if that axiom be not general
and broad, I do not see what foundation it can ever seem to
have to a reasonable man.

But further, the Bible surely teaches us that every function
among men is a copy of some Divine function, and not a
copy only, but an operative and representative image of it.
Thus human priests are representatives of the High Priest,
not substitutes or vicars for Him, but discharging partially His
functions to men, setting forth what He is ; fathers likewise
represent the Great Father, and so with other functions.

Surely it is most natural to suppose that, analogously to the
other parts of this Divine plan, we shall have representative
kings, setting forth the Divine King of mankind, deriving their
authority and commission directly from Him, and in no wise
invested with them merely by the free-will of their subjects,
' the people.'

But we should also naturally expect that many rulers would
seek to hold power by a very different tenure, not to exhibit
themselves as true officers of the Righteous Governor of all
by themselves exercising Righteous Government, but to set
up their own will as law, delighting not in doing what is right,
but what they pleased ; *such* a kingship God Himself cannot
exercise. By the very law of His nature His will must be a
righteous, cannot be an arbitrary will, and that righteous will is
the true fountain of law for all who bear His title of king. Such,
briefly, I believe to be God's primal plan for the government
of the nations. Men have caused all sorts of deviations from
it, even as myriads of sects and heresies have obscured the
true type of the Church. The more fully, as I believe, that

this plan is carried out, the more perfect will be the liberty of subjects, the more will all arbitrary and unjust barriers be broken down; for neither for God, nor angel, nor man can I admit liberty to consist in unbounded scope for arbitrary will, but in perfect willing obedience to a perfect law.

As for the course of events, they are evidently tending to democracy. Kings have forgotten their mission and set themselves up as devil-tyrants. So far as I can read God's ways in history, it is His purpose by these (?)[1] means to work out the liberation of all mankind from the thraldom of all kinds of kingly oppression, and then, when at the same time the barriers true as well as false have been broken down, and the nations are howling in all the horrors of anarchy, to set up anew His true representatives, kings exercising righteous judgement.

With regard to the case of the Israelites, I think Maurice is right. At the time of Saul they were scarcely enough formed into a nation to be fit for a king, more especially as it was needful that they should first be taught the primary truth (the title by which David reigned), that the Lord was their King; but clearly it was intended that they should ultimately have an earthly king. Their sin was that they desired one who should treat them as slaves, and not as the free subjects of a true king.

Thus much concerning my Toryism. I might write for ever, but space has bounds. The question of rebellion, which in some measure follows as a corollary, it is less important to touch on, more especially as it is well treated in the *Kingdom of Christ*, vol. iii. 1st ed.[2] But perhaps you will fancy that this has little to do with Communism. I can only say that it was through the region of pure politics that I myself approacht Communism, and I cannot help feeling that I thereby was delivered from some very unpleasant paradoxes.

Most persons think of it merely as connected with property; others with rank and social station; others with family and especially conjugal relations. All these are, I believe, most intimately connected; at all events, I never heard of a Com-

---

[1] The word is indistinct.
[2] See postscript to this letter, p. 144.

munist who was not a Radical. (I use the word in no offensive sense.)

I have no intention of going through all these phases ; but if you allow the truth of what I have alleged in favour of inequality of power and authority, you will, I think, see that consistently the same must be true with regard to property. Let me say once for all what appears to me to be the real nature of the difference between the several opinions on the subject. Political economists, ' Millocrats ' (?),[1] aristocrats, etc. etc., practically and often avowedly declare that their superiorities of wealth, or station, or birth are intended for their own special enjoyment, are, so long as they possess them, exclusively their own, and that they may do what they like with their own.

The Communistic or rather Socialistic theorist accepts this selfish view of property, etc., and appeals to mankind whether it is right that these gradations of enjoyment or ' happiness ' should be recognised and allowed. All men, he contends, have an equal right to enjoy themselves, to have an equal portion of the pabulum of enjoyment. But it seems to me that the deadly poison of Socialism is its deification of selfishness, that it is based upon the notion of a balance of interests, as many in number as there are human beings on the globe. Surely, surely the doctrine which Kingsley pours forth so gloriously in *The Saint's Tragedy* is the *true* doctrine, that nothing in the universe, which lives its true life, lives for itself.

Surely every man is meant to be God's steward of every blessing and ' talent ' (power, wealth, influence, station, birth, etc. etc.) which He gives him, for the benefit of his neighbours. Taken simply *per se*, this doctrine would probably lead to much fanaticism, constantly to the saddest confusions and perversions of God's laws ; but, if we remember that His Spirit is at every moment teaching us how to be faithful and wise stewards, reminding us that we are not mere bottomless buckets (letting God's gifts run straight through us as fast as we receive them) but responsible living men, bound, as on the one hand not to seek our own enjoyment, so on the other to remember constantly (the hardest of tasks to the ' well-mean-

[1] The word is indistinct.

ing '!) that neither is enjoyment the right end of the lives of others, and that the truest and highest way of spending and being spent for our brethren is to educate them constantly especially to the highest education, the knowledge of God,— if we do this, I say, we shall see why God gives more to one than to another, and learn how to be workers together with Him for His great glory; for this again is an important consideration. He uses all sorts of means in the education of mankind; and even so may and must we use all that are in our hands, not stepping out of our place and endeavouring to be greater philanthropists than He is, but laboring to discern and keep in harmony with the present laws of His operation.

To be without responsibility, to be in no degree our 'brother's keeper,' would be the heaviest curse imaginable. This seems true universally, but surely there is no material of responsibility so powerful as wealth; how men could be educated without it, I cannot see.

But I am far from shutting my eyes to the awful abuses of property now existing; but for those, I think, if possible, partial or temporal remedies must be devised. I cannot at present see any objection to a limit being placed by the State upon the amount of property which any one person may possess, or even to sumptuary laws of various kinds; on such points we might learn much from the Romans. I believe the true idea of property to be set forth in Maurice's sermon, on "Give us this day our daily bread." "Mine and yet not mine, but mankind's" is its formula, logically self-contradictory, even as is the similar formula of moral action, "I and yet not I, but Christ that dwelleth in me." The doctrine of human merit is the corruption on the one side, of the negation of virtue and the substitution of vicarious virtuous acts of Christ's, on the other, of the latter idea;[1] and in like manner the common selfish notion of property is the corruption on the one side, socialism on the other, of the former.

But you will protest that, true or false, this seems not to

---

[1] This sentence is obscurely worded. Apparently the right sense would be given by rewriting thus: "Of the latter idea the doctrine of human merit is the corruption on the one side; that of the negation of virtue and the substitution of vicarious virtuous acts of Christ is its corruption on the other."

touch the frightfully practical question of Competition; you rejoice because Maurice seems to you to state broadly that competition is *per se* a bad thing.   To the best of my recollection this is not his real doctrine.   I think he says—at all events *I* would say—that the co-operative *principle* is a better and a mightier than the competitive *principle ;* for I know no meaning for the competitive principle but a rivalry, a jealous and selfish rivalry, of interests.   It seems to me that *competition* is not in itself a bad thing, if we mean by that that several men separately gain their living by the same means ; I would rather say that the co-operative principle attains its fullest realization in competition, and that competition is self-ruinous, self-destructive without it.   Would that all thought so and acted so !   To denounce competition as purely evil is to say (as a little reflexion will show you) that trade is purely evil, and commerce, and all interchange of goods.

    This is certainly a startling doctrine.   Possibly if trade were more generally regulated by the principles of the book of Proverbs, no one would dream of admitting such a doctrine for a moment.   But when the co-operative principle seeks to frame for itself a spell [?] [1] drawn out of itself,—in short, to solidify itself into a system of its own,—it must lose its own meaning.   Its beauty and excellence are moral, not mechanically inherent ; co-operation is fellow-work, the work of brother *men* for and with each other.   Here each is a spring of life, each's responsibility is daily proved, each renders to his brethren willing, cheerful, reasonable service.   But co-operation turned into a system becomes simply co-machination ; the true individuality of each is lost, all that constitutes him a man, a moral being, is lost ; he is merely a conjointly-working wheel. Nor is selfishness a whit removed ; he seeks ' *our* interest,' ' the interest of that of which *I* am a part,' instead of ' *my* interest ' ; and I own I do not see what is gained by the change.   Of course he may be unselfish under such circumstances, but not more so than under a state of competition.

    I am quite willing to allow that as temporary and partial alleviations of present material suffering, nay, possibly as examples suggestive of the principle which should guide all

[1] The word is indistinct.

dealings of trade, such associations as Maurice is setting up may be most useful. But I contend that such devices must be but grease and springs to relieve the jars and strains and jerks of our social system, but never can rightly, or even (for any time) possibly, form its substantive elements, much less its motive power. The very important question of birth and nobility I have not much studied, but assuming that normally there are inequalities of station, I cannot imagine any better foundation of inequality, any more effectual corrective of a mere ploutocracy or titanocracy.

There is a most common feeling to which one cannot but in great measure assent, that power and dignity should belong to those, and those alone, who are worthy of them, and would exercise them wisely and graciously. Yet after much reflexion on this point (especially in connexion with Carlyle's demand of only Able-men for kings) I have come to the conclusion that God most wisely ordains that men should be looked up to for other than personal excellencies; otherwise it would, I feel, be next to impossible to think of Him as the Source of everything bright and good, and not to look upon their excellencies as inherent in themselves. These seemingly arbitrary grounds of distinction are so many witnesses that it is God Himself who must choose whom He will 'delight to honour.' There is also a most evident connexion between pre-eminence of birth and the idea of family, which I think you will readily allow to have been the simplest type of order which God has set forth to men in all ages, the trunk of the tree of society. Further, whatever may be the case when all mankind shall have understood and recovered their true position, there is now at least great good in the attaching honour to those who distinctly preserve practically the idea of race, the main medium of setting forth true individualism together with true blood-unity, as separated *pro tanto* from 'the masses,' from those who mostly forget their connexion with the past and the future, and more or less are but particles of a lump. (See Maurice's comment on the Beast in *The Songs of the Church.*) But however the horrors of competition and aristocratic insolence may act as ever-present goads to you, I believe the main root of your Communism,

and of all true Communism (*i.e.* Socialism *plus* what I am
going to mention), is the feeling that men are meant to be
not only free, brothers of each other, equals of each other,
but one with each other.

I think Maurice was wrong in substituting Unity for Equality
in the Communistic triad, for Unity being a far deeper idea
than Equality, he disturbed the co-ordination of the three;
Unity is rather the central root from which they all spring.
And I for one do most firmly hold that all men are equal, as
well as that men are unequal, and that their equality is deeper
than their inequality.   I mean it not merely in the pseudo-
religious way in which it is often acknowledged in the pulpit
on Sunday, but really substantially as a fundamental principle
of true Christian action.   But I should think it a hungry, dry,
theoretical principle if it were not sustained by the principle
of the unity of mankind, the deepest in men's hearts and the
hardest to express in any formula, revolutionary or otherwise.

And as I believe that men are equal in spite of the divine
inequalities of paternity, kingship, etc. etc., because the Father
and the Son are co-equal in spite of the subordination of the
Son to the Father, even so I believe that men, though many
persons, are one, because the Father and the Son are one, and
that in each case the unition is in and through the Spirit, not
begotten, but proceeding from both the Father and the Son.

The distinctness of the Three Persons of the Godhead is
the ground of the personal distinctness of men, which personal
distinctness is hated by genuine Communists ; witness the
rejection of individual names on the part of the Count and
Countess in *La Comtesse de Rudolstadt,* who will acknowledge no name but the common name of 'man.'   This
principle of unity may take, and has taken, a thousand different
shapes.   I will not enter upon its connexion with the Church,
but merely refer to 'A man's a man for a' that' and the
Bothie as good practical expressions of it.   It has much to
do (especially in connexion with the opposite pole of Individu-
ality) with various mysterious but most important questions—
that, for instance, of the relation of ἔρως to στοργή and of
ἀγάπη to both, but these, tho' quite *ad rem*, must be left now
untouched.

Instead of giving you now any *a posteriori* arguments to connect Communism with Pantheism, I will leave you to follow out such thoughts as what I have already said may suggest.   Neither will I bother you with showing that to be consistent you must follow Plato, and believe permanence of marriage to be a pernicious bondage.   Lawless right, formless substance, bodiless spirit,—these are, I believe, the general formulæ common to all the aspects of Pantheism ; arbitrary law, naked form, lifeless matter, of pure Monotheism.   The mutual correlation and reciprocal necessity of the twin sets of ideas, as grounded upon a Trinity in Unity, are set forth and interwoven into the daily life of men by the two great Universal Sacraments, and in a lesser degree by the lesser Sacraments.   I ask you not to conclude too hastily that this conflict and this reconciliation, which are found in every other region, are wanting in the region of Politics.   May God lead us both into all truth in these and all other mysteries of His Kingdom !—Ever, my dear Ellerton, most affectionately yours,   FENTON J. A. HORT.

[Postscript]

On second thoughts it seems better to say a word on 'loyalty' and rebellion.   I do not profess to be able to answer every objection, but I think I see my way clearly in one or two directions.   There is a certain Divine plan upon which God would have all kingdoms formed, even as there is a certain Divine plan for all churches and religious bodies ; but, as religious bodies have forsaken the Apostolic type, even so have states forsaken their true Davidean type, becoming tyrannies and democracies in various modifications. Nevertheless all these violations of God's own order are part of His providential government.   It behoves men therefore, who find themselves in an abnormal and irregular state of things, while they maintain in their hearts and advance, so far as God's will is made manifest to them, the truer and higher state, to submit themselves to the lower, and more corrupt, as still in a lower sense ordained by Him, and not to rebel against it in self-will ; thus the Apostles rightly did not resist the Emperors, but the Nonjurors acted wrongly.   Submission to *de facto* rule is a duty. It was for their maintaining this rule in opposition to the Sacheverel doctrine that James I. refused to sign the Canons of 1606 (I think), commonly called Bishop Overall's *Convocation Book*, after they had been adopted by both Houses of Convocation and Parliament. Loyalty I cannot define, but it seems to me to be a peculiar *filial* feeling toward God's Anointed King, which could never in any considerable degree be shown to any one, whose authority was in any sense our own creature. It is customary to call it slavish ; but a slave, a human labouring machine, cannot be loyal ; freedom and personal independence are implied in it.

The following letter was written and sent before the last was completed :—

To THE REV. JOHN ELLERTON

BATH, *March* 30*th*, 1850.

. . . I cannot let Easter-tide altogether pass away without sending you a line or two of good wishes and ordinary babble. As for No. 1, you seem to take that individual's misfortunes (?) to heart much more than he does himself; there is really nothing very appalling in being two places lower than one might have been, tho' it is vexatious, especially as Tait seems disappointed, as well as several of my friends. I should infer from your letter that you fancy Beamont to be above me ; *that* is not the case ; he merely begins with a B, I with an H (I wish for the nonce the examiners had spelt me as some tradesmen do, ' Aught ' !). Schreiber and Beamont have got the medals, and are, I should think, the best of those in for them. After all I have the Moral and Natural Science Triposes still before me, to say nothing of my Fellowship ; I wish I had any chance of the latter for this year, but I have none. If during the next eighteen or twenty months I read half what I have in mind to do, I shall do very well, but indolent ways are not easily overcome.

I have made several valuable acquaintances ; among others that of Markland (who founded the sermon for the Propagation of the Gospel Society). . . . He had a glorious library, heaps of interesting portraits, etc. etc., and pleased me much. I heard once at St. Michael's, a splendid modern Early English church, ——. I was half asleep, but he seemed a man with real brave stuff in him. I was twice or three times at the Octagon Chapel. These chapels are curious places, quite Bathonian.

I heard John Parry the other night; he is laughable enough, has a noble voice and most marvellous power over the piano, but his 'entertainments' are not particularly intellectual.

This is a most beautiful city. The Abbey is not very much, late Perpendicular, unfinished; but the hollows and combes, where the soft lias of the vales melts into its harder beds, where they join on to the oolite of the hills, are most varied and rich. We are about the junction of the strata, half-way up Lansdown, in the last row in Bath, looking out on the breezy Victoria Park.

Perhaps it will be as well to keep Maurice's letter till I am in Cambridge, which will be (*D. V.*) in a fortnight. You are most welcome to take a copy *for yourself;* but no one has seen it but the Macmillans, their friend H. Gotobed, W. Howard, and Blunt, and it is very doubtful whether I shall show it to any one else.

I wish Kingsley's tract *Cheap Clothes and Nasty* was out. I am not now going to talk on the subject, but simply protest against being associated with the *Economist*, or any other political economic quack. You shall have more of the new *Princess* from Cambridge; there is a song between each canto, and the 'conclusion' is considerably altered and enlarged; minor changes occur throughout. Don't abuse Kingsley's War-song; it is not flute-like, but surely it has a rude gigantesque tromboon vigour about its music; it occurs in one of a beautiful series of articles on 'N. Devon,' and is sung by Claude Mellot in a boat of fishermen and fisherwomen, old and young, going out from Clovelly to Lundy Isle. I am much pleased with No. 2 of Carlyle; he has boldly set forth *justice* as a ground of punishment, and made the sentimentalists furious. The authoress of *Shirley* is older than you fancy;

she is twenty-six, and wears light flowing hair down to her
waist. She lives quite in solitude with her father (her two
sisters died a year or two ago), and he knew nothing of the
matter till she simultaneously presented him with *Jane Eyre*
and the reviews of it. Clark reviewed *Shirley* in *Fraser*. I
saw in the *North American* an amusing review of *Lady Alice*.
It is much vext to find that the book is written by an American,
and grieves that a model republican should write so superstitious,
aristocratic, indecent a book; it certainly has faults enough,
but no nation need be ashamed of it. I want much to skim
Southey's *Life*, but have not yet seen it.

I wish I saw into that φρόνημα σαρκός question ; Maurice
gave me no answer about it. Two things at least are certain :
first, that Christ has redeemed the flesh and taken it into the
Divine Nature by the Incarnation ; second, that " the flesh
lusteth against the spirit." The reconciliation I cannot see.

I am afraid I cannot help you on Gen. iii. Probably
Revelations are, as you hint, the best guide ; the beginning of
the Bible is elucidated by the end. I have often thought of
asking Maurice in conversation, but there are more impera-
tively engrossing points. Thinking over the time when I used
to exult in despising Revelations, etc., I cannot help thinking
of Clough's lines, and longing for more of that

> Courage to let the courage sink,
> Itself a coward base to think,
> Rather than not for heavenly light
> Wait on, to show the truly right.

I wrote to Macmillan about Midhurst ; I know no one myself.
Respecting your work in Scotland, remember that noble sonnet
by one of the Ragged School teachers, prefixt to the volume of
the *Politics for the People*, beginning—

> Not all who seem to fail, have failed indeed.

To his Mother

CAMBRIDGE, *May* 10*th*, 1850.

. . . The Exhibition of Antient and Mediæval Art, which
I especially wished to see, interested me a good deal, though I

was in some measure disappointed; I had expected to see a good deal of beauty of form, especially in the goldsmiths' work, but found scarcely any. On the other hand, the elaborateness and richness of the carving was perfectly wonderful. Many of the best objects had been sent for exhibition by the Queen, and several were of historical as well as artistic interest; one of the finest of these was a magnificent shield (attributed to Benvenuto Cellini) given by Francis I. to Henry VIII., probably at the Field of the Cloth of Gold.

. . . Babington will be much pleased if I can join him at Edinburgh for the British Association, which meets there on July 31st, and then take a run with him and Balfour (the Edinburgh Professor of Botany) into Ross-shire and Sutherland-shire, and either the Hebrides or the Orkneys for scientific exploration. I was glad on reaching Cambridge, and examining the Ilfracombe sea-weeds which I had myself gathered, and a few of which I had laid out, to find that, with few exceptions, you and I had hit on different species.

To the Rev. Gerald Blunt

CAMBRIDGE, *Ascension Day*, 1850.
(Finisht *May 12th.*)

. . . You ask me about the liberty to be allowed to clergymen in their views of Baptism. For my own part, I would gladly admit to the ministry such as hold Gorham's view, much more such as hold the ordinary confused Evangelical notions, tho' I would on no account alter the Prayer-book or Catechism to make them more palatable to them. But for all that I could not have signed the famous Judgement, because I do not think that the Formularies will fairly bear the meaning there pronounced admissible. But if a clergyman says *he* can honestly use them, I would not molest him. I do not think that Gorham's views would have been tolerated in the early ages. I am not aware of their existence for many centuries except in notorious heretics.

Of course you have seen by this time *Cheap Clothes and Nasty*, and the three numbers of the *Tracts on Christian*

Socialism, 1 and 3 by Maurice, and 2 by a barrister of the name of Hughes. They are fully worth study ; but I still hold back from Socialism. . . .

I think Maurice's letter to me sufficiently showed that we have no sure knowledge respecting the duration of future punishment, and that the word 'eternal' has a far higher meaning than the merely material one of excessively long duration ; extinction always grates against my mind as something impossible. . . .

You will be glad to hear that Sir James Stephen has been delivering a really splendid course of lectures on the mediæval history of France, . . . full of matter and thought.

Hare's charge is good and interesting ; he has twice indignant protests against the persecution of Miss Sellon ; his letter to Cavendish is not remarkable. I daresay you will have seen the article in the *Quarterly* on Maurice and Queen's College, as well as Maurice's magnificent pamphlet in reply ; I never saw charges so completely flung back on the accuser. As a piece of controversial writing, it surpasses even Henry of Exeter's works.

To the Rev. John Ellerton

CAMBRIDGE, *May* 16*th*, 1850.

. . . A few days afterwards Kingsley was here for an hour or two merely on business, so that I did not see him, but Macmillan told him of you and Serres (that's the name I think) ; he said that he would give anything to know you, and desired that his request might be conveyed to you to call upon him at Eversley, or write to him, and he would call upon you at Easebourne, or do anything else to bring you together.

I was in town from Sunday to Tuesday last but one, to see the Mediæval Exhibition ; heard Maurice preach on Sunday, went to breakfast with him on Monday and Tuesday, and tea on Monday, and saw and made acquaintance with Ludlow, Hughes (the author of Tract No. 2), Furnival, Vansittart Neale, Chevallier, and others of the set, as well as the Tailors. A. Macmillan (who was with me) told them I was an enemy,

but I had a friend Ellerton down in the country, a most
determined Socialist; they shouted, Hughes especially, O that
they must at once get him to fraternize and make him an
agent, and Hughes asked me where you dwelt; I told him, and
shall not be surprized if you hear something of them; at all
events, the door is opened for you.

Of course you've seen Maurice's magnificent smasher of the
Quarterly's pitiful attack.   Kingsley is coming out with a three-
volume Socialist novel, *Alton Locke, Poet and Tailor: an
Autobiography;* I have to-day seen the two first proof-sheets.

TO THE REV. JOHN ELLERTON

CAMBRIDGE, *Trinity Sunday* [*May 26th*], 1850.

My dear Ellerton—After spending the greater part of to-
day in reading Maurice's *History of Philosophy*, from the
beginning of Plato down to the Christian period (no small
amount), I sit down to begin to you an answer due above a
month ago.

. . . I heard a fair amount of music at Bath.   Catherine
Hayes disgusted me; they call her pretty, but she is merely
like a painted doll.   I don't know whether you remember
a pair of popular Cambridge engravings, each of a rustic
girl sitting in an attitude on a bank simpering vilely; the
prettiest of them is exactly a portrait of her, and all her
ways and manners are equally mincing.   Her crack song,
'Savourneen Deelish,' was to me horrible; she dolorously
drawled and whined and spun out the notes to half a minute
apiece, in a manner most unpathetic and unballad-like.   She
has a wonderful, rich, powerful voice (of course far below
Jenny Lind's), but, I think, no genius.   This came out most
strongly in '*Ah non giunge*,' which she had the bad taste to
sing in rivalry of Jenny Lind; she sung it very well, but it was
merely the pretty, varied, sensuous air of Bellini, while Jenny
threw the very soul of music into it.   I must in justice mention
that she was picked out of a charity school at Limerick by the
late Bishop, educated, and sent to Italy at his expense.
Meanwhile he got into difficulties and had to sell the furniture

of his palace ; she chanced to hear of it, instantaneously turned every article she possest into money, and redeemed the furniture. I did not like Kate Loder's piano-playing, it was so monotonous and tastelessly rapid ; but she had the disadvantage of a detestable piano.

While I think of it, will you be kind enough to send me Maurice's letter, if you have really done with it ?

How noble Carlyle continues in spite of some nonsense ! We had a capital Union debate on the Latter-Day Pamphlets ; of course I defended him most warmly. Davies [1] (our scholar) sent Carlyle a copy of a pamphlet he has just published (on admitting the Clergy to Parliament), and mentioned the debate and its favorable result, and received a most characteristic but hearty and kind note in return. It was Mill who answered Carlyle on 'Quashee and Pumpkin,' etc. *Apropos* of him, 1st, because I see that in England Socialism begins in the region of Political Economy, and to study it rightly one should occupy the ground ; 2nd, because the subject is in the Moral Science Tripos, I have just got his *Political Economy*, and hope to read it *cum multis aliis* in the Long.

Poor, poor Lord Lincoln ! ! Yet perhaps his heavy sorrows are meant to ripen him for future holding of the helm of the State. So after all the mighty spring of half the life of the century is dried up. Wordsworth is dead ! Well ! I believe we shall find men to take his place, not altogether unworthily in course of time. There is a large committee of great names to collect subscriptions for a bust in Westminster Abbey, a monument at Grasmere, and some institution to his memory ; Maurice, Hare, and two others form the acting committee.

On Tuesday last I had a sort of link to you, being at one end of that long belt of Lower Green Sand on the other end of which you are fixed ; all the vegetation is wonderfully fresh and warm upon it.

Maurice told me that he hoped to have the first (ante-Christian) part of his *History of Philosophy* out in June, the est not for ever so long, as a vast deal would have to be done to it in the way of expansion, etc. He had entirely re-written the Jewish period, but intended only to touch up the Greek.

[1] Now the Rev. J. Ll. Davies.

I know nothing of the *Warburtonian Lectures* and *Sermons on the Occasional Services* except the advertisement; but Macmillan has just had a note to say that he and Mrs. Maurice are ordered abroad by their medico for three months for health's sake. He laughs as far as regards himself, tho' I am sure he greatly overworks himself, but his wife is certainly very ill. I have got Coleridge's new book, but not read much; it is (except a few pages transcribed in Gillman's *Life*) entirely new, consisting of a gathering up, as complete as possible, of his articles in the *Courier, Morning Post*, etc., and his early *Watchman* effusions. These latter are wild enough, but fully bear out his protestation that he never was a Jacobin. At the end are a few new poems, chiefly epigrams. *Voici* the best of them.

> In vain I praise thee, Zoilus,
> In vain thou railst at me.
> Me no one credits, Zoilus,
> And no one credits thee.

I have F. Newman's *Soul* in hand, but find it awfully dull and saccharine and vapid. I have scarcely seen his new *Phases of Faith* (the last being, I suppose, 'New Moon'). They seem stronger, but full of the same placid, self-complacent, boudoir scepticism which exasperates me beyond measure. I have also a long while begun G. Sand's *Lelia*, in order to see her worst, but have made little way through its jungles of dreary Werterism, setting up people as the objects of the greatest interest—almost worship—in proportion to the amount of sins they have committed.

I have a sort of fancy that I never told you of my having written to Maurice about three weeks before going to Bath, to ask about a course of Moral Philosophy reading, etc., and to know whether he still thought that Englishmen should attend more to Ethics than to Metaphysics. Just then I heard of the forthcoming Socialist Tracts, and added a postscript wishing him success, but protesting against the cant of praising the meritoriousness and benevolence of those who joined an association. At last I got an answer, which you shall see when you are with me, but is hardly worth sending unless you are methodically attacking the subject—valuable enough for its own purposes, and containing some beautiful remarks on Plato and Aristotle. To the former, he says, he owes more than to any book but the Bible. I will transcribe what he says on Socialism ; of course he begins it in connexion with the previous subjects :—

"On the whole I should hold fast to Plato and Aristotle, and make the other books of the course illustrative of them. Our modern Socialist questions, which, as you say, must press more and more upon us, will, I conceive, present themselves to you again and again while you are busy with those ancients. And it is a grand thing to read the newspapers by the light of them, and them by the light of the newspapers. I send you my tract in this letter. You shall have the second soon. I do not suppose they will be read much, but they may set some people thinking who will do something better themselves. I do not wish to represent it as any *merit* in the working men to join a trading fraternity ; but neither do I think it is any merit to join a purely religious or benevolent fraternity. It seems to me the right thing to do both one and the other kind of work according to the Gospel, and that is all I see about it."

On my return hither I wrote to thank him, and explained that I did not mean *merit* theologically, but could not ascribe moral excellence to what was done from motives of self-interest. A few days afterwards I went up to town, and of that visit I must now give you some account. Mackenzie was eating his term at Lincoln's Inn, and I agreed to run up on the Monday and go with him to see the ' Mediæval Show ' (as Maurice called it). I wrote three or four days before to Maurice to ask what time I should find him at home on Monday or Tuesday, knowing (and telling him) that he was not to be found at ordinary hours. He begged me to come to breakfast on Monday if I were so early in town, and at all events he would try to meet me at the 'Show,' and I must take tea with him in the evening, when 'some barristers and others to whom he would like to introduce me ' met 'to read the Scriptures—not at all in a formal way,' and must breakfast with him the next morning. I knew of this ' Crotchet Club,' as A. Macmillan calls it, and had chosen

Monday with that view.   I answered that I could not resist
his whole invitation, and would go up on Sunday.   Meanwhile the thought struck me, why not hear him preach as
well?   And as I found A. Macmillan was going up on Sunday
morning to attend a sale, I agreed to go with him.   We deposited our luggage at Wood's, Furnival's Inn, secured beds,
and sallied forth to look at Lincoln's Inn and the neighbourhood, and finally to go to service.   We got in the pew
diagonally furthest from Maurice, and he was already in his
desk.   It was a dark afternoon, and the stained glass was dim,
and I would hardly believe that that was the Maurice of the
portrait.   His reading of the service did not seem to me nearly
so marked and varied as you described and Blunt confirmed,
but it was wonderfully beautiful; not a particle of effect or
mouthing, but the calmest, solemnest, yet never monotonous,
prayer.   The anthem was a long, dreary anthology of scraps
from old English composers; but it was curious to watch his
face looking out into the chapel, with the dark hollows of his
deep-set eyes strongly contrasted with the rest of his face in
the sort of twilight.   His text was 1 John i. 8, 9. . . . Such
a sermon in every respect I never heard; his quiet, deep voice,
piercing you so softly and firmly through and through, never
pausing or relaxing in its strain of eloquence, every syllable,
as it were, weighted with the energy and might of his whole
soul (and what a soul!), kept me crouched in a kind of spell,
such as I could not have conceived.   After chapel we dined
and then went to see Ludovici (an odd Red Republican
German artist of some genius, who was here for some time) at
a curious foreign boarding-house; and truly a more strange
Sunday evening I never past: there were one or two male
singing notabilities and Hurwitz, the great chess-player.   The
next (rainy) morning we were at Maurice's before nine; he
received me most kindly, and apologized that he had brought
me unawares but unintentionally into a Socialist breakfast; a
committee had to meet, and his breakfast-table was most
speedy and convenient.   Accordingly I was introduced to
Ludlow and one or two others (Hughes, a most glorious, free,
hearty fellow Macmillan had introduced to me after chapel on
Sunday).   Ludlow, with his quiet, earnest, strong, gentle manner,

pleased me much. Among the others were Vansittart Neale, who supplies most of the cash (he is cousin to Vansittart, who is now among the promoters, but was that day at Cambridge), and Chevallier, a French political economist. They are coming out with a book on the subject likely to be very strong, and to contain an honest attack on property, root and branch. Maurice's evanescent smiles and occasional quiet, overwhelming observations, the force of which they did not in the least perceive, amused me much. I had not much conversation with him then, but in his presence everything was delight. . . . I called for Mackenzie in Wimpole Street, and thence to the 'Mediæval Show,' which certainly disappointed me, interesting as it was ; I expected beauty of form and found none. Thence to the Old Water-Colours Exhibition, but any details of this and the Royal Academy I must reserve, or this letter will not be able to go to-night. Thence with him as far as Regent Circus, Oxford Street, whence we parted, and I to Lincoln's Inn. I had still some time before meeting Macmillan, so walked to the National Gallery to see John Bellini's ' Doge,' and lounged there for half an hour ; thence joined Macmillan at Nutt's, went and dined and called on Furnival. He took us to see the Shoemakers' and Tailors' Associations. Thence to the Central Committee room in New Oxford Street, where Maurice presided over a large court of promoters, some of whom I fancied, others I didn't ; they received a *third* shoemakers' deputation for an association. Thence we all walked, I coupled with Ludlow, to Maurice's house, it being past 9 P.M., and I had a great deal of most interesting talk with him (Ludlow), which I must also reserve, only saying that it enormously strengthened all my previous feeling and judgement against the system of Socialism. After tea Gen. xxii. was read, and Ludlow and Furnival made some critical remarks. Maurice said but little—of course there was good in it—but nothing particular. The next morning I went alone to Maurice's, and breakfasted quietly, no one being there but Mrs. Maurice (who was miserably ill, so that I could not judge much of her), a sort of governess, and his second boy (the eldest was gone to his day school), a most dear little fellow, who made great friends with me. I had much interest-

ing talk with him, and still more as I half-walked half-cabbed
with him to Harley Street, where he was going to Queen's
College.   Cambridge, Plato, etc., and the ecclesiastical horizon
were our chief topics.   Much that he said, on the last especially, will be interesting to you, but I must most reluctantly
postpone it.   He parted from me in the most cordial way.   I
then went to the Academy Exhibition, and spent some three
hours there; thence joined Macmillan at the sale, and finally
dined and returned to Cambridge.   I know I had much more
to say besides what I have reserved, but I cannot at this
moment remember what.

To the Rev. John Ellerton

Newland, *June* 30*th*, 1850.

. . . What an unspeakable loss we have sustained in
poor Sir R. Peel !   It is very gratifying to see that the regret
seems universal; I am sure, however, that his death was a
necessary step to a new order of things.   Gladstone is
evidently not unconscious of his own position.   His tone, and
Lord John's to him, in the Foreign Affairs debate showed
this; so also the *Dublin Mail*, which is very well informed
on Government affairs, said during the debate that Lord
Stanley had been down to the House of Commons and had a
long conference with Gladstone, and it was understood that
they had formed a coalition.   Moreover, Stanley has deserted
the Protectionist squallers; but I sincerely hope that Gladstone
will not consent merely to head a party of Conservatives such
as they were before Peel Liberalised them.

I hope you are reading *David Copperfield;* it is very
beautiful.

But I must tell you something of my present locality.
You perhaps know that the upper part of the district between
the Wye and Severn is a small coal basin (though elevated
ground) called the Forest of the Dean, and is royal property
above ground.   The course of the Wye below Ross to
Chepstow lies along a range of mountain limestone, forming
beautiful wooded hills, sometimes in cliffs and nearly always

steep. At Monmouth, where a more level country opens into Herefordshire, disclosing a view of the distant Brecon mountains, the Wye begins to run nearly due south, through hills of endless variety, but never interrupted by depressions. Our village is on the map about two miles and a half from Monmouth (by road four and a half); exactly south-east of that town, but lying in Gloucestershire, about a mile and a half from the Wye; I believe we are on Millstone grit, but there is limestone all round. We have the deepest and most beautiful wooded undulations, but less romantic than those close to the Wye. We are some two or three miles from the Forest, most of which is richly timbered, but we have seen very little of it. The drive to Chepstow is magnificent. Tintern is very beautiful, but disappointed me; it seems all late Early English, but all the large windows are utterly gutted (I fancy, by Cromwell) except the west. Of course I have plenty to do in the way of plants, especially my favorite *Rubi*. Our village was called in Elizabeth's time 'the aristocratickal village of Newland,' and there are now more gentlemen's houses than others in the village, but the parish embraces a vast part of the Forest. Our church is a big late Perpendicular building, with countless vile changes and additions, but having a respectable tower; it looks well in its noble situation.

The following letter has reference to the sufferings, physical and mental, of a friend, and may illustrate some characteristics of the writer, without knowledge of the particular circumstances :—

To a Friend

Cambridge, 1850.

I scarcely know what to write to you, feeling how completely you must be occupied with the accounts of poor ——. Yet painfully harassing as this protracted duration of suffering cannot but be, we cannot—at least we ought not—to forget how often such sufferings are medicinal in all their bitterness, and are turned into blessed instruments of softening and purifying. Even the words in ——'s letter of "more comfort of mind, as well as body," without attaching to them too much significance, do yet, I think, seem to support a strong hope that it is even so in this case. A mind disappointed and ill at ease with itself cannot pass through such fires uninfluenced the one way or the other; if it be not driven in upon itself with tenfold bitterness swelling almost to madness, it must be suffering its dross to be purged away and approaching a more peaceful and happy state. But the truer and deeper the improvement, the less noise and outward trumpeting of it shall we hear; we must be content with any chance intimation of the improvement that may reach us,—here a little sign, and there a little sign. And even if we hear none at all, and can perceive from a distance no stirring of a genuine life, still we have no right—nay, we should be presumptuous and impious—to infer that there is no life there. I do not know what your experience in this matter is, but hardly a month passes without showing me how blind even the keenest-sighted of such judgements are. It is hardest to think well where there is manifest hypocrisy; yet even there our uncharitable thoughts are often rebuked. But how much more reason have we to hope, where there is an outward crust of hardness, that there may be a well of life springing within! There may be a long and weary strife, but remembering Who it is that is even now fighting, and that He is stronger than the devil (hard as it is to remember), how *dare* we *despair* of the victory? And then—the last enemy that shall be overcome is Death.

To the Rev. John Ellerton

WESTFIELD HOUSE, WESTON ROAD, BATH,
July 23*rd*, 1850 [finished *July* 31*st*].

. . . I hope you will be able to see the Exhibition before it closes. E. Landseer's large picture is a total failure; only individual details are good. His 'Good Doggie' is excellent, and nothing more of his. As I have the Catalogue by me, it may save you some time if I mention a few of those, as far as I can remember them, which struck me most. Creswick's 'Wind on Shore' is excellent. Frost's 'Disarming of Cupid' and Pickersgill's 'Samson Betrayed' are tolerable in a style that is bad unless first-rate; the former is too lady's-maid-ish. Stanfield's 'Macbeth,' the best in the Exhibition, and the only imaginative picture of his that I have ever seen; a true natural mountain scene on a lowering day, the figures very (rightly) subordinate. Turner's three or four I hadn't time to try to see in the crowd, but think they would repay a week or two's study; they consist chiefly of effused Seville orange pulp. . . . The 'Water-Colours' are rather poor. Gastineau's are, I think, the best, though some of Copley Fielding's quite rival his; but I own I care little for any of them. Some of, I think, Fripp's would amuse you as miracles of colouring in a passion.[1] . . .

Well, I must now try to recall some of Maurice's conversation when I was in London. He spoke of the University Commission as capable of doing some good, and laught at Prince Albert having aught to say to it; hoped they might hit upon some plan for allowing fellows or, at all events, tutors to marry, on the ground of the vast good an improved female society would do in the University. . . . He asked what was the state of things in Cambridge? I told him we were clogged and deadened by Via Mediaism. "In short, Eclecticism?" he askt. 'Yes,' I said; 'it had, however, one advantage; we were nearly free from party spirit.' His answer was, "I am sure that is anything but a healthy sign among young men. It is just the same at Oxford; all is stagnant and dead." I said, 'I fancied there had been something stirring in Clough's line.' 'No, he thought not; there might be infidelity in plenty, but if so it was passive, 'stagnant' infidelity. The only strong feeling he saw there was a general discontent of the younger men with everything, the University, and above all, with the apathy of the higher Dons.' He talked a good deal of Grote's account of Socrates and the Sophists, especially his vindication (?) of the latter, agreeing with his facts, but thinking that they were precisely to be condemned for what Grote praised them for, viz. especially their aim to make the young

[1] These notes on pictures are selected from a long list of similar criticisms.

men *clever* and powerful by persuasion. He expatiated most lovingly on Socrates as the Athenian of Athenians, the man who above all others threw himself into the feelings and cravings of his age, especially of its young men ; and dwelt on the fact that, so far from being the sublimely abstracted and denationalized sage of Grote, he could not have been so mighty for all future ages and nations had he not been the man of his own age and nation.

He did not talk much of the Gorham question, but hoped the Bishops might do something good ; he seemed chiefly pained and disappointed at what he called the want of confidence of the High Churchmen in their own principle, the feeling they seemed to have that the truth was made more true or false by decisions of synods or judgements of courts. He spoke in very high terms of Thompson as a 'solid, substantial man,' and seemed greatly delighted at Whewell's having lately declared him to be the most valuable man in Cambridge. Hardly a word past on Socialism.

I am afraid I have forgotten several subjects, but in one especially you will be interested. Altho' you have said nothing, I have had a feeling that you fully shared with me the consciousness of how much reflexion was rendered necessary by the three or four last pages of his anonymous pamphlet on the Gorham case,—I mean where he contemplates a secession in case the Government and Evangelicals should succeed in altering the Baptismal Services. I had been much perplext to discover the right course in such a case, and had been inclined to think that lay communion was the only right thing, as it seemed schismatical to leave the body of the Church because it had abolisht one of its former doctrines. I was determined, as I went with Maurice from his house to Harley Street, to sound him well, and get him to remove this objection if possible. Of course I did it very gently and cautiously, lest he should think I was hot-headedly agog for secession and a *Mons Sacer*, nor did I allude to the pamphlet. I spoke of the gloomy prospect, should the Evangelicals carry on their present victory so as to alter the Services. He trusted God would spare us such a trial. I assented, but urged that it was a more than possible contingency. This he allowed, but exprest an opinion that there was dormant in the middle classes a most strong feeling which would resist a proclamation that their children were Sons of the Devil. I trusted it might be so, but said that surely such a feeling was not now active, and that it would require such a preliminary event as the alteration of the Services to rouse the feeling into life, and that nothing but experience would show them what the denial of Baptism involved. To this he assented. I said that, if so, this middle-class resistance would avail but little, in the first instance, to ward off the calamity. What did he think we should be bound to do in such a case ? He at last (the whole was reluctant, evidently from the fear I have already mentioned, manifested in the pamphlet) said he feared we must give up the emoluments of the Church. I said that was not what I was thinking of, but I felt it hard to decide whether or not it were schism so to leave the body. He said that undoubtedly to cut oneself off would be schism ; that he had always contended that the act must be our adversaries', not our own (this he had already more than once repeated). Then, I supposed, he considered the alteration of the Services as such a schismatical act ? " Doubtless," he said ; " it would be declaring themselves held together not by sacraments but opinions." " Then," I said, " if I understand you right, you think that by such an act they would be voluntarily cutting themselves off from the body of the Church, and declaring themselves to be only a sect, inasmuch as they would be professing that the ground of their communion was not union in the body of Christ, but the accident of their holding intellectually the same opinions." " Exactly," was his answer. (I cannot be sure of the words ; the sense I have given correctly). Much subsequent reflexion has convinced me that his view is right, and that by such an act the Establishment would float off on its own raft, leaving us standing as before on the rock of our old Catholic ground.

I wish I could remember well my very interesting conversation with Ludlow as we walked from the Central Association Office in New Oxford Street to Maurice's house. I can recall but two or three points. I remember saying, " Then you regard the relation of employer to employed as essentially evil, and would do your utmost to destroy it altogether?" "Certainly

I object altogether to the relation of master and hired servant, for this reason, that the hire or wages will always be dependent on the rate of wages in the market." "But supposing the amount of wages in any case *not* to depend on the market rate?" " I cannot entertain such a supposition, because wages always must be regulated by the market rate." I prest him no further here, being quite satisfied at having made a profest assailer of political economy doctrines entirely rest his support of one of the main elements of Socialism upon an assumed axiom of political economy, which goes on the assumption that selfishness is the law of men's actions ! Again, I urged that I fully adopted the Christian principle of co-operation, but repudiated the Socialistic scheme as substituting a mechanical for a moral co-operation ; that I thought a real fellow-working was chiefly, if not only, possible under the old so-called ' competitive ' machinery. To this he replied that practically, as men are selfish, mutual assistance and co-operation, springing from merely moral motives instead of from machinery, are impossible. Another strange confession ! Further, I asked him whether he wished to carry out the machinery to the utmost and universally. " Doubtless." " Then have you thought of the time when individual tradesmen shall have been swallowed up into a number of trading associations ? Will there not then be a competition between rival associations infinitely more terrible and crushing than the present competition of individuals ? or how will you be able to blend the associations ? " " That," said he, " is *the* rock ahead of Christian Socialism. I do not see my way at all through those difficulties ; only, feeling sure that we are on the right way, I trust that, when the time comes, we shall be guided to what is right." He further added that Co-operation was not intended to stand alone without Exchange, and that the latter principle would remove some of these difficulties. " Exchange ! " I exclaimed ; " that is quite new to me. I never heard before of Exchange in connexion with Socialism ; that is an element so totally new and important, that I must take time to think about it." " Why ! we always look on Exchange as essential to Co-operation." He then turned round to A. Macmillan, who was walking behind with Furnival, and shouted, " Macmillan, have

you never told Hort about the principle of Exchange in connexion with Socialism ? " " No," he shouted back, " I don't
know anything about it, and I don't want ; Socialism is enough
for me ! " Ludlow laughed, but by this time we were more
than half down Queen's Square, and the conversation ceased.
One or two more things. Some one said that Kingsley either
had just had, or was just going to have, a long controversial
correspondence on the subject with J. S. Mill. Maurice told
me that he heard that throughout the manufacturing districts
the men were beginning to find that machinery (material) was
really their friend, and that its seeming injuries must be re-
butted by changes in the relations of employment. Mrs.
Maurice told me that of the many poor needlewomen who
had been to her to be examined, not above three or four were
even tolerable workers. I wish much to hear more about this
' Exchange,' but shall not, I suppose, till Chevallier's lectures
are published ; at present it seems to me negative to the idea
of Socialism. I have never yet been able to ascertain from
any of you wherein the Socialistic part, *i.e.* the machinery of
' Christian Socialism,' differs from that of other Socialism ;
the moral principle of co-operation I fully recognise, but think
that Maurice makes his definition deceptive and arbitrary by
including it. I told them at the Office that they must consider me as a spy in the enemy's camp. Furnival protested
that this was not true, and that, as I allowed their ' principle,'
I was really a ' Christian Socialist '; doubtless I fall under
Maurice's verbal definition, but utterly repudiate the name, as
I am not what you all understand by it.

This letter has been kept shamefully long ; I was at Bath
all last week. Sunday evening and Monday I was tortured
with toothache, and nearly maddened on Tuesday, so I went
in all speed to Cheltenham and had the offender extracted,
returning to-day (July 31st) to Newland. I am sorry to see
the Exhibition is closed already. I have not yet seen Wordsworth's new poem. I observe the new *Christian Observer*
has a review of Kingsley's Sermons. How magnificent and
humiliating Carlyle's ' Hudson's Statue ' is ! I have not yet
been able to get hold of either the June or July *Pendennis.*
Well, I am getting sleepy, so will say good-night.]

To the Rev. John Ellerton

Weston-super-Mare, *September 12th*, 1850.

. . . I have got Emerson's last book, but only dipt; his remarks on Plato seemed acute taken singly, but I thought his whole idea of him absolutely false; he seemed to try to make out the most εὐσεβής of the antients to be an atheist like unto himself. As for Maurice writing in the *Leader*, Ch. Wordsworth is about as likely; even *Open Council* is not much in his way. The letter on Queen's College is indeed wonderful and valuable; I wish he oftener spoke out in like manner. Ludlow's in *Fraser* was very inferior, tho' good. I forget whether I ever recommended to you Massingberd's pamphlet on W. Goode's publication of P. Martyr's letter. It is most excellent and of great permanent value, as showing the real behaviour of Cranmer, etc., as to Baptism; I need not say it is at once charitable and most hearty. I gave up the Hulsean because the necessary reading was impracticable—even had I been at Cambridge; and I could not carry down a library into the country. The Burney[1] subject is, 'The unity of design displayed in the successive dispensations of religion recorded in Scripture, as an argument for the truth of Revelation.' I have written a few pages, expanding the passage quoted pp. 21, 22 of Maurice's letter on revelation, general to all mankind, as well as special (as in the Bible) to the Jews and Christian Church; then I am about asking what kinds of revelation demand an unity; not the mere teaching of practical sagacity, nor the Paleyan notion of future rewards and punishments; but that we cannot give an answer about the higher wisdom (whether a revelation of that demands an unity) till we find what is its object, Truth; in short, that what gives all its unity to Revelation is that its central subject is the Being of God. I then hope to trace the development of this revelation through the 'dispensations' of the Bible, showing how all is connected with the gradual disclosure of the full Name of God. I am writing very soberly, but fear I shall be too philosophical in language for them.

I am not going in for the Fellowship.

[1] The Burney prize is for a theological essay, and is open to graduates.

The next two letters are to a friend who was perplexed with conscientious difficulties about the marriage
of the clergy.

TO A FRIEND

NEWLAND, *June* 1850.

. . . I think I can enter into your present feeling. You
fully concur, I fancy, in all that I said about the wrong of
setting for oneself a special saint-morality which will not fit
other people ; but still you feel that at all hazards, at the risk
of any conceivable inconsistency, you cannot conscientiously
do that which seems now so often to lead to sin and misery.
You find no reconciliation of this present war of your conscience and reason ; only do not assume that the reconciliation
is impossible or, at all events, impracticable for you.   God
cannot be the author of anomaly, but to those who wait for
the light He will in His own way show the Harmony and
Order which He has establisht.   Do not then, whatever
present appearances may be, take it for granted that God
demands of you to contravene His earliest law for man,
" It is not good for the man to be alone," but believe firmly
that His Truth cannot be shaken by all the lies of men and
devils, and that in due time He will make known to you
His Will concerning you and all men in the way which shall
seem to Him good ; and, believing this, you will not willingly
set up any theory or resolution which may hereafter blind
your eyes from discerning His ways, or clog your feet from
following them.

TO THE SAME

NEWLAND, *October 4th*, 1850.

. . . With regard to Luke xx. 27-38 and the parallel passages, I merely meant that our Lord, when asked vexatious
questions by the Pharisees or Sadducees, hardly ever or
never gave them real answers, but either made expressly *ad
hominem* appeals, or asserted some truth which in some manner
superseded the question, or showed that there were more im-

portant ones; thus I infer that our Lord's words here were not
meant as an answer to the Sadducees' question, as they would
have been had they been given to the disciples. At all
events I must remind you that, except by remote inference,
the verses will not support your theory, for tho' γαμοῦσιν and
ἐκγαμίσκονται should deny that marriages are made after
death, they certainly cannot assert anything about the dissolu-
tion of previously-made marriages. The passage is most
hard, nor do I expect to understand it till I can see more of
the relation of sex to the image of God. The difficulty is
greatly increased by the way in which v. 36 is made to support
v. 35. Our translators were not scholars enough to see that
they were destroying the true connexion by missing the force
of οὔτε γάρ. . . .

The 'self-anatomy' you speak of may surely be either
good or evil; to be free from it altogether, as is the case
with many of the noblest women, is no doubt a blessing,
and suited to their nature. I much doubt whether it be
the same with men; a more distinct introspection of our
own motives and feelings seems natural to us, and we are
likely to go wrong without it. On the other hand, it is apt to
become a dangerous and 'morbid trick,' when its predomi-
nance makes the judgement chiefly analytical; then we come
practically to look upon ourselves as a collection of wheels
and springs, moved mechanically by 'motives,' and we are
suspicious and jealous of ourselves in a way the reverse of true
Christian humility and watchfulness, misinterpreting our best
and noblest impulses either by persuading ourselves that they
are merely imaginary, or by resolving them into corrupt
wishes. We then act in the same way towards others, especially those who may be in, or may be brought into, any near
relation to ourselves, mistrusting in them all that is not com-
prehensible. Yet I doubt not that self-anatomy is in some
form needful to deliver us from carnal delusions; and wisely-
tempered self-consciousness, if it has its miseries, may also
bring blessings unspeakable both on ourselves and on those
who have it not. True knowledge is neither of parts nor of
wholes exclusively, but of each in each. And they must be
very peculiar and miserable circumstances indeed that can

ever make blindness a blessing or a thing to be desired; ἐν δὲ φάει καὶ ὄλεσσον is of universal application. Hence the venerable fancy of making Love blind always seems to me rather a half-falsehood than a half-truth. It suits the Pantheistic leaven now spread everywhere to picture God as tolerant of evil, sorry for it, but too much averse to giving pain to use stern remedies for its extirpation, and this, forsooth, because He is Love! Yet surely He whose love is best exprest in the sacrifice of His Son must, by the very force of His love, have the keenest vision and the intensest hatred of any, even the least spot of sin in the children whom He loves. . . . Again, tho' in the picture you have drawn 'instinct' may 'stop short,' 'reason' need not 'ply her office' alone, but take the child instinct by the hand, whose eyes may often see things hidden from the wise and prudent. If reason, so accompanied, find it hard to tell whether what she views be merely 'fancy's brook,' that may soon be 'waterless and dry,' or

> The gift for which, all gifts above,
> Him praise we, who is God, the Giver,

it may indeed be true love, yet, it would seem, it must be so immature and imperfect that reason may safely ponder whether it be advisable to let it ripen ; if so, *vogue la galère !* if not, crushing may be a duty ; but, however painful at first, it is not likely to leave permanent rankling. I do not mean that even the riper gift must not sometimes needs be trodden down, but then much more than 'advisableness' is requisite ; this, methinks, must often be God's last gracious hammer to bruise a stubborn and flinty heart.

To the Rev. John Ellerton

Cambridge, *October 29th*, 1850.

. . . I send you by this post *Alton Locke*, thinking you may like to read it. Of course either of our Bepton friends are welcome to do the same, though I am not sure that it is the wholesomest food imaginable. During the early part I was intensely delighted, though driven nearly to desperation every other page with something which disgusted me. The middle I was rather indifferent to, though of course much interested in it; but the last six chapters left me in a most uncomfortable and annoyed state of mind. I cannot at all take to her Ladyship, your namesake; she is apparently intended as a sort of female Maurice, but she only disgusts me. And all that theology at the end, true as much of it was, seemed quite stagnant as I read it,—so different from the burning words in *Yeast*, that used to make me almost bound from the floor at the Union. The chapter on Miracles seems a strange perversion of a beautiful idea of Maurice's, or of Trench's, or of both; but, taken by itself, as far as I understand it, it *denies* miracles. And, in spite of all the talk about God, I do—I grieve to say it—feel that the idea of Him is wholly absent from the book, except in bits of Sandy Mackaye. The book is pure Humanitarianism, with God as the instrument to bring it about. But Sandy Mackaye is almost always thoroughly delightful; he is no mere portrait of Carlyle, but Kingsley evidently had him in his mind all the while. You will chuckle greatly over the Emersonian sermon. Kingsley is cruelly unjust to Lillian. Granted that she is frivolous, she need not be so always; surely her type of character is a necessary and beautiful one, albeit not the highest by many degrees; and then the absurdity of that 'serene imperial Eleanore' telling Alton that he had been in love only with her physical beauty. Granted that the difference of their stations made him to feel chiefly adorative admiration such as (even as Kingsley observes) that felt by the Greek youth for the statue, still that was not all. Surely Alton would any day have risked his life for hers in a way he would not have done for any other human creature, and we are assured it was a most pure feeling. Why then give him such a pedantic jobation? The book grieves me much.

The heathenish old porch in front of St. Mary's is knocked away, and a really beautiful, though almost too elaborate, Perpendicular doorway put in its place.

I may mention in passing that we had on Sunday night 'Plead thou my cause,' and I was raised, I verily believe, to the tenth heaven.

To THE REV. JOHN ELLERTON

CAMBRIDGE, *December 3rd*, 1850.

. . . I did not send in for the 'Burney' after all; I found it very hard to move on without infinitely more thought than 'twas possible to bestow. . . . At Degree Time I am to get new rooms, second floor Nevill's Court, the first staircase from the arches going towards the Hall; they are exactly what I wanted.

. . . Lees of Christ's, who has been reading with Kingsley, describes a rich scene.   Maurice was there at Eversley for two nights, and on one of them the house was attacked by burglars. The noise made by our heroes in getting up dispersed them, but as their dodge is to wait till inmates are sounder asleep after the first disturbance, they resolved to sit up all night with a light; so there sat our dear sage in his trousers and shirt, with his sleeves turned up ready for action.   The others had each their cigar and brandy and water, and with the greatest difficulty got him to join them in the latter.   Oh, what would I have given to see it ?

To THE REV. JOHN ELLERTON

NEWLAND, *Christmas Eve*, 1850.

Though this cannot reach you till the 26th or 27th, I must not omit to send a line to wish you all the blessings of this season of life in the midst of death. . . .

These Advent lessons and anthems do indeed, as you say, thunder the Law and whisper the Gospel in our ears.   I had to read two Sundays ago Isa. xxvi. in Chapel.   It was hard not to make a fool of one's self ; those verses, the 12th, 13th, 15th, 17th, culminating in the 18th, and answered by the voice from heaven of the 19th, and then the Athanasian chant of the 20th and 21st, wedding Advent to Christmas, the triumph of judgement to the angels' song of peace and goodwill. Well, the day of the Nativity is begun, and I must go to bed.

Have you seen Maurice's delic. us letters on Education in the *Christian Socialist?*   I will send the *Leaders* when I get to Cambridge, which will probably be in a fortnight.

CHAPTER IV

THE year 1851 saw the introduction at Cambridge of the 'new Triposes' in Moral and in Natural Sciences, for both of which Hort entered, and in each of which he was placed in the First Class ; in the former he obtained the Moral Philosophy prize, and in the latter he was 'distinguished in Physiology and Botany.' The examinations themselves were severe ; in each there were set, on one of the days, two papers of four hours each, and there was an interval of only a few weeks between the Triposes.   Nor were these his only examinations in the year ; he competed in October for a fellowship, and, four days after the conclusion of that ordeal, entered on the Voluntary Theological Examination.   His own letters give sufficient account of the scope of the new Triposes, as also of his comparative failure in the fellowship examination.   The amount of reading got through in this and the preceding year must have been enormous.   Yet he found time to attend the meetings of various societies, and in June joined the mysterious company of the 'Apostles.'   The first paper which he contributed was on the subject 'Might is Right,' in defence of

Carlyle. The titles of other papers read by him were: 'Can Pope teach our young poets to sing?' (a criticism of a *dictum* of C. Kingsley); 'Is government an evil?' (a defence of authority); 'Must the giants live apart?' (on a saying of Thackeray); 'Is irony less true than matter of fact?' 'Is wealth the foundation of rank?' 'Should all honours be given to the horrible?' 'Can anything be proved by Logic?' Most of these were not so much essays as challenges to discussion, couched in a paradoxical form. He remained always a grateful and loyal member of the secret Club, which has now become famous for the number of distinguished men who have belonged to it. In his time the Club was in a manner reinvigorated, and he was mainly responsible for the wording of the oath which binds the members to a conspiracy of silence. Mr. Vernon Lushington remembers that at the Apostles' meetings he considered Hort "the most remarkable figure of our time," and that he "always spoke very seriously on these occasions." That he considered his membership as a great responsibility is shown by the fact that, before consenting to join, he asked Maurice's advice.[1]

Two other societies of widely different aims were started in this same year, in both of which Hort seems to have been the moving spirit; one a small club formed for the practice of choral music, the other called by its members the 'Ghostly Guild,'

---

[1] A good account of the Club, whose proper name is the 'Cambridge Conversazione Society,' is given in Mr. Leslie Stephen's *Life of Sir J. Fitzjames Stephen* (pp. 99 foll.); he refers to a historical article by Mr. W. D. Christie in *Macmillan's Magazine* for November 1864. A description of it was given recently by the late Hon. Roden Noel in the *New Review*. This paper contained some very inaccurate statements about Hort, for which Mr. Roden Noel afterwards expressed his regret.

the object of which was to collect and classify authenticated instances of what are now called 'psychical
phenomena,' for which purpose an elaborate schedule
of questions was issued. The 'Bogie Club,' as scoffers
called it, aroused a certain amount of derision, and
even some alarm ; it was apparently born too soon.

A Shakespeare Society must also be added to the
list ; and, as Hort's attendance at meetings of these
various kinds seems from his journal to have been
regular, one finds little difficulty in believing that
work must sometimes have been driven into very
unconventional hours. At this time, if not earlier,
began the habit of sitting up far into the night, a
habit for which his friends continually rebuked him,
which left permanent ill effects on his health, and
which he afterwards bitterly regretted. He never
spoke of it but to point a warning. On one occasion
he went to sleep in the small hours over his books,
and his 'Facciolati' caught fire from a candle ; the
consequences were within a little of being serious.
His friends, coming in to see him in the morning, were
often confronted with a notice bidding his bedmaker
not to call him till mid-day.

In politics the movement which most interested him
at this time was 'Christian Socialism' ; the subject was
debated at the Union, and he was chiefly responsible
for an amendment (which was carried) ' condemning the
substitution of Socialism for the present trade while
allowing possible benefit from single associations.'
The *Christian Socialist* newspaper he read regularly,
and contributed to it in October 1851 an interesting
'Prayer for Landlords' of the sixteenth century, which
he had discovered in Professor Blunt's *History of
the Reformation*. About the same time there was

great excitement in Cambridge on the subject of
'Papal Aggression,' and an indignation meeting at
the Union approved Lord John Russell's conduct.
Hort was strongly opposed to the whole agitation.
A few months later he rejoiced in the fall of Lord
John Russell's ministry. The future of the Irish
Church was a subject much in his mind, and the
duties of the English Church towards it. In January
1852, when he was under twenty-four years of age,
he wrote a letter to a friend suggesting what he considered the right course for the English bishops to
take ; this letter was shown to the Bishop of Oxford
(S. Wilberforce), and drew from him a careful and
courteous answer.

Among the notable experiences of 1851 were the
Great Exhibition, hearing the ' Elijah ' at Exeter
Hall and two operas at Covent Garden, and Thack-
eray's Lectures on the English Humorists at Cambridge. In the summer Hort saw much of Maurice,
and was introduced by him to Archdeacon Hare. At
Cambridge he gained a new and abiding friendship,
that of Henry Bradshaw, who, as well as Mr. B. F.
Westcott and Mr. G. M. Gorham, belonged to the
Choral Society ; another musical friend was Mr. R.
B. Litchfield, and he saw much also of George
Brimley, whose acute intellect he warmly appreciated ;
and of Mr. W. Mathews, his companion a few years
later in many Alpine excursions. The history of his
friendship with Charles Kingsley may be gleaned
from the long and interesting letter written to him on
24th February in the brief interval between two Tripos
examinations. A few days of the long vacation were
spent in an excursion to Newport (Monmouth), Caer-
leon, etc., in company with Mr. Babington and mem-

bers of the Archæological Institute. He reviewed, besides other botanical books, the third edition of Babington's *British Flora* in the *Annals of Botany*, and in the *Guardian* Mr. Westcott's first publication on the *Elements of a Gospel Harmony*. The latter notice concludes with the words: "We trust that this will not be Mr. Westcott's last contribution to our stock of exegetical divinity."

In one of the latest letters of 1851 will be observed what are, perhaps, the first signs of interest in the text of the Greek Testament, the subject which was to claim his chief attention for little less than thirty years.

The year 1852 was for the most part quietly spent in reading at Cambridge, from which he seems not to have been absent for more than three weeks at a time all the year. His only holidays, except short botanical excursions, were visits to his father's new home at Chepstow ; to Mr. Gerald Blunt, now married and settled at his first curacy ; and, to London for the annual Apostles' dinner, where he met a distinguished Apostle of an earlier generation, W. Monckton Milnes (afterwards Lord Houghton), with whom he breakfasted next morning.

Success in the Fellowship examination could hardly be doubtful after his performance the year before. The others elected were C. Schreiber, W. J. Beamont, and J. B. Lightfoot, the first two of whom had been placed second and third (bracketed with Hort) respectively in the Classical Tripos of 1850. At the customary 'Fellowship Dinner' to celebrate his election Hort entertained W. G. Clark, E. A. Scott, C. B. Scott, A. A. Vansittart, G. Brimley, W. W. Howard, H. W. Watson, C. Schreiber, J. B. Lightfoot, H. M. Butler,

G. V. Yool, G. M. Gorham, J. D. Williams, F. V. Hawkins, H. Bradshaw, and W. D. Freshfield. Besides work for the Fellowship examination, Hort spent much time over an essay for the Hulsean Prize on the 'Evidences of Christianity as exhibited in the writings of the early Apologists down to Augustine inclusively.' He had meant if successful to work up his essay into a book.[1] On its original scope he wrote as follows in a letter to the Rev. W. Cureton, asking for information about early apologetic literature contained in unpublished manuscripts in the British Museum :—

Half the essay, according to my plan, is to consist of a critical and historical account of the different Apologies, in the widest sense of the word, containing original abstracts, with occasional extracts, of the extant works, translations of all the more important fragments, all the particulars that I can glean respecting lost works, and in each case such biographical details as may illustrate and enliven the subject,—the whole being set in a continuous brief narrative of the persecutions and other outward occasions of Apologies, and of the successive relations in which Paganism and Judaism stood to the Christian Church and *vice versâ*. This is an ambitious scheme, too large to carry out altogether in the first instance . . . but [my idea is to treat the ante-Eusebian period in the way described as fully as I can, and give a much slighter and more superficial account of the second period. It is not likely that any one else will follow so elaborate a plan, and therefore I may have a reasonable chance of success ; in that event I should wish to complete the second period on the same scale as the first before publication.

---

[1] The MS. of this essay is still extant, and, being found to contain valuable matter of permanent interest, is likely to be (in part) reproduced ; it is in the hands of Prof. Armitage Robinson.

One of Hort's earliest articles in the *Journal of Classical and Sacred Philology*, that on the Date of Justin Martyr, was an expansion of a note made for the same essay.

Maurice, who was delighted with the Introduction, wrote to Hort about his essay as follows :—

You must think again of your division of heresies. I do not say that it is wrong, but it requires a good deal of reflection before you put it forth even roughly. I should be disposed a little to expand what you have said about internal and external evidence ; it is a point which requires so much clearing to make people aware of your meaning. You are on the right tack, I am convinced. The external evidences of the last century substituted Nature, or at best a Demiurgus, for God. The reaction against that mischievous dogma is the substitution of human intuitions, or at best the Reason from which they flow, for God. The Living and True God reveals Himself to the Reason ; that is the Mesothesis of the external and internal. The idea of Revelation in the seventeenth and eighteenth centuries was the announcement of certain decrees, imperative Laws enacted by God. In the nineteenth it is the discovery of an endless flux, of which the source is in the creature energy of man. The gospel of God concerning Himself in His Son is, as you have happily indicated, the reconciliation of two ideas each of which by itself tends to Atheism *and* to superstition.

The prize did not fall to Hort ; his friend J. F. Stephen also competed unsuccessfully. Hort's defeat was a considerable mortification ; more important, however, than success or failure in this particular competition was the impetus given, by reading the necessary books, to his desire to devote himself to the study of ecclesiastical history, and that on a scale very different from that of most Church histories. The subject was not new to him, but his ideas were now beginning to take definite shape. The breadth of the scheme which he proposed to himself is seen in the important letter to Ellerton of 14th November–14th December 1852. Perhaps the realisation of such a plan is beyond the grasp of one man ; perhaps also he was the one man who could approximately have carried it out. Forty years later the stores of various knowledge had been accumulated, and, had he possessed greater readiness of expression, some noble fragment of the great design might have been given to the world.

By the end of 1852 therefore it is possible to distinguish two chief lines of future study now becoming clearer in his mind : the Text and Interpretation of the New Testament, and Early Church History in the widest sense. When accordingly, on becoming a Fellow of Trinity, he settled down to work at Cambridge, it was with the definite conviction that a student's life was that for which he was best fitted. To live, however, altogether at Cambridge was never part of his plan, nor, as will be seen, did he regard active parochial work, to which he looked forward by and bye, as incompatible with the pursuit of the above objects. For the present he was content to remain at Trinity, reading and taking pupils, and was perhaps rather freer than before to enter into the varied intellectual life of the University. The value of this graduate period he always estimated highly, for the sake both of what a graduate may then best learn, and of what he may be in his relations with younger men.

In the October term of 1852 he was President of the Union. Between the years 1846 and 1852 he appears to have made twenty-four speeches at Union debates ; he defended the Crusades, upheld the poetical merits of Tennyson, and slighted those of Byron ; expressed sympathy with the Continental 'progressive' movement of 1848, condemned Palmerston's policy on the Greek question (1850), approved of the principles of Carlyle's 'Latter-Day Pamphlets,' maintained the superiority of the novelists of 'this generation to those of the last.' In questions of party politics he spoke most often on subjects connected with Convocation, the Irish Church, and colonial policy.

It may be of interest here to collect Hort's contributions (besides reviews) to botanical publications ; I am indebted for the following list to an obituary notice in the *Journal of Botany* for February 1893, by Mr. G. S. Boulger, who remarks that "forty years ago Hort might have been styled one of the rising hopes of the Cambridge school of botanists."

In the second vol. of the *Phytologist* (pp. 1047-9) appear a 'Notice of a few Plants growing at Weston-super-Mare,' and a 'Note on *Centaurea nigra*, var. *radiata* and *C. nigrescens*,' both bearing date November 5th, 1847, when the young undergraduate was not yet twenty ; and in the third vol. (pp. 321-2) is a 'Note on *Alsine rubra*, var. *media* Bab.,' dated 'Torquay, Sept. 27th, 1848.' In the first vol. of Henfrey's *Botanical Gazette* (1849), pp. 197, 200, he has a paper 'On *Viola sylvatica* and *canina*,' and in the second vol. (1850), pp. 1, 2, a 'Notice on *Potamogeton fluitans* Roth and *Ulex Gallii* Planch.'

In 1851 he found time to publish, in the third vol. of the *Botanical Gazette* (pp. 15-17) a note 'On *Euphorbia stricta* and *platyphylla*,' and in the same volume (pp. 155-7) appears a 'Note on *Athyrium filix-femina*, var. *latifolium*,' dated November 12th, 1851, which was reprinted in the *Phytologist*, vol. iv. pp. 440-2. To this year also belongs his paper 'On a supposed new Species of *Rubus*' (*Rubus imbricatus* Hort), which appeared in the *Annals and Magazine of Natural History of the Botanical Society of Edinburgh* (vol. iv. pp. 113-6), to which it had been communi-

cated.   In the fourth vol. of the *Phytologist* (1852),
pp. 640-1, is a note by him on the 'Occurrence of
Orobanche cærulea Vill. and *Aconitum Napellus* L. in
Monmouthshire,' dated July 21st, 1852 ; and a 'Note
on the Third Volume of Mr. H. C. Watson's *Cybele
Britannica*,' frankly corrected some blunders that had
found their way into that work from his own list of
Weston-super-Mare plants.   He appears in *Topo-
graphical Botany* as a correspondent of Watson's from
no less than eleven vice-counties, viz. North Somerset,
East and West Gloucester, Monmouth, Merioneth,
Carnarvon, North Lancashire and Westmoreland,
Cumberland, Durham, West Suffolk, and Cambridge.

His Cambridge friend and contemporary, the Rev.
W. W. Newbould, used always to speak of Hort's
abandonment of botany in favour of biblical studies
in much the same manner as Watson regretted that
Edward Forbes' "attention had been drawn from
botany to the more showy studies, in which he became
eminent."

To his Mother

CAMBRIDGE, *February 3rd*, 1851.

My dearest Mother—I hope you will forgive me if you find
me brief and stupid to-night, for indeed I have good reason
for it, having been to-day in at two examination papers of four
hours each, which is heavy work. . . .

I am quite comfortable in my new rooms, though the floor
is still encumbered with books, as the shelves are not all right
yet, and the Tripos has kept me too busy to think of much
else.   I have two windows looking north into Nevile's Court,
and one looking south into the New Court, which is very comfortable.[1] . . . I am quite ashamed to let such a letter go, but

---

[1] The rooms were in Nevile's Court, Staircase C, first floor.

if you knew how my ears are full of 'Springs of Human
Action,' 'Things Allowable,' 'Price,' 'Circulating Capital,'
'Rent of Land,' etc., and how dismal and dismal-making this
drizzly night is, you would be indulgent.—Ever, my dearest
mother, your affectionate son,   FENTON J. A. HORT.

TO THE REV. JOHN ELLERTON

CAMBRIDGE, *February 7th*, 1851.

My dear Ellerton—I really don't know how long I have
been silent, but I am afraid it has been some considerable
fraction of a century.   I suppose it was first the theoretical
preparation for the Moral Tripos, and then the actual preparation, and finally, the Tripos itself that withheld me.   Whatever
it was, it was unpardonable.   As I have mentioned the Tripos,
I may as well go on.   It began on Monday, 9-1, with a
good paper of Whewell's, which I did very fairly ; 2-6, Pryme's
Political Economy, of which I thought myself lucky to do half,
as I had spent (irrespective of a chapter or two in the summer)
just half an hour upon it.   Tuesday, 9-12, Maine, General
Jurisprudence,—a capital paper, of which I did about half ;
1-4, a detestable mass of bad poetry, puns, and anecdotic
gossip, with a screed or two of absurd law, called Laws of
England.   Wednesday, 9-2, History : Gibbes, corrected by
Sir J. Stephen, whereof I did about half.   Yesterday, 9-2,
General Paper, nominally Holden, but each subject set by its
professor.   I did all the Moral Philosophy very fully, about
half the History, and two or three scraps of the other things.
There have been but five of us in : Mackenzie and A. Wilson
of Trinity, Bruce of Jesus, and Pooley of Christ's.   I don't
know when the lists will be out.   I shall look for them rather
anxiously, as I hope I have a fair chance of a Whewell (Moral
Philosophy) prize.   I am now going to read for the Natural
Science Tripos, which I hope I shall be much better prepared
for ; it comes on March 3rd.   I have plenty of work before
me, as I mean to make a desperate effort for my Fellowship
this time, and I have to read lots for the Voluntary, Justin
Martyr, Apol. I., being the Patristic subject.   Likewise there

are the Siren voices of two essays — the Hulsean, on the extinction of Paganism in connexion with the evidences of Christianity, and the Members' Prize, 'Why the Reformation got no further in Europe'; both alluring, especially the former, which I should like to treat by showing how all that Julian and Proclus, and Plotinus and Celsus, etc., could do by piecing Paganism with what people nowadays call the kernel of Christianity was of no avail, but only faith in the living, dying, and risen Nazarene.

Talking of essays, Westcott is just coming out with his Norrisian on 'The Elements of the Gospel Harmony.' I have seen the first sheet on Inspiration, which is a wonderful step in advance of common orthodox heresy. He has a full catena from the Ante-Nicene Fathers on the subject. Altogether, I doubt not, it will be a most valuable book.

February 10*th.*—The scrap[1] which I sent you on Saturday will have told you the result of the Moral Examination. It is a bore that they have not placed us alphabetically, as they seemed to promise, but certainly I do not deserve to be higher, if reading is any criterion of merit, and after all it is a first class, so I don't care, especially as I have got what I most cared for, the Moral Philosophy prize, which I shall value in many ways ; it is likely to get me into the Master's good graces for a Fellowship, to say nothing of £15 worth of books, which thing is not to be despised.

Now to turn to your letter, I don't know whether to feel comfort or pain at your 'difficulty of speaking to the poor as you ought to speak,'—I mean, as regards myself. I always fancy, whenever I think about the matter, that I shall never be able to get out anything but commonplaces. And, tho' it is something of a melancholy satisfaction to find that I am not alone in this respect, it is not very favorable to the hope I have felt that, when the time actually came, the difficulty would vanish. But of one thing I am sure, that the more we seek to be but God's spokesmen, and not to dwell on our own thoughts, the more will our lips be opened. You will remem-

[1] Moral Sciences Tripos, 1851. First class. —Ds. Mackenzie, Trin. ; *Wilson, A., Trin. ; Bruce, Hon. T. C., Jesus ; *Hort, Trin. (* Moral Philosophy prizemen.)

ber how Maurice dwells on the four Gospels as pre-eminently setting forth the ministerial office even more than the Christian life; and there is no more perplexing or more valuable precept than that to the Apostles to take no thought what they should speak, for the Holy Ghost should teach them what they should speak. Maintain a firm, live conviction that we have the Word dwelling in us, the Word who Himself took flesh and partook of every form of sorrow, known or unknown to us, and His sympathy will become ours, and we shall be able to use the strength which He won in subduing all His enemies by the word of our mouths.

Thank you much for your note received this day, February 13th. I may as well mention that I got 96 out of 100 marks for the Master's paper. Holden and Gibbes wanted to place me second, but the Master (very justly) contended that the order must be not by merit but by marks. They are all enthusiastic in our praise; say we should be thoroughly First Class in any such examinations, most agreeably surprized them, etc.

I have just struck up a most delightful acquaintance with Lees of Christ's, who has been Kingsley's pupil for some months. But this and heaps more that I want to say I really must defer.

To his Mother

CAMBRIDGE, *February 14th*, 1851.

. . . Thank you all for your congratulations. There is no limitation about the prize. Whewell sent for me on Monday and paid me the money; he was remarkably gracious (I should mention that this is the first time I have come personally in contact with him), and asked after a Mr. Fenton Hort whom he remembered very well; he hoped that, if ever he were in Cambridge again, he would call at the Lodge, as he should be very glad to renew his acquaintance; he also asked after my uncle.[1] I mean to get five or six volumes to bear on their backs the University Arms, but I shall find the rest of the money very serviceable, as I have a very large book bill,

---

[1] Sir William Hort, Mr. Fenton Hort's elder brother.

caused partly by these very Triposes; that is to say, reading for them has been the occasion of my getting permanently good and important books rather more than usual. The same may be said of the examination itself; independently of the prize and honour, and still more valuable objects of various kinds consequent thereupon, I have read and learned much valuable matter, that would otherwise have been lost or acquired more loosely. I only regret that I did not pursue this advantage to anything like the same extent that I might have done. Since I wrote, I have seen the marks given, and heard various particulars, chiefly from Holden himself, the 'additional examiner.' They have all taken every opportunity of praising us all, as having been fully up to the First Class mark, 'so that we should have been no lower had there been a hundred competitors' . . . they have dwelt especially on the 'good style,' particularly of Mackenzie and myself (style, not so much of composition as of treatment). . . . Holden says he does not at all understand why I was not published as *first* Whewell's prizeman. All this sounds painfully egotistic, but I know you will be glad to hear it, and I do not see how otherwise you can know of it. I will send to-morrow a *Cambridge Chronicle*, if they print the papers in it. I am now at work for the Natural Sciences Tripos, the examination for which begins on Monday fortnight. I am at present at Structural and Physiological Botany, which (reading as I do in the highest books) is anything but child's play, and is a region nearly new to me.

Many thanks to Kate for her letter, which I hope to answer in two or three days. Perhaps she will be good enough to dry a snowdrop for me, bulb and all, if possible; it will soon flatten down. Do they grow *generally*, or only near the gardens and houses? I do not see why they should not be really wild in that part of England. Babington has no doubt they are sometimes really indigenous. I wish I could see them. Well, I must close ; love without end to you all.—Ever your affectionate son,   FENTON J. A. HORT.

The occasion of the following letter was the publication by Kingsley of some remarks on the state of the universities, the nature of which will be apparent from Hort's criticisms thereon.

To the Rev. C. Kingsley

CAMBRIDGE, *February 24th*, 1851.

My dear Mr. Kingsley—I have been so much delighted this afternoon by the receipt of your most generous letter, that I cannot rest till I have thanked you very heartily for it. . . . Of the state of London I can know nothing. Of that of Oxford I thought some little while ago much as you do now, except that I was more hopeful of future well-being by the possibility of a sound direction being given to activities and energies which I supposed to be really working, though in a wild and confused way. But my somewhat vague impressions were changed by a very interesting conversation in (I think) October last (but possibly it was May) with Mr. Maurice (to whom we both, I believe, owe under God nearly all the better part of our being, and not least the desire, and in part the power, of calling no man our master, but learning the truth from the strangest and most dissimilar quarters). He had been staying with Arthur Stanley at Oxford, and seemed very desponding about the state of matters there ; all, he said, was stagnant, and lifeless, and hopeless; the only apparent feeling was a vague but bitter one of distrust and dislike of the authorities as idle pedants on the part of the younger men. I asked if there were no outwardly infidel movement, which gave promise of ending in a real and active faith, and mentioned in illustration Mr. Clough's poems. 'No,' he thought not ; there might perhaps be some infidelity, but if there were, it was quite *stagnant* (that word, or one like it, was what he dwelt mostly on) and hopeless. He then asked me about Cambridge. I could not give a more lively account, but observed that at least we had one great blessing, in being free from party spirit (a blessing which I had good reason to appreciate, having been maddened by a residence of some years in the midst of Cheltenham) ; he much doubted this being a healthy sign among young men. I spoke of the

kindred mischief of via-mediaism and a cowardly shrinking
from 'extremes' merely because they are extremes; he
assented, and lamented that this Eclecticism was equally
prevalent at Oxford.   I mention this conversation in order to
show you how I came to regard stagnation as the leading
characteristic of both Universities; only I have seldom been
able to trace discontent against superiors at Cambridge.   Now
certainly I can find in your letters statements agreeable to
most of those contained in my letter to ——; but I still
think that the total impression conveyed by your words is that
our curse is misdirected activity.   In your last letter to the
Spectator I think you partly meet my statement by attributing
the deadness to the mass of the University, and the activity
to its leading intellects,—at least so I understand you; but it
appears to me that all alike suffer from the general apathy,
though it shows itself in very different forms.   I cannot easily
guess what description —— has given you of the better men
among us.   That there is a vast deal of good, I thankfully
acknowledge; it is perpetually springing up where I have
least expected it, and putting to rebuke my uncharitable
thoughts; yet since last May I have not had one friend in
residence to whom I could open myself freely and unreservedly
without feeling that there was something cold and dark
between us, which kept us up to a certain point apart; and
yet I *know* that I am not suspicious.   ——, I think, might
become an exception, but I have not known him at all till a
few days ago.   Of course it would be absurd in the extreme
for me to assume that there are no noble minds of the highest
class—noble especially as having struggled and now become
victorious—with which I am unacquainted; still I think I can
say that from various concurrent causes I have at least as
good means of discovering such minds, in Trinity at least,
as any one here.   There is one circumstance in the present
state of Trinity, and probably in a less degree of the whole
University, which not only makes such discovery very difficult,
but actually checks and confines the growth of the very highest
minds; I mean the amount of respectable cultivation existing
in probably nearly half our number; and yet this is so valuable
an advance upon previous inanity and brutality, that no one can

wish for its removal. Modern literature is extensively read in a way that, though neither earnest nor profound, is still rather humanizing and genial than otherwise. A 'reading man' is distinguished not from one who does not read, but from one who does not read University subjects enough to obtain moderately high honours; and the two kinds of reading usually progress together; so that, though there may be a few really well-read men who do not pursue the studies of the place, still on the whole the best scholars and mathematicians in Trinity (in any year) are, with very few exceptions, the best acquainted with modern literature. And theology is usually by no means excluded from their attention, and that not in a merely sectarian way; so that stolid, pharisaical orthodoxy is all but unknown among undergraduates, bachelors, and younger masters, except in a small and inferior class. This is of course a partial good, but it is accompanied by a fatal evil of a peculiar kind. Enough easy and comfortable exercise is given to men's conscience and faculties to remove the restless *ennui* of perfect idleness, and still more the impatience and rebelliousness which mere restraint and 'obscurantism' would produce. Religious difficulties are not often, I think, *stifled*, but rather met with half lazy solutions, not absolutely untrue, but weak and imperfect. Then comes the friendly intercourse which prevails between men of all opinions, rubbing off many asperities, but rubbing off also, alas! much vigour and distinctness; truth is seen not to be the exclusive possession of any one party, and every question is found to have two sides. The total result is not ignorance of the questions which are being asked all around, but universal trimming; the doubts, which, if treated roughly, must before long have imperiously claimed to be heard, and ultimately have led their victims into utter scepticism or Romanism, or else to perfect faith, because nothing less would have satisfied them, are judiciously humoured and coaxed away. I do not want to deny the good that must be mixed up with all this specious evil; I am sure that God is daily leading many into His truth by ways of His own that I know not; and it cannot be but that much is really learnt from the books which are the main *instruments* of the mischief. Maurice's more popular

writings are among the most common, though I seldom see or
hear of his more profound ones, and none are really *studied*.
But the disheartening thing is to see so few symptoms of any
one knowing what it is to be ever craving and unsatisfied till
one has reached the very ground and bottom of a question,
and to care little for consequences in the pursuit.   What is to
be the end of these things, it is not easy to predict ; you
think it will be a violent revulsion "in the direction of
Strauss, Emerson, and [Francis] Newman." It may be so,—
especially in the direction of Newman ; for the degree of
intelligence and cultivation which pervades our orthodox (if
so it can be called !) Epicurism is likely, I think, to make
our infidelity also Epicurean ; and more luxurious, complacent
hands-in-the-breeches-pocket infidelity than prevails in the
little of Newman's writings that I have read, I cannot imagine.
I could greedily devour *The Nemesis of Faith* every week,
but it is an irksome labour to me to get through one chapter
of *The Soul*.   But surely the evil seed is sown in many
more effective ways than by these books, especially such a
cold laborious criticism as I take the *Leben Jesu* to be.   If the
root of all unbelief be, as the Bible teaches us, in our selfish
and cowardly hearts, the devil will never want innumerable
direct means to plant it where it may grow most rank.   I can
hardly think that the infidelity of even educated Englishmen
will be often German in its character ; nay, there seem to
be signs that not theology, but questions concerning social
relations, and, above all, that which daily more strongly
appears to me to lie at the root of all social problems, the
relation of the sexes, will be the *prominent* subjects of
unbelief.   But indeed, if I seemed to you to doubt your
gloomy prophecies of a coming time of shattered faith,
it was merely from my bitter sense of our present awful
quiescence, of those "evils that," as Ruskin says, "vex less
and mortify more, that suck the blood though they do not
shed it, and ossify the heart though they do not torture
it."   But when one thinks what tremendous responsibilities
rest on those whose feet God has in any wise set upon
the living Rock, it is yet more horrible to feel by daily
experience how every vain or unkind word and every un-

clean thought brings back doubts which seemed vanquished for ever.

I must say a word or two on other points of your letters. It is with pain I allude to our 'chapel-keeping,' knowing how constantly I am thinking, speaking, and acting as if it were the merest disciplinary form.   But if you were to attend our service a few times, especially in the morning and at the more orderly end of the chapel, I think you would find it far less ' soul-less ' than you suppose ; certainly in no other congregation have I had at all an equal sense of united worship.   And I am sure that, far as the College system is from what it ought to be, its effects are still up to a certain point truly healthy and beneficial ; and that Mr. Sewell's plan of professors in provincial towns, however useful for disseminating information, would be totally wanting in that which makes Oxford and Cambridge to be even now, with all their shortcomings, almost the only places of education in England ; and surely the professor's office is rather to guide students in their studies than to teach.   You allow that meddling with machinery is ineffectual to infuse life ; but still you look to the Commission to effect that object by compelling the Universities to reform themselves.   But how ?   ' Reforming themselves' in ordinary parlance means a change of machinery *ab intra* instead of *ab extra*.   But *you* can hardly mean this only.   You must be thinking of vital spiritual reform, yet that is not definite enough to be a subject of outward compulsion ; and as for the moral compulsion of the public, made wise by the blue-books, will the public really understand the evils and their remedies ?   Do you think that the state of feeling in any class is so much higher than it is here that our fathers generally will scent out the true poison ?   Are they not yet more infected by it ?   Will they not rather rejoice to find that their sons are studiously reading their Latin and Greek and Mathematics, with literature and the newspapers and the sciences of the new Triposes superadded, and just minding their own bread and butter like practical, common-sense Englishmen, and pleasing their tutors, without troubling their heads about wild, dangerous notions in morals, theology, or politics ?   I am *not* speaking from personal experience, or at least very slightly; but I think the state of society generally bears out my statement. And again, supposing the compulsion existing, if the University authorities *have* not life, how can they bring it into operation ? And yet how will the public be able to get living men to fill their places ? The best sign I have seen yet is a strong and rapidly increasing tendency among the younger masters to make Honours far less the object of the University System than at present ; such a spirit can hardly fail to produce other good fruits. There is reason to hope that much will be done in this direction by the Syndicate now employed to revise the University Statutes, which comprises most of the best and most thoughtful men in the University. And the new Regius Professor of Divinity announced yesterday approaching changes in the now troublesome yet almost useless Voluntary Theological Examination. Without such divisions as would introduce rivalry, we are to be distinguished (I suppose by two alphabetical classes) into those who have really prepared themselves for Holy Orders, and those who go in as a matter of form.

.   .   .   .

I must hasten to conclude this long letter. I am sure you hate receiving compliments as much as I hate paying them. But you must allow me *for this once* the pleasure of telling you how much love—even more than admiration—I owe you. I cannot adequately thank you for all I have learnt from many of your writings, especially from *Yeast*. But I think of you rather as one that had felt and was feeling what it contains, as a flesh-and-blood man than as an author. And so, without seeing you, I have come to love you as a very dear friend, even when you sometimes made me angry with you.—I know you will excuse the freedom with which I write.—And now I have to thank you for the offer of your friendship made on the strength of a letter in which I misrepresent and abuse you. You may well believe how thankfully I accept it. But I give you warning you will find me a troublesome friend. I have read your writings too carefully not to know how completely we differ on some important points. In various ways I shall be perpetually exasperating you. I am hampered and logged every way with vanity and selfishness, and very impatient of

corrective measures; but if you have any regard for me,
you will knock them out of me any way you think best, without mercy; and if I wince and turn fractious, you must not
mind.   Only do not despair of me, or cast me off.—Yours
most truly,   FENTON J. A. HORT.

To HIS MOTHER

CAMBRIDGE, *March 2nd*, 1851.

. . . Poor old Duke! he has enough on his hands just
now, as *bonâ fide* the Queen's Privy Councillor.   It is something to feel, even for a week, that we are a kingdom again,
and not a cabinet-dom!   The Queen seems to have been
acting capitally.

I do not, from your description, at all doubt the wildness
of the snowdrops; still less of the daffodils, which occur, I
believe, in many of the really native woods of the west of
England.   As I have a conscience, I won't ask Kate to dry
one.   They grow in a wood at Whitwell, three miles from
Cambridge, but there escaped a century ago from a garden.
Nothing is out with us yet but a few daisies and a bilious,
disgruntled - looking dandelion or two.   If it will be any
pleasure to you to collect the mosses, pray do; *you* need not
be afraid of my despising them.   Perhaps I have seemed not
to pursue them very warmly.   This is chiefly because I do
not want to get any book (no thoroughly good one exists)
which will be superseded as soon as Mr. Wilson's appears;
but, if you like, we will try what we can do with Hooker's old
descriptions, which are respectable, but have no plates.

To HIS MOTHER

Saturday Night [*March 8th*], 1851.

My dearest Mother—I have not much to add to the
above.[1]   In Physiology I was very high—far the first.   In

---

[1] Viz. the class list of the Natural Sciences Tripos, in which Hort was
placed second in the first class (Liveing being first), with the note, ' Distinguished in Physiology and Botany.'

Botany I did also very well, and was quite first.   In Chemistry
and Mineralogy of course I got very little.   Geology seems
to have been tolerably done by all, brilliantly by none.   If
the paper had been a quarter of the length, it would have been
more satisfactory to all parties.   Fuller says Sedgwick boasted
of having made it a 'very complete' paper, and got *all*
geology into it, to be written out in four hours !   We all (*i.e.*
all the 1st class) did very well in the general paper.   I was
glad to find that Fuller thinks two subjects as much as any
one can manage.

I have had a talk with Babington.   He recommends what
I thought of, viz. Lindley's *Ladies' Botany*, Bohn's edition in
12mo (mind this).   He knows of no book short of a full
systematic one which would be of use to find out plants'
names by, but this seems easy and nicely done ; and Lindley's
name is enough for its scientific excellence.   It takes a hedge
or common garden flower (such as a Buttercup, Poppy, or
Strawberry) in each of the principal Natural Orders by their
English as well as their Latin names, and, as it were, pulls it
to pieces before you, explaining the parts in a familiar way,
not by getting rid of the science, but by putting it in an easy
and English form ; not telling you how to put plants in the
shelves and compartments of any system invented by learned
men, but helping you to see for yourself how they are actually
related to each other in the unchangeable order of nature.
Now this, it seems to me, is of all things the most delightful
to a child.   It will soon tire of the mechanical process of
counting stamens, but will always feel a burst of pleasure at
catching a glimpse of a fresh family likeness — even among
plants.   Some sage people will tell you that this is putting
mysterious fancies into a child's head, and mischievously keeping it from the influence of 'plain common-sense.'   But I
have yet to learn that it is a good thing for any one, whether
child or grown-up, to despise and cast off mysteries. . . .
I can assure you I do not forget how very much I owe both
to you and to grandmamma, whether in leading me to love
plants or in anything else.   I do not grudge you any amount
of 'the credit.'   If I have ever seemed to do anything of the
kind, you must not judge it too harshly.   Doubtless I have

sometimes done so, for what thoughts will not a hard pride suggest? but not habitually, nor deliberately, nor, I would hope, in my truer self. You must not measure me by what I say, or do not say ; but I know you do not.

To Mr. C. H. Chambers

CAMBRIDGE, *March 8th*, 1851.

I am afraid you and I should not agree about the Papal affair, unless the crisis, as they call it, in which our precious Ministers got themselves a few days ago have changed your views, as it seems to be doing those of some people. I cannot see what right we have to molest the Romanist bishops for taking what titles they please. Of course it is a bore, but so are many other things. There are no new pretensions made ; the Romanists have always claimed, as we do, the allegiance of the whole nation, and not their own adherents only. They would have been monstrously inconsistent if they had not, while they claimed to be a Church and not a sect. The real insult and grievance, if insult and grievance there be, is the existence of such a body as the Romish Communion in England ; but the only way I see of redressing it is to fry every Jack man of them at Smithfield, or —let them alone. However, 'the Provisional Government' cannot last, and I suspect that Anti-Aggression Bills will fall when falls the Complete Letter-writer.

To his Mother

CAMBRIDGE, *March* 13th, 1851.

. . . The glass house[1] is certainly a wonderful affair, though, from its extreme lowness, you do not take in its size, except by running your eye along the infinity of compartments. One wonders where all the glass could come from. I felt a sort of impulsive wish to put on a good strong glove and scrunch the whole affair with a single elephantine pat. It

[1] The Exhibition building.

looks so unsubstantial, and so like an edifice of spun sugar, that it seems only made to be scrunched. . . .

If you can find the true Dog Violet, which has a bluer flower with a bright yellow spur, I shall be pleased, but it is not worth much search. It is most likely to grow at the edges of the meadows by the banks of the Wye, between Redbrook and Monmouth. There will probably soon be a blaze of Marsh Marygolds all along the river. One other beautiful violet you are pretty sure to see wherever there is limestone, that is on most of the higher ground, including that part of the tramway, but not in the sandy hollows. Like the sweet violet, it has flowers springing directly from the root without any apparent stem, but they are bluer and scentless. Their spurs are slightly hooked instead of straight, and the hairs on the leafstalks are spreading instead of curving downwards ; it is the Hairy Violet. I have seen it in magnificent masses of blue on railway embankments near Cheltenham.

To THE REV. JOHN ELLERTON

CAMBRIDGE, *March* 19*th*, 1851.

. . . I am just now doing that same (revelling in enjoy-ment) over Hartley Coleridge. Derwent has done him honestly and lovingly, but too clerically, and given too few of his letters,—about the most thoroughly delightful I ever read. . . . Two volumes of Essays and Marginalia are to follow, and a reprint of the *Northern Worthies*. The memoirs and letters show indirectly how cruelly S. T. C. has been called an un-natural father.

To THE REV. JOHN ELLERTON

NEWLAND, *Good Friday* [*April* 18*th*], 1851.

I called on Furnival (in town) and had a long and inter-esting chat ; he told me that Lloyd Jones was going to lecture at 8 at Charlotte Street, where many Promoters and possibly Maurice might be. I went and saw all, Maurice included (who looked very ill), but of course could get no conversation, and had to leave almost immediately ; Kingsley unluckily was not there.   I am writing to Blunt to Jerusalem, as the Syrian Mail is closed on the 20th.

Westcott's excellent, though not faultless, book on the Gospels is out (and with me).   I have written a Review of it, which Macmillan is going to get into the *Guardian.*   Hardwick has just published what seems a good History of the Articles ; Westcott likes it much, and says he brings out well their Lutheran and *plusquam* Lutheran character against the Calvinistic bodies, especially on Justification.   At his advice I have been getting a whole heap of the Symbolical books of all the Churches, real and so called, and am going to read Moehler's *Symbolik* and Guericke's (Lutheran and anti-Prussian) *Allgemeine Symbolik,* both of which he likes exceedingly.

I am sadly afraid poor Manning is gone [1] at last, and of course numbers will follow.

To the Rev. John Ellerton

CAMBRIDGE, *May* 15*th,* 1851.

. . . Vol. i. of Sir F. Palgrave's *History of Normandy and England* is out, and seems very delightful, and a noble defence of the Middle Ages.

—— says he is so bewildered about Socialism he scarcely dares think of it, and is proportionately truculent and dogmatic if I hint disparagement.   He says the *Guardian* is thoroughly Romish (which is almost entirely false), yet the other day, talking of Newman, Manning, etc., he said they evidently saw that the great movement of the day is the ' Neo-catholic ' (*i.e.* chiefly Oratorian) movement, and that more good could be done by working in it than in any other, and that he was by no means sure they were not right.   I exclaimed indignantly against joining oneself to a Lie, merely because it promised to do most good ; but he only jeered at me, and asked how we were to know what is true except by its consequence of doing good.   Truly a curious symptom of the approaching union of Romanism and Communism, which I have been some time expecting.

[1] Viz. over to Rome.

To the Rev. John Ellerton

12 Marlborough Street, Bath,
June 20*th,* 1851.

. . . I am anxious to see the Pre-Raphaelites, but expect to be much annoyed. Ruskin's second letter was a remarkable one ; but the point for which he praises them, and which is the most characteristic thing in *Modern Painters*, is just what has been the burden of my song for six or seven years, viz. that truth and not falsehood is the subject of art. I suppose he means only to consider them as clumsy but promising infants. I have just finisht all that is out of the *Stones of Venice*. It is, all but the first and last chapters, a technical account of the necessary elements, constructive and decorative, of all possible architecture. Venice is to come in vol. ii. Vol. i. is full of most valuable, but what many would call dry matter ; it is not often eloquent, and frequently very perverse, but on the whole I read it with great delight. The fag end of a note on the Crystal Palace is excellent ; he calls it good as a piece of human work and industry, worthless as architecture, as being *cast*, and therefore bearing no impress of human hearts and heart-directed hands. What a marvellous tearful power Maurice's tales have ! *T. Bradfoot*[1] moves me almost fearfully ; every line is rich too in practical wisdom.

Do have some patience with ——, in spite of all his absurdities ; an Oxford 'Protestant' and clever man, who has just found his way into something like Catholic views, is likely to caper away with some strange antics.

Not very long after my last letter I wrote to Maurice, giving him my crude impressions of the Education question, and asking his advice, being much puzzled by his recent effusions in the *Christian Socialist*. He wrote me a strange passionate reply, which I took for a rebuke ; you shall see it some time. . . .

I wrote a long and rather warm reply, which he answered like himself, disclaiming any wish to censure what I had said,

[1] *The Experiences of Thomas Bradfoot, Schoolmaster*, in the *Christian Socialist*, 1851, beginning 26th April.

but saying that he was merely vindicating his conduct in now deserting the 'unsatisfactory go-between' which he had formerly (not very warmly) supported. He also says a little about Socialism, but not to the point; and recommends to me Kingsley's lecture on agriculture, which (with one or two exceptions) I liked thoroughly. Meanwhile I had (don't open your eyes too wide!) been asked to join the 'Apostles'; I declined, but after hearing a good deal which shook me, begged time to consider. Meanwhile I wrote to Maurice for impartial counsel, telling my objection, and his second letter contained a P.S. which left me no alternative. He said he 'could not advise me impartially.' His 'connection with them had moulded his character and determined the whole course of his life'; he 'owed them more than he could express in any words; was aware of the tendency to self-conceit and trifling which I spoke of; could not but desire fervently that it should be counteracted by the influence and co-operation of earnest men; 'twas not possible therefore for him to advise me to stand aloof from them; believed there must be evil attaching to every exclusive society; the counteracting good in this he had found very great.' Could there be a more beautiful or delicate recommendation? So I joined, and attended one semi-meeting, but must tell you more when I know more. I had written to Kingsley a few days before, but, without acknowledging it, he wrote me a very kind note to ask me to read Maurice's letter in the *Christian Socialist* on his most painful fight with the *Guardian*, and to offer to dry plants for me in Germany, whither he is going with his father and mother. On Wednesday afternoon I left Cambridge and then went down to Blackwall, and there had a most pleasant (annual) dinner with the 'Apostles' old and new. Doune of Bury was President, and I, as junior member, Vice - President. Maurice, Alford, Thompson, F. Lushington, T. Taylor, James Spedding, Blakesley, Venables, etc. etc., were there; Monckton Milnes and Trench were unable to come. Maurice made a beautiful speech. We drove back to Farringdon Street together on the box of the Bus, and thence walked together as far as Holborn. In the morning I got (late) to Lincoln's Inn Chapel, and walked up with him to Queen Square, but he was engaged out to breakfast. We talked partly of Scotch Church matters, but chiefly about F. Robertson of Brighton, who has happily got acquainted with him. He was as kind as possible. At noon I started for Bath, and here I am till Wednesday or Thursday, when we all move to town for a week to see the Exhibition, etc.

TO THE REV. JOHN ELLERTON

56 SOUTH AUDLEY STREET, LONDON,
June 26*th*, 1851.

. . . On Thursday and Friday I was at the Great Exhibition, which is a wonderful sight indeed as a whole ; but I was much disappointed with the details. The designs are, I think, mostly very poor. But in all respects we appear superior to other nations ; I do not think the much-talked-of Italian sculpture at all equal to our own. The 'Veiled Eve' (or some such name) is an unnatural block representing what is absolutely contrary to the laws of gravity. The 'Greek Slave' (American) is not '*tall*' or 'loud,' and that is its merit ; but it has few others. It seems correct anatomy without being graceful, but is absolutely meaningless, and that is the character of most of the sculpture ; any names would do equally well for them all. Bell's 'Una' is worth them all put together ; it is a Christian version of Danacker's 'Ariadne.' Friday night we heard 'Elijah' at Exeter Hall, very fine certainly, but many degrees below Handel.

Saturday we were at the Zoological Gardens. We saw the Hippopotamus to perfection, and truly he was a comical sight ; his lubberly good-humour and fondness for his keeper are indescribably ridiculous. Yesterday afternoon I walkt to Lincoln's Inn, and heard a grand sermon from Maurice on Deborah, Jael, and the Judges generally (*N.B.* He is delivering a course on the O. T.) ; shook hands with him afterwards, and he introduced me to Hare, who is much better. I breakfast with Maurice to-morrow. In the evening I went with my father and sisters to Westminster Abbey ; we had to stand an hour outside in the crowd, and were almost equally prest inside ; had very poor music and a dreary sermon on the fear of God. Fear generally, we were told, was the cause of most good things, of prudence in marriage, for instance, etc. etc. One main instance was fear when we hear a great noise in the night, from which we might understand what is meant by the fear of God. This morning I saw the Water-Colours, which have some noble Copley Fieldings, and the Royal Academy, which is very poor, one or two passable Stanfields, a capital 'Titania and Bottom' of Landseer's, and the usual Danbys, Lees, and Creswicks. I can't make up my mind about the Pre-Raphaelites; they are very gaudy and precious ugly, but the faces are more like living human faces than any I have seen in modern pictures.

To the Rev. John Ellerton

Hardwick, Chepstow, *July* 10*th*, 1851.

. . . I think I am as anxious as you are for real synodical church government, but do not think that God has yet shown us the right way. The other day we had a tolerable debate on the subject at the Union, when I spoke long and strongly in its favor, and I hope did some good; we were very amicable, except an absurd man who got up, when Temple spoke of 'scientific theology,' to protest solemnly against the profanity of 'placing science on a level with theology.'

I fear you scarcely tolerate my having joined the 'Apostles,' but you must not judge too much by vague impressions. The record book of proceedings is very amusing; think of Maurice voting that virtue in women proceeds more from fear than modesty! It is a good sign that there is always a large number of neutral votes. Some of ——'s are ludicrous enough; *e.g.* on the question whether we ought to follow the text of Scripture or the discoveries of science as to the formation of the earth, etc. He votes the latter, adding a note that he considers the question of very little consequence, as he 'does not believe in matter'!

I am very glad that Browne is so fond of the young Lutherans Guericke is a brave, genial, uncompromising fellow; if I have time and space, I will copy an amazing note from his *Allgemeine Symbolik*. Of Stier I know very little. Dorner's name always fills me with shame to think that Germans should now occupy the chosen English ground of solid dogmatic theology, and that he is the real representative of Pearson, Bull, and Waterland. His great historical treatise 'on the Person of Christ' is, I believe, above praise; Wilberforce is honest enough to acknowledge his great obligations to it in his book on the Incarnation. I should much like to know Morrison of Truro (who translated Kant and has lately done Guericke's *Antiquities*); he is an 'Apostle' and a great friend of Thompson's. He has revised for Bohn the American translation of Neander, and the half-dozen words which he lets fall *in propria persona* here and there give me a very high idea of him. I think I should admire the 'Elijah' more, were I familiar with it, but that is all; it is admirable and very grand, but not deep or spiritual. It exactly answers to Mendelssohn's own face, noble enough in its way, but with none of the strange mysterious depth of poor Beethoven's face and eyes; and *he*, you know, tho' anything but fond of yielding place to others, was never tired of setting up Handel as unsurpassable, and chose to die with his works piled on his bed. It seems to me that Mendelssohn is genial and moving only in petty things, such as some of the exquisite *Lieder ohne Worte*.

The authoress of *Mary Barton* (I forget her name) is now, I know, on intimate terms with the Maurices, but she has certainly been long married, and is, I think, nearer fifty than thirty.

I must say a word or two of my breakfast with Maurice on Tuesday week. I had some pleasant talk with him, first on various things, and learnt that Kingsley was to come if possible. He did come before long, and I cannot say how charmed I was with him. The moment he came in, Maurice tossed him a letter for him (evidently on his late sermon); he read it with a curling lip, and then protested the world was like a cur dog, which first barks and snarls at you, but, when it finds that others do not repudiate you, comes up to you in a patronising way and smells (here he suited the action to the

word) at you; at which Maurice laught more than I should
have thought possible. In the middle of breakfast the Archdeacon [1] and his wife came down, and very delightful was our
talk. But think of the luxury after breakfast; thundery rain
was falling, so we four men lounged and sat round the window
talking for more than an hour. They were all very unjust to
Ruskin, of whose writings none were really *au fait*, and I was
unexpectedly obliged to parry some of their charges. . . . One
circumstance I shall not easily forget. All were attacking
Ruskin for not doing justice to Raffaelle's later pictures; I
suggested that this judgement was distorted by his strong disgust
for Raffaelle's later immoral life. Maurice said that he had
lately been greatly cleared, and urged that he was at all events
purer than any one round him, and dwelt on his strange position in that horrible city with his infinite capacities for enjoying
beauty; and finally Kingsley said slowly and solemnly, "They
jest at scars who never felt a wound."

On Thursday I saw the British Institute Exhibition. It
had two or three wonderful Leonardo da Vincis (especially
the 'Vierge aux Rochers'), some capital Rembrandt and
Vandyke portraits, one or two sweet Murillos, etc. Kingsley
had urged me by all means to see the Dudley Gallery at the
Egyptian Hall, mentioning particularly the duplicate original
of Correggio's well-known Dresden 'Magdalen.' So we all
went on Friday, and I never enjoyed such a feast of art; it is
chiefly a collection by some cardinal of the early religious
Italian schools, whom, in spite of Ruskin, I was not prepared
to like. The forms were often stiff and flat, but the beauty
was inconceivably *divine* (I can use no other word); the
monkery lay very lightly upon them. I scarcely know what I
liked best. Giotto, Francia, Fra Bartolomeo, and Fra Angelico
were all wonderful. One picture by Garofalo (I don't know
his name) contained, I think, the most glorious woman's head
I ever saw; Raffaelle could not surpass it. Then there were
some inexpressibly delightful Leonardos and J. Bellinis, a
good Titian or two, and a large very early Raffaelle. I was
just going to propose departure when I met Brimley, who
told me Kingsley and his wife would soon be there; so I

---

[1] Hare.

began examining anew with Brimley, to whom the class of pictures was almost as new as to me, and who was almost equally pleased; by and bye Kingsley came and introduced me to his wife. It was delicious to look at such pictures with Kingsley, and I was delighted to find that he chiefly enjoyed the same things that I had done, as well as pointed out others; I had no idea how catholic he was. He showed me in poor Fra Angelico's 'Last Judgement' the meeting in heaven of him and his love, who died young, and on whose death he became through grief a monk.

On Sunday afternoon I took my father and Kate to Lincoln's Inn, where we had from Maurice the most magnificent (I do not say most valuable) sermon I ever heard or read, being the last of his series on the early books of the O. T. It was on Samuel iii. 14, the character of Eli, and atheistical priests, and prophets raised up to testify against the priests (with a long digression on Savonarola), and the speaking by the mouth of a child. You can conceive his applications to our own times; the eloquence was marvellous, especially when he summed up the number of ways in which " we, the priests of the English Church, cause the offering of the Lord to be abhorred," and prayed solemnly for the prophets, Carlyle being evidently in his mind; yet now I feel it was a one-sided sermon.

To the Rev. G. M. Gorham

HARDWICK, CHEPSTOW, *September 1st*, 1851.

. . . The day after I left Cambridge I went down to Bath, and was there nearly a week, and was then about a fortnight in London, seeing the big glass toyshop and other London sights. Unluckily I am singular in being rather disappointed with the individual toys, grand as is the general effect. The designs seemed to me for the most part either tame or rabid. . . . At last we came down to this house, which my father bought in the spring; and having been living in hired abodes for fourteen years,—in short, ever since we left Ireland for educational purposes,—we are most glad to get truly settled again, especially in such a beautiful neighbourhood, with all the Wye scenery easily approachable, and Tintern within five miles. Here I have been 'reading' rather better than usual, but have not done much beyond some Plato, and the Master's *Philosophy of the Inductive Sciences*, and a little Theology. However, the Master's book is good in itself, and indispensable for Fellowship purposes.

Thank you much for your account of yourself and your doings. Such things are never 'uninteresting' to me, and, as for their being 'selfish,' that they cannot be except made so by a selfish spirit ; personal they may be, but that is quite another matter. I am glad you have found such pleasant and congenial quarters. If your pupil seems disposed to go out in the Natural Tripos, by all means encourage him, so far as you can do so without relaxing his Mathematics. He certainly should learn Botany on the Natural System.

. . . With regard to Moral Philosophy, I asked Maurice exactly the same question a year and a half ago. Unluckily his letter is at Cambridge, but I will try to recall its substance. He said he doubted whether on the whole he could improve the 'special subjects' marked out by Whewell ; but that, at all events, he was convinced the right thing in all such cases was to follow the prescribed course, and obedience would bring its own blessing. He urged me to give the greatest attention to the Plato and Aristotle, and to make them the central points of my reading, and the other books subsidiary. I did not myself go through anything like the whole course, but read all the Plato. The Aristotle I would read, if I were you, if possible—in Chase's translation if not in Greek ; and, next to that, Cousin and Sanderson. I need not tell you that Butler is always good, and the Master upon him. I would also briefly skim Macintosh's *Dissertation on Ethical Philosophy*, and perhaps Whewell's preface to it. In the quarto *Encyc. Metrop.* Maurice devotes 44 pages to an account of Modern Philosophy. It is of course valuable, but far too brief and sketchy ; in short, with the exception of the elaborate account and defence of the Schoolmen (evidently written against Hampden), and a clear indication of the progress from Locke to Kant, it is little more than a series of hints, and not a history at all. Blackstone of course is good, but I know next to nothing about Law. I must read Mill more before I can judge of him. It is very hard, but very necessary, to distinguish his own deductions and applications from the scientific principles which he lays down. I suspect the inconclusiveness lieš in the former. — Ever, my dear Gorham, very truly yours,   FENTON J. A. HORT.

TO A FRIEND

CAMBRIDGE, *September 29th*, 1851.

. . . You have been led by God in all your past thoughts and ways in a direction which involved most painful contradictions. You will not forget that the same God has brought you in like manner out of those painful contradictions, and has cut a knot for you which you could not cut yourself. That the process brings bitter pain is certain, but pain is only a secondary evil, and well is it for us if we can recognize it as a token of our sonship. So at least am I beginning at length in some slight degree to feel, having a thousand times refused to listen. We can still pray with not the less energy, "Despise not then the work of thine own hands," though we may feel that we have misinterpreted the form for which the work was destined.—God bless you, ever your affectionate friend,   FENTON J. A. HORT.

TO HIS MOTHER

CAMBRIDGE, *October 10th*, 1851.   9.30 A.M.

Trinity Fellowships

Rowe	.	.	3rd year
H. Tayler	.	.	3rd year
Westlake	.	.	2nd year
Watson	.	.	2nd year

I needed the humbling.

To his Mother

CAMBRIDGE, *October* 18*th*, 1851.

My dearest Mother—It seems such a time since the Fellowship List came out that I can hardly believe I have not long ago told you all about it. During the vacation I rather on the whole expected to succeed, but on arriving here soon realized that Watson's place would make him tolerably safe. Still, though not expecting success, I should not have been surprized by it; and so felt some little annoyance at first, but in an hour had forgotten all about the matter. This day week I called on Thompson, and had an hour and a half's talk with him, in which, of course, I learned much. He welcomed me very cordially, and said he was anxious to tell me what a very favourable impression I had made on the Examiners generally, himself included; he said that I had been very near indeed being elected; at one period I had actually a majority of votes. The Master expressed very superlative opinions about my Philosophy paper; apparently I was most successful in that subject, both in the specially-appropriated paper and in the translation of Plato and Aristotle. I was fully ahead of every one in my year (not elected), Schreiber being second and Beamont third; and Thompson told me that, unless I fall off woefully in the course of the year, which he did not see the least reason to suppose, I shall be elected as a matter of course next year. Accordingly I have received divers anticipatory congratulations; and I suppose, if I go in, I shall be safe enough. This week I have had enough to do with the (so-called) Voluntary Theological Examination, a troublesome but not particularly difficult one. I was not so well prepared as I could have wished, as it was no easy matter to work much last week after emerging from the Fellowship drudgery. However it mattered little, for the papers were badly set, and, if I had tried ever so much, I should have done very little more. I left very little undone, and probably beat nineteen-twentieths of those in, but cannot look upon it as anything more than a bothersome but necessary job got done with, for it is impossible to give satisfactory answers to unsatisfactory questions,—at least in a long examination. I have had a great enjoyment this week in Blunt's company; he came up on Saturday, and we have almost lived together; he started this morning for Brighton. Well! I think I have by this time said enough about my precious self! . . . I have not given you at all an equivalent for your delightful letter, but *I* have no garden to lay out, and you would hardly care to hear how my kettle sings, so I must say good-night.—Ever, dearest mother, your affectionate son,   FENTON J. A. HORT.

To Mr. C. H. CHAMBERS

CAMBRIDGE, *October 19th*, 1851.

. . . Thompson expressed a wish (to me) that Mackenzie would publish his essay. I do not know whether it is absolutely necessary to correct and annotate it; if not, I shall be only too happy to correct the proofs, and help in any way in getting it through the press.

I have very little Cambridge news to tell. Westcott has been ordained, and [has been] doing duty in Birmingham, but is come up for the term. The usual crowd of what Thompson calls 'the early Fathers' has of course brought up the usual crowd of 'nice' young men, and chapel swarmed to-night to overflowing with astonished surplices.

To THE REV. JOHN ELLERTON

CAMBRIDGE, *October 21st*, 1851.

. . . Carlyle's *Sterling* is very fine; if you cannot get hold of it, I will send it as soon as Stephen returns my copy. It is, however, very perverse—partly from its keen sight; you cannot imagine his bitter hatred of Coleridge, to whom he (truly enough) ascribes the existence of 'Puseyism,' etc. etc., and whose influence he considers to be the one thing which still keeps some intelligent men from abandoning the Church and her crucified Lord and Formulæ, for the 'Destinies,'

'Eternal Radiancies,' etc. etc. The picture of Sterling is doubtless almost true, as far as it goes, and an exquisitely beautiful one it is; but Hare's is no less true. Many incidental portraitures are wonderfully done,—Sterling's mother, for instance. Of Hare he always speaks with respect and regard, but never strongly—"*surely* a man of much piety," etc. He bestows not a single epithet on Maurice; but the tone and the silence is, and is meant to be, a deeper and more reverential compliment than words could convey. Altogether I cannot regret the publication of the book, for all the calumnies it may generate, and the unjust impression which dear Carlyle conveys of himself. Thank you much for *Harold.* I cannot express how much I like it; its *strength* is marvellous. Lees, who has been up here (as has also W. Howard, whom, alas! I have scarcely seen, but hope to see again in a few days), says it was written ages ago, long before *The Saint's Tragedy.* Kingsley is getting on with his new fourth century novel *Hypatia.* I doubt Kingsley's power to appreciate that age, but at all events he will throw great light on its strange events, having read most largely in almost unknown books. Perhaps you do not know Hypatia's story, as told by Socrates; how, being young, beautiful, noble, of spotless purity, and a teacher of the so-called Platonic philosophy, she somehow incurred the hatred of that bloody bigot Cyril of Alexandria, and how, with his connivance, a band of fanatics pursued her to the altar, and there tore the living flesh from her bones with oyster shells. Have you seen Croker's attack on Maurice and Kingsley in the new *Quarterly?* Brimley wrote an excellent answer ten days ago in the *Spectator.* I wish he would complete it with instances. I like Ruskin's pamphlet, but don't think it has much to do with the Pre-Raphaelites. Dyce's answer to the 'Sheepfolds' is not bad. I have just got a nice volume of poems by one Meredith;[1] they are not deep, but show a rare eye and ear. There is a Keatsian sensuousness about them; but the activity and *go* prevent it from being enervating and immoral. . . .

I am going to work at Hebrew, and have likewise *Modern Painters,* Bentley (the critic, not publisher), Bull, F. Newman,

[1] George Meredith.

Comte's *Politique Positive*, and ($\beta o\hat{v}\varsigma$ $\epsilon\pi\grave{\iota}$ $\gamma\lambda\acute{\omega}\sigma\sigma\eta$ [1]) an article [2] on Christian Socialism on hand ; *satis, puto.*

TO HIS MOTHER

CAMBRIDGE, *November 3rd*, 1851.

My dearest Mother—I wonder whether you are hugging the fire as affectionately at this moment as I am doing.   This is the first real frost we have had, and it has been bitterly cold to-day, though very fine and excellent for walking.

> But still I'm all froz
> From the tip of my noz
> To the tips of my toz,

at least I was just now, coming in from chapel through the cold courts, till I got˙ thawed.   It is pleasant to realise that you are able to write about out-of-door things as being really familiar friends, after being used to eschew all acquaintance with them (pavements, door-steps, and brick walls excepted) in the intervals between summer and summer.   To be sure it was in a great measure the same last winter at Newland ; but still we were too palpably there rather town mice come to visit country mice, than genuine country mice. . . .

As you suppose, I have lost the company of many friends, and have not made many new ones ; but still I have plenty to walk with—Westlake, Beamont, Brimley, E. Scott, Westcott, Babington, Mathews, etc. etc. ; and I hope to extend my acquaintance among the younger men, especially under- graduate scholars of Trinity.   My attendance at chapel varies mostly from six or seven to ten or twelve times a week, of which a respectable and increasing number are in the morning. I am not reading very hard, but am not idle, having various things on hand ; Classics, Theology, and Hebrew (which I am beginning to take up again) are the most staple subjects, and I have always plenty of miscellaneous reading—Politics, and Biography, and Poetry, and all manner of things—on hand to

---

[1] *Anglice*, ' Tell it not in Gath.'
[2] This article was apparently not finished.

a greater or less degree. Westcott and I have started a small chorus—Gorham, Freshfield, Howard, and Bradshaw, besides ourselves—to meet once a week, and get Amps, the organist of St. Andrews, and deputy organist of Trinity, an excellent musician and master, to teach us part singing. As yet we have only met once to try voices, and are pronounced to have two basses and four tenors, mine being of the former ; but on Thursday we begin regularly. Amps is to provide for the treble and alto parts one or two boys each. We anticipate much pleasure without much expense. They had on Saturday a great Football Match at Rugby—old Rugbeians against present Rugbeians ; where the former, though 35 against 400, kicked one goal and completely penned up the great host in one part of the Close all the afternoon.

To Mr. C. H. Chambers

CAMBRIDGE, *November* 28*th*, 1851.

. . . Even when long looked for, it is some time before we realise the sharpness of a very severe blow. People may say that must arise from the first effect being to stun ; but the result is the same when there has been no stunning, but conscious and intelligent acquiescence.

I can quite understand what you say about your genealogical researches, though I have very little taste that way myself ; but I suppose it is rather undeveloped than nonexistent, for not very long ago, in reading a novel (*Lady Alice*), I took the trouble to make out the pedigrees and write them on paper (being very intricate) in order to understand the story better ; and the *Stemmata Cæsarum, Ptolemæorum*, etc., in Smith's Dictionary smite me rather with respectful admiration than with fear and disgust.

To the Rev. John Ellerton

HARDWICK, *December* 22*nd*, 1851.

. . . There is great satisfaction in the assurance that nothing in which God has been a guide and a worker can

truly come to an end and lack fulfilment. I cannot describe
the rest I have sometimes found in those wondrous words of
Tauler's which Trench quotes (*Parables*, p. 177), "Upon the
way in which we may have restored to us 'the years which the
cankerworm has eaten,'" respecting "that Now of eternity,
wherein God essentially dwells in a steadfast Now; where is
neither anything past, neither to come; where the beginning
and the end of the whole sum of time stand present; where,
that is, in God, all things lost are found; how, finally, all things
that we have let go or lost we may find again, and gather up
again even in that most precious storehouse of the Lord's
Passion."

Christmas Eve.—I hoped to have gone on yesterday, but
was prevented, and as I am anxious to wish you a happy and
blessed Christmas I must be brief, for it is near virtual post
hour. I must write again to tell you of Blunt's wedding, at
which I was, as you suppose, present, to my great joy. I
don't understand what 'the fancies and speculations' are, on
which you want 'sun and air' to be let in, and am, indeed,
apt to be far too deeply plunged in that cloudland myself to
be very Phœbus—or Boreas—like for you to any practical
purpose. Nevertheless sprout away.

I send a scrap of Meredith, copied for you weeks and
weeks ago; is it not sweet and perfect in itself as a song?
Talk of Moore and Herrick! It seems to me more like
Shakespeare's songs. Well! to-morrow brings glad tidings of
great joy to us, as to all people; may we rejoice in it! God
bless you.

To the Rev. John Ellerton

HARDWICK, *December 29th and 30th*, 1851.

. . . With regard to F. Newman, it may perhaps be well
to read his *Soul*, on account of his curious dread of pantheism;
but I confess I would rather read some man of stronger mind
from the same point of view doing the same thing, *i.e.* trying
to construct a religion from within, *i.e.* from the pantheistic or
anthropocentric principle. I have looked a little at his friend
Mackay's *Progress of the Intellect*, an intelligent and very

learned book, but horribly dull, lifeless, and dreadfully
tolerant of us poor Christians, which is a thing I can't
abide.   (This reminds me of a story Stephen told me.
Some Whig was remonstrating with some High Church clergyman for disliking Lord Lansdowne: "Why, surely, you
can't deny Lord Lansdowne tolerates the Church."   "Bah,
that's the very reason we hate him," was the answer, "*because*
he tolerates the Church.")   I have read Maurice's new book [1]
but once, but like it much better than his last.   The first is
surely a most beautiful application of the Kantian Noumena
and Phenomena doctrine.   The talk about the Fall is rather
confusing to me.   But I must read the whole again.   It is,
as you say, a great thing that he sticks so close to the letter.
But I wish he knew Hebrew, and I also.   I had not heard of
the panic at King's College; if you learn more, pray tell me.
I think I must write to Maurice himself soon.

    . . . Certes we never wanted true Teutonic Protestantism
as we do now; it is the only thing that can keep true catholicism
from rotting into one of the legion forms of pseudo-catholicism
which swarm around us.   Have you heard of a new book,
Wilson's *Bampton Lectures*, which are making a great stir at
Oxford?   I have read part of them (he was one of the 'five
tutors' who protested against Tract 90), and they seem to
me perfectly horrible; people will quote them as instances of
Germanising, but the Germanism lies only on the surface.
Locke and Zwingle are the real originators of the book, which
is dreadfully and calmly philosophically destructive.   It is on
the Communion of Saints, and the object is to show that there
is no communion between the living and the dead, and that
Communion of Saints can mean only good action in different
Christians, assisted by 'separate rays' from the same divine
source; incidentally he intimates his hatred of doctrines and
contempt for historical Christianity.   Truly it is the dreariest
of all the Gospels (Bentham's not excluded) preached to our
poor age.

    I am doing some little steady work.   Every night after
prayers I lug down a big pile of books,—Bruder's *Concordance*,
Olshausen, De Wette, Tischendorf's text, Bagster's *Critical*

[1] Probably *Patriarchs and Lawgivers.*

Greek Testament, and a German dictionary,—and work at St. Paul chronologically. I have been two nights at 2 Thess. ii. and have at last got some light, which has much pleased me and encouraged me; I find it altogether a most interesting and all-ways profitable study. I had no idea till the last few weeks of the importance of texts, having read so little Greek Testament, and dragged on with the villainous *Textus Receptus.* Westcott recommended me to get Bagster's *Critical,* which has Scholz's text, and is most convenient in small quarto, with parallel Greek and English, and a wide margin on purpose for notes. This pleased me much; so many little alterations on good MS. authority made things clear not in a vulgar, notional way, but by giving a deeper and fuller meaning. But after all Scholz is very capricious and sparing in introducing good readings; and Tischendorf I find a great acquisition, above all, because he gives the various readings at the bottom of his page, and his Prolegomena are invaluable. Think of that vile *Textus Receptus* leaning entirely on late MSS. ; it is a blessing there are such early ones. . . .

Westcott, Gorham, C. B. Scott, Benson, Bradshaw, Luard, etc., and I have started a society for the investigation of ghosts and all supernatural appearances and effects, being all disposed to believe that such things really exist, and ought to be discriminated from hoaxes and mere subjective delusions; we shall be happy to obtain any good accounts well authenticated with names. Westcott is drawing up a schedule of questions. Cope calls us the 'Cock and Bull Club'; our own temporary name is the 'Ghostly Guild.' Westcott himself is, I fear, about to leave us. . . . His book has been wonderfully well received. He is preparing a companion volume for the epistles, *Elements of the Apostolical Harmony,* which will, I think, be rather odd. I am getting to know more younger 'live' men, which is a great pleasure. E. A. Scott of Rugby I like exceedingly; he is thick with the A. P. Stanley set. Benson also, and some of those just going out, seem likely to be valuable friends. He gave us a beautiful declamation in Hall on George Herbert, which he is printing (not publishing) at Martin's request. We had Thackeray at Cambridge to deliver his six lectures on English Humorists of last century; I heard all but the last.

They were very delightful and on the whole good.   I did not meet him while he was there.

I have now had a term of the 'Apostles,' and, on the whole, like them; *ridentem dicere verum* seems their motto, and, of course, the *verum* is now and then sunk in the *risus*, but not, I think, substantially.

And so poor Turner is gone at last! and even the *Times* says calmly, "The fine arts in England have not produced a more remarkable man than Joseph Mallard William Turner." I have not seen any other critiques.   Only think how fast the giants fall—Wordsworth, and Peel, and Turner; and soon, I fear, the glorious old Duke.   I got a number of delightful anecdotes, etc., about Turner three or four weeks ago from W. T. Kingsley, and saw part of the *Liber Studiorum* (and hope to see the rest next term), and one or two glorious water-color drawings of his.   While I think of it, let me beg you to look up on the heath near you for ripe seed of *Ulex nanus;* to make sure, you had better gather from unmistakably dwarf furze bushes.   We want them much for the Cambridge Botanical Garden; if not ripe now, you may possibly get them before you leave Easebourne.

I think it is since I wrote at Cambridge that the Voluntary List has come out.   It is scarcely worth mentioning, but you may be glad to hear that, when I went for my certificate to Blunt, he told me he had had very great pleasure in looking over my papers, etc.   He asked if I were residing to go in for a fellowship.   I told him I had just missed one, and that of course my reading for it had greatly interfered with my reading for the Voluntary.   He said he should not have thought it. At going out he wished me all success very warmly.

To the Rev. B. F. Westcott

Hardwick, Chepstow, *January 2nd*, 1852.

. . . Your prophecy has proved seemingly true; I *am* sticking at 2 Thess. ii.   But, for all that, you are no true prophet, I make bold to say.   I work very regularly from half-past ten to half-past eleven every evening, and get on so (comparatively) smoothly that there is a good chance of getting through a respectable proportion of my prescribed task. That troublesome chapter has occupied many hours, but it is a great satisfaction that at last I have gained some light upon the matter, though a great deal remains to be cleared up. What assures me most is that my view seems to combine in a certain degree all others, to be analogous to the acknowledged inter-pretation of other prophecies, and to make the whole passage a beautiful illustration of the meaning of prophecy and inspiration, getting completely rid of Olshausen's preliminary discussion as to the 'subjective' or 'objective' nature of the passage. Verses 6 and 7 seem to me to have been quite misunderstood as to their construction. I wish I could make up my mind as to whether a *Menschwerdung des Satans* really *widerstrebt dem denkenden Verstande* and *dem frommen Gefühle*, but incline to think not. But this and other points must be kept for conversation.

To the Rev. B. F. Westcott

HARDWICK, CHEPSTOW, *January 24th*, 1852.

. . . We must have some talk about 2 Thess. ii. when we meet. Apparently we shall agree in most points ; but is there any real ground for applying ὁ κατέχων to the Roman Empire ? if so, what was the *immediate* anti-christian manifestation that was to follow its removal ? I take the immediate fulfilment of the whole to be the Fall of Jerusalem, which, from my view of the connexion of O. and N. T., I probably think of more importance than you do. God Himself seems to me to be ὁ κατέχων ; but of course, in that case, I should adopt a differ-ent grammatical construction from the usual one ; as, indeed, I should do on other grounds. I can make nothing of the order of τῆς ἀνομίας.

To the Rev. John Ellerton

HARDWICK, *January 26th*, 1852.

. . . I heard that *Hypatia* was to be an exposition of modern politics ; the Church the friend of democracy, the heathen, and especially the Neo-Platonists (whom he wants to make out Emersonians), of aristocracy; and so poor Hypatia's murder a most proper and Christian punishment for the sin of being an aristocrat! I hope this is not true, but have my fears.

Do you feel warm on National Defences? I confess I do, and have distant visions of taking to rifle practice and I know not what.

To Mr. C. H. Chambers

Hardwick, *January 27th*, 1852.

. . . It is strange, the placid disgust with which one (at least I can answer for one fraction of that indefinite pronoun) hears of the successive developments of the famous Coodytar.[1] Have you any strong opinions about National Defences? I confess I have, and have indeed had for several years; only it is no use indulging them at times when nobody cares about the subject. But I hope people are at last beginning to open their dull eyes. It will be not a little fun if we get rifle corps (what is the plural of 'corps'? not 'corpses,' I hope) all over the country. This business of the Iron Engineers is likewise painfully interesting; but it is rare to find the justice so wholly monopolised by one side of quarrelling folks. I did not give the masters credit for so much courage and firmness, but I fear they are by no means sure of success.

To the Rev. John Ellerton

Cambridge, *February 8th*, 1852.

. . . I am in the midst of Gladstone's most significant and invaluable Letter to the Bishop of Aberdeen on lay membership of synods. I don't know that I agree with him on the final result—at least as a matter of principle, for in practice it may perhaps be necessary, but the letter is a model of calm, practical, Christian wisdom.

I am at work for the Hulsean, and have an awful list of

[1] = *Coup d'état.*

Apologists before me. I long to be rid of dear, good, prosy Justin Martyr, and in the midst of Tertullian and Origen, and still more Athanasius, Theodoret, and Augustin. I rather like *Hypatia*, but think it shows signs of the perversion I spoke of before. By the way, those good monks are not, I think, the real live Manichæans; the latter are surely yet to come—followers of Mani, I mane (forgive me!) Indeed I am beginning to think that Maurice, etc., are not strictly right in giving the name Manichæans to the *Latin* Tertullianistic and monkish glorification of 'holy virginity'; the more exact counterpart of Manichæism, I think, occurs in Origen and the very opposite Alexandrine school. Maurice (whom I saw in passing through London) told me that Kingsley prefaced *Hypatia* by stating that all the seeming modernisms were literal translations from the Greek; I have seen no such preface. Maurice said, significantly, that he was sure Kingsley would not intentionally misrepresent old circumstances. Maurice recommended me *Babylon and Jerusalem*, a pamphlet by Dr. Abeken in reply to some furious anti-Protestant publications of Countess Ida Hahn Hahn, who has emerged from the vanities of the world into the seriosities of Romanism. Parker has published a nice translation of it. Maurice called it the best book published in Germany for some years. It certainly is a grand book, honest, hearty, and wise, and without a particle of German philosophism, though there are defects, natural to a Lutheran.

To Mr. C. H. Chambers

CAMBRIDGE, *February 26th*, 1852.

. . . If you see the *Spectator*, you must have been somewhat startled to learn by its publication of last Saturday that " The Hall of Trinity College, Cambridge, was destroyed by fire yesterday. Nothing but the walls remain !" A friend of mine wrote to me in much natural agitation about it. You will probably, however, have learned by the other papers that the scene of the conflagration was Trinity Hall College, much of the front building of which was really gutted by fire on

Friday. My bedmaker woke me violently about half-past 6 saying that it was on fire, and Latham had sent to rouse Trinity. When I reached the spot, the flames were bursting out in fine style, but there was a dearth of buckets. So I ran back and routed out the bedmakers on every staircase in the New Court, and made them bring all their 'young gentlemen's' pails. Of course we had several lines of buckets, but the disposition of lanes and buildings was not favourable to those mysterious concatenations of human beings. However I got away at half-past 9, the fire being then effectually got under, though the engines were obliged to go on playing till half-past 12. Five sets of rooms were destroyed, and several others injured, as well as much furniture, etc. The College is scatheless, having put on an additional insurance of some thousands only a few days before. A marvellous number of watches vanished from their owners' pockets in the confusion.

Westcott has been away from Cambridge this term, having been taking Keary's place at Harrow during the latter's illness, and now to-day we hear that he is dead. I suppose Westcott will remain there permanently.

To his Mother

CAMBRIDGE, *February* 28*th*, 1852.

. . . In the autumn the Botanical Society of London announced that they were going to distribute a good stock of specimens of foreign plants to such of their members as wished for them. I should not have thought it worth while to spend any money upon them; but, as they were to be had for the asking, and I knew I should make at least as good use of them as nineteen-twentieths of the members, I applied for a list of what they had, and marked all I in decency could. And this morning they have arrived with some rare British plants, and very beautiful some of them are, especially the Swiss grasses; I find also among them a piece of olive from Athens, and something else from the slopes of Hymettus. You will be somewhat amused at something I did last week.

On the Tuesday (at 4) I got a kind letter from Gerald Blunt, describing his forlorn state, as he was left in sole charge of the parish in his rector's absence, and he was unwell and always found the work hard. Near the end he said, " If you want employment, send me down by Thursday a little sermon," giving a text, as it was to be part of a series. When I read it, I took it for a joke ; but in the evening it struck me that he really was in a hard plight, and that it would be great fun to surprize him with a sermon, *if* only I could manage it, but I feared it would take me days to write one ; and it must go the next morning at 10, or it would be of no use. However I sat down to make the attempt, though I had not a moment to spare for thought or arrangement, and expected very soon to stick and have to give it up as a bad job. But somehow I went on and on, time slipping away imperceptibly ; at last finished it (in exactly five hours), sealed it, and sent it the next morning ; and have since had the pleasure of receiving very warm thanks for it.[1]

To THE REV. B. F. WESTCOTT

CAMBRIDGE, *March 26th (vel potius* 1 A.M. *March 27th*), 1852.

. . . I have just learned from Scott that you are coming up early next week, but he does not know the day. I hope you will be here for our last musical meeting of the term, which is to be on Wednesday night. We have got Mozart's Mass in very tolerable order (except the movement *cum Sancto Spiritu*, which we have sung but twice, and one or two runs elsewhere), and shall be delighted to have you joining in it ; I fear I am getting a most Popish predilection for the Latin words.

. . . The 'ghostly' papers have at last arrived un- mutilated from Barry, whom Gordon has brought into the Society ; we are also going to ask Thrupp to join, who has just arrived from the East, without, however, many additions to his languages, excepting barbarous theories about pronouncing Greek by accent entirely, and purism as to gutturals.

---

[1] Mr. Blunt found the sermon in question too long, and cut it in half.

To THE REV. JOHN ELLERTON

HARDWICK, *April 8th*, 1852.

. . . I have been working pretty hard for the Hulsean, for which I have laid down a sufficiently ambitious plan. It would be a physical impossibility to realise it for the whole period before October; but I mean to try to do so tolerably for the Ante-Nicene period (so as, if possible, to bear down all competition), treating the subsequent centuries superficially; meaning, if successful, to work them up to the standard of the early part before publication. If I have but time, I think I shall be able to make a serviceable book, but the reading required is prodigious. All in Church and State seems hidden behind a thick veil; no one can guess what is coming, We have been this term occupied at Cambridge with two successive lectures on 'Electrobiology,' which certainly affords most extraordinary phenomena. I did not choose to pay a guinea to be taught the art; but yet I succeeded perfectly up to a certain point with a gentleman two nights ago.

To THE REV. JOHN ELLERTON

HARDWICK, *April 15th*, 1852.

. . . I do not know whether the Society for Promoting Association has itself helped the strike, but suspect not; I will try to find out at Cambridge through the Macmillans, but do not like asking Maurice or Kingsley about it, as I wish to avoid the subject with them as far as possible. Davies tells me that Maurice's name appeared some time ago prominently in the committee of an Omnibus Drivers' Association, but that it has lately been withdrawn, which is somewhat significant. I do hope the Masters will now use the noble opportunity they have to be gracious, and show that they really wish to treat their workmen like men, though they will not for a moment tolerate rebellious dictation. But, I should think, the time can hardly be far off when Government will really think the commercial fabric of the country not beneath their notice and government.

To Mr. C. H. Chambers

CAMBRIDGE, *May 11th*, 1852.

. . . I send you two 'ghostly' papers ;[1] you can have more if you want them, but I find they go very fast, and the 750 copies which we printed go by no means far enough. We are promised a large number of well-authenticated private stories, but they have not arrived yet. Our most active members are, however, absent from Cambridge ; to wit, Westcott at Harrow, and Gordon[2] at Wells. The latter says that Macaulay is horrified at the paper, as a proof how much ' Puseyism ' is spreading in Cambridge ! and some other eminent Edinburgh Reviewer (I forget who) thinks it highly unphilosophical in us to assume the existence of angels—which, by the way, we don't do (for our classification is only of 'phenomena'), though I don't suppose any of us would shrink from the 'assumption.'

To the Rev. B. F. Westcott

CAMBRIDGE, *May 11th and 21st*, 1852.

My dear Westcott—I can hardly believe that it is nearly six weeks since I saw you here ; but so it is, and I must not put off writing any longer. My vacation was curiously broken up. The new tubular suspension-bridge at Chepstow was in process of being got into its place (*i.e.* the tube thereof), and, thanks to the several steps of the process, and the numerous procrastinations and false alarms connected with each, a great number of hours was lost from enjoyment of home. . . .

During the vacation I distributed some eight or ten 'ghostly' papers, and have been promised some narratives from Scotland. Blunt showed me one MS. of what appears to be a well-known story concerning Lady Tyrone ; the account was known to have come originally from her family, but the paper was marked as copied in 1805 (I think), and there was no means of ascertaining its exact parentage.

[1] *i.e.* Prospectuses of the ' Ghostly Guild.'
[2] The Hon. A. H. Gordon, now Lord Stanmore.

I left a paper on my table the other evening when the Ray met here, and it excited some attention, but not, I think, much sympathy. Dr. —— was appalled to find such a spot of mediæval darkness flecking the light serene of Cambridge University in the nineteenth century. There were also grave smiles and civil questions; and finally several copies were carried off. . . .

I have just had (May 21st) a young Tübingen theological student here, who came bringing an introduction from a friend, and was visiting England to learn something about English theology and English Universities. He was very intelligent and gentlemanly, but I have had a great job in describing to him University organisation. Schleiermacher he spoke of as the man who is exerting most influence in Germany. Moral questions seem intermixed with theology in a very un-Whewellian fashion. He says that even the most orthodox care nothing for the theology of the three Creeds, even where they accept it; which is itself rare with many whom we should on other accounts call 'orthodox.' The great problem, he says, is agreed on nearly all hands to be the adjusting of a Christian faith which shall touch other parts of man besides his mere intellect. One would think that they would not have far to go in their quest before finding the thing sought—if only they could learn to find some divine meaning in the words 'Church' or 'Creeds.'

To the Rev. John Ellerton

CAMBRIDGE, *May 28th*, 1852.

. . . The 'Peelites' do, as you say, seem the only hope of the country, but more minute study of Gladstone's speeches, etc., and talk with Gordon about him, have made me doubt his possessing the unity and harmony of mind requisite to make him a second Burke, though he towers far above nearly, if not quite, all our other 'statesmen.' Walpole seems to promise something; this ministry will at least have achieved the good of bringing him out. Of course I agree with all you say of your views of social politics (with the possible exception of association—which, however, I am disposed to allow *remedially* in small doses), and am thankful that you have reached them, though I felt sure it would be only a question of time.

I know more or less your several spots of halting, having spent some weeks at Ryde in the summer of '42 before it was made a semi-royal watering-place ; though even then it was dashing enough. Southsea always took my fancy; there is something so jolly about that comfortably stout, well-to-do castle, squatted independently plump on the flat shore, as if the architect had sent it down with a pat like a lump of stiff clay or putty. The *teeth* of Portsmouth and the Solent are truly wonderful. I know no place where the beaverism [1] (?) of the nineteenth century becomes so human and, as it were, spiritual as the dockyard; all is stern work for a stern purpose—no pomps and vanities and no greediness of pelf. I confess I didn't like Ventnor, but Bonchurch is perfection ; and now the exquisite loveliness of the place is strangely intertwined with mournful associations. One cannot forget poor Sterling there, and Adams, and others whom I cannot recall just now. But Bonchurch is not genuine Undercliff, and therefore I hope you went on to Niton ; the view of the sea and shore from the beach near Black Gang Chine is grander than anything in the Island. Alum Bay is pretty, but a mere toy. The Needles and Freshwater cliffs are, however, noble, but I saw them only on a voyage round the Isle.

To the Rev. John Ellerton

Hardwick, *June 29th*, 1852.

. . . When I was in London I saw the Royal Academy. The pre-Raphaelites (Millais at least) are past description. I was disappointed at first at the first of them I looked at, Millais's ' Huguenot,' but found that the deficiencies arose simply from his scrupulous and honest humility ; he can't yet paint a background, or air, or distance at all, and so he doesn't try it, but arranges his picture so as to get rid of them, and

Word nearly illegible.

place all in simple noontide sunshine. One is struck at the
utter absence of even the quietest melodramatic or even true
attitudinising. There is no clinging, no convulsion. The
points of contact and union are simply the eyes, and the faces
as ministering to the eyes; and further, all four hands are
strained to the utmost; the girl's two at the two ends of the
white badge, the man's right (which passes lightly round her head
and his own left arm, *not* embracing her) holding the loop of
it from being drawn tight, and his left smoothing, or rather
pressing, back the hair from her right temple and compressing
her head at the same time. Neither face is very intellectual
or beautiful; both are common, and yet both people on whom
one could lean instinctively, so true and strong and tender and
free from all frivolity. Then the desperately calm, intense (not
at all violent) look of her uplifted, quiet eyes, and the strange
answer which his face gives; at first I thought that he rather
pitied and despised her emotion, but really loving her, tried to
look concerned in the midst of his smile; but I did him cruel
wrong. He is intensely moved (though not a whit shaken), but
tries to put on a calm and resigned and almost cheerful look
for her sake. So thoroughly human a picture I never saw,
full also of the deepest and purest Wordsworthian beauty.
'Ophelia' is hard to describe, but it is scarcely if at all
inferior, though less interesting. It is indeed like the beginning
of a new era to other things than painting.

It is very pleasant to see what good service Gladstone has
been doing of late in the House of Commons, but I fear he is
damaging himself with the public.

To the Rev. B. F. Westcott

HARDWICK, CHEPSTOW, *June 29th*, 1852.

. . . Certainly I cannot but be pleased at your having
bought (and, may it be hoped? read) Maurice's *Kingdom
of Christ*, for you seem to me to have misunderstood his
position and objects. But I have thought for years, 1st,
that he is intelligible and profitable to a person so far as
that person needs him, and no farther; 2nd, that the most

substantial benefit which he confers is that of enabling us to
enter into, sympathize with, and profit by the writings of
others ; in short, to realize truly the connexion between their
sayings and their selves.   Similarly, he seems to me to be a
most acute interpreter to us of our own confused thoughts.
You will therefore easily see that I regard him as a man to be
valued and loved, far more than admired and glorified.

. . . I have hardly ever come into contact with anything
belonging to German Theology without being chilled by the
way in which it seems almost universally regarded by its
warmest cultivators as an interesting' scholastic speculation
(Dr. Abeken's *Babylon and Jerusalem* is a notable exception),
and feeling thankful that we English *cannot* forget that the
Truth is that in which we daily live, whatever penalty we may
pay for our privilege in the shape of theological factions.

. . . It will not do to get too discursive, but the newspapers have of late given us plenty of food for thought ;
every week seems to bring us nearer to the consummation,
the separation of Church and State.   Thank you very much
for asking me to come to you at Harrow.   I do hope to give
myself that enjoyment some time, but I am going to be at
Cambridge all the Long, partly for Fellowship, but chiefly for
Hulsean, which I am very anxious to do serviceably.

To the Rev. B. F. Westcott

CAMBRIDGE, *August 5th*, 1852.

. . . On the whole I am not sorry at being thus restricted
to the Hulsean, respecting which you kindly ask.   I have
roughly completed the Chronology, including innumerable
notes or dissertations (for appendices) on chronological, historical, and critical points, and a few fragments of translations
or analysis ; likewise three or four pages of the Introduction,
which requires very delicate and cautious treatment, as it is
mostly on the subject how development is applicable to a
revelation, the object being to show that, in spite of theological
changes, the defences made by the Fathers are useful to us
now.

To his Mother

CAMBRIDGE, *August 6th*, 1852.

. . . We who have been rovers all our lives have perhaps no great right to urge others not to migrate ; but
even gypsies, I suppose, would hardly advise all the world
to follow their vagabond example.   I have been anything
but shaken by lately meeting with precisely the opposite
advice by an American, who says that "human nature will
not flourish, any more than a potato, if it be planted and
replanted, for too long a series of generations, in the same
worn-out soil."   Can you imagine a more cruel insult to the
poor potato, who is kept by transplanting in a state of perpetual gout for our benefit, and gets twitted when he tries to
get back to his natural state by making himself a home ?   By
the way, this reminds me of a very curious discovery (lately
published in the *Gardener's Chronicle*) made by some French
practical botanists.   The origin and native country of our
cultivated corn has been for ages a question of great difficulty.
The true wheat was said three or four years ago to have been
found on the Altai mountains, in the heart of Asia ; but there
appears to be some doubt as to whether it was not even there
the remains of old cultivation.   But these botanists have been
for years experimenting on the cultivation of several grasses,
and have at last obtained, by sowing and resowing from two
species of the genus *Ægilops*, two common 'varieties' of
wheat, the. common wheat being produced from *Ægilops*
triticea or 'wheat-like *Ægilops*.'   Some botanists are in a
terrible fright, and think that this discovery unsettles the
whole foundations of the science of botany; but that only
shows how vague their own notions of science are.   Thank
you about the bramble, but I do not wish it cut, even for
specimens, which could be obtained at Itton ; what I wanted
was to have a good healthy bush near home, to study growing.
I felt so convinced of its distinctness from all well-known
species, that I gave it to Babington with a new name, but told
him I should not publish it till I was more familiar with it.
I am glad now I did so ; for strolling with him the other day

in the Botanic Garden, I came on some brambles grown from
seed, some of mine and some from Mr. Bloxam in Leicester-
shire ; among the latter I immediately recognised one bush as
the Monmouthshire kind.　It came under the name of a species
which has always puzzled me, having seen but two or three
dried specimens ; it was only known to grow at Rugby.　So
the already published name comes in very conveniently to be
joined on to the observations which I had made independently.
Babington is very glad, as a double scandal is thus avoided,
1st, of describing a new species, and 2nd, of dropping an old
one.　The *Orobanche* which I found the day I walked with
you to New House proves, as I expected, to be *O. cærulea.*
There is a record above half a century old of its having been
found somewhere in Glamorganshire ; but it has been doubted,
as it is known to grow only in Hants, Herts, and Norfolk.
You would be amused at the duties which fall to me this
vacation as senior bachelor in residence.　I have every day
after dinner to order second course for the next (taking with
me one or two counsellors) ; but fortunately the cheapness of
fruit renders it no very hard matter to provide for our table.
One of my colleagues the other day wished for Norfolk
dumplings ; and they sent us up dry doughboys, which required
to be cut with a knife !

　　I will certainly read Forsyth's life, if you wish, if I see it
again ; but I have looked into it before two or three times,
and, I confess, been somewhat repelled.　Pray do not fancy
that I think I do not want such 'spurs,' or set myself above
them.　But there is about that and most similar books an
artificial atmosphere which stifles me, and makes me unable to
appropriate the genuine good which is there.　But do not the
less believe that I am more than ever your affectionate son,

　　　　　　　　　　　　　　　　　　FENTON J. A. HORT.

　　　　　　To THE REV. JOHN ELLERTON

　　　　　　　CAMBRIDGE, *August* 15*th*, 1852.

　　. . . On the 23rd I got a line from Blunt to say that he,
his wife, sister, and mother were in town, and when would I
go and see them, as I had already more than half promised to

VOL. I　　　　　　　　　　　　　　　　　　　　　　Q

do. I wrote to say I would be there next day (Saturday), and delightful hours those forty-eight were. The Chevalier Bunsen had pounced upon them the moment they were in town, and been as kind as could be to them; they had dined at the Embassy, and now he (Blunt) had to call there, and I called with him. Luckily the Chevalier was at home, and so we had a most cosy and friendly chat with him for the best part of an hour, mostly about his book (now in the press) on St. Hippolytus, and in fact on many things in early Church History and theology. It would be too long to talk much about it now; but it will evidently be a very interesting book, but, I fear, sadly heretical. It concludes with an 'Apology of St. Hippolytus to the English people, at the Great Exhibition of all nations, May 1851.' On Sunday afternoon Gerald and Julia Blunt and I walked through the thunderous rain to Lincoln's Inn, and had the usual luxuries there in service and sermon (on the mischief of compromise in *re* Protestantism *v.* Catholicism) not very new or striking; afterwards I had just time to shake hands with Maurice and introduce Blunt. In the evening I read them a MS. sermon of Maurice's (whereof more anon) which I had brought with me as a thing which they would like to see.

On the 29th I went with Babington and Newbould for thirty-six hours to Newmarket, to explore the botany of the country north of it.

Maurice has written and is revising two new volumes of sermons on the *Kings and Prophets*. He sent down here the first six, which Macmillan lent me, and it was one of them I took to London. The first (on Samuel as prophet, and last of the judges anointing the first king) is very good and beautiful, with a strange pathetic apology (so I take it) for himself as taking part in things which he dislikes, because they seem part of the coming act in the great world drama which is all part of God's order. The second is indescribably wonderful; it literally makes one quiver, and is rich in poetry to a marvellous extent; it is on 'Saul among the Prophets'—in short, Saul's life. The third is not much less beautiful, on David before his accession. The fourth also good, on David as king. Fifth not *so* good, on Solomon. Sixth ditto, but interesting and pregnant, on Rehoboam and the schism in the tribes, taken as a type of all schisms.

I am not in a very comfortable way as to Fellowships. Against me there are in my own year Schreiber and Beamont, both medallists and therefore 'senior ops,' one above, the other equal to me in the Tripos, both having read at least quadruple my amount of classics. In the other year is Lightfoot, a double man of boundless reading, who would have got one last time, Thompson said, if he had tried. . . .

I am getting on with my Essay slowly enough, and yet have written a vast deal; but I am working more regularly than I have done since I have been at Cambridge, at all events since my first term.

To the Rev. John Ellerton

CAMBRIDGE, *August* 23rd, 1852.

. ¦ . Please mention your Brighton address, as I want to lose no time in writing to Henry Bradshaw of King's, whose mother has just taken a house there in permanence, and I want to put in a line asking him to call on you. He is young (between his second and third year, I think), but, I am inclined to think, about the nicest fellow in Cambridge.

To the Rev. C. Kingsley

CAMBRIDGE, *August* 31st, 1852.

Dear Mr. Kingsley—As you gave a gracious reception to the notes which I wrote on your Dialogue[1] the other day at Macmillan's request, I make bold to add two fresh suggestions. No. 1 comes from Macmillan himself, who is far better versed in Bohn's translations of Plato than I am in the original. Surely 'Euthyphron'[2] is a bad name for your *ingenui vultus puer*. He was a μάντις in some sense or other, a pious one, who thought to show off his piety by prosecuting his father for murder. Either 'Charmides' or 'Glaucon' would

[1] 'Phaethon.'

[2] Apparently the name first chosen for the interlocutor, afterwards called 'Phaethon.'

suit you exactly, if you didn't mind their beauty. Glaucon at the beginning of the second book of the *Republic* does very much as your Euthyphro, but his name is not so attractive as the others, and I do not know whether his age and that of Alcibiades agreed. On the other hand, Charmides, a dear boy, was certainly his contemporary. But, if beauty is a disqualification, I despair of finding you a substitute for Euthyphro. Ugly boys were rarities in Athens, I fancy. So apparently you must put up with a pretty one, and drop the disparaging words.[1] Suggestion No. 2 relates to the Pnyx. As the place of Assembly was on the N.E. side of the Pnyx-hill, Sunium would be hidden from persons standing there, even if there are no spurs of Hymettus in the way. Further, as Sunium is due S.E. of Athens, the sun could hardly rise there ; and it will not do to say that you do not mean that it rises exactly over Sunium, for then Hymettus himself is in your way. The simplest way will be to say nothing about Sunium. By the bye, the regular hour of meeting was daybreak, which leaves little time for the Dialogue ; but the passage in the *Acharnians* which gives the rule, shows likewise that the magistrates were not always punctual. I have hardly space to say how much I liked both Dialogue and Prologue, but that is no matter.—Ever most truly yours,   FENTON J. A. HORT.

The above notes are perhaps in themselves trivial enough, but any who in later years sought literary criticism from Hort before publication, will appreciate the jealous accuracy of which his friends' no less than his own books reaped the benefit. More serious criticism of the finished Dialogue will be found later on.

TO THE REV. B. F. WESTCOTT

CAMBRIDGE, *September* 14*th*, 1852.

. . . I have never read the *Tracts for the Times*, but the perfect clearness and keenness of Newman always gives me

---

[1] This appears to have been done.

pleasure ; at the same time it is rather like a very pure knife-edge of ice.   I believe he has really a warm heart, but he has put it to school in a truly diabolic way.

By the way, have you read *Uncle Tom's Cabin* ? if not, do. I cannot at all understand how so good a book has come to be so praised.   If you saw the *Times* review, however (which is an exception), you will need no further recommendation ; it could be no poor or trivial book which could stir up such deep blasphemy against the Holy Ghost.

I once spent a most delightful week at Lynmouth, but I enjoy Ilfracombe far more.   I do hope you not only saw it, but encamped there for some days.   The breezy freshness, the free toss of the wavelike 'Tors,' the swelling hills with woody ravines ending in such sweet combes, and its rocky shore with transparent pools, full of the richest forms of life, give it for me a charm like very few other places.

To his Mother

CAMBRIDGE, *September 26th*, 1852.

My dearest Mother—Will you have the kindness to abstain from calling your letters 'great stuff' till you obtain leave from me ?   Not that I am likely, I hope, ever to give you leave, but that makes no matter ; one's thoughts and one's sayings do sometimes coincide ; so till you get leave, abstain. But I am far from uninterested in your details of household arrangements. . . . There is not a wide sphere here for me to have domestic arrangements in, much less to describe them, gyps and bedmakers being only charmen (are there such beings ?) and charwomen.   The whole family consists of my-self and my books, and the latter are very silent (so indeed is the former).   I had the other day seventy volumes of them on the table, more or less in use ; but as the libraries close on Wednesday, I shall be quite deserted then.   The remaining member of the family—that marked No. 1—has been attain-ing a comparatively wonderful amount of regularity and punctuality, seldom missing Morning Chapel, taking a spunge bath every morning, taking constant walks, and working more steadily and continuously than for several years.

To his Mother

My dearest Mother—Very many thanks for your congratulations, which are not the less welcome or valued because of their seeming limitation. For my own part, I value the Fellowship [1] chiefly as means of future, even more than present influence. But of course the more efficacious it is in that respect, the greater is the responsibility; and therefore I shall need your affectionate prayers more than ever,—and I know I shall have them. It is, as you say, a very odd feeling, but the prominent one is increased pride and interest in the College; but the charm would be snapped instantaneously if I thought of it for a moment as anything but a temporary resting-place.

The Essay, such as it is, must be sent in to-morrow week. It is on the early defenders of Christianity against heathens and Jews in the first four centuries.—With much love, your affectionate son,   FENTON J. A. HORT.

To the Rev. B. F. Westcott

. . . You evidently estimate the event [2] as I do, not so much as an honour as an acquisition of a vantage ground from which whatever message may be committed to us is likely to be listened to with more attention. But it makes one tremble the more lest any 'idle words' should bring discredit on a body which has inherited such a weight of authority earned by speaking the full truth.

I have got the *Beiträge*, but have hardly had time to look at them yet. But, so far as I have used Credner's *Introduction* (which is not much), I can quite confirm your high opinion of him; and his abstinence from unnecessary verbiage is a very great merit indeed. But it seems to me

[1] The following were admitted Fellows in 1852 : C. Schreiber, W. J. Beamont, F. J. A. Hort, J. B. Lightfoot.
[2] His election to a Fellowship.

pretty plain that well-trained English classical scholars are likely to become much better sacred critics than Germans. The union of the two characters seems rare in Germany, and not usually felicitous where it does take place.

You must have misunderstood me about Newman. Many of his sayings and doings I cannot but condemn most strongly. But they are not Newman ; and him I all but worship. Few men have been privileged to be the authors of such incalculable blessings to the world (though perhaps not a hundred acknowledge the fact), and therefore few have had his temptations. Unhappily the hard-hearted, scornful, and lying persecution which he had so long to bear did its work upon him but too effectually. Still even now it were most wrong to 'confound the cry of agony with a mocking laugh,' or rather to forget how both may be mingled in the same sound.

To the Rev. John Ellerton

CAMBRIDGE, *November* 14*th*,
HARDWICK, *December* 14*th*, } 1852.

My dear Ellerton—Time passes terribly, and it is with no little shame that I see your last letter bears date exactly a month back. One thing is that I am President of the Union, and debates, private business meetings, adjourned private business meetings, library committees, standing committees, and private consultations about all manner of meetings and committees, take up a good deal of time. Likewise I have begun to take pupils, or, to speak correctly, *a* pupil, for no more have come to me. As it turns out, I am not so sorry that I have no more ; for he is a good one, and occupies my time largely, I have to make so much preparation for him. In fact I am learning Greek far more rapidly than I have done all the time I have been up. Then C. B. Scott and I read Hebrew together any time that I can spare on Monday, Wednesday, and ¿Friday evenings. On Wednesday there is the Ray, on Friday our musical class (in which we are singing Beethoven's wonderful Mass in C, the treble of the accompaniment of the Kyrie Eleison of which I played (?) to you in a manner when you were here), and on Saturday the 'Apostles,' to the college of whom we last night admitted Farrar. Further, I have been constantly correcting the sheets of Maurice's *Kings and Prophets*, which come 'revised' from his hands in the most ludicrous state of inaccuracy; I am sure six corrections a page would be under the average, but the majority of these belong to punctuation. You will now be able partly to understand how, not having yet recovered regular hours, I have found myself short of time, and have not even done any reading of my own of any regular kind.

I promised to give you some details about the Fellowship, but really there is very little to tell. In Classics Lightfoot was of course first, and Benson second, chiefly, I believe, from a beautiful translation of "Then quickly rose Sir Bedivere, and ran," in *Morte d'Arthur*, into Greek Hexameters. I gather that I was third in Classics, but I am not absolutely sure; I was at all events, Thompson told me, quite sure from the very first (which was said of no one else), and all the early papers were classical. Mathematics were almost zero to me. The History papers were so absurd (mostly technicalities about *modii*, rates of interest, etc.) that no one but Beamont did respectably. In Philosophy I was far ahead of everybody. I wrote a good deal on one question about Natural and Artificial systems, to be illustrated from Botany, and my answer seems to have made quite a sensation. Sedgwick, I hear, has been talking in the most extravagant way about it, saying that no man in England could have written such a one, and indignantly trampling on somebody who suggested that Henslow might write as good a one!!! Beamont came out considerably, and did very much better than last year; he was next to me in Philosophy. He is gone off to the East alone, with the intention of making his way to Mecca, disguised as a Mahometan pilgrim! I believe that there is no more to say about the Fellowship except that I was elected unanimously.

My Essay went in on the 20th (or rather A.M. 21st) at great length, but in a singularly imperfect state; all the period from Tertullian to Augustine being merely a catalogue of names and dates, interspersed with fragments and critical and chronological notes. It would take too long, or I would tell you the extraordinary hurry in which it was written out, greatly increased by the unexpected arrival of my Bury cousins, the Colletts, to be lionised over Cambridge two days before. Suffice it to say, that I was forty-eight hours out of bed, and that E. A. Scott, Bradshaw, an hired amanuensis, and myself were writing for the bare life in my rooms continuously from half-past 7 P.M. till about 6 A.M., and to some of us that was only the finale. I meant to have gone on rapidly with it this time, and my rooms are full of books for the purpose; but I have had no time to do anything. I have a long and very delightful letter to thank you for, especially for its account of Brighton affairs and your doings, of which I am quite insatiably greedy. I am afraid I must have talked big and misled you when you were here, for I really know very little actually of Church History; I only know *of* regions of Church History which are popularly ignored. *The* sources are the Fathers. Eusebius himself, the Burnet of the early ages, unmethodical and unfair, is yet full of interesting information, especially in his numerous quotations. But after all it is very hard to sit down regularly to read history without some definite object; and that was one great object I had in attempting this Essay. I have at least, however, gained the negative advantage of ascertaining that there is nothing deserving the name of a Church History in existence. Neander is exceedingly useful as a handbook, but he is very unfair in his own demure way, besides writing no history at all, properly so called. I forget whether when you were with me I had got the first (and, as yet, only) volume of Thiersch, translated by the Irvingite Carlyle. That is the nearest approach to a history that I have seen ; and a very good one too, being learned, sensible, spirited, and orthodox. The history of the N. T. books seems excellent, so far as I have looked at it, and know the subject ; but unluckily the volume does not go beyond the Apostolic age.

My thoughts have for some time converged towards making Church History the central object of my reading, with a view perhaps to writing a great history years hence, especially containing a full landscape, foreground and background, of the

times, independently of religious and ecclesiastical matters.
But the necessary preparation will be enormous. Independently of the entire contemporary literature sacred and profane,
and all the principal modern comments and digests of the
same from the fifteenth century till now, I shall have to devote
great labour to discovering and constructing an accurate view
of the world in all aspects (especially the social) before the
coming of Christ. Independently of smaller centres, which
become very important in subsequent Church History, there
are at least five large distinct heads—Rome, Greece, Judaism,
Persianism, and Egypt. Then there are all the very curious
mixtures of these, the Græcising of victorious Rome,—the
multitudinous effects of Alexander's conquests, as the Græcising of Persia, resulting in the stifling of the old faith for several
centuries and the rise of that strange Parthian empire, and the
Græcising of Egypt under the Ptolemies with all its strange
literature, producing Lycophron and Theocritus side by side,
—the Jewish mixtures especially in Samaria and Egypt and
Leontopolis, the rival Jerusalem of the Egyptian Jews. Then
there are all the minor tribes, many of them Semitic, of North
Africa, Pontus, Phrygia, etc., and *their* mixtures, especially with
Hellenic culture. All this will, I fear, require much ethno-
logical study. Then this whole state of things arises from the
fusion of decaying powers, which must therefore be studied in
their youth and manhood; you will easily see how much is
thus rendered necessary. It seems to me that, whether I write
and publish or not, I shall have to work up three distinct
treatises : (1) a history of the Jewish nation from Abraham to
B.C. 300. This will involve all the questions of Hebrew criticism, not only historical but philological, and thus require
study of the whole range of Semitic languages, not only the
Aramaic with Syriac and Chaldee, but Arabic, Persian, and
Æthiopic. (2) A history of Greek philosophy from Thales to
Aristotle's immediate disciples, Theophrastus, etc., paying
especial attention to the ante-Socratics (Pythagoras, Hera-
clitus, and Empedocles in particular), and trying to bring out
their relation to their unphilosophical contemporaries, especially the early poets, and to the state of the Greek cities
generally before the corruption of the fifth century. This will

involve imbuing oneself with all the good Greek literature—
a pleasant task enough, but a heavy one. (3) A history of
the Hellenic world from the death of Alexander the Great
to the birth of Christ. This will be almost entirely new
ground; the materials are scanty, and politics had by that
time reached such a state that philosophy and religion, such
as they were, must form the main element. The προπαρα-
σκευὴ εὐαγγελική has been often enough touched theologically
for theological purposes; but I do not think it has been
attempted with any fulness with a genuine historical purpose;
yet few things are more necessary to give the starting-point of
Church History. This is an alarming catalogue of labours,
not a tenth part of which will, I suppose, ever be realised.
At all events, these dreams are between ourselves; anybody
else would have just reason to laugh at me for them. But
they may at least give some little purpose and method to
reading.

By the way, I was immensely taken the other day by an
exquisite song, words and music one inseparable whole; the
latter by Schubert, the former by I don't know whom; it is
called 'Einsam? einsam?'

Gordon was kind enough to give me a ticket for St. Paul's
at the funeral,[1] and the temptation was too great to be resisted.
Unluckily, though near enough to hear everything, and well
placed for seeing such of the procession as entered the
building, I was hindered by one of Wren's clumsy, shapeless
piers from seeing the 'area' and ceremony. But it was an
infinite pleasure to take part in what I felt to be the real fast
and humiliation of the nation for all its sins, and solemn service in celebration of the last sixty-three years. It is no use
attempting any description; the impression, never, I hope, to
be forgotten, was not a matter of words. To me, perhaps,
the solemnest part of the whole was the exquisitely chanted,
"Lord, Thou hast been our refuge from one generation to
another," so humble and quiet and prostrate and suppliant,
finally bursting with such perfect and harmonious sequence
into, "And the Glorious Majesty of the Lord our God be
upon us: prosper Thou the work of our hands upon us, O

[1] Of the Duke of Wellington.

prosper Thou our handywork." People found fault with the
'inappropriateness' of the concluding anthem from the 'St.
Paul,' "Sleepers wake! a voice is calling!" I don't know
what Milman meant by it; but I imposed my own meaning, and found it more than appropriate. Dear old Blunt
gave us a very nice sermon at St. Mary's: the beginning
commonplace, but he waxed warm, and you can imagine how
he honoured such a kindred spirit as the Duke. I hope you
enjoy Tennyson's Ode, which I hear sadly abused here. At
first I could not make it out; the words *seemed* nothing
remarkable, but there was a mystery about the music of them.
Another reading, however, enabled me to get into the spirit of
them and feel their grandeur. For metre I know nothing
equal. A man named Evans of Emmanuel has got Macmillan
to publish some more than respectable sonnets on the occasion.
So much has come before one's mind of late that I am overwhelmed with matter. But I am sure you must have been
rejoiced by the debût (oh, what a word!) of Convocation, and
Hare's delightful speech and fraternization, and Thirlwall's
perhaps still more valuable mediation in the Upper House.
Trinity shone out in her proper place; it was pleasant to see
Peacock stand up so manfully for dear old Mill. We owe
much thanks to S. Oxon, who has been the prime mover in
the whole.

We had a most noble commemoration sermon at St. Mary's
from Harvey Goodwin on 'Reasonable Service.' Think of
his having the boldness to condemn the 'cropping and
pollarding' young men into a proper clerical state of mind!
I am curious to hear what is your opinion of the *Restoration
of Belief;* I fear I stand alone in disliking No. 2.

You will be much delighted with Maurice's *Kings and
Prophets;* they take quite a new flight; but I suppose you
will see them in a day or two. I am anxious also to see the
little fugitive volume of sermons on the Sabbath, etc., which
Parker is publishing for him. He gets on very slowly with
the *History of Philosophy*, but prints as he goes. I have
seen all the sheets as yet; they go to St. Clement of Alexandria, and are a vast improvement, though far from perfection.
I have also now in my possession, and am reading, the sheets

of the new *Warburtonian Lectures ;* they go as far as the Synoptic Gospels and their differences, and part of the writings of SS. Peter, James, and Paul.   Have you seen M. Arnold's new poems, *Empedocles on Etna,* etc. ? they are full of genuine beauty, but lack strength and purpose, and show painfully how an epicurean, making pleasure the chief good (so far as there is good at all), does virtually annihilate or sour pleasure ; in a way very satisfactory to me, who always contend might and main that pleasure is *a* good and divine.

To THE REV. C. KINGSLEY

HARDWICK, CHEPSTOW, *December* 15*th,* 1852.

My dear Mr. Kingsley—This is rather late to thank you for ' Phaethon,' [1] but you must excuse one of my procrastinating habits.   I put it off in the first instance with the intention of writing you a long letter, which I afterwards resolved to spare you.   —— did not show me the letter which he finally sent you, but I saw his manuscript notes in the margin of his copy, and also your reply to his letter, besides having had abundance of talk with him on the subject.   The impression left on my mind exactly coincides with what I have long felt, that *his* state of mind cannot effectually be reached by direct attacks of that kind.   It is quiet, incidental observations that really sink into his mind, and therefore I never seek controversy with him, but am always ready to talk freely as much as ever he likes.   I doubt whether you realise how very deeply his scepticism is seated. . . . His talk brought clearly before me what might, I think, be expressed more fully in the Dialogue with advantage, viz. that your doctrine finds an antagonist not only in a sophistical habit of mind, but in the honest philosophical (or unphilosophical) opinion that words ought to be, if they are not always, definite labels of definite notions, and that it is illogical to give the same name, ' spirit of truth,' to the vague notion with which Alcibiades starts, and the notion of a personal Spirit of truth which is ultimately arrived at ; and that no argument drawn

[1] Sent to Hort in MS.

from the accidental coincidence of name can be valid. Now
such an opposition can only be met by acknowledging
candidly and distinctly the plausibility and *prima facie* probability of the opinion on which it rests, and then pointing
out how nevertheless the instinct of mankind (guided, as you
or I would say, by the Divine Word) has, consciously or unconsciously, discovered and recorded in language affinities
which a deliberate logician, *making* language, would discard as
tending to confusion. Again, the worshippers of 'subjective
truth' might fairly, I think, come down on you and say,
"All your arguments to prove the superiority of objective
truth will be pertinent enough when you have shown us that
it is within our reach; till then, forgive us for holding fast by
subjective truth, not from preference but from necessity."
You give the true answer in the latter part of the Dialogue,
by saying that the Spirit of truth reveals truth to men, not
that they discover it for themselves. But I think you do not
exhibit the relation between that part of the Dialogue and the
earlier with sufficient expressness. If I am to cavil, I would
say that you are throughout rather one-sided. This is, I
think, the respect in which you are least Socratic. You start
with a certain definite conclusion in your mind, to which you
conduct your interlocutors. In short, you and your Socrates
are entirely teachers of what you have learned, and not fellow-
learners with Alcibiades and Phaethon. Now in Plato we are
always, I think, *feeling our way* in certain distinct lines, which
are at last found to converge, though we do not pursue them
(indeed, he could not lead us) to the point of convergence,
but are made to feel that without holding securely certain
sound clues, we shall only lose our way in speculation. And
forgive my expressing a wish that you had put (as I understood you intended) a word or two of qualification into
Socrates' last speech, so as to hint that, however absolutely
the light and the power of receiving it are the gift of God,
there must nevertheless be a corresponding act of reception
on the part of man—in short, that he has the awful power of
refusing to receive the fullest light. You asked for all manner
of criticisms, so I have sent them without scruple. ——'s plea
for Emerson himself seemed to me very frivolous. Emerson

is full of wise and beautiful sayings, but they no more grow
in him than holly in a plum pudding. You might, perhaps,
have distinguished more clearly between Emerson and his
ill-educated but far from 'uncultivated' sect, though you
certainly were explicit enough for most readers' comprehen-
sions, and your main drift was to show that his atheism
implicitly contains and must issue in the debasing superstitions
of which they already give sign. In this I entirely agree, and
had (curiously enough) put on paper a similar prophecy the
night before your MS. arrived. By the way, I hope you will
be glad to learn that old Dr. Mill praised ' Phaethon ' without
qualification, ascending through a climax of phrases to " A
very valuable tract indeed." This letter has somehow spun
itself out to some length, and all about ' Phaethon.' So I will
only wish you and Mrs. Kingsley and all your belongings a
happy Christmas, with all the blessings included in it, and
remain, very affectionately yours,   FENTON J. A. HORT.

The above criticisms, as well as those contained
in an earlier letter (on the setting of ' Phaethon '),
were written in the midst of heavy work. Kingsley
was very grateful for the suggestions, "sent straight
to me, instead of twitting me in a review, as three-
quarters of the world would." The criticism of more
important points in the Dialogue induced him to stop
the press, and add three or four pages to his work.

In 1853 Hort began to devote himself more
definitely to work on the lines recently laid down
for himself. But unfortunately interruption came
from health. A troublesome skin disorder, the outcome probably of the scarlet fever of undergraduate
days, was a source of constant vexation now and for
some time to come. It led, at the beginning of 1853,
to his trying the experiment of a water-cure, and he
spent many weeks under the rather irksome conditions of Umberslade Hydropathic establishment, near

Knowle. It was during these weeks, in the course of a walk with Mr. Westcott, who had come to see him at Umberslade, that the plan of a joint revision of the text of the Greek Testament was first definitely agreed upon. The hydropathic experiment was only a partial success. In April Hort returned to Cambridge. In this year he became a Major Fellow of Trinity, and took his M.A. degree. He undertook some MS. work in the University Library, and was appointed examiner for the Le Bas Prize, and for the Moral Sciences Tripos of 1854.

Meanwhile his circle of friends widened: he had interesting letters from F. W. Robertson of Brighton, whom he only knew through correspondence; he visited Mr. Augustus Jessopp, to whom he gave literary help by verifying quotations in the works of Dr. Donne. Dr. Jessopp recalls that, two years later, it was Hort who introduced him to Mr. George Meredith's poems, a volume of which he was carrying in his pocket. Through the 'Apostles' he now became acquainted with Clerk Maxwell, afterwards one of his greatest Cambridge friends, who in this year read to the 'Apostles' a paper with the characteristically baffling title of 'Idiotic Traps.'

Early in the year Hort had thought of applying to Archdeacon Hare for a curacy, and in June the offer was actually made through Maurice, whose influence, however, decided Hort to remain at Cambridge for the present. He was reading for Ordination, for which the Bishop of Oxford accepted his fellowship as sufficient title. About this time Mr. Daniel Macmillan suggested to him that he should take part in an interesting and comprehensive 'New Testament Scheme.' Hort was to edit the text in conjunction with Mr. Westcott;

the latter was to be responsible for a commentary,
and Lightfoot was to contribute a New Testament
Grammar and Lexicon. Another piece of work came
upon his shoulders through the death of his friend
Henry Mackenzie.[1] He was of the same standing as
Hort, and had come up to Trinity after a brilliant
course at Glasgow. The freshness and vigour of his
mind are shown in many delightful and humorous
letters. In 1851 his health had begun to give way,
and in 1853 he died, after a long and trying illness,
borne with splendid courage and cheerfulness. In
1850 he had obtained the Hulsean Prize for an
essay on 'The Beneficial Influence of the Christian
Clergy on European Progress in the First Ten Centuries.' During his illness he employed himself in
working up his essay for publication. He was busy
with it till the last, even when he had become too
weak to lift by himself the books by which his bed
was surrounded. After his death it was his mother's
wish that her son's work should be prepared for the
press by his friend Hort, and he cheerfully undertook
the charge. Whewell was much interested in it, and
highly praised the language of the essay. Mackenzie
had compiled an enormous mass of notes, many of
them intended for future use, and not as immediate
illustration of his subject. For instance, according
to his editor, his notes from Bede were " in fact a most
complete analysis of everything of any value in that
author." The work of editing proved heavier than had
been anticipated, and the essay did not appear till the
autumn of 1855. The editor's part was done with

---

[1] Son of Lord Mackenzie, a friend of Sir W. Scott (see Scott's
Journal, vol. i. p. 207, etc.), and grandson of the author of *The Man of
Feeling.*

characteristic care and devotion, which were warmly
appreciated by Mackenzie's friends, whose only complaint was that the extent of Hort's own work on
Mackenzie's notes did not sufficiently appear. He must
have verified an enormous number of references. One
passage from his introduction to the essay deserves to
be quoted : " Those who knew Henry Mackenzie will
recognise these last few words " (a quotation from a letter
about the essay) " as altogether characteristic of his mind.
They well convey his hatred of all special pleading,
most of all in defence of the Faith which was so dear
to him, along with that trust in history as a guide to
truth which is happily taking possession of the more
thoughtful men of England, France, and Germany."
This sentence shows how nearly akin was Mackenzie's
mind in some important respects to the editor's own.

Maurice's expulsion from his posts at King's
College was of course a great grief to Hort, whose
first introduction to him had been through correspondence on the very questions on which Maurice's position
was now pronounced to be heretical. The controversy
needs not to be now revived. Hort's chief part in it
was the circulation of an address of sympathy, which
entailed a great deal of correspondence, and over
which he took endless trouble and care, although the
terms of the address did not altogether satisfy him.

In the winter of 1853 the *Journal of Classical and
Sacred Philology* was projected, and in 1854 the first
number appeared. Hort took from the first an active
part in establishing this useful publication, which was
described by one of his friends as a " Kitto's Theological Journal, Arnold's Theological Critic, and Dobree's
Adversaria all in one."   It received a welcome, amongst
others, from the Chevalier Bunsen. The inception of

the undertaking was due to Mr. (now the Rev. Professor) J. E. B. Mayor. The project was warmly
taken up in Trinity, especially by A. A. Vansittart.
W. G. Clark, H. A. J. Munro, W. H. Thompson, and
E. M. Cope also helped with criticisms and suggestions. The first editors were J. E. B. Mayor, Lightfoot, and Hort. Hort had only just taken his M.A.
degree, and Lightfoot was still a B.A.—a striking
recognition of what was even then expected of these
young scholars. Hort himself wrote largely in the
Journal, articles, reviews, and notes (see Appendix III.)

Meanwhile Hort was diligently preparing for his
Ordination. This was with him no mere matter of
course, required by the existing college statutes ; the
purpose which he had declared when a boy at Rugby
eight years before seems always to have been kept
steadily before him. The careful answer which he gave
shortly after his own Ordination to his friend Blunt's
questions about the nature of a ' call ' to take holy
orders, is sufficient evidence of the devout deliberation
with which he had himself taken this step.

In the summer of the same year he went abroad
for the first time, except for the early school-days at
Boulogne. His foreign letters show an extraordinary
vigour of mind and body. It has seemed worth while
to print rather long specimens of them, since they
illustrate his character in more ways than one. Not
least noticeable is his assurance that his family and
friends will care to enter into all that he is seeing and
doing. He did not shrink from the trouble of writing
two or three elaborate accounts of the same events,
each of which shows that he was all the time considering who it was to whom he was writing, and in which
of his experiences that particular correspondent would

be specially interested. His own vivid imagination enabled him thoroughly to enjoy the recorded experiences of others, and he was therefore eager to share with others every pleasure that fell to his own lot. In the last year of his life, a short tour which I took in Greece was to him the source of almost as much delight and excitement as if he had been himself carrying out the long-cherished desire of seeing Delphi and Athens, instead of reading of them on a sofa at home.

After this year health generally required that the time available for foreign travel should be spent in the Alps. Venice he saw on this first trip, but Florence and Rome not till thirty years later. This tour lasted nearly three months. Both before and after it much time at Cambridge was taken up with the Library Syndicate—the first appointed—and other reforms now being discussed in the internal government of the University. He felt much anxiety about the proposed changes in the condition of the Bachelor's Degree, and especially about the proposed introduction of a Theological Tripos. On this subject he wrote a careful letter to the *Spectator*, defending the rejection of the Tripos. He also printed and circulated a pamphlet on what he considered 'mischievous measures,' but acquiesced in the scheme which was eventually adopted. The reasons for his dissatisfaction will better appear at a later [1] stage.

To his Mother

LILLESHALL, *January 4th*, 1853.

. . . The christening [2] passed off very well on Sunday. Baby behaved with the utmost fortitude, though the water was not of the sweetest, having been brought from the

---

[1] See p. 275.   [2] Of Mr. Gerald Blunt's first child.

Jordan in a small flask. There was at first some doubt which was the Jordan flask and which the Dead Sea flask ! You would have been amused to see me on Friday night at the Lilleshall school feast, surrounded by some dozen little girls, who were eagerly being puzzled, and in turn puzzling me with making words out of card letters. However, we got on famously. Much love to all, specially to yourself for to-morrow, and, I hope, many happy to-morrows. Ever your affectionate son, FENTON J. A. HORT.

TO THE REV. F. D. MAURICE

;LILLESHALL, NEWPORT, SALOP,
January 5th, 1853.

My dear Mr. Maurice—Let me at once thank you for your Sabbath sermons. . . . The volume was very delightful to me on several accounts ; on this especially, that, without masking or in any wise glozing over a single conviction which it was needful for you to utter boldly, you have avoided giving needless offence to many candid and reasonable but timid readers. You have sometimes seemed to me, in your anxiety not to quench the smoking flax of earnest men assailed by scepticism, to have been too careless of those who are similarly assailed by pseudo-orthodoxy. But it is not so in this little volume. The latter class is seldom attended to but by merely mischievous teachers ; yet it is a very large and important one. I have been often astonished to find how honest and godly a spirit is hidden under a pharisaical intellect and even speech. Thousands, I suspect, who might easily be led into the fulness of truth, would be stopped at the threshold by anything which *seemed* to interfere with their devotion to their Bible or their Church, as the case might be. The claims of sceptics are beginning to be acknowledged (and at all events are sufficiently canted about), but it will be no less necessary to recognize the claims of the orthodox. . . . But to return to your book. . . . There is another view—what some people would call the common-sense view—which you hardly meet : . . . surely there are numbers in all classes, really needing the divine message, who would be tempted away by pleasurable excitement from the most perfect and divine preacher of it. If our lips lost all their coldness and insincerity, there would still be multitudes, by no means thoroughly vicious, who would not listen to them. I do not say that this consideration necessarily vitiates your conclusion, but it ought to be remembered. . . . Of the perfect truth of the principles you have laid down I have no sort of doubt. I hope it is not wrong to rest undecided about their application. While on the subject I may as well call your attention to a suggestive note of Dorner's (you will find it by the word 'Sonntag' in the index: mine is the second edition), which I was looking at the other day; it illustrates much that you say, and connects the Sabbath with a thought that has often occurred to me, how important is the view which the conflict with gnosticism led the early Fathers to take of our Lord's life and ministry, as especially the work of One who was the Creator. By the way, I think you will find that the modern pharisaical view of the Sabbath mainly dates from Constantine's enactments on the subject. This ought to have some weight with religious people.

I am not anxious to decide too hastily whether to continue and complete my Essay on the Apologists or not. It might be published in a way which would not show any defiance to the Examiners (let me observe in passing that, though bigotry *may* have interfered with my success, the very fragmentary and unfinished state in which the production was sent in is quite as likely to have stood in my way). And it would be affectation to say that I do not think it contains good matter, worthy of being published. But on the other hand, many things have long been leading me to feel that, unless I receive some clear intimation otherwise, my work must chiefly lie in Church History, especially in connexion with the previous and contemporary state of the world. So that a good deal of what I have now worked out might be used up years hence in other forms. Still I confess I have a hankering after trying to say something on the real nature of Apologetics ; and the historical seems the most appropriate and effectual form to use, at all events for me. The upshot of the matter is that I shall probably send or bring you my rough copy of the MS., and ask you to look at it and give me your advice, though I cannot promise explicitly to follow it.

I am staying with Blunt for a few days for the baptism of his little girl, to whom I am godfather. He sends kind regards from self and wife to you and Mrs. Maurice. . . . All manner of best New Year's wishes to yourself, Mrs. Maurice, and the boys (who, I hope, have not quite forgotten me).—Ever yours affectionately,   FENTON J. A. HORT.

What a pleasure to see a Government expressly repudiating any 'interest' or party !

To THE REV. GERALD BLUNT

UMBERSLADE, *January 29th*, 1853.

. . . A great deal of time will necessarily be wasted here, but I shall never lack something to do, having brought with me my botanical books, Origen against Celsus, Tertullian's *Apology*, Dorner on the Person of Christ, Tauler's *Sermons*, a book of Erskine's, Thiersch's *Church History*, Gk. Test. (and have written for De Wette's Commentary), Palgrave's *History of Normandy*, Niebuhr's *Lectures on Ancient History*, etc.

To THE REV. GERALD BLUNT

UMBERSLADE, *February 13th*, 1853.

. . . The failure with Hare [1] and Maurice's strong request (for such it is) not to leave Cambridge form, I think, a very decided call to me to give up the curacy idea altogether for the present, and to look resolutely at Cambridge as my sphere of work for some time to come. Perhaps I ought to add my Fellowship (as Maurice does) as a third call; but I don't feel that so strongly as he does. So heigho ! my doom is lectures and chapels and gyps, and for my new master's gown to get rusty-fusty by brushing against dons at the high table, instead of being scraped by rickety pulpits in the effort to speak the words of life to men, women, and

[1] *i.e.* to obtain a curacy at Hurstmonceux.

children.   Well! that too has its blessings and advantages, especially perhaps for me, though I am more impatient of it than most would be.

Macmillan wants to know whether you have heard anything from Bunsen about the MS. of Muratori's fragment on the Canon ; but I told him the Chevalier had not been at Lilleshall for ages.

. . . Bunsen wrote very kindly to send me an extract from a MS. of his father about the 'Star of the Messiah,' which he had mentioned in his last sermon and I had catechised him about ; and also to comment on my message about Lachmann.   My answer was a long and, I fear, not very temperate onslaught on the last-named personage.

To the Rev. John Ellerton

Umberslade Hall, Hockley Heath,
Birmingham, *February* 20*th*, 1853.

My dear Ellerton—Our letters have somehow become rather angelic in their frequency of late, so I will not delay longer to give you some account of this place and the rather peculiar life here. . . .

Maurice is going to preach sermons and make a book [1] on Unitarianism, from money left him some time ago by a lady. And he is hard at work on his Warburtonians and *History of Philosophy*.   I have seen two or three sheets of the latter, and much of the former.   In the latter he describes many of the Fathers—always well but still quite imperfectly.   I feel more and more that he is right in calling his books collections of hints.   But they seem to me every day more pregnant, even where one-sided.

To the Rev. Gerald Blunt

Umberslade, *March* 6*th*, 1853.

. . . I have only looked at *Visiting my Relations* enough to make me wish to read it, without caring much about it.   I

---

[1] See the advertisement to Maurice's *Theological Essays*, dated May 24, 1853.

have a dreadful suspicion from your words that you have been misled, like many others, by type, etc., into ascribing it to Helps ; but any one page ought to undeceive you.   It is by an old lady who lives at Newmarket.   I have just read *Esmond*, which you certainly should get hold of as soon as possible ; it is a right wise and noble book, though not one in a thousand will appreciate it.   I cannot forbear sending you a bit which I copied, as strangely echoing what I have so often felt and uttered to you.   Please send it back.   It reads artificial on paper, but it is true.   I hope you noticed a review in the *Guardian* (last but three) of the *Heir of Redclyffe*.   The extract given, a scene in Switzerland, makes me long to read the book.

TO MR. HENRY BRADSHAW

UMBERSLADE HALL, BIRMINGHAM, *March* 30*th*, 1853.

My dear Bradshaw—I have been intending to write to you nearly every day for the last two months ; but, as you know something of the multitude of my intentions, and the paucity of the accomplishments thereof, you will not be surprized that I have not written.   Gorham or Scott will doubtless have told you how it is that I have been absent from Cambridge ; so I will not repeat, but only add that I am getting on satisfactorily but slowly. . . . But I am far from dull here.   I have many more books with me than I can possibly read, and really do not find time to look at them much.   Going through the text of St. Paul's Epistles and dabbling in Oriental alphabets are almost my only work.   Baths and the disciplinal exercise before and after baths take up much of the day ; and so do billiards, battledore, and (in the evening) cards.   We have also abundance of music of all kinds, as one of the patients is Miss Stevens, the great singer, who is an exceedingly good performer, and is never tired of playing or of helping others to sing.   So that we often get up something like quartetts and choruses, and have learnt a good part of the ' Elijah ' after a fashion.

You   and   Gorham   (but   especially   Gorham)   are   never sufficiently to be anathematized for allowing our Cambridge music[1] to drop in that disgraceful manner. I cannot imagine what spirit of laziness and discord can have possessed you.

I did the pilgrimage to Stratford-on-Avon, but felt sadly unpoetic. However, it was a real pleasure to see Shakspere's tomb with one's own eyes, and though I wrote no verses about it, I trust I did at least as much homage as those who do. . . . I forgot to mention that Anglo-Saxon is one of my 'intentions,' and I expect every day the requisite books from Cambridge. I wish you would learn it too : every educated Englishman ought to know it. If you see Ellerton (supposing him to be alive, of which I have my doubts), please give him a dig in the ribs, and let it be a severe one; his own conscience will tell him the why. Write soon, like a good fellow, such as is not your affectionate friend,

FENTON J. A. HORT.

TO THE REV. JOHN ELLERTON

UMBERSLADE HALL, BIRMINGHAM, April 19th, 1853.

. . . Hydropathy has done me some good, but not much, and I am impatient to get to Cambridge from the expense and idleness of this place. I have not seen anybody that I know except Westcott, whom, being with his wife at his father's at Moseley, close to Birmingham, a fortnight ago, I visited for a few hours. One result of our talk I may as well tell you. He and I are going to edit a Greek text of the N. T. some two or three years hence, if possible. Lachmann and Tischendorf will supply rich materials, but not nearly enough ; and we hope to do a good deal with the Oriental versions. Our object is to supply clergymen generally, schools, etc., with a portable Gk. Test., which shall not be disfigured with Byzantine corruptions. But we *may* find the work too irksome.

[1] *i.e.* the Choral Club.

To Rev. B. F. Westcott

UMBERSLADE, *April* 19*th*, 1853.

. . . We have been having abundance of pleasant music here. Miss Stevens brought over the other day from Birmingham Rossini's 'Stabat Mater,' which I was very anxious to hear, being puzzled with the strong opinions expressed both for and against it. However, if I am right, the discrepance is easily explained : it seems to me to have a great deal of very fine music in it, but to be *utterly* unspiritual, and, as applied to these words, absolutely blasphemous. This morning we sang one of the least inappropriate movements, the *In-flammatus*, with the chorus *In die judicii*, immediately after having gone through the 'Mount of Olives,' and then we sang the Kyrie of Mozart's 'Twelfth Mass,' and you may imagine the dreadful earthiness it had between two such neighbours.

To the Rev. Gerald Blunt

CAMBRIDGE, *May* 25*th*, 1853.

. . . The journey to Cambridge would not have been unpleasant but for two malefactors who smoked weeds (in the strictest sense of the word) of genuine home growth. And when it got cold, I dared not shut the window for fear of being poisoned. Ultimately I entered Trinity as it was striking twelve, after a more delightful day than I have had for months, or am likely to have for many more. I lighted my fire, made tea, got in my easy-chair, and, as I looked at the backs of the critical books on my table, came with bitter decision to a conclusion the very opposite of that which was the 'Professor's' under similar circumstances. So you will see there is hope for me yet. I sought in vain for a book that would not be discordant : the Psalms would hardly do with one's tea, and ultimately I had recourse to *In Memoriam* as the best food I could find ; but still one wanted some moral marmalade to that bread of tears and water of affliction.

To the Rev. John Ellerton

CAMBRIDGE, *June 5th*, 1853.

. . . I am very glad you like Bradshaw; I have certainly taken a great fancy to him ; it is always a pleasure to be with him.

Perhaps I may go on with the Hulsean Essay—indeed, last night I analyzed a little Origen for it—but it is doubtful, as the labor will be very great, and perhaps not commensurate with the very moderate worth.   But at times I feel vehement bursts of anxiety to finish it, and say my say on divers points of history and of Christian Evidences, which I should shrink from putting in any other form.

Hare has just been made a royal preacher.   I hear his reception the other day at Hurstmonceux on his return with restored health was most delightful.   By the way, while I think of it, I should mention that, as a compliment, Peterbro' Deanery was offered to old Sedgwick, who refused it by return of post.

About Mat. Arnold . . . I know few finer and more ex- quisite things in modern objective (*i.e.* quasi-objective) poetry than Callicles' final song and some other parts of *Empedocles*. *Tristram and Iseult* I liked less at first ; but I read it to the three Blunts, who have all excellent taste, and they were enchanted with it, and I have come pretty nearly to their view of it.   I know nothing of *Preciosa*. *Margaret Fuller* is a wonderful book—too much so to talk of now ; it has, I hope, made me more charitable to America, and more thankful for elements of English life which we take as a matter of course like daily bread : it is as sad a search for freedom without obedience as the world has often seen.

To his Mother

CAMBRIDGE, *June 13th*, 1853.

. . . Cambridge is always very enjoyable at this time of the year ; and I have been wishing that you could see it now, to take away the hard and frosty recollections of it which you seem to have carried away from your last visit.   One is never tired of looking up or down the narrow aisle of tall limes at the back of Trinity, with the blue sky quivering through the delicate green young leaves at the top of the long, long arch, and the huge, cumbrous old horse-chestnuts with their white spikes (men in surplices climbing up green mountains, as somebody called them) seen between the trunks of the avenue. One of the appurtenances of a Fellowship is a key of the 'Roundabout' or Fellows' garden of Trinity, a badly kept place, consisting of a great roundish meadow with a gravel walk bordered with shrubs round it, and here and there straggling beds of flowers; it is a most delightful place for an after-dinner stroll in this colourless region, and we have been revelling in its lilacs, laburnums, and barberries, but they are fading now. Three or four weeks ago we had plenty of *Daphne Cneorum,* just as it used to be in the green garden at Leopardstown. By the way, I do not think I have told you of another privilege I now possess, which will make you laugh : I can walk across the turf about the College without being fined half-a-crown ! The College is nearly empty. I have no one on my staircase, and to-day we were but four at table in Hall. Fortunately one of these is Sedgwick, who has but lately been released from his duties at Norwich, and he keeps everybody alive.

To the Rev. Gerald Blunt

CAMBRIDGE, *June* 19*th*, 1853.

. . . Soon after I left you in London, I went with Babington to pay W. H. Stokes (of Caius) a visit in his newly-occupied living at Denver, just out of the fens twelve miles below Ely. You know he was one of our Ray fellows. We walked and drove to divers places in the neighbourhood, botanizing, anti-quarianizing, ecclesiologizing, etc. We were not far from the scene of the great floods of the winter (indeed there was a tolerable lake still), and the sight of what had been rich corn-fields utterly desolate and bedraggled with mud and rubbish, waste and useless for many months to come, made a stronger impression than I could at all have anticipated.

This has been the week of the 'Apostles'' dinner. On

Tuesday I went to London, and to a concert of the Musical
Union at Willis' Rooms, which was a treat indeed. The per-
formers were a M. Hiller, pianoforte; Vieuxtemps and Goffrie,
violins; Blagrove, viola; and Piatti, violoncello. We had first
an exquisite stringed quartet of Haydn's, full of sportive fairy
music; but then came *such* a trio of Beethoven's (piano,
violin, and violoncello). At the third or fourth bar one was
shivering through and through, yet that was nothing to what
came soon after. The second movement did indeed lift one
up, I don't know where. There were the vast disadvantages of
being alone without a soul that I knew in the room, of the
room itself being much too large for so small a body of sound
so subtly modulated, of my being rather far off, and of my
unfamiliarity with the music; but still there was a taste of
heaven about it, and one thought that after all, in moderation,
the angels with their harps may not be such a bore as they
sometimes appear,—at least, if they play Beethoven. Our third
piece was a very fine quartet of Mendelssohn's, which it was
hard to do justice to after its predecessor.

Next morning I got to early service (eight) at Lincoln's Inn,
waited for Maurice, and went to breakfast with him. He was
in excellent spirits, and I had a very delightful talk on many
subjects, which I prolonged by walking with him to Somerset
House. . . . At last we got to dinner (the 'Apostles''), but
it was rather a dull affair, our numbers being small, and our
best members wanting. Maurice had to preach at the opening of the church of some High Church friend; Thompson
was at Ely, being made a canon of (*i.e.* being 'bored,' as
somebody explained it); Stephen was ill; Monckton Milnes
was at the Queen's state ball; and Trench, Alford, Blakesley,
and others were away on different accounts.

Next morning I was up rather late, but was at the Exhibition soon after twelve by appointment to meet Ellerton, who
came up for the day. We went carefully over all the chief
rooms of the Exhibition, and saw it very well. I got to understand and appreciate the Pre-Raphaelite pictures much better
than on the former day, particularly the 'Proscribed Royalist'
and 'Claudio and Isabella,'[1] tho' I still object to the direc-

[1] By Holman Hunt.

tion of Isabella's eyes. Montague's 'Children, they have
nailed Him to a Cross,' also improved much on acquaintance.
Ellerton and I, after leaving the Exhibition, went into the
Green Park, and sat and talked there till it was time for him
to go, and then took a boat for London Bridge. I never
was at that London Bridge Station before, and I can't say
what a strange thrill it gave me (and I daresay will, more
or less, all my life) to see it and be in it. There is interest
enough in its being the gate from this dear confined island to
the mysterious world beyond seas ; but it was naturally linked
in my mind with several departures for the Continent, in which
I have had a deep interest. . . . Next morning at eight I returned hither. And now you have a full account of all my
doings, the rest of the time since I saw you having been spent
in doing nothing, except burrowing in the libraries among MSS.
The other day, in one of them, I came upon a monkish
couplet, which gave me a rough, savage sensation of pleasure
by stirring up a concentration of all one's antipathies into action
against itself. Here it is for your benefit—

> *Femina corpus, opes, animam, vim, lumina, vocem*
> *Polluit, annihilat, necat, eripit, orbat, acerbat.*

Could more atrocities be condensed into two lines ?
By degrees I am getting through my arrears of novels. I
have finished *Villette* and *Ruth*, both of which are most excellent, and make one proud of one's country. I know scarcely
any book equal to *Ruth* in holiness and tenderness. Truly,
we parsons have no monopoly of preaching the Gospel nowadays. *Cyrilla* I have heard abused on good authority, but
the four chapters which I have hitherto read are delightful,
and quite equal to *The Initials*.[1]

To his Mother

CAMBRIDGE, *July 6th*, 1853.

. . . I doubt whether I have mentioned an employment which
I have undertaken, which is, along with two or three others [2]

---

[1] By Baroness Tautphœus.

[2] The most active of these was C. B. Scott.

(who happen to be friends of my own), to examine minutely and form a *catalogue raisonnée* of the theological Manuscripts in the University Library. At first I began *en amateur*, but am now formally placed on the committee by the Pitt Press Syndicate, with power of taking out MSS. It is slow and laborious work, but often very interesting; and one picks up indirectly a good deal of knowledge which may be of great use hereafter, and would be almost impossible to acquire in any other way.

TO THE REV. GERALD BLUNT

CAMBRIDGE, July 14th, ⎱ 1853.
BRIGHTON, July 23rd, ⎰

. . . Degree time was very pleasant from the number of old faces and hands, though the last gathering of an University 'year' for the lifetimes of most of its members is rather a gloomy occasion. Unluckily —— asked me to look over the proofs of his Latin Essay, which he had to recite in the Senate House; and, as it abounded in atrocious blunders from first to last, it took me from twenty to thirty hours. —— came to my rooms several times and talked very pleasantly, and still more so when we strolled out in the warm evening and wound in and out among the flowers and green turf of the Trinity Roundabout. He seemed overflowing with quiet happiness, and it did one good to see him.

Three or four weeks ago I, after divers refusals, accepted an invitation from Jessopp[1] to visit him and his wife at Papworth St. Agnes, not far from St. Ives, from Saturday to Monday. I went, and stayed till Tuesday, and have not often had three pleasanter days. On the Tuesday they drove me over to Cambridge, as Jessopp wished to join me a little in collating MS. in our Library; so we spent the afternoon collating, while Mrs. Jessopp looked out references in St. Gregory in another part of the Library, and then we went to dinner in my rooms; but lo and behold! my bedmaker was not aware of my arrival, and had not appeared; so there was the dinner waiting and no preparation made for it! Luckily we found in

[1] Now the Rev. Augustus Jessopp, D.D.

my cupboard a tablecloth, some bread, four knives, and some teaspoons. So I lighted a fire to warm the plates, and then rushed off to the nearest friend's rooms in quest of forks, spoons, and, above all, salt. I arrived first at ———'s, and burst in upon him as he was sitting over his wine with a prim Oxford Fellow of Magdalen. However, there was no help for it but to explain my strange mission, and I bore off in triumph the needful plate and salt wrapped up in scribbling paper. At length we got to dinner ; it was a scrambling affair, a kind of domestic picnic, but far from unpleasant, as both my guests entered fully into the fun of the thing, and made themselves useful in divers ways.

A large proportion of our year seemed to have taken unto themselves wives and babies, though they seemed shy of bringing them up for 'the year' to see. So that I felt more than ever like what Sedgwick gave the other day as the definition of a Fellow to a French guest of his, who had supposed us to be '*élèves* — in fact, a kind of *professeurs*,' — namely, 'a Protestant monk,' a *frère*, and no more. However, there was hope in our good vice-master's further explanation that we differed from French monks in being allowed to marry. "What ! can your Féloes marry ? " "Oh yes ! exceedingly," shouted old Sedgwick, in great excitement, adding soon after with equal energy, "A man's thought a most wretched fellow, if he doesn't marry when he leaves us ! " You may imagine my amusement at the whole scene ; but the dear old ' Féloe ' evidently spoke feelingly.

I got a line from Maurice saying that he had just been at Hurstmonceux, where Hare asked him if he could recommend a curate. Maurice mentioned me "as at least possible," and Hare "was evidently much pleased," and "begged him to make me the offer," "which," says Maurice, " I do accordingly." "If," he proceeds, "you have made up your mind to stay at Cambridge, I shall think you are doing very right ; but, if you wish for a curacy, Hurstmonceux has certainly many recommendations," etc. etc. I wrote by return of post how much I was tempted by the offer, but gave the substance of my letter to you ; but said I still thought it my duty to stay at Cambridge, unless I had some decided call to leave it, and I could not consider such an offer as such, however alluring.

..⁋ I had to lionise and help a pleasant young German, Dr. Osiander, who came accredited by Maurice and Bunsen, being sent over by the German Orientalists to see the contents of the Arabic MSS. in England.   I took him to Power, and got him access to the valuable Arabic MSS. of the University Library, where he found much of interest, and talked of coming again.

I am glad you enjoy *Ruth.*   I understand, and perhaps partly agree with, your objection, which I have heard before. The best answer to it, I think, is,—that Mrs. Gaskell does not mean to say that Ruth did not know she was sinning.   You must remember that, when she entered the carriage, she thought she was going to be driven *home*, and Mrs. Gaskell's delicacy has, perhaps not wisely, allowed us to see nothing whatever of her till two months later, in Wales.   That Ruth's conscience had not been silent is, I think, clearly implied in many of her subsequent thoughts and sayings.   My own feeling is that no sin can be so great but that circumstances may reduce the guilt to a very small remnant, and no sin so small that any amount of circumstances can altogether take away its guilt. Now Mrs. Gaskell's object primarily was to show how the fall of a creature like Ruth could take place easily and naturally without any great previous moral depravation, and how many natural and harmless circumstances tend in such cases to diminish the guilt.   Perhaps it is better as it is ; but my com-plaint would rather be that she has not put her case strongly enough.   That *any* so tempted should ever keep from falling is to me one of the most stupendous of miracles : I wonder how many of us men could so stand.

To the Rev. G. M. Gorham

Hardwick, Chepstow, *September* 17*th*, 1853.

. . . I hope that meanwhile you have been getting on swimmingly with the Hulsean.   I should have been glad to have been of any service to you, but really I have known but little (and fear I have mostly forgotten that) beyond the chronology of some four or five select Bishops of Rome, or rather some points in their chronology, for I have never worked even that out to completion. With the first two or three Bishops of Rome (and their relation to St. Peter) and the history of the other sees I have hardly meddled at all, though hoping to study them well some day or other. But the subject is far more extensive than it looks at first sight. The best book, I imagine, is Rothe's *Anfänge der Christlichen Kirche*, which has not been translated; and Ritschl and Bunsen (not *Hippolytus*, but *Ignatius von Antiochien und seine Zeit*), not to mention others, should be consulted, though of course not to the exclusion of others, such as Pearson, Dodwell, Pagi, etc. But, after all, the whole labour may be superfluous, for the last book that I read before leaving Cambridge, Mr. Shepherd's so-called *History of Rome* (which seems to be written to show that it has no history, as Daillé wrote *On the Use of the Fathers*, to show that they were of no use), left two serious doubts sticking in my mind—(1) whether Rome ever existed, and (2) whether there were ever any Bishops of Rome. The second doubt must be left for future considera-tion ; the first I am inclined to embrace at once, as it would save one a world of troubles and annoyances of all kinds, and Dr. Cumming's occupation would at once be gone. However, I suppose the 'vested interests' will prevent that desirable consummation from being accepted as credible.

To his Mother

CAMBRIDGE, *October 24th*, 1853.

. . . I spent yesterday at Harrow with my friend Westcott, and came back this afternoon, or rather evening, after a very pleasant visit. I was very glad of the opportunity of seeing Harrow, the new Rugby. No one can doubt its excellencies, but it rather disappointed me, and is certainly in some respects unequal to Rugby. In the morning Rendall[1] preached a most excellent sermon in the School Chapel. . . . He came

---

[1] The Rev. F. Rendall, Hort's first classical tutor at Cambridge.

in in the evening to see me, and talked with much kindness
and interest.   In the afternoon Dr. Vaughan preached, and
pleased me much.   After chapel we walked up to see the
noble church, which, as I daresay you know, is beautifully
placed on the top of a hill rising abruptly on all sides but
one from the great plain of London, and the view is so extensive that I could see the Crystal Palace at Sydenham across
London on one side, and Windsor Castle on the other, though
it was not a very clear day.   Between services we took a stroll
with Bradby,[1] an old Rugby friend of mine, a late scholar of
Balliol, who has likewise become a master of Harrow; and
talking to him at Harrow seemed really to recall Rugby days.

To the Rev. John Ellerton

CAMBRIDGE, *October* 31st, 1853.

. . . I must write you a line to tell you, if you do not know
it already, that Maurice was expelled from King's College by
a vote of the Council on Thursday last   They met a fortnight
earlier, when the correspondence between him and Jelf, which
has been going on all the Long, was placed printed in the
hands of the members to digest.   Gladstone and Anderson,
who were unavoidably absent Thursday last, wrote to the
Council earnestly pressing them to delay, but in vain : Jelf
would not allow him even to lecture on English literature the
next day.   He was condemned exclusively on the last Essay,
Jelf's charges being—(1) that he " threw a cloudiness about the
meaning of the word 'eternal'"; and (2) that he seemed to
tend towards the belief that the wicked might perhaps find
mercy at last,—or words to that effect.   All the correspondence
is printed, but I have seen only Maurice's last letter to Jelf;
the whole will be published in a few days.   That letter is
crushing.   I fear he loses £500 a year at one swoop, which
he can ill afford, but it remains to be seen whether any one
will have the courage to give him a living or institute him.
He has no idea whether the Bishop of London will take any
further step against him *in propria persona.*   My own feeling

---

[1] The late Rev. E. H. Bradby, D.D.

is that a considerable number of High Churchmen will support him. On the first head he only repeats Plato's doctrine, which Augustine lays down in the most emphatic terms in the *Confessions;* on the second he goes no further than is implied in prayers for the dead.

To the Rev. Gerald Blunt

CAMBRIDGE, *November 4th,* 1853.

. . . First of all I must give you some details of the sad event which is haunting my mind incessantly. All the Long Maurice and Jelf have been having a correspondence about the former's Essay on Eternal Life and Death. When it had reached a certain point, crowned with Jelf's final charge, they agreed that the whole should be printed, as containing all that Jelf had to say against him. Maurice in like manner was to write and print a final answer. These two documents were placed in the hands of the King's College Council, at their first meeting for the term yesterday three weeks, at which meeting great altercation is said to have passed between his friends and opponents. They took a fortnight to read and digest, and yesterday week met again. Having heard that they considered his tone to Jelf disrespectful, he appeared before the meeting to say that in this matter he stood to Jelf not in the relation of inferior to superior, but of accused to accuser. Jelf made some euphuistic reply, and Maurice retired. The result of the meeting was a vote for Maurice's expulsion from both his Professorships. What the majority was is not known. A statement in the papers that Gladstone was the only dissentient is pure fiction, proceeding from a violent letter in the *Morning Herald,* in which this statement was made rather doubtfully, as a belief. Both Gladstone and James Anderson were unable to be present, and both wrote strong letters, intended to be shown to the Council, most strongly protesting against unseemly haste in so solemn a matter, and urging them on no account to come to a vote that afternoon ; but their exhortations were vain. On the receipt of the minutes of the Council, Maurice wrote to the secretary to ask whether the Council wished him to continue at his post till a successor should be appointed ; Jelf sent back a message that he would never be allowed to deliver another lecture in King's College. And so the matter stands. Jelf's publication, *i.e.* the correspondence with later footnotes, if not out already in London, will probably be out to-morrow ; Maurice's publication, *i.e.* his final letter to Jelf, also with a few notes and an explanatory preface, will be out soon after. You shall have them as soon as they are both out. I have seen the original of the latter, which is a masterpiece of calm, clear, controversial writing ; it will be an historical document to future Church historians. . . . I hear that Maurice included in his first letter to Jelf (which is, of course, printed) a verbatim copy of the greater part of his letter[1] to me. Indeed, his whole defence seems to have been an expansion of that letter, with an indignant repudiation of Universalism, although that is just the charge for which most people suppose he has been condemned. I ought to add that Jelf (and, I believe, the Council) urged Maurice to resign quietly, but he positively refused, denying that a professor at King's College could be subjected to any test of orthodoxy beyond the Creeds, Prayer-book, and Articles, all of which he cheerfully accepted. Maurice desires every one to know, therefore, that it was an *expulsion.* The first public intimation of the fact was a paragraph in the *Morning Herald*, stating that unbounded indignation at the dismissal prevailed in King's College and elsewhere. Next day appeared the letter I have mentioned, protesting against the paragraph. There was also a pretty good article in the *Chronicle* on Maurice's behalf, but written in ignorance that the vote was already past. . . . The *Record* you will doubtless have seen, as also its extracts from the *Morning Advertiser*. I send you the *Guardian*, which writes under a misapprehension of facts, but is very kind and generous ; pray note also O. P.'s extravagant but noble letter. The *English Churchman*, misapprehending the real charge, expresses kind regret at a result which they approve, but awaits the publication of documents. These are all the public notices I know of. A letter from Sir J. Stephen to Macmillan says it

[1] See pp. 116-123.

has caused no small stir in London. Here Hardwick and Harvey Goodwin seem to give a kind of neutral adhesion to Maurice. My own feeling is that a large proportion of High Churchmen will stand by him : I am sure they will mainly agree with him. If they speak out, an immense good will indeed arise out of this present evil, and we shall have one more proof how the antient Catholic faith is the only one really capable of meeting the wants of the age. Meanwhile it is a time of great anxiety for us all. The feeling seems general, that the matter will have to be tried before the Bishop of London as Bishop of London, and ultimately before the higher courts, and God only knows what the end will be. . . . General indifference seems to prevail here, though divers individuals are deeply interested. Plans of testimonials, etc., have been talked of, but will, I hope and think, come to nothing : unless they carried the weight of names of known and established orthodoxy, they would be worse than useless ; but I think every one who is grateful to Maurice ought to send him a line of sympathy privately. Kingsbury, whom I regard as by far Maurice's ablest and most intelligent theological disciple, has, I rejoice to say, written most warmly and energetically.

Now for your letters. I rejoice to hear of the pony : it will be the thing of things for you. Something physical of the kind is excellent to let off one's steam. Football is good, and fighting, and dancing (such as, I hope, the Church of the Future will see and foster) ; but under existing circumstances a gallop across country must be not a bad substitute, and, in spite of my own incapacity, I quite enter into Kingsley's praise of the moral worth of hunting.

I am bound to say that I never met with a purer and holier mind than Novalis'. He is always fundamentally reverent in treating of mysteries, but he is fond of mysteries, and of comparing one with another, and that the English mind habitually is not. He is certainly no atheist, but a warm Lutheran, with perhaps a faint Romeward hankering ; but, like every great mystic, has a considerable infusion of what, if carried out, would amount to Pantheism ; and being a German, a philosopher, and a poet, he is especially open to that temptation.

. . . I suspect you are too anxious to find 'plain' enough texts. I don't know any really plain *subjects* in the Bible : the plainness should lie in the treatment. I can't now discuss Maurice's doctrine about the Resurrection, etc. Much seems to me good. . . . Carlyle's *Cromwell* is certainly not such pleasant reading as his *Sterling*, but is still very valuable and interesting ; remember that it is not a biography but a series of documents, 'with elucidations.' *My Novel* I have not yet read.

I have undertaken to edit poor Henry Mackenzie's Hulsean Essay (who died at last some three weeks ago) for his mother, and she wants it to be out by Christmas, if possible. I went down and spent a Sunday with Westcott at Harrow very pleasantly, and saw divers old friends. We came to a distinct and positive understanding about our Gk. Test. and the details thereof. We still do not wish it to be talked about, but are going to work at once, and hope we may perhaps have it out in little more than a year. This, of course, gives me good employment. I have likewise University MSS. work, Trinity Library MS. work, ordination work, Apologists work, and general reading, so am tolerably occupied.

Love to your wife and to the thing with the dear little hands.—From your ever affectionate friend,

FENTON J. A. HORT.

To his Mother

CAMBRIDGE, *November 8th*, 1853.

. . . Your query about the Moral Sciences Examinership I partly answered last week. It will certainly take some reading, though not, I hope, an exorbitant amount, the subjects I shall chiefly have to look up being Political Economy and General Jurisprudence. But my present plan (in which I am much encouraged by the friends here whom I have consulted) is—(1) not to confine myself to the special books or divisions embraced in the Professor's lectures, but to take my questions from the subjects at large, with a preference for such as bring out principles of general application ; and (2) to try, according to the original idea of the Tripos, to bind the five sciences together by asking questions which bear on the mutual connexion of the sciences, and the joint application of them to practice in actual history. This will be an innovation upon the doings—I cannot speak of a *custom*, where there have been but three examinations—of my two predecessors, who have contented themselves with cramming into one paper questions on the special subjects of five sciences, similar and supplementary to those of the Professors. But I feel sure that the change will be generally approved. I was somewhat amazed and amused two days ago to be told that I had just been elected a member of the Council of the Philosophical Society. Fortunately the inspection of papers is rather of a routine kind, for otherwise there would be something ludicrous indeed in my sitting in judgement on Augustus de Morgan's mathematical disquisitions, which form a large proportion of our papers.

To the Rev. John Ellerton

CAMBRIDGE, *December* 11th, 1853.

. . . I hope you got the pamphlets about dear Maurice's sad affair. It is too long to talk much about now ; but you will be glad to hear that at the second meeting (at which the vote of censure was passed) Gladstone, who moved an amendment, was not the only opponent of Jelf; indeed, at the first or preliminary meeting there was great fighting, but between whom, I have not heard. At the third meeting the Bishop of Lichfield and Milman formally protested against the rejection of Maurice's protest and appeal. Others (*e.g.* Judge Patteson) were also on his side, but how far, I know not. Edition 2nd, greatly altered, is just coming out ; he will publish the new preface and last Essay separately. The former I have seen, and it is a most beautiful, dignified, gentle piece of writing.

Last week I wrote to S. Oxon, asking his leave to be ordained in Lent, and I have had a very kind letter of consent.

To the Rev. B. F. Westcott

HARDWICK, CHEPSTOW, *December* 31*st*, 1853;
January 3*rd*, 1854.

. . . You will doubtless have been following with interest the incidents of Maurice's expulsion from King's College, which took place just after I left you.

. . . I have been astonished at the small number of even thoughtful men at Cambridge who were able to recognise the distinction between time and eternity. The prevalent idea seemed to be that, right or wrong, Maurice had invented it to meet a particular case. No one seemed to enter into the impossibility of a theology, or of the existence of a spiritual world, without it. Thompson was the only one I met who knew that it was to be found in Plato. I do not know what you will say to an address which is being circulated; you shall have a copy when I get some more; Thompson says that Dr. Vaughan is going to sign it.

What a sad loss dear old Mill's death is. I was looking at his hair, with less of gray in it than my own, last term, and thinking how long we were likely to have his services, and how much we should need them.

. . . I believe it is since my very pleasant visit to Harrow that Whewell asked me to take the additional examinership of the Moral Science Tripos, which involves a good deal of reading and other trouble; but I am not sorry to have an opportunity of doing something to widen and deepen the Cambridge study of the subjects. Scott also induced me to take the Le Bas Examinership. . . .

There has been however, in one way or another, quite enough to take up my time and prevent me from making much progress with the Greek New Testament. But what I have done has been pretty efficiently done.

. . . I forgot to tell you I saw a tempting bramble on Harrow Hill, thought I would cut it, thought I hadn't time, went on, came back, caught a vehicle, got a lift, and so was in time.

TO THE REV. JOHN ELLERTON

HARDWICK, *January* 20*th*, 1854.

. . . I believe in writing to you last time I passed over your queries about my fears respecting Convocation. I have not time now to explain myself fully, but I must say a word or two. It seems to me that many who clamour for Convocation speak of that as the Church's rightful government, and as if she had no government now. Now this seems to me a direct denial of the apostolical constitution and polity, of which Convocation forms no part. Practically our bishops may, through inability, cowardice, overwork, etc. etc., have ceased for the most part to govern; but they are there, and their functions are there, and may be revived. They, and subordinate officers deriving authority from them, have alone paramount authority in the Catholic Church. The authority of a representative and democratic assembly, derived from the wills of individual members and not from Christ's ordination, is anarchic except so far as it is subordinate to that of the successors of the Apostles. Moreover, in the early Church synods were assembled at particular periods, whether rare or frequent; they never formed a regular standing part of the Church's constitution. This I do not urge as a reason why they should not practically become such now; there are many reasons why they should. I only protest against their interfering with the apostolic rule. Many High Churchmen seem dangerously disposed to think of bishops merely as 'channels of grace,' not as rulers, and to exalt the presbyterate against them; and of this I have a great dread. About the mode of election I have not thought much; but of course, whoever might be the electing power, the commission would be equally apostolic. Guizot however seems to have confused them grievously in his *European Civilisation*. Edward Strachey's book I have not yet seen, but want to see.

I am getting on with my paper for the Moral Sciences Tripos, which gives me a good deal of trouble; ordination also takes up my time. I am working through Pearson *on the Creed* for the first time, and am much struck with its clear, sound logic and the marvellous scholarship of the notes. When this is done (besides Bible and Gk. Test.), Hooker's fifth book, Augustin *de Doctrina Christiana*, Butler's *Sermons*, and Burton and Blunt await me; so that S. O.[1] gives his candidates quite enough to do. Indeed his Christmas papers included Mediæval Church History, which is rather too bad.

One book I have lately read with the most thorough delight, the *Heir of Redclyffe;* I don't think anything has so stirred me since I read *Yeast* in *Fraser.* Yet the contrast is most singular. It is a most convincing sign of the thorough depth and geniality of the Catholic movement in England; its main deficiency (if so it may be called) is the absolute ignoring of all the perplexing questions in theology and morals which are now being stirred,—in short, it is bread without yeast. But the perfectly Christian and noble *Theodicée,*—the true poetical justice,—is beyond all praise.

I am very anxious to hear what you think of dear Maurice's sad business. In spite of all the pain and anxiety of it, one cannot but rejoice at his giving sceptical literary men so bright an example of clerical honesty and boldness. I cannot talk much about the matter now, but you will like to hear some of the details. At the first meeting of the Council after the vacation an angry altercation took place. Copies of Jelf's and Maurice's pamphlets were then given or sent to all the members. At the next meeting (a fortnight later) some rabid member proposed a vote of instant expulsion; the Bishop of London thought this violent, and proposed a gentler string of resolutions (those afterwards carried). Gladstone strongly dissented, urged the utter incompetence of such a tribunal to try so delicate and mysterious a point of theology, and moved an amendment that the matter be left in the Bishop of London's hands, to be by him referred to a committee of theologians nominated by him, who should report to the Council. The Bishop readily acceded to this amendment, and so did most of the Council, but Lords Howe, Harrowby, Cholmondeley, and Radstock made such a violent outcry, protesting against betraying the Gospel of Christ, that Gladstone in disgust withdrew his amendment,—the Bishop's

[1] *i.e.* S. Oxon.

resolutions were carried without a division. The forbidding Maurice to lecture was Jelf's own act. At the next meeting was read Maurice's letter (which you must have seen in the *Guardian*), asking the Council to interpret their own resolutions, and demanding to know what formulary he had contradicted, and by what words of his own. This was refused ; on which the Bishop of Lichfield, Milman, and James Anderson handed in formal protests against the proceedings : Justice Patteson, Sir B. Brodie, and Green the surgeon (Coleridge's philosophical executor), if not others, also voted against the refusal. I am glad that Maurice has kept his temper so admirably in the preface to the 2nd edition. You may perhaps be interested in a passage of St. Clement, bearing on the question, which I found some weeks ago and translated literally ; so I send it, but should like to have it back again. You will see that the whole passage is in exposition of the common patristic but wrong interpreta- tion of St. Peter's words about Christ's preaching to the spirits in prison, but the possibility of a *locus pœnitentiæ* after death is clearly assumed throughout. You will doubtless have been grieving over dear old Professor Mill's sad and unexpected death. We never wanted him more. Of late he has been rather better appreciated ; but he was indeed as a prophet in his own country, and will be more honoured a century hence than now.

I forgot to mention (what perhaps you know already) that a rather mild address to Maurice is being got up by Hare, Thompson, etc. My copy is abroad at present, but you shall see it when I get it back. Davies [1] (St. Mark's Parsonage, Whitechapel) receives signatures, viz. of clergymen and graduates.

To his Mother

CAMBRIDGE, *February* 13*th*, 1854.

My dearest Mother—The worry of the Moral Sciences Tripos is at last over, and thoroughly glad I am of it. You have, I hope, long ago received the paper itself, which I sent off on Thursday as soon as it was set. I gave them

---

[1] The Rev. J. Llewelyn Davies.

five and a half hours to do it in, and when that period of hard work for them was over, mine began. I had undertaken to Whewell to have the answers all looked over and marked, and the marks added up by eleven on Saturday morning, and I kept my word; but it was a close run, and I had to use the greatest exertions. . . .

The government of the University Library has just been reformed, and the Vice-Chancellor has nominated me among the sixteen who form the first Syndicate under the new régime. We began our work to-day, and there seems every prospect of our getting on well.

To THE REV. B. F. WESTCOTT

CAMBRIDGE, *February* 23*rd*, 1854.

. . . I am now deep in St. Augustin's *De Doctrina Christiana* for ordination, and am greatly delighted with its beauty and wisdom, on the whole. It is certainly to the Bishop's (or Trench's?[1]) credit to set such a book before candidates. By this day fortnight I shall probably be at Cuddesdon, and the ordination is on the following Sunday. I am sure you will remember me on that day.

To HIS MOTHER

CUDDESDON PALACE, *March* 9*th*, 1854.

My dearest Mother—Before going to bed, I want to scribble you a line to say that I have arrived here safely, and have had one day of the examination. I reached Oxford yesterday a little after four alone, Gorham being detained a day or two in town by urgent business. As soon as I had tidied myself a little, I called on Pinder[2] in Trinity, but he was already in hall. A search for John Ormerod was more successful, and I dined with him in Brasenose. Late in the evening Gorham arrived. At a quarter past nine this morning we started in a fly, and reached this place

[1] Examining chaplain to the Bishop of Oxford.
[2] Now the Rev. North Pinder.

about ten. The servants showed us to our rooms, but before long we assembled (nineteen in number) in a sort of hall-room. The bell soon rang, and we made our way to the Bishop's beautiful little chapel. Presently the Bishop arrived with his two chaplains, Trench and Randall, and Pott,[1] who all took part in the service, but it was performed as quietly as possible. The lessons were Lev. viii. and Luke vi. 1-19. The second was read by the Bishop, who thereupon delivered a short but most beautiful and every way excellent address. Soon after chapel we had a short piece of Hooker to turn into Latin for half an hour, and then two hours nominally on the New Testament, but including various things. I began in the middle, and did not find time to attempt many questions, as I wrote rather carefully. Next followed a bread-and-cheese lunch, and then half an hour for air and exercise. They might have allowed us more, for after our return we had to kick our heels forty minutes. Then we had two hours for a sermon on 1 Cor. x. 13. Then chapel again (at about half-past six), the lessons being Lev. xxi. and 1 John ii., with another address from the Bishop. Then a few minutes to dress, followed by dinner. The Bishop made me sit by his side, which I found a very agreeable post. After sitting a short time, coffee was brought in, and then the Bishop rang the bell, went to the door and shook every one by the hand and said good-night as he went out, and we were dismissed to our rooms. Mine is a very excellent and comfortable one, with a blazing fire. And so ends a very pleasant, but exceedingly fatiguing day. My expectations were so high that it would have been strange indeed if they had been surpassed, but I have certainly not been disappointed.

Good-night to you all.—Ever your affectionate son,

FENTON J. A. HORT.

TO HIS MOTHER

CUDDESDON PALACE, *March 11th*, 1854.

. . . The Bishop had a talk with me this morning, and told me that I had done very well indeed (especially in the

---

[1] The Vicar of Cuddesdon.

doctrinal paper) in all but the Old Testament History, in which my answers, though above the average, were not so good as he should have expected from my other papers. These have been three very pleasant days. The Bishop is kindness and goodness itself, and his chaplains both pleasant in their several ways. I wish you could have heard his morning and evening comments on the special lessons in chapel. I do not know any one who would have enjoyed them more.

To his Mother

' Oxford, March 12th, 1854.

My dearest Mother—I am sure you will like to receive a line from me written before this awful day has quite gone by, although it be no more than a line ; and indeed I do not feel disposed to write more. My thoughts about the event (even if I knew how to express them to myself, which I do not) are as nothing to the event itself. All took place as could have been wished, and there were no unpleasant accessions to disturb and vex one's thoughts. The Bishop of Grahamstown preached the sermon—very good but rather dry. He also read the Epistle. I had to read the Gospel, which I managed pretty well, though at first it was difficult to see the letters. I was not sorry at the Communion to receive the bread from Bishop Armstrong. He shook hands with me most affectionately both before and after the service. In the afternoon I heard the Bishop of Oxford preach before the University at St. Mary's ; the sermon was mainly practical, and addressed to the undergraduates, but (not to speak of its astonishing power and eloquence) it would not be easy to imagine a more valuable or appropriate conclusion to the services of the morning. At half-past six Bishop Armstrong was to preach again before the University, but we had had enough. At five we went to Christ Church to receive our Letters of Orders, and the Bishop of Oxford again twice said good-bye to me with especial cordiality.

Gorham and I have been fortunate in getting these quarters. Butler[1] has been most kind and pleasant, and his wife

---

[1] George Butler, eldest son of the then Dean of Peterborough.

thoroughly delightful. In the evening two or three pleasant friends of his came in,—among them William Thomson, the author of the *Bampton Lectures* that you were reading.

Now good-night, and God bless you all.—Believe me, ever your affectionate son,   FENTON J. A. HORT.

The first part of the following letter gives an account of the ordination almost identical with that sent to his mother ; a third detailed account was sent to Mr. G. Blunt.

TO THE REV. JOHN ELLERTON

CAMBRIDGE, *March 19th and April 2nd*, 1854.

. . . . Gorham and I made acquaintance with George Butler, and he very kindly offered us beds at his lodgings, which of course we were only too glad to accept. Pleasanter quarters we could not have had. I ought to have mentioned that, as the Bishop likes taking his candidates to different towns to familiarize the people with ordination, we should probably have gone to Reading, or some such place, had not the Bishop been obliged to preach before the University in the afternoon, and therefore tied to Oxford, which I did not at all regret. A little before 9 A.M. we met at the church-warden's house. To my great delight Bishop Armstrong was outside, and greeted me very warmly. We (the candidates) then walked in procession in our surplices and hoods to St. Peter's Church, the oldest in Oxford ; it was dreadfully mauled in Perpendicular times, but retains much glorious Norman work, especially in the chancel. There was an air of life and reality about the whole church, congregation, and service which was very invigorating and enjoyable. The whole service was musical (as you will have seen by the *Guardian*), and that for the first time, I believe (in an ordina-tion), for centuries. The rector intoned the prayers very well. The choir consisted of the Plainsong and another musical society of the University ; but the singing was tolerably congregational. The chanting was all Gregorian. Arm-

strong's sermon was in many respects good. The Bishop's
chair was then placed in the entrance of the altar rails, and
he very solemnly and pointedly addressed the congregation as
appointed. When we came to the Litany, he turned round
to the East, kneeling at his chair ; and Archdeacon Clark and
Randall (Trench was gone back to Itchenstoke) knelt at the
rails on one side and the rector and chief curate on the other,
and all five at once intoned or almost sung the petitions of
the Litany, the Bishop leading magnificently, and the choir
and congregation sang the responses. The effect was
perfectly wonderful,—far beyond what I could have supposed.
I had to read the Gospel. A great many of the congregation
stayed for the Communion, which was very solemn and congenial. . . . At a little after one the great service was finished.
Gorham and I dined quietly with the Butlers. In the
evening W. Thomson of Queen's, James of Queen's, and Max
Müller (the great Sanskrit scholar) came in, and we had some
pleasant talk. When they were gone, Gorham asked for some
music. Mrs. Butler had there no 'sacred' music, so called ;
but she played Beethoven's divine second sonata, and so
appropriately ended the day. Next morning Conington came
to breakfast, and we had a good talk about our *Journal of
Philology*. After breakfast we strolled round the Bodleian.
I have not time to talk about Cuddesdon, the Bishop, etc.,
but can only say that I came to love and value him very
highly indeed ; it is not easy at a distance altogether to
appreciate his temptations and his character. His arrangements were most admirable ; from the time I reached
Cuddesdon on Thursday till I said good-bye, when I went for
my Letters of Orders at Christ's Church on Sunday afternoon,
there was nothing whatever to meet one's eye or ear that was
not harmonious with the occasion. Oxford too I enjoyed
much, and wished for a longer stay.

I am delighted to hear you speak so of the Government ;
I doubt whether there has been such a one since Elizabeth's
time. . . . But, in praising the Government, one must not
forget the misdeeds of single members. . . . It is very
delightful to find England in so noble a moral position as the
publication of the secret correspondence gives her. And

what a blessed thing this French alliance is ! what prospects it seems to open for the world and the Church ! Surely it must do more for France than centuries of *entente cordiale* and Louis Philippisme ; Frenchmen will hardly know themselves in the doubly new position of fighting along with England, and in defence of the right. But it is fearful to read the wild exultation with which some of the papers (representing but too faithfully, I fear, the minds of their readers) are looking forward to the war. I have a sad foreboding that—over and above the cruel carnage which must inevitably touch every corner of the land—we shall be visited by some fearful national calamity, for, alas ! we need it.

I must not speak at any length about Maurice's business. I agree with you in thinking it a pity that Maurice verbally repudiates purgatory, but I fully and unwaveringly agree with him in the three cardinal points of the controversy : (1) that eternity is independent of duration ; (2) that the power of repentance is not limited to this life ; (3) that it is not revealed whether or not all will ultimately repent. The modern denial of the second has, I suppose, had more to do with the despiritualizing of theology than almost any[thing] that could be named. How contrary it is to the spirit of the Fathers of *all* schools may be seen from the notes to Pearson on the Descent into Hell. The cool *a priori* paragraph (beginning, "Again, as the authority"), in which he flings antiquity boldly aside, because it clashes with the modern dogma, is well worthy of remark. . . .

Great changes are taking place here. The University Library is already half reformed, and the Pitt Press will soon have much greater changes. Unluckily they propose most dangerous schemes for future degrees, Theological Tripos, etc. etc., which we shall have to vote on next term ; and I am not sure that I shall not perpetrate a pamphlet. We are getting up a society for Church music, and hope to get Helmore to start it ; luckily we have Harvey Goodwin, but some furious High Church undergrads give much trouble. How pleasant to think of Lord Aberdeen offering dear old Blunt the Bishoprick !

If you come across Charles Reade's *Peg Woffington*, read

it; it is obviously sprung from Thackeray's influence. Robert Curzon's *Armenia* is of course delightful, but it ought to be more so, and more of it.

TO THE REV. GERALD BLUNT

HARDWICK, *April 11th and 14th,* 1854.

. . . On Saturday the new complications of railways made my train so late at Shoreditch that I could not get to Paddington in time for the express ; but ——[1] of King's, being in the same predicament, said that he meant under the circumstances to go by the short train to Eton (where he is now a master) for the two nights, and urged me to do the same, offering me a bed, which I accepted, and was quite repaid.   Eton is truly a great place, and it is no wonder that Eton men are so extravagantly proud of it.   I am sure I should be the same, if I had been brought up there, though I would not take it in exchange for Arnold and homespun Rugby.   On Sunday morning we went up to Windsor Castle, and attended service in St. George's Chapel.   I was glad to attend service there at the beginning of the war.   In the afternoon we had a congenial service at Eton Chapel, a noble building in spite of its second-rate architecture.   After service we strolled through the beautiful bright green meadows by the Thames, making a circuit to the Castle, where we enjoyed the air and the glorious view from the terrace for some time. . . .

I have not heard of the address to Maurice being yet presented.   He is very busy at a ' People's College' which he is trying to establish, and on behalf of which he is going to deliver public lectures in London.   He also talks of answering Dr. Candlish's Exeter Hall attack, when it is published. Kingsley is publishing the lectures on Alexandrine Philosophy which he delivered at Edinbro ; I wonder they are not out yet. . . .

It is an age since I have heard anything about your wife or my dear little godchild ; do tell me all about them.   Can the latter walk, speak, or do anything human ?   Even teeth

[1] Name indistinct ; probably [W.] Wayte.

would, I think, interest me. If I go on longer, you will get no breakfast, so good-night and God bless you all,—always dear, but never so dear as at this old Justin Martyr sofa-table.[1]—Ever your affectionate friend,

FENTON J. A. HORT.

To THE REV. B. F. WESTCOTT

HARDWICK, CHEPSTOW, *Easter Eve*, 1854.

. . . I thank you very much for your kind wishes ; I am sure they are true, though my time for fully realising their truth in practice does not seem to be yet come. You must not expect a long account from me now ; but I spent most happy days at Cuddesdon and Oxford, without anything discordant to violate the sacredness of the time, and was specially delighted with the calumniated Bishop himself. I must just allude to some publications which Trench mentioned to me then, and has since lent to me. A most singular movement is taking place among the German 'Reformation' settled in America, the centre of the move-ment being Mercersburg. The leading man is Dr. Nevin, who has written in the *Mercersburg Review* a series of passionate articles against the 'baptistic' and 'anti-creed' theory of Christianity, pleading earnestly for continuity of development in Church History, and especially for an affectionate study of the early Church, as the only way of getting a standing ground for interpreting the Bible, taking the Apostles' Creed as a guide. I can compare him to no one but Newman, and higher praise it would be difficult to give. I fear he is fast drifting Romewards.

To HIS MOTHER

CAMBRIDGE, *May 24th*, 1854.

. . . Thank you for John's[2] interesting dispatches, which I duly forwarded to Kingstown. They are a great help

[1] A table at which Hort and Mr. Blunt read Justin together, and talked, one summer vacation at Hardwick.

[2] His first cousin, afterwards Lieutenant-General Sir John Hort, then serving in the Crimea.

towards making the newspapers intelligible. I see by yesterday's *Times* that on the 7th (I think) the 4th and its companion regiments were moved to Bulair, as John expected,
to take their turn at digging the entrenchments across the
isthmus above Gallipoli. I will send my father by the next
post a sixpenny reprint of an article in *Fraser*, the best
and most authentic account that has yet been published
of the Russian defences in the Baltic and the Russian fleet
generally. The author is one of our *attachés* at St. Peters-
burgh, driven home by the war; he is a very sharp-eyed and
intelligent little creature, and had access to all documents
likely to be of much use in drawing up such an account. I
hope my father showed you Du Hamelin's French dispatch
about the affair at Odessa; it is the only really satisfactory
account that I have seen. The anxious care taken by our
fleets to spare private property is very pleasant to see at the
beginning of the war. I have been since told (not having
myself noticed the fact) that the gunner of the *Terrible* has
been disrated for not being able to abstain from firing (and
but too skilfully) a shell at the temptingly smooth round white
dome of some mosque or similar building.

The following letter is an answer to questions about
the ' call ' to take holy orders.

To the Rev. Gerald Blunt

Cambridge, *May* 31*st*, 1854.

My dear Blunt—It is not very easy to answer your question fairly without seeming to beat about the bush ; but I will
try. I think you have rather confused the ' inward motion of
the Spirit ' with the ' call,' which are not exactly coincident,
though they must be mostly considered together.

First observe the distinct phrase used by the Church, " Do
you *trust* that you are inwardly moved ? " etc. The matter is
frankly set forth as one of faith, not of sensible consciousness.
The motion of the Spirit is to be inferred from its effects in

and on our spirit ; any other view is likely to degrade and car-
nalize our apprehensions of spiritual operations, not exalt
them. Now I do not think it possible for one man to lay
down absolutely for another what inward thoughts and aspira-
tions are or are not trustworthy indices to a genuine motion of
the Holy Ghost; but the Church's words do themselves suggest some necessary elements of them,—a direct and unmixed
(I mean, clearly realizable and distinguishable) desire to be
specially employed in promoting God's glory and building up
His people. You will say that this is after all the duty, not
specially of a clergyman, but of every Christian man. I cannot
deny it, though I do not know why I should wish to deny an
inference to which the Church herself so plainly leads me.
Perhaps we may find it a most pregnant and significant intimation of the real nature of the priestly and the simply
Christian life, and their relation to each other. The one
great work of a priest is to set forth what a man is and is
meant to be ; if we set this fundamental truth aside, we affect
a more saintly eminence than our High Priest, the Son of
Man. We have therefore, I quite allow, the strongest reasons
for saying that the glory of God and the building up of his
brethren must be the common daily work-day aim of every
man ; but this may be done mediately or immediately. Plato
has taught us that every craft and profession has some special
human work (some particular way of glorifying God, as we
should say), which must not be confused with its adjuncts and
accessories. The healing of bodies is the work of a physician,
so far as he is a physician,—not the supporting himself, etc.
These subsidiary results must follow, not lead or even, in some
sense, accompany, the primary work. And so it is with the
clergyman's work. He must have a desire to set forth the
glory of God simply and directly, in those forms which show
it forth most nakedly. He must not only act it out but speak
of it, make men know it and consciously enter into it. None
of the phenomena of life are primarily his province, but the
glory and the love which underlie them all. He is not simply
an officer or servant of God or workman of God, but His
ambassador and herald to tell men about God Himself. He
must bring distinctly before men the reality of the heaven, of

which the earth and all that it contains is but the symbol and
vesture.   And, since all human teaching is but the purging of
the ear to hear God's teaching, and since the whole man, and
not certain faculties only, must enter into the divine presence,
the sacraments must be the centre and crown (I don't mean
central *subject*) of his teaching, for there the real heights and
depths of heaven are most fully revealed, and at the same
time the commonest acts and things of earth are most closely
and clearly connected with the highest heaven.   This is,
briefly, my view of a clergyman's work ; and by this, I think,
must the nature of the Spirit's inward motion be determined.
If a man does not feel a clear paramount desire,—often interrupted and diluted and even counteracted, but still distinctly
present whenever he is in his right mind,—to tell men of God
and Jesus Christ whom He has sent,—in a word, to preach
the Gospel, that is, announce the Good Tidings,—I very
much doubt whether he has a right to 'trust that' he is 'inwardly moved by the Holy Ghost.'

But this desire may be present in a greater or less degree,
and with a greater or less commixture of other thoughts.   In
some it is so strong that any other way of accomplishing God's
glory would be irksome to them, except as a subsidiary part of
their lives.   But in the vast majority of cases where the desire
is really present, it is not so overwhelming but that it may be
subordinated to others, if circumstances should be unfavourable.   I do not think that this at all necessarily implies any
moral declension.   A man may honestly and truly desire to
preach the Gospel, and yet he may best do God's will by
becoming squire, attorney, or shoemaker.   It is here, I think,
that the wishes of parents or other circumstances may and
must have their effect.   Of course I cannot shrink from considering the converse case.   A man's own thoughts may have
lain in another direction, and yet subsequent external circumstances may, I think, justify his taking orders, but only under
certain conditions.   If he cannot find in himself any of the
special desires which mark God's inspiration of His own
special priests and prophets, I do not think that any outward
circumstances can supply the place.   But it must be remembered that circumstances do not act upon us only at one

crisis of our lives ; they belong to our childhood and youth as well as our manhood. And therefore it may be that the genuine desire has been really latent in a man's mind for years, hidden and kept down by one set of circumstances and brought to light and consciousness by the pressure of another. In short, when we speak of a 'call,' we must take great care lest we introduce notions which may altogether distort our views of the Spirit and His operations. We must not think of ourselves as cut off from the complicated mass of events and influences around us, or forget that the same God, who holds them all in His hand, does also call us to His work, and inspire us with the desire and the strength to accomplish it. We do not honour the Spirit, but subject Him to our own private fancies, when we refuse to recognize a call in His ordering of events. I do not mean that *outward* events or things independent of ourselves entirely constitute our circumstances ; our own inward history, our present inclinations, even our felt capacities, are all, I think, part of our circumstances, but in these we need more care to avoid self-delusion, and it is not often that we are justified in consulting them alone. But no circumstances can justify us in following a profession for the work of which we have *no* desire.—I say 'work,' because that seems the best word ; but of course I do not mean outward employments, except in a subordinate sense ; they are but the outcome and embodiment of our real inward 'work.'—The case is precisely analogous to that of ordinary morality, which requires us to be led by circumstances and not to yield to them. The eternal laws of morality are paramount over all temporal circumstances. If they were not, there could be no such thing as sin. Ordination is no exception to the general rule. The Church requires a trust that we are inwardly moved (" Lord, we believe ! help Thou our unbelief ! ") by the Holy Ghost ; and that must be present, or else we become the slaves of circumstances and so fall into sin.

I have doubts whether you will think this letter a satisfactory answer to your question. But I am convinced that no answer can be a righteous and true one, which supplies a mechanical test easy of application, and exempts a man from the awful responsibility of deciding for himself alone before God.

But there are two obvious truths, which ought to be kept distinctly in mind, if duty and responsibility are not to remain in a cold and cheerless light, which is by no means divine. If it is the Spirit that moves the inward man, and the Spirit that gives the call in whatever shape it may come, it is the same Spirit that clears the eye and strengthens the heart to decide truly whether either the motion or the call do really exist.   And again it is the same Spirit who fills us with Himself at ordination.   The Reformers may have been quite right in denying the name 'Sacrament' to an institution belonging only to a part of mankind; but it is most truly (what the Greeks called Sacraments) a mystery and sacramental.   It is God that makes us priests, and not we ourselves; and so it is not our own previous or succeeding desire to set forth His glory that enables us to do anything for Him, but only the anointing of His grace.—Ever yours affectionately,

FENTON J. A. HORT.

P.S.—One word more on a point that I forgot.   You seem to speak as if a love of outdoor occupations were something like a disqualification for a clergyman.   I cannot allow this.   I do not think my standard is lower than the popular one, but it is certainly different.   With regard to such employments in themselves, the whole of society has relinquished them to a most injurious extent; and I cannot see harm, looking especially to the future, in a clergyman's cultivating in due proportion that which I believe to be an integral part of a healthy human life; and still more with respect to the tone of mind which such employments induce and from which the love of them springs.   Nothing is more wanted for the regeneration of England than a vast increase of manliness, courage, and simplicity in English clergymen.   These are moral qualities; but the breezes of heaven and the use of the muscles have not a little effect in cultivating them.   God knows there are temptations enough in this direction as in every other; but better be anything than an effeminate sneak.

To Mr. C. H. Chambers

CAMBRIDGE [*May 29th ?*], 1854.

. . . There is a good deal of University business going on. A fierce struggle took place at the beginning of this term on the proposal of the great Studies Syndicate (*alias* the XXXIX. Articles) to allow men after Little-go to proceed *ad libitum* in Mathematics, Classics, Morals, Physics, or Theology, and take a degree accordingly, a new Theological Tripos being proposed at the same time. Fortunately we succeeded in throwing out all except the exemption of Classics from subjection to Mathematics. But plans for wiser reform are already afloat, and I am on a new Syndicate to adjust the Little-go and Pol.[1] The Pitt Press will likewise be revolutionised on Wednesday next, and will, I trust, be greatly improved. The newly-organised Library Syndicate has been sitting two terms. We have been working very hard, and have already done much good work.

The last University intelligence is the Whewell Pot. Our artistic Master has been crowning a chimney in the Great Court with a row of bright blue pots surrounded by a double border of bright yellow fleurs-de-lys ! We are threatened with similar ornaments all round the College.

We had Bishop Selwyn here yesterday, and he preached a grand sermon at St. Mary's. Politics would give much food for talk, if one had time. On the whole I am hopeful about the war, though not without grave misgivings. The French alliance is, however, a great and solid satisfaction. At home I never expected to see so good a government. Gladstone has always been a favourite of mine ; and it is now doubly pleasant to see how he confounds the politics and frustrates the knavish tricks of those rascally Derbyites.

To his Mother

HOTEL DE L'ECU, GENEVA, *June 24th*, 1854.

My dearest Mother—You will be thankful to hear that I have come thus far safe and sound without anything like a

---

[1] *i.e.* the examinations for the ordinary degree.

mishap. . . . Soon after midnight I woke up in time to get
some refreshment at Tonnerre, and again at 3.10 just in time
to get out of the train at Dijon.   The diligence stood ready-
horsed a few yards off, and at the half-hour we drove away.
It was a queer affair, not unlike an English coach but for the
conducteur's *banquette* on the top.   Inside there was nothing
but a small *intérieure*.   A dim creature (whom, after some
mutual boggling in French, of which he knew, to speak, even
less than I did, I discovered to be a Scotchman) had the first
place, a Frenchman the second, myself the third, and our
plaids, hats, etc., the fourth.   In passing by twilight through
the quaint streets of Dijon, I had just such a glimpse of the
Cathedral as to make me wish to see more.   The country, as
well as I could make out at intervals between snoozes, was
interesting from its novelty, but not very striking.   At length
we crossed the Saône, a noble river, and entered the strongly-
fortified town of Auxonne.   An hour or so more brought us
to Dôle, a large and interesting place, at 6.25; here we
crossed the Doubs.   From this onwards the country was
rather flat till Poligni, a most striking place, which we reached
at 8.45.   Here our passports were demanded for the first time
since leaving Boulogne.   Here the plain suddenly ceases, and
the lower outskirts of the Jura rise abruptly, covered with
vineyards.   The vineyards themselves rather disappointed me,
but I had formed in England no conception of the exceeding
grace and beauty of the single vines, with their leaves and
tendrils of tender golden green glistening in the sunlight.
Our enjoyment of the beautiful ascent from Poligni was much
spoiled by the intrusion of an enormous Frenchman into our
fourth place, besides half of *my* place; fortunately this nuisance
lasted only two stages.   A mile or two brought us to the top
of the hill, and then we had a long drive on a tolerably level
plateau of rugged ground, which was very delightful from its
wildness, and the beautiful flowers, especially some beautiful
Spurges and *Genistæ*.   At 10.25 we crossed a rapid river in a
gorge below us and entered Champagnole, where a *petit quart
d'heure* was allowed us for breakfast.   We were famously
hungry, and soon devoured no small amount of *café au lait*,
trout fried in oil, omelette, raspberries, and wild strawberries.

We proceeded, much revived, up and down all manner of beautiful vallies and ravines for many miles.   The vegetation (which had begun to change the moment I left Boulogne) was very interesting to watch, but probably three-quarters of it was common to England, and it was a pleasure to recognize old friends (such as the bugloss) among the brightest flowers. The vallies (barring the pines) might all have occurred in England, and once I had just noticed a striking rezemblance to parts of Teesdale, when we burst on an acre of globe flowers, growing just as you may remember them at Caldron Snout, and in the following ten miles I noticed almost all the characteristic Teesdale rarities. . . . At half-past three we reached the highest point of the Jura, and Mt. Blanc suddenly burst upon us in all his glory, his top quite clear from the thin clouds which hung here and there about his sides and lower peaks, sometimes rising into white mounds which looked like rival Alps, till the eye learnt to distinguish the filmy precision and sharp deep shadows of the genuine snows.   Half a minute more discovered a reach of the blue Leman ; and then every turn, as we zigzagged rapidly down the mountain, opened out some new aspect of the glorious valley.   We were soon at the bottom, and then (except for the distant Alps) the level ground, vegetation and all, could scarcely have been distinguished from that of England.   Our passports were taken from us at the entrance of Geneva. . . .

This morning I went to the pretty new English Church, and meeting there my Scotch friend of yesterday, who had much interested me, strolled with him up the old town (after getting a magnificent view of Mt. Blanc, now quite free from cloud), and then into the cemetery (where we wandered a long time among the plane-trees, looking at the epitaphs), to see the plain square stone with ' J. C.' which marks Calvin's grave.   My fellow-traveller was a young ' Free Kirk ' minister of Glasgow, who was going to-morrow to join his family at Chamouni : otherwise he would gladly have accompanied me.   We had a long and most delightful talk on theological matters ; and, though he was a stout disciple of John Knox, it was a very long time before he found out that I was anything else.   We parted the best of friends, both, I hope, the better for our meeting. . . . I have just been wandering about the fine old streets up to the curious cathedral, and down again along the lake, and about the bridges, listening to the rushing Rhône. I am well lodged here in a nice though small room *au quatrième* (there are two higher stories !). My windows look out on the busy *Place* in front of the Messageries Imperiales, with the level lake and all its strange boats, and two streets, one containing a cluster of low planes.

Last night I felt very odd here—more like my first night at Laleham than anything else that I can remember ; but the situation is at least as amusing as desolate, and I have enjoyed myself very much. I have been singularly little tired with the journey, which had its pleasures in every part.

To the Rev. John Ellerton

BAIERISCHER HOF, MUNICH,
August 13*th and* 15*th,* 1854.

My dear Ellerton—Before leaving England I made no promises to write to you from abroad, as I foresaw there would be great difficulties, and I have quite enough broken vows to answer for already. But still I know you will be glad to hear from these regions.

I left England on June 23rd, reached Dijon next day, travelled from thence by *malle-poste* to Geneva. . . . Next day I steamed up the lake to Vevay, slept there, took the early boat next morning to Lausanne, wandered about the city and cathedral (on which I have writ something in the incepted journal), and took the late boat to Geneva. I did not see the lake to advantage, for clouds hid the highest mountains both days. Thursday the 29th [June] I went by diligence to Sallanches, and thence by *char-à-banc* to Chamonix. July 1st I got a good (botanist) guide, Payot, and walked round through the grand gorge of the Tête Noire to Trient, and back over the Col de Balme (in the clouds, and therefore no view) to Chamonix. A Mr. Mills had taken the duty at Chamonix for some weeks, and a very pleasant man I found him—scientific, to boot. He gave us good services and sermons. He had with him six ladies. An agreeable Oxford man, Theobald, was also there. On Monday we all made a famous party up the Flégère to see the view, especially of Mt. Blanc. In the evening at half-past nine Theobald, Mills, and I started with two guides and a lantern up the forest on the flank of Mt. Blanc to the little inn at Montanvert, which we reached at midnight; slept there, and next day had a glorious expedition to the so-called 'Jardin,' high among the glaciers in the hollow heart of Mt. Blanc, returning to Chamonix in the evening, unluckily in much rain. Next day I only strolled about. On the 6th I set out alone with Payot for the Tour of Mt. Blanc; that day we only crossed the Col de Vosa to Contamines. Next day it began to rain soon after we had started, and continued all the way to the first top of the Col du Bonhomme; then we had cloud for the next hour along the dangerous part between the first and second top, and then heavy rain again all the way down to the little hamlet of Chapin (at the extreme S.W. corner of Mt. Blanc), where we slept. Next day we had a fine day for the inexpressibly glorious views over the Col de la Seigne and down the Allée Blanche to Cormayeur in Piedmont, where we slept two nights, passing a dull Sunday. The 10th was a hard day. We walked up the Val and over the Col de Ferrêt, and then over the Col de la Fenêtre (with much deep wading in steeply-inclined wet snow), down some way and then up again to the Hospice of the Great S. Bernard, where we slept. The said hospice by no means pleased me. Next day I walked down to St. Pierre, and there took a *char* to Martigny, where I slept. Next morning (July 12th) I parted with Payot, and P.M. went by diligence up the rather monotonous valley of the Rhône to Visp, where I slept. Next day I had a beautiful walk up the Valley of St. Nicolas to Zermatt, near the Matterhorn and M. Rosa. Next day I went up the Untere Rothhorn (with a famous young guide, Kronig) for the magnificent panoramic view of the highest peaks, rising out of beds of glacier; and above all of that mountain of mountains, the wonderful pyramidal Matterhorn. Next day I had (with two guides, Kronig and an old hunter) a delightful glacier excursion (altogether 11½ hours), ending with a long and difficult climb, to the Stockhorn of the Zmutt Glacier. No tourist has made the excursion before, except the very very few who have crossed the dangerous Col d'Erin, among whom is James Forbes, from whose book I gathered my resolution to make the attempt. The view is grand indeed, and, above all, it enabled me to see well the W. side of the Matterhorn. Sunday I passed at Zermatt. Monday the 17th I went with my two guides to the top of the Matterjoch (*alias* Pass of St. Théodule, *alias* Col du Mt. Cervin), with splendid glacier views at every step, then down across the Furgga Glacier and up the Hörnli : this is a spur running out from the base of the Matterhorn, and is described (without the name) in Ruskin's splendid and no less faithful portrait of the Matterhorn (in *Stones of Venice*, vol. i.), which portrait it was one great object of mine to verify, and most strikingly true I found it in all points but one, and in that the error was very natural. From the Hörnli again the view was magnificent ; but the truth is, that this astonishing region round Zermatt affords an inexhaustible supply of excursions and points of view, all first-rate. I meant in the two following days to have taken a new and much-including course over the glaciers of M. Rosa to the head of the valley of Saas, and *so* descended to Visp again. But on that Monday evening, having been for hours wading across deep pure snow under a cloudless sky, I was attacked (in spite of a green veil) so severely with snow-blindness that I dared not trust myself to the glaciers so soon again, and next day merely walked down to Stalden, where the vallies of Saas and St. Nicolas meet. Next day I walked up to the village of Saas, and still higher to Fée (which has, I think, the finest single glacier in the Alps), and down again past Stalden to Visp, where I again slept. Next day I dismissed Kronig and took a car down the Rhône valley to Leuk, and thence walked up to the Baths of Leuk, a most strange place. Next morning I walked over the Gemmi Pass (which begins, or almost begins, with scaling a vertical precipice of a good many hundreds of feet by zigzag galleries), through a most savage and thoroughly enjoyable region down to Kandersteg, whence I took car to Thun. Next morning I met James of

Trinity with two friends (one an old Rugby contemporary of mine), and we went by diligence together to Berne and dined there, and then they went on to Basle. At dinner I was lucky enough to fall in with a Mr. and Mrs. Lee. They are very delightful people, and the next day (Sunday) at Berne was a very happy one. Monday I went by diligence back to Thun, and thence by steamer along the lake of Thun to Neuhaus, and thence by car to Interlachen. Here I met Lord Rollo. Finding that our routes would partly coincide, we agreed to travel together for the next day or two, and I enjoyed his company much. Next day (the 25th) we took a carriage to Lauterbrunnen, walked to the Staubbach, and then he rode and I walked to the top of the Wengern Alp, where we slept in the little inn full in front of the superb Jungfrau. This is a famous place for avalanches; but we saw only one worth mentioning. Next morning we descended on the other side to Grindelwald, and thence up the Faul-horn, in ascending which we were overtaken by a very pleasant English party. Unluckily the rain came on again, and we saw little from the summit that evening. We slept in tolerable comfort up in the region of snow, and next morning were rewarded with as splendid a sunrise as man could desire, having the whole cluster of Oberland Alps ranged close before us, only just far enough off to enable us to take them all in. After coffee we had a most merry walk and ride all together over the great Scheideck down to Rosenlaui. Lord Rollo and I went up to the exceedingly pretty little glacier of Rosenlaui, and then down the valley past the fine Reichenbach Fall to Meyringen, where we slept. Next morn-ing we separated, and I started with my Interlachen guide Gaultier up the beautiful valley of Hasli, stopped at Handeck to see the truly magnificent fall ('see' is not the right word, for two-thirds of the fall is quite hidden by the spray), and then mounted the gloriously wild pass of the Grimsel, all bestrewed with huge sloping flakes of granite, to the new Hotel near the top, where we slept. Next morning we finished the pass, and descended the Maienwand, a steep mountain-slope covered with the richest alpine vegetation, to the foot of the big glacier of the Rhône. We had then a

fatiguing and rather dull ascent of the Furka (relieved by
some backward views of the Oberland), and a still duller
descent on the other side to Hospenthal. At dinner I struck
up an acquaintance with two Brighton men. . . . Next morning
I read service to them and to two English ladies, and P.M.
we walked leisurely to the Hospice at the top of the St.
Gothard Pass, and back to Hospenthal. On Monday we set
out walking down the wild but too much praised defile of the
Devil's Bridge to Amsteg, and after dinner took *chars* to
Altdorf, walking up in the sultry evening to see Tell's birthplace at Bürglen. Tuesday morning was wet, but P.M. we
walked to Fluelen, and thence took steamer to Luzern, walking in the evening to see the really great Lion (designed by
Thorwaldsen) in honour of Louis XVI.'s Swiss guards.
Next morning, during a lull in the rain, we steamed to
Küssnacht, and later walked up the Righi, getting some
tolerable partial views during the ascent, but nothing at the
top except the singular 'Spectre,' consisting of our figures
thrown on a cloud encircled with a double iris. We were
not roused by the usual horn next morning, for nothing was
to be seen but clouds. We walked down in rain to Goldau,
saw the strange desolation caused by the landslip of the
Rossberg, and then took a carriage to Zurich. In the
morning I went by steamer and diligence combined, along
the lakes of Zurich and Wallenstadt to Ragatz, and then
walked up to see the extraordinary limestone rift containing
the hot spring that supplies Pfeffers' Baths. I had meant to
stay two or three days in the neighbourhood, but the badness
of the weather and other reasons induced me to leave Ragatz
next morning by diligence and descend the rather dull valley
of the Rhine to Rorschach, there take steamer, and sleep at
Constance, where I also spent the following day (Sunday).
My six weeks for Switzerland were now finished, and I was in
the Grand Duchy of Baden; but next day I returned to
Switzerland for a few hours by taking diligence to Schaff-
hausen, and walking to see the rather poor Falls of the Rhine,
and then returned by steamer to Constance. On Tuesday I
steamed to Lindau (there entering Bavaria) and sailed to
Augsburg, where I slept at the famous old hotel of the Three

Moors.   Here I met Thacker, and have been with him ever
since.   Next day we railed to Munich, and I have been
engaged ever since in seeing its wonders, which would, alas !
require months to exhaust.   The present Industrial Exhibition, a Crystal Palace on a small scale, is not remarkable,
except for the superb Bohemian glass.   The artistic interest
of Munich is twofold: (1) the modern revived German art
seen in perfection, partly in architecture (which is chiefly so-
called ' Byzantine ' and full of instructive experiments, though
never, I think, quite successful, and always rather mechanical),
great learning, great skill, thorough good taste, and hardly a
spark of life or inspiration ; and (2) the treasures of antient
sculpture and painting in the Glyptothek and Pinacothek.
The former, chiefly Greek, include many very exquisite things,
the latter form an admirably-arranged exhibition of all schools
(except the English), but especially the early German, Rubens
per se, and early Italian.   You may imagine how rich it is in
the early German schools, when I tell you that the first day
I got no further than Albert Dürer, who comes out in all
his glory ; but it is vain to begin to talk about the pictures
now.

To THE REV. JOHN ELLERTON

ISOLA BELLA, LAGO MAGGIORE,
September 10th, 1854.

. . . I left Munich the evening of August 16th and
reached Innsbrück the next afternoon by a pretty drive
across the mountains.   Next evening I took the Verona
diligence across the Brenner Pass (which I crossed in the
night), the fine gorge from Brixen to Botzen, the great flat
sultry valley of the Adige from Botzen to below Trent,
and crossed the back of Mt. Baldo in the night, reaching
Verona early on Sunday morning.   Trent, the only place
worth mentioning on the route, is a fine city, in a dreadfully
hot and confined situation, embowered in rank fields of white
mulberry, vines (chiefly sprawling over divers trees), maize,
and pumpkins — altogether as unlikely a place for such a
Council as one could easily imagine.   You will observe, by

the way, how many places connected with the Reformation I
shall have seen this summer—Geneva, Zurich, Constance,
Augsburg, and Trent; Prague would have been added, if I
had gone home by E. Germany. At Verona I stayed two
days, and saw it after a manner; but I cannot seek lions with
any energy when alone.   It is full of beautiful canopied tombs,
especially those of the Scaligers.   On the 22nd (August) I
took the train to Padua, walked up into the city and saw
divers things, but, above all, Giotto's most exquisite frescoes
in the Arena chapel.   No panel pictures of his that I have
seen give any idea of the sweetness and graceful dignity of
these frescoes.   The groupings are mostly conventional, but
most of the figures themselves are very great indeed ; the
'Last Judgement' is alone painful and vulgar.   In the evening I went on to Venice and took up my quarters at the Hotel
de la Ville, *alias* the Grassi (Renaissance) Palace. . . .

It would convey no idea to you to give a bulletin of each
day at Venice, nor can I give you now more than very short
results ; but I feel the mere fact of having been there to be an
important event in my life ; there is a magic in it which I
cannot account for.   St. Mark's is most truly not 'barbarous,'
but it *is barbaric*.   The effect is certainly beautiful as well as
peculiar ; but it is by no means so impressive as a great Gothic
church, though the odd power exercised by its richness and
bizarrerie might easily be mistaken for impressiveness.   In *detail* it is always most interesting and generally most beautiful.
The mosaics alone would take weeks to study and decipher,
and would repay it ; but Ruskin's plates give a very fair idea of
the exquisiteness of the Byzantine capitals and other carving.
The Doges' Palace looked lovely at first and looked more
lovely every day ; it is, however, quite beyond description. . . .
Of the beauty and other excellencies of the Venetian-Gothic
and Byzantine palaces there can be no doubt ; but I have not
been able to make up my mind whether they would be in any
way available in England.   The churches, one and all (except
St. Mark's, Torcello, and Murano), miserably disappointed me ;
their Gothic is generally very finicking and cramped ; literally
half the parish churches of England would, I think, supply
better.   Their use of moulded brick and their intermixture of

colours of brick and stone are, however, well worthy of study and imitation. I must be brief about pictures, though (just now, at least) a knowledge of Venetian painting seems to me the greatest treasure of this summer. One result greatly surprised me : Titian went down immensely in my estimation. Assuredly he excels most painters in manliness ; but at Venice he looks shallow and theatrical by the side of others, who more than equal him in manliness. I went to Venice with great misgivings as to Ruskin's exaltation of Tintoretto ; nor can I now agree in all his praises of particular pictures, but my impression is that he rather underrates the man than otherwise. He seems to me a man of lordly, energetic, fiery spirit, usually disdaining to throw off a sort of dogged composure, revelling in all kinds of beauty and yet almost always liking to veil it from profane or vulgar eyes, full of subtle mysticism and yet often even painfully realistic, rejoicing in the earth and all that is upon it, but not the less inwardly religious, in the best sense of the word. I have always enjoyed Titian most in mythology (as our 'Ganymede' and 'Venus and Adonis '), but in power and grace he is as nothing when you look at three Tintorets in the Doges' Palace (especially a most perfect 'Venus crowning Ariadne ') and two somewhat similar ones (the 'Fall' and the 'Death of Abel') in the Academy. The 'Paradise' of the Doges' Palace must be *sui generis;* there can be no picture like it in the world. But the precious Scuola S. Rocco is the place where Tintoret is most completely and distinctively himself. Those acres of rapid sketchy brown and grey tell one more of God and man (chiefly, I fancy, because they have entered so deeply into the Incarnation) than any other human utterance that I can recollect. Æschylus, Dante, and Beethoven are the illustrative names that first occur, but they are only illustrative. Pray read again Ruskin's excellent analysis in the Appendix to the *Stones*, vol. iii. ; it is almost all true, except that he has failed to see as much as he might have done. The last four of the N. T. series I hope I shall never forget,—that thin, ghostly, white, lonely figure standing with the sad quiet face bent down as Pilate washes his hands, the robe unfolded to show the bleeding, sinking, exhausted body (*Ecce Homo*), the slow tramp of the crosses up the zigzag of the hill, and then that unutterable Crucifixion,—such a scene of bustle and confusion and sight-seeing, one of the side-crosses in the act of being hoisted up by ropes which stretch across one side of the picture, the other lying on the ground, and just receiving the thief who is being laid upon it and unbound, all in a crowd of soldiers, workmen, holiday parties, etc., with two or three quiet gazers, and the heap of mourning women round the foot of the one upright sullen cross, bearing the motionless figure with its head bent down in gloom.   There are several other pictures of Tintoret's that I should like to talk about, such as the 'Last Judgement,' another 'Crucifixion,' the 'Descent into Hades,' etc., but I have not time. But Paul Veronese, whom long before I left Venice I learned to love most thoroughly, must have a few words.   He has nothing of Tintoret's depth and awfulness, but his most rich and pure delight in beauty (especially of colour), without an atom of sensuality, in any sense of the word, and united usually to most vigorous manhood, is inexpressibly delightful. It was also a great pleasure to learn to know Bonifazio, Giorgione, etc., not to speak of the elder school, Carpaccio, Catena, Cima di Conegliano, etc.   About John Bellini I must have some talk with you another time.   I must, however, just mention (not as Venetian !) one most glorious Garofalo in the Academy.   On my return from Venice with the Bullers I again saw Padua; unluckily we were much hurried at S. Antonio's Church, one Gothic chapel of which was very striking.   The Palazzo della Ragione is also worth telling about another time. At Verona I was compelled to stay another day, and saw San Zenone and the Amphitheatre very enjoyably in company with the Bullers.   The former, as you perhaps know, is one of the finest and most characteristic late Lombard churches, and full of interest ; the cloister is very exquisite, with hardly a particle of ornament.   On Friday I came on alone to Milan, meaning to start for the Simplon at midnight, but was ashamed to pass by everything unseen, and therefore stayed a day.   Yesterday I saw first of all Leonardo's 'Last Supper.'   I will only say now that it is far greater even in its ruin and bedaubment than any of the engravings ; but it does not satisfy me, though it is impossible not to love it very dearly ; it reminds me of one of

Manning's sermons ; one longs for a little more honest realism, even at the cost of some sweetness and refinement. My next sight was Sant' Ambrogio, a most peculiar Lombard Church of the ninth century, as interesting as San Zenone, though ruder and less beautiful. Next I went to the Brera Gallery, where, unluckily, there was an exhibition of shiny new Milanese pictures hiding the old ones in a great measure. Moreover, we were turned out by a file of soldiers at a very early hour, so that about the only good picture I had any time for was Raffaelle's 'Marriage of the Virgin'; and I caught flying glimpses of a glorious Francia and a similar Garofalo. (By the way, I forgot to mention two most beautiful Peruginos in the Venice Manfrini Gallery, both of which I took at first for excellent second-rate Raffaelles.) From the Brera I went to the Cathedral, a *very* queer building, and not at all to my taste. Unluckily the haze spoiled the view from the highest point of the lantern that can be ascended. The Cathedral is like a monstrous chapel in the style of the ' Mediæval ' Court of the Great Exhibition, stuck all over with innumerable large slender pinnacles, each bearing a statue, and one of them (to use a medical phrase) *hypertrophied.*

To the Rev. John Ellerton

Hardwick, *September 29th*, 1854.

. . . My last was, I think, closed at Isola Bella. . . . On the 11th I took a boat to Baveno and then joined the Simplon diligence. At 6 [A.M.] one of the passengers and myself got out at Isella, the last village in Italy, and walked up the pass through the very fine gorge of Gondo to the village of Simplon, where we breakfasted. Just as we were setting out afresh, the diligence came up ; and it finally over-took us about a third of the way down the pass on the Swiss side. At Brieg I found great difficulties (of expense, time, etc.) in the way of my glacier plans ; so that, to cut a long story short, I was obliged to abandon them, and started next day by diligence for Turtman. I saw at Turtman a very pretty fall, and made arrangements for a walk next day over

the Loetschberg.   This is a glacier pass from the Vallais into
the Berne valleys a few miles east of that of the Gemmi, and
some 1200 or 1400 feet higher; the walk is very long at both
ends.   I was a good deal tired when I reached Kandersteg
late in the evening after a day of magnificent and rarely visited
views ; however, it did me a world of good.   Next day I
thought it safer to do no more than wander about the
Oeschinen Thal, luxuriating in the alpine air and vegetation
and the splendid glaciers and crags around me. . . .

On Wednesday morning I went by rail to Frankfurt, and
thence again to Castel, the fortified suburb of Mainz across
the Rhine.   Here, after some delay, I embarked, but before
very long we stuck in the mud.   This and the necessity of
returning some way in order to get into a deeper channel
made us some hours late, and the lout of a captain would not
venture as far as Cologne that night, but deposited us at
Coblenz.   I was able, however, before it got dark, to see the
best part of the Rhine, which fell below even my very low
expectations.   At 5 A.M. we again embarked, and reached
Cologne.   I stayed there and saw the Cathedral and some of
the churches.   I hardly knew what to expect as to the quality
of the Cathedral, but its size is not very great.   As well as I
could make out, the very oldest part must have been in the
usual German Gothic style, to which I cannot get reconciled,—
the windows all elaborate exaggerated lancets very close
together, and the whole stuck over with a forest of vapid
pinnacles, the high-pitched roof being the redeeming point.
There is, however, in the choir (the original part) much very
beautiful work inside and some excellent windows.   Being
alone, I did not pay the extravagant sum for admission to see
the shrine of the Three Kings ; but the Dombild, a most
lovely specimen of early Cologne painting, delighted me
exceedingly.   It is difficult to judge properly of the nave and
aisles, as they have at present a false roof, but the general
effect is good, and the clerestory undeniably beautiful, though
wanting in real freedom.   The modern carving is much
praised, but seemed to me hard and lifeless.   On the whole
it will, when finished, be a noble building, but, methinks,
vastly below its reputation, and not to be compared to the

better English Cathedrals for all that constitutes real beauty. I much doubt whether the Germans enter at all into the genuine Gothic spirit. . . .

As at present advised, I hope to go up to Cambridge about the 10th. I have two freshmen to look after, and this will be a very busy term with me. The Le Bas Prize, Mackenzie's *Essay*, the *Journal of Philology*, the new Degree Syndicate, besides the University Library and its Syndicate, and all my own readings and writings, are quite enough to make me wish to lose no time in getting to work. I have said very little about my tour on the whole; and indeed I must leave that as it is : my own thoughts are hardly collected, and will by degrees find their own places. I must just, however, say that the politics of Italy now seem to me a more fearful problem than ever. Of course it is impossible to acquiesce in the occupation of the country by unblending foreigners; but I felt often tempted to think that the N. Italians are only too lucky and honoured in being governed by Germans. Their degradation did not at all seem to be that of crushed and disabled men, but hopeless decrepitude of body and spirit, the slow result of their own fearful wickedness. Piedmont is the only visible door of hope, and that is unsatisfactory enough; most of its reputed partiality for Protestantism means only, I fear, secularization, often of the most unprincipled kind. Of course life can return, if it ever return at all, only through the Church; but that is just the most seemingly hopeless region of all.

It is exceedingly annoying that I could not be at Cambridge when you were there. I hope you found time to see Ely. The choir is now becoming so magnificent that there can be few greater architectural glories in England.

To THE REV. JOHN ELLERTON

CAMBRIDGE, *November* 17*th*, 1854.

. . . My time gets more and more occupied. Besides the Library Syndicate I am this term on a new and important Syndicate for reforming Little-go and the Pol. You may guess we are pretty active, as we met yesterday and meet again to-morrow. We have already agreed to many recommendations, but it remains to be seen whether the Senate will adopt them ; *inter alia* we propose to abolish Paley's *Moral Philosophy*. I have also been appointed a Trinity Examiner, and shall have to take the Butler's *Sermons* and Whewell at Christmas, and the *Gorgias*, Butler's *Analogy*, and Church History in the May. I have also (without my consent being asked) been made a classical examiner for the Pol (*Cic. de off.* iii. and the *Hippolytus*), which is a great bore, as it involves coming up in the middle of January.

Then I am getting on well with Mackenzie's *Essay*, and have plenty to do for the *Journal of Philology* to get it out by the end of the month. This evening I have been correcting the proof of a stiff but, I suppose, valuable paper of H. Browne's on Clement of Alexandria's N. T. chronology,—a slow and laborious process from the multiplicity of figures. I am also at work as usual at the University Library MSS., and occasionally do a little at Greek Testament, as a treat. I have just finished *Heartsease* with much delight ; but, with all its beauty and wisdom, I can hardly enjoy it so much as the *Heir of Redclyffe*. But it says much for Miss Yonge that one does not get sick of Violet ; and Theodora is perfect, and Percy scarcely less. I have nibbled at a very different book, Ferrier's long-expected *Institutes of Metaphysic*, which is readable and seemingly not without value ; it is at all events something to find an absolutist Scotchman, however fantastic a one. I should like much to know your views of Maurice's new book on Sacrifice. There is nothing, I believe, that positively repels me (as parts of the *Essays* did), and there is much (especially the last sermon) which makes him dearer than ever. The Working Men's College is far more hopeful ; it does seem as if he had at last found a thoroughly healthy *modus* of social improvement ; and is it not grand, Ruskin's joining in the teaching ?

Time and space alike are wanting to do more than allude to the one engrossing subject of these fearful days of suspense. It is somewhat paradoxical, but I believe I feel far more happy than otherwise even at the losses we have sustained ; every despatch seems to carry fresh assurance that God has not ceased to go forth with our armies, even though He may allow every man in the Crimea to perish by the enemy. Sometimes I fancy it is well for us Churchmen to have our love for England thus quickened and deepened before we are tempted to hate her for outrages against Christ's Church. But I believe these are faithless thoughts, though they *will* come.— Ever yours affectionately,   FENTON J. A. HORT.

TO THE REV. JOHN ELLERTON

HARDWICK, *December* 30*th*, 1854 ;
January 2*nd*, 1855.

. . . You will have seen that the new Theological Tripos was passed 'unanimously'; the truth is, there were but few in the Senate House. Some who objected were unwilling to give the first *nonplacet;* others (myself included) did not discover that the graces were being read till the whole was over. I am not, however, very sorry ; the present plan is infinitely less objectionable than the other, and perhaps it is not altogether amiss that the experiment should be tried. Some changes of detail will by and bye have to be made ; *e.g.* it is not only ridiculous but very mischievous that candidates for Honours in Theology should be required to know no more Church History than that of the first three centuries and the Reformation. The proposed changes in Little-go and the Pol do not come before the Senate till next term, when we shall also, I suppose, have a report from the St. Mary's Syndicate, which is at present divided against itself. Whewell and Willis are violent upholders of Golgotha and the 'preaching house' theory of St. Mary's : Harvey Goodwin (whom I am glad to see appointed Hulsean Lecturer) is, I believe, leader of the opposition.

There has been some excitement at Cambridge about Rowland Williams' sermons before the University this month. Unluckily I did not hear any of them ; but I suspect they must have been really very heterodox, and certainly very odd, though, it is said, beautiful compositions. Selwyn's sermons were, as you may well suppose, a great treat. It was very interesting to see how with a mind unphilosophical and nearly untheological he was driven by the realities of his life to feed on the highest Catholic truths. The subject of his Ramsden sermon seemed perpetually to dwell in his mind, — 'the prayers of the Son of God.' It was amusing to see how he seemed to fancy that all Cambridge was troubled with doubts about Unity and in danger of going over to Rome! But his speech at the Propagation Society meeting was the grandest thing of all. He began in a low voice with administering one of the most terrible rebukes I ever heard in the gentlest and most gentlemanly form, and then spoke with extraordinary rapidity for a considerable while, every minute making one feel more strongly the depth of his wisdom. Dear old Blunt then said a few words, which I could not catch; and Harvey Goodwin made a speech which would have been good at an earlier hour, but was then too long and fell flat. I hope we shall not lose altogether the quickening effects of his visits to Cambridge.

One of the most important events of the year 1855, as showing Hort's active interest in other matters than those directly concerning a scholar, was the establishment of a Working Men's College at Cambridge. In the following year he, along with Maurice, assisted at the inauguration of a similar institution at Oxford, one of the very few occasions on which he made a public speech. On the occasion of this visit to Oxford he took an *ad eundem* degree. His diary and correspondence about this time are for some reason very scanty. The Crimean War was much in his mind. His thoughts on the tragedy of the war were given a personal turn by the death at Malta of a young officer's wife, for whom he and his friend Blunt had a great regard. Their feeling about the war, thus intensified by sympathy with the sorrow of common friends, took shape in the anonymous

joint publication of a little volume of verse called
Peace in War. The last only of the poems, that
called 'Tintern,' was by Hort ; it was suggested by
a walk taken in October 1855 to the ruined abbey,
which was one of the chief delights in the neighbourhood of his new Chepstow home. The poem,
somewhat difficult and compressed as is its style, ex-
hibits a command of language which the writer did
not at all times possess. Apart from its beauty,
this, his one original poetic utterance, is interesting on
that ground alone, but it is perhaps chiefly remarkable biographically as evidence of a mind which
regarded every passing event not in isolation, but as
part of the great scheme of human life, which even
in early manhood 'saw life steadily, and saw it
whole.' The occasion which had prompted his friend's
verses is merged in the thought of the general tragedy
of the war, while the war itself is treated as part of
the universal mystery of pain and death ; and, characteristically, pain becomes the ground of a manly
optimism ; the 'peace' is like that of which a more
recent poet speaks :

Not Peace that grows by Lethe, scentless flower,
There in white languors to decline and cease ;
But Peace whose names are also Rapture, Power,
Clear sight and Love, for these are parts of Peace.[1]

TINTERN, October 1855

So stood the clustering hills
About the sacred nest,
When first stern English wills
Disturbed its grassy rest ;
So glowed or gloomed the narrowed sky
On labouring limb and praying eye.

[1] William Watson, 'Wordsworth's Grave.'

When round the crumbling walls
    May's brightest blooms are shed,
And earth's fresh glory falls
    Alive athwart the dead ;
The heart within us *will* rejoice,
And answer with its human voice.

For then her choicest stores
    The foster-mother brings,
And duteously adores
    Her ancient priests and kings ;
New decking after winter's rage
The tomb that marks a perished age.

And we are of to-day ;
    The spring in leaf and bud
More meetly than decay
    Beats time to dancing blood :
Our wayward eye will scarcely brook
On unattempered death to look.

But holier yet the sight,
    When summer's glare is gone,
And chill autumnal light
    Is searching every stone,
Till faint amid the paling blue
Calm golden stars steal trembling through.

For now in lonely air
    The ruin lonely stands ;
The beauty still is there
    That grew by human hands :
The year's young glory dying lies ;
But *this* endures through wintry skies.

Through no deceitful mask
    The foster-mother still
Pursues her gracious task,
    Is bright or dark at will :
The promise of her spring were less
But for her autumn mournfulness.

And giving of her mirth,
And taking of their tears,
She soothes mankind from birth
Through all the fitful years :
The face whose gladness wakes their own
Diviner yet in grief is known.

'Tis better far to stand
Full face to face with death,
To grip his grinding hand,
To feel his stiffening breath,
Than heap vain veils to hide away
The tokens of his certain sway.

For when we know him well,
We know him conquered too ;
Unknown, the depths of hell
Breed phantoms ever new ;
But they who dwell within the light
Need fear no shade that haunts the night.

Deep autumn's solemn voice
Is music to the ear,
When we would fain rejoice,
But cannot stifle fear :
Such evening tones give strength to gaze
On threatening dawns of latter days.

For, while the hurrying years
Flash by to join the past,
A swarm of nameless fears
Buzz round us thick and fast ;
We cower from ghosts of coming ill,
And hug the present closer still.

Its joys are all we crave,
Its voice seems always true ;
We long that one deep grave
Might swallow old and new ;
Cling blindly to life's outer crust,
And only live because we must.

The works of elder time
  Afflict us with their peace ;
Their presence seems a crime ;
  Though dead they *will* not cease :
In vain we strive alone to dwell,
Unbidden faces mock the spell.

And round the aimless dance
  Of mad unrest within
The outer lightnings glance,
  World-thunders shake their din ;
From nook to nook in grief or dread
The pulses of the tempest spread.

With fiercer, blinder pride
  Death gluts his shortened reign ;
His cunning poisons glide
  Through many a living vein ;
And swifter struck with sudden might
His thousands pass from mortal sight.

Yet blest be every power
  That breaks the dreadful trance ;
In such tumultuous hour
  The hosts of truth advance ;
And welcome all, though rough its guise,
That rends the film from dreamy eyes.

What but a coward breast
  Would sigh for only calm ?
And he, that woos his rest,
  Knows neither peace nor palm ;
But richer joys will heal the smarts
Of valiant arms and loving hearts.

Then ask we not the tomb
  To render back the past.
From time's all-fruitful womb
  The fairest springs the last ;
And long-forgotten years obey
The works and glories of to-day.

Yet 'mid the roaring throng
　'Tis well to hear arise
The silent evening song
　Of yonder autumn skies,
Bring back yon roofless aisles, and hold
Strange converse with the times of old.

So from the inner shrine
　Yet holier strains may steal,
And all the heart divine
　Of earthly forms reveal ;
Weak moulds of dust no longer hide
The dead and living side by side.

Then back to earth once more.
　She hath her glory too ;
Nor lacks she heavenly lore
　For them that read her true ;
And changeful gleams may show aright
The changeless and eternal light.

When Christmas bells shall ring
　Across the lifeless snow,
We too will gladly sing
　The joy above the woe ;
No storm of earth shall keep afar
The peace that cannot turn to war.

And, when through budding trees
　Blithe Easter chimes shall bound,
Tossed on the quickening breeze
　In waves of throbbing sound,
We will not scorn the bliss of spring
For all our autumn murmuring ;

But cherish, as we may,
　The living fire that burns
In growth and in decay,
　In light and shade by turns ;
And greet through veils of sunlit tears
The perfect sum of deathless years.

The authorship of 'Tintern' was not disclosed; it was guessed, however, by Daniel Macmillan.

In 1856 Hort took priest's orders at Ely. In the same year he examined, for the first time, for the Natural Sciences Tripos. The Councils of the Working Men's College and of the Cambridge Philosophical Society occupied much time. Much also was given to the composition of the monograph on S. T. Coleridge, which appeared in the *Cambridge Essays* for 1856. The essay itself is compressed, and its scope could hardly be indicated by any attempt at further abstraction ; it considers Coleridge as a man, a poet, a theologian, a philosopher, and shows a remarkably deep and wide acquaintance both with Coleridge and with Coleridge's teachers. Mr. Leslie Stephen once spoke of it to me as the only serious attempt known to him to give a coherent account of Coleridge's philosophy. The nervous vigour of the style seems to show that composition, in spite of the difficulty of the subject, came easier to the writer at this age (twenty-eight) than at most periods of his life ; but the appearance may after all be deceptive.

In the May term Hort had a short experience of the work of a college lecturer. In the Long Vacation he spent nearly two months in Switzerland, chiefly in company with Lightfoot. The principal climbing event of the tour was the ascent of the Jungfrau, of which Hort's own description may be read in the Eggischhorn climbing-book. Later in the month he engaged the afterwards famous guide, Melchior Anderegg, with whom he crossed by a little known pass from Schwarenbach to Sierre in the Rhône valley. The rest of the time was spent mainly in the Mont Blanc region, in company partly with four other Fellows of Trinity,

—Lightfoot, the Rev. J. Ll. Davies, Mr. F. Vaughan Hawkins, and Mr. (now the Rev. Dr.) H. W. Watson. The chief object of the tour had been to ascend Mont Blanc from the St. Gervais side ; four attempts were made, but all were frustrated by bad weather. Hort, who took part in the last three of the excursions, wrote very full accounts to his parents and to Ellerton, some of which, familiar as the ground is now, are interesting as showing what kind of difficulties confronted the pioneers of the science of mountaineering. The story of these experiences is also told by Mr. Vaughan Hawkins in *Peaks, Passes, and Glaciers* (1st series, 1859, pp. 58-74).

A notable feature of these expeditions was Hort's attempt at photography in the high Alps. He carried to considerable heights a full-plate camera of the cumbrous make of the period, and took several pictures. Unluckily the waxed paper was kept too long undeveloped, and all Hort's efforts, assisted by his friend W. T. Kingsley, with whom he did much photographic work, could not produce a presentable picture.

To Mr. H. Bradshaw

CAMBRIDGE, *February 4th*, 1855.

. . . I have just been reading in the *sheets* of Kingsley's *Westward Ho!* a capital description of the attempt of the Spaniards to effect a lodgement in Munster in 1580, and have been so much interested by it that I daresay I shall some day make an effort to discover what your books[1] may contain about it. Kingsley's novel is the very thing to come out now,—judging by so much of it as I have read ; and I think you will enjoy it thoroughly. The only fault I have to find with it is that he will not leave those poor Stuarts alone.

[1] Bradshaw had recently become a master at St. Columba's College, near Dublin.

To THE REV. GARNONS WILLIAMS (his Brother-in-law)

CAMBRIDGE, *March 8th*, 1855.

. . . I am glad you find some spirit still left even in the printed text of Selwyn's *Sermons*. To myself, who heard three of them delivered, they seem in reading almost tame as compared with what they sounded from the pulpit,—as indeed I felt was likely to be the case, when I heard them. Now it is necessary to conjure up his face and voice and combine them with the words, before I can really enter into the sermons. This fact, however, does not make them less valuable to readers. It only confirms my previous impression that his greatness lies rather in his energy, resolution, generosity, and singleness of heart than in any specially intellectual brilliancy.

We have lately had a magnificent gift to our College Library. Dear old Archdeacon Hare left us his whole German library of 3000 volumes, by far the best in this country, and rich in valuable books and tracts hard to meet with even in Germany; he also sent a message that he would have given us his classical and theological books besides, but that he feared to burden us with duplicates of books that we had already. Mrs. Hare, however, entreated that we would send some one to choose out any that we pleased. Before he arrived, however, she had herself picked out and sent off some valuable large serial works, for fear we might have scruples about taking them! Altogether we have from 4500 to 5000 volumes. He has also given us busts of Coleridge and of your bishop,[1] which I have not yet seen. Poor Thirlwall is sadly cut up, I hear from those who saw him at the funeral. Hare was his dearest friend; and the very great benefits which they have both rendered to English literature were mainly connected with the employments in which they were associated together. Well, here is the end of a sheet; so I will say good-night.—Ever your affectionate brother,

FENTON J. A. HORT.

[1] Viz. the Bishop of St. David's.

To the Rev. Gerald Blunt

CAMBRIDGE, *March 11th and 20th*, 1855.

. . . You ask about Ellis.[1]   I never knew him personally, I am sorry to say ; but, when a freshman, I often saw him.   I should suspect that he knows more than any man living, and is among the deepest thinkers ; he is also one of the purest and humblest Christians.   But his living martyrdom cannot last much longer ; for months he has not been able to move a limb.

I have heard but little about dear old Hare.   One hardly knew how one loved him till he was gone.   You gave me a sad shock in writing about him ; telling me that I "must gird up my loins and take up the ——" here the page ended ; when I turned it, and saw the next words "prophetic mantle," they gave a thorough chill.   But just then the conclusion of that precious sermon on Saul, which I remember so well describing to you as we shouldered our way through the confusion of Bishopsgate Street, occurred to me, and relieved me by making me feel that in *that* sense I could accept your words and wish their fulfilment, to "desire not the power of the prophets but their obedience, not to speak inspired words, but to have the humble and contrite heart which He does not despise."   But enough of this.

. . . A large number of books worth mention have come out lately, but I must only speak of one or two.   First and foremost is Kingsley's *Westward Ho !* which is published to-morrow.   He has quite surpassed himself ; all his old energy and geniality, tempered with thorough self-restraint and real *Christian* wisdom.   The suffering and anxiety he has endured now for some time have obviously much purified and chastened him, and rather increased than lessened his strength and elasticity.   I hardly know a more *wholesome* book for any one to read.   Personally I feel deeply indebted to it, though I suppose its lessons, like most others, will prove transitory enough.   Don't smile ; but my first impulse, after reading it, was to wish myself chaplain of the *Dauntless*.   For the first

[1] Robert Leslie Ellis.

time, while I have been writing this down, the thought of one
John Brimblecombe has flashed upon me, as likely when you
read the book to appear whimsically to you to have suggested
to me that wish ; but the fact is I never thought of him and
his chaplaincy in connexion with the subject till this moment.
It is some time since I read the book, and the wish is not yet
quite melted away, but I suppose it is sufficiently fantastic. I
ought to say that *Westward Ho !* will very possibly not be
popular.   Some will say that it is too like a book of travels ;
others, like a common novel, etc. etc.   Its great fault is its
dearness, so that I must wait for the cheap edition.   Kingsley
has also printed (anonymously) a little tract for soldiers,
Brave Words for Brave Men, a dilution of a passage in that
astonishing sermon of Maurice's on 'the Word of God
conquering by sacrifice.'   It is very spirited and good, but
not all I could wish.   Great numbers have been already sold
for distribution.   Maurice's Edinburgh Lectures, and also those
on *Learning and Working,* will soon be out in one volume ;
I have not seen them.   Parker has started as a speculation
two yearly volumes like reviews, *Oxford Essays* and *Cambridge
Essays.*   The latter will be out in the autumn ; the former has
been out some weeks.   They are mainly pleasant, but not
very substantial reading, except one invaluable paper by
Froude on the study of English History, full of the best kind
of toryism.   Trench has brought out another nice little book
on the English language, *Past and Present.*   Another genuine
poet has arisen, to whom I hope some day to introduce you,
one Coventry Patmore.   His (anonymous) *Angel in the House*
is coming into notice, at least at Cambridge ; but his previous
volume (*Tamerton Church Tower*), which I have read to-day,
is better still.

Do pray give me a good long letter very soon, such a letter
as you used sometimes to write in days when you had neither
wife nor bairns ; for I am always less bad when there is anything of you to help me.   All love to aforesaid wife and
bairns.—Ever your affectionate friend,

FENTON J. A. HORT.

To the Rev. Gerald Blunt

HARDWICK, *April* 10*th,* ⎫
LLOWES,[1] *April* 16*th,* ⎭ 1855.

. . . You have been, I think, a little wilful in your way
of understanding my implied accusation. I never charged
you with writing worse letters in quality, since you became a
noun of multitude. But I have enough materialism in me to
think that quantity has its merits as well as quality; and I do
say that for the last three years your letters have been too
often seasoned with 'the soul of wit,' to a height unpleasing
to my dainty palate and insatiable maw.

The London trip was a very pleasant one. We are thinking of establishing a Working Men's College in Cambridge,
something like that in London. They were going on the
Thursday to have the tea which opens their term, and
Davies wanted some of us to come and be present, which I
was not sorry to do, as I wanted much to consult him and
Maurice on some points. So Vesey[2] and I went up together,
he being quartered on the Butlers, I on Davies. We had a
pleasant evening enough; I sat next to Maurice and had some
talk. Friday was chiefly spent with Vesey and Butler,[3] seeing
the great new church in Margaret Street. By the way, you
ask about Butler, as if you ought to have known him. But
the fact is, he has but just taken his degree, being senior
classic. He is a son of the late Dean of Peterborough, brother
of Spencer Butler (in the year below ours), an old Rugby
friend of mine, and of George Butler, who was my host at
Oxford when I was ordained. He is a very noble fellow;
indeed I do not think I love any one now at Cambridge so
well. I dined with the Butlers in Westbournia, and then we
went to Exeter Hall to hear Mendelssohn's 'Lobgesang' and
Mozart's 'Requiem.' Next day I dined with Maurice alone
at two, and then had a thoroughly enjoyable talk with him of
two or three hours about the College and other matters, and

[1] In Herefordshire, the parish of his brother-in-law, the Rev. Garnons
Williams.
[2] The Rev. F. G. (now Archdeacon) Vesey.
[3] H. Montagu Butler, now Master of Trinity College, Cambridge.

he gave me his new book, *Learning and Working*, which is worth its weight in gold. Next morning I went to Davies' church, and heard him preach; in the afternoon to Lincoln's Inn, and heard a good sermon from Maurice; and in the evening to St. Bartholomew's, Stepney, where Kingsley was to preach for Vivian, Davies' friend and neighbour. Kingsley was almost late; he looked very haggard, worn, and wild; but the sermon was one which few who heard it are likely ever to forget. You know I don't like his printed sermons in general, but this was quite another thing. It showed even more than *Westward Ho!* how deeply his distresses had worked in purifying and chastening him, and making him more of a Christian, as well as more of a man. After church he came for a few moments into the parsonage. I shook hands with him, but he had forgotten my face, for which he was almost ready to go on his knees when I told him my name; but we had no opportunity for talk. As he was going, the drawing-room being crowded, I went after him into the room where the hats were, with Vivian and some one else. When he saw me, he reproached himself violently for having been on the point of going without saying good-bye, took me by both hands, and asked when we could really meet. Fortunately he will be in London (he even *talks* of Cambridge) all June, and indeed will be hanging about London most of the year, as he is going to rebuild his parsonage in a less noxious spot. When I saw and heard and felt him again, I thought of what you had said last summer, and forgave you for your preference of him to Maurice, though my own judgement was unchanged. The grip of his hand would be a cordial for almost any ill; and it seems impossible to despair of anything while he is among the living.

Llowes, April 16*th.*—I meant to have finished this letter before, but find it hard to get time for writing here. . . . The new church here, though small, is one of the most beautiful modern ones I have seen; it has its blemishes, but it is a real luxury to look at it, and would be still more so to have for one's own church. Yesterday I preached my first sermon, but it was necessarily only in the schoolroom.

. . . I ought not to forget to mention Maurice's Lectures

on *Learning and Working* and on Roman Religion. They are some of the profoundest, cleverest, and most delightful things he has written, and full of invaluable hints on education and politics. I must now have done, only expressing a hope that you will continue to uphold the honour of wife and children (to whom all love) by the excellence of your correspondence.—Ever yours affectionately,

FENTON J. A. HORT.

TO THE REV. B. F. WESTCOTT

HARDWICK, *October 2nd*, 1855.

. . . I am sorry to say I have not read more than half a volume of Jowett[1] as yet. But the day before yesterday I read his essay on Natural Religion. Few, if any, of the thoughts were new to me; but it gives one a high impression of his goodness and wisdom. The facts (at least the modern facts) are indisputable, but is not his conclusion, so far as he has a conclusion, blank scepticism? After all he says very little about *physical* 'theology,' which seems to be your subject just now. I confess I have thought and care comparatively little for that aspect of the matter, and have a strong Job-like feeling, "The deep saith, It is not in me," etc., but I should much like a talk with you.

TO HIS MOTHER

CAMBRIDGE, *October 24th*, 1855.

. . . Mackenzie's *Essay* is at last really published, I am happy to say, and looks very well. I forgot to order to-day a copy for my father, as he asked me, but I will send one to-morrow. We have had several visitors the last few days, which partly accounts for the flight of time. One of these is a friend of mine who has been away some years, and is a brother worshipper of brambles. We spent a considerable part of a day in looking and talking over the large bundle

---

[1] Viz. Professor Jowett's edition of *St. Paul's Epistles to the Thessalonians, Galatians, and Romans.*

that I had brought home this year. But it was curious to find how few of my forms he could recognize as Worcestershire friends. Another visitor, who is here still, is Dr. Tregelles of Plymouth, whose life is completely given up to the restoration of the Greek text of the New Testament, and whom I was therefore particularly glad to know personally, though we had exchanged several letters before.

To the Rev. Gerald Blunt

CAMBRIDGE, *November 18th and 26th*, 1855.

My dear Blunt—The time has slipped away unaccountably without my writing, but I will not waste any more in making excuses. I do not know that I have anything more to say about the subject of subjects.[1] I suppose you are right in thinking that the last generation did not die away in the same fearful way. This we owe partly, I suppose, to their and their fathers' escapes ; partly also, perhaps, to the fierce and furious life which we live within nowadays ; at least I have not noticed such mortality among thick-skinned and tepid persons. But if we live fewer years, we have far more of *life* crowded into every year. And after all, could we desire to live in a time when God was less sharply and pertinaciously forcing the sensation of His presence upon us ? I for one wish always to keep in mind the motto to *Yeast*, " The days will come, when ye shall desire to see one of the days of the Son of Man, and ye shall not see it." And—once more—have we not a miserable, cowardly dread of physical death, such as no Christian age ever had before, and do we in our hearts sufficiently believe that *all* live unto God ? . . .

I have been induced to take fresh work in the shape of examining for the Natural Science Tripos in the spring, and also for the different Professorial certificate examinations in the same subjects. There is so much now to draw me away from natural science that I am not sorry to be compelled to stick to it, as I am sure that in moderation it is good for me in particular, and partly for everybody ; besides, it is a great

[1] The Crimean War.

enjoyment. I am just treating myself to a first-rate micro-scope, which will be a great accession. By the way, I am also going to start Photography.

I have never told you, I believe, about the Working Men's College which we have set up here like that in town. It is too long a story for a letter, but I will send you Harvey Goodwin's Inaugural Lecture when it appears, which will tell you something. I take the second Latin class, and lecture for an hour on Thursday evening, chiefly catechetically. Even if the educational results are poor, it is a vast gain to both sides that the University men and any kind of working men should be brought into that kind of intercourse. It is a strangely happy feeling to see the softened and bright kindly eyes of those young fellows looking up at one. Maurice is coming here on Friday for a night to see how we get on (though he has no connexion with us), and we are all to meet him at Goodwin's house.

About Jowett, I don't think you could go beyond me in enjoying and praising him. His wonderful sympathy, depth of insight into men, and thorough love of truth and fact are above praise; but, alas! his theological *conclusions* seem to me blank atheism, though *he* is anything but an atheist. Even the learning and scholarship of the book you must not accept on trust. It is nearly always second-hand, and often quite wrong. I have not yet been able to do much more than look over Sydney Smith, but it seems very delightful. It is very obvious that we have never done him justice. Still we should be in a very bad way now if we had not had at the same time far deeper men, whom he probably both mis-understood and despised. Miss Forssteen will probably have told you of the volume of Lectures to Ladies, which even now I have not finished. Several are invaluable,—Maurice's of course, also Dr. Chambers', Davies', and a thoroughly practical and sensible one of Kingsley's; it is remarkable as the only place where I remember to have seen him speak despondingly of the state of England, and it is a sad confirmation of one's own fears. Bunsen will of course have shown you the delightful translations of German hymns which another Miss Winkworth has published. If you remember any of our talks about Novalis, you will read with interest "What had I been if Thou wert not?" She has much shortened and demysticized it; but I cannot say spoiled it. I hope you noticed Godfrey Arnold's "How blest to all Thy followers, Lord, the road." Maurice has written a preface to the new edition of the Old Testament [Sermons] (now called *Patriarchs and Lawgivers*), in answer to Mansel's pamphlet on Eternity, or rather pointing out how much must be consistently given up by those who profess to adopt Mansel's philosophical scheme against him. He has also written a preface of 100 pages to Hare's *Charges*, which are going to be collected into one volume (including the unprinted ones). The preface will be, as he intimates himself, a comment on the English Church History of the last fifteen years. A very noble Scotchman named Campbell, who was turned out of the Kirk with Irving, Alex. Scott, etc., for asserting that God does not will the death of a sinner, is publishing at Macmillan's a valuable book on the Atonement, much of which I have read. It is quiet and evangelical in tone, and not at all alarming; I do not think it meets all sides of the question, but it expresses my own ideas better than any book I ever saw.

To his Mother

CAMBRIDGE, *November 30th*, 1855.

. . . I had an extremely kind note from Mrs. Mackenzie, thankfully praising the book, and telling me that all friends, Lord Murray in particular, wrote to her to the same effect. I can honestly say that I was perfectly disinterested in undertaking the labour; but I have no doubt that, if ever I go to Edinburgh, as Mrs. Mackenzie has often pressed me to do, I shall find there that it has gained me several kindly-disposed friends.

To the Rev. John Ellerton

HARDWICK, *January 2nd and 7th*, 1856.

My dear Ellerton—I feel some shame at having acted on what looks like commercial principles in not writing because you owe me a letter; but I have written hardly any letters the last few months beyond what have been absolutely necessary, and it really seems as if every month I had less and less time for anything, while yet the results are painfully empty.

I have not much to tell you about myself. What chiefly occupied me last year was Mackenzie's *Essay*, of which I hope you received a copy that I sent by post. This last term I hardly know what I have been doing, except the ordinary work of our *Journal of Philology*, and preparing a rather elaborate article on the date of Justin Martyr,[1] which I have not yet finished. Examinations also take up time. . . . As for plans for the year, it is far too early to think of them, and I now never know my fate for a month beforehand. But Lightfoot and I have some vague ideas of getting three or four weeks together at Paris to collate MSS., he of Clement of Alexandria, and I of Epiphanius; and the experience of eighteen months ago was so favourable as to my health, that I dream of trying to get four or five weeks more among the glaciers. But this is all among the clouds.

You would be surprized at the changes at Cambridge. The tutors now are Mathison, Thacker, and Munro. Dear old Munro groans under the infliction, but I think it will do him a great deal of good. We have had a great loss in Scott,[2] but one could not grudge him to Westminster. The most important man, I think, now in Trinity is Lightfoot, from whom I expect a great deal. He always seemed solid, a good scholar, and disposed to be a learned and thoughtful theologian; but I was hardly prepared for the vivacity and liberality which he has shown in the last few months. He is certainly West-cott's best pupil. At St. John's we have lost Hutchinson, who has just married and gone to Birmingham ; but the two Mayors and Roby are invaluable in their several ways.

But perhaps the most important Cambridge matter of all has been the establishment of the Working Men's College. . . . Somewhere about October 1854 Montagu Butler (a most excellent fellow,—and brother ' Apostle,'—senior classic last spring, and elected Fellow of Trinity his first time) spoke to

---

[1] See *Journal of Classical and Sacred Philology*, No. viii. p. 155.
[2] The Rev. C. B. Scott.

me on the subject, having been of course stimulated by the
then recent foundation of the College in London.   Whether
he or Vesey was the first to suggest it for Cambridge, I don't
know ; but they consulted together.   My advice was to wait
a while, till the London experiment had been fairly tried, and
then see what could be done.   In December I was introduced
to Vesey, and he spoke to me about it, and I gave the same
answer.   He had been similarly advised by ¡H. Goodwin.
Early last spring, however, they moved again, and this time
H. Goodwin consented to act at once ; and of course, entirely
approving the project in itself, I could not refuse to do the
same, though I should have preferred further delay.   We four,
with A. Macmillan and Joe Mayor, met repeatedly and got our
ideas into shape ; we then called a meeting of friends well
disposed to the plan [and] voted (after much discussion)
several fundamental principles, the chief being that the
Council should consist exclusively of teachers and such as
should be ready to teach if called upon.   Those present who
were willing to subscribe to this condition then became *ipso
facto* the Council, all future members being admitted on
similar terms by ballot.   Harvey Goodwin was elected
Principal.   After many meetings in that and May term, we
took and furnished rooms at the back of a house in the
market-place, and in October started the classes.   Hitherto
the success has been in most respects all we could desire, in
number of students most remarkably so.   The great principle
we have started from is to substitute for Mechanics' Institute
orations and 'lectures' a *bonâ fide* education by means of
carefully catechetical lessons.   Even if the education actually
given should prove to be small in amount, which we have no
right to assume, two great benefits must, I think, arise : 1st,
the men (who are chiefly young) will be shown practically what
accurate learning and knowledge is, and will at least receive a
good lesson in genuine self-education ; and 2nd, and above
all, the University and the town will be brought face to face
in a way that cannot fail to be of the greatest possible service
to both.   Indeed, over and above the object of bridging over
the chasm between classes, I am sanguine enough to hope that
the rest of the University will receive a healthy impulse towards

a real combination of 'learning and work,' and a practical
horrour of keeping knowledge, or anything else, 'hid in a
napkin.' I think you will allow that these are strong reasons
for doing what we can at Cambridge ; and of course the
assemblage of a good staff of teachers, such as only an
University town could furnish, is a very great help. I must not
write longer on this point, but I hope we shall soon have an
opportunity of talking it over. Maurice is of course greatly
interested in our experiment, and actually came down to us for
three nights (including Sunday) at the beginning of December.
In the morning he preached at St. Edward's for H. Goodwin,
in the evening for Tayler at St. Mary's, and you may imagine
what a pleasure it was to hear him from that pulpit. Tayler
opened the galleries (they have been closed in the evenings
since Carus' departure), and every part of the church was
crammed. He gave us a very simple and affecting sermon on
godly sorrow and the sorrow of the world, and I have some
reason to hope it conquered some prejudices. Poor dear old
—— was aghast at such a pollution of St. Mary's pulpit, and
doubly so when he heard that Maurice had preached a most
inoffensive sermon, remarking that he was very sorry to hear
it, as it would only delude people into a false security.
Maurice seems to have gone back to London greatly delighted
and encouraged by his visit. He has left us a pleasant relic
of it in his portrait, which Macmillan induced him to have
taken by a photographer on Parker's Piece. Well ! unless
something fresh occurs to me, I think this must do for
Cambridge news. . . .

I cannot remember whether I mentioned to you Westcott's
new book on the N. T. Canon, as solid and thorough a book
as you will often see. A very valuable book on the Atonement (of which I have read four or five chapters) is just
coming out by Campbell, a great friend of Alexander Scott,
and expelled with him from the Kirk. He was at Cambridge
last term, and a milder and more beautiful spirit I have
seldom seen, with much of the wisdom that it might be
expected to produce. . . . Maurice is getting on with the
Mediæval Philosophy, but his thoughts chiefly turn to the
last instalment of the Warburtonian Lectures, the commentary

on St. John's writings. When that shall have been published, he tells Macmillan (but of course it must not be repeated) he feels that his work on earth will be done. Birks has just published at Macmillan's a book, *The Difficulties of Belief.* The leading ideas seem to be a strong faith in man's freedom, and the necessity of recognizing it in all theology, and a horrour of attributing arbitrary and 'potter'-like conduct to God; and from such premises some rather weighty results may be worked out. I hope you will see Kingsley's new book 'for children,' *The Heroes.* It is nearly free from preaching, and a singularly beautiful and truthful rendering of the stories of Perseus, the Argonauts, and Theseus. The engravings are by his own hand, and surprised me exceedingly after his failure in *Glaucus.* As pictures they are for the most part very lovely, and they have caught the true Greek spirit in a way that I do not remember to have seen even approached. The figure of Andromeda in the frontispiece is, I think, the best, and exquisite it is. In speaking of Cambridge I might have mentioned the *Cambridge Essays.* Most of the best contributors called off for one reason or another when the time came, and so this number is below what I had hoped, but still interesting. The gem of it is Brimley's article on Tennyson, a genuine burst of hearty enthusiasm ludicrously at variance with all dear Brimley's pet theories (he now professes to believe in nothing but 'nervous tissue'!), and, except in one or two groundless cavils, a worthy vindication against the populace. The next best article is one by Hughes of Magdalen, on the 'Future Prospects of the British Navy,' with which should be read his 'Cruise of the Pet,' a capital account of his voyages to the Baltic (including Bomarsund and Sveaborg) in '54 and '55. . . . Clark's [1] (who is the editor) is too slight (on Classical Education), but has two or three inimitable pages. Clark has asked me to write in the next number, and I have undertaken a paper on Coleridge, but rather shrink from all the reading that ought to be accomplished beforehand. Otherwise it would be difficult to find a more convenient way of uttering several things that I want to say, especially about the

[1] W. G. Clark.

tendencies of English philosophy.   I am anxious to hear
what you have been doing in certain proposed plans.   Several
promising titles of hymn-books have been advertised in the
papers during the last year, but I have seen hardly any of
them.   Miss Winkworth has published under the name of
Lyra Germanica a very good selection of German hymns
from Bunsen's great collection, for the most part admirably
translated ; but they are few, and a large proportion fit only
for private use.   Some of the so-called Christmas and Easter
Carols done by J. M. Neale are also, to my surprise, extremely good hymns for church use ; others are simply
absurd.   When I was with you at Brighton you were at
work on a scheme for a book in conjunction with your
Canterbury friends (I forget the name).   I hope that is not
given up.   I may as well tell you at once that in four or five
days you will receive a poem of Blunt's.   The verses headed
'Tintern, October 1855,' are my own.

It is rather too late at the end of this tolerably long letter
to begin talking politics, but I must own I should be glad to
know what you are thinking of the progress of affairs.   I find
so few to agree with me, that every accession gains double
the value to me that it would have for its own sake.   The
preface to poor Henry Lushington's *Poems* seems to me still
incomparably the truest word that has yet been spoken about
the war ; and no one else seems really to feel what is at
stake.   The blind ferocity of the war party and the narrow
Guizotian aims of even the noblest and bravest of the men
of peace repel one's thoughts almost alike.   How one
almost curses that word civilization !   And then what a
glorious future the new seers promise us !   First, a military
despotism, whether it be Russian or Occidental, and then a
China, a hive of 'industry.'   And then how many centuries' work is undone in that Concordat !   Still there is hope
in this new Swedish alliance.   Sweden itself, I fear, is half
rotten, morally and politically, but in Norway and Denmark,
if anywhere, can I see any promise of genuine life.   I had
better stop ; so I will only send kind regards to your mother,
and, though late, every best wish for the new year.—Ever
yours affectionately,   FENTON J. A. HORT.

To his Mother

CAMBRIDGE, *February 28th*, 1856.

. . . You will perhaps have been expecting to hear something about my ordination at Ely last Sunday week, but really there was nothing about it on which I could write with any pleasure. Nothing could well be more frigid and perfunctory without being absolutely offensive.

.   .   .   .   .

That little creature (*Chelifer* by name), which I found in the wood, turns out to be a real curiosity. It is exactly as I supposed, intermediate between scorpions, spiders, and mites. Both Babington and William Kingsley have known it some years, but hardly anything has been written on the curious little tribe to which it belongs. They are chiefly to be found behind the loosened bark of trees. My capture is now safely mounted in Canada balsam, and it is fortunate that our first attempt failed, and that he was laid by in spirits of wine, though he suffered some injuries then, and some more since.

To the Rev. Gerald Blunt

CAMBRIDGE, *March 20th*, 1856.

. . . In the new number of our *Journal of Philology* is a most excellent review[1] of Stanley and Jowett *as critics* by Lightfoot, but he purposely avoids the theology. I have, however, just seen in MS. a big pamphlet or small book which Davies is going to print against Jowett's theology; in nearly every word of which I concur, though I should like to say a good deal more of both praise and blame. . . . I think I mentioned to you before Campbell's book on the Atonement, which is invaluable as far as it goes; but unluckily he knows nothing except Protestant theology. . . .

You will all this while be wondering at my being up here at this time. The reason will perhaps surprise you also. Montagu Butler has accepted the post of secretary to William Cowper, President of the Board of Health, and has just been

---

[1] *Journal of Classical and Sacred Philology*, No. VII.

suddenly summoned to his duties. The result is that his
lecture-room is left mouthless for next term. He has accordingly, after consultation with Mathison, asked me to
lecture for him for next term, not as assistant tutor, but simply
as a temporary substitute. This I have agreed to do ; and am
therefore staying up to coach Tacitus for the benefit of
Mathison's freshmen. I hope it may make me regular. At
all events I like the work, though it will be laborious ; and I
shall be my own master after next term.

This last result may be of some consequence, if I carry
out a dream that I have gradually been forming of going to
Egypt, Palestine, and Syria for about January to July next.
I don't know that I shall be able to afford it, but I think I
ought to try. It is possible that I might join a probable party
consisting of Butler, Vesey, Gibson, and Lightfoot. Again I
am pretty nearly resolved to go somewhere this summer, but
where I cannot say. Health, however, is a great object ; and
that combined with pleasure point very strongly to M. Rosa
and the glaciers. . . .

We had an election of a musical professor a little while
ago (when Sterndale Bennett, to my great joy, was elected
triumphantly), and Trench came up to vote ; he breakfasted
with me next morning, and I meant to have given him *Peace
in War*, but forgot it. I have now, however, sent it to him.
I have also sent it anonymously to Ruskin and Keble.

I have done very little for Coleridge yet, but must work at
him this term ; the essay will be far less elaborate than I had
once thought of making it. I have not yet finished off Justin
Martyr, but hope to do so very soon. By the way, any news
from the Roman Bishops? I have had a vague idea of
writing a (much wanted) pamphlet on examinations, but shall
probably not have time. The ground is also partly occupied
by a good book lately published by Donaldson on classical
learning and scholarship. Much the most interesting and
substantial book come out lately is Archer Butler's *Lectures on
Ancient Philosophy* (*i.e.* Plato and his predecessors, Aristotle's
Psychology, and a little of the Neoplatonists), with very
excellent notes by Thompson. I have just got and begun a
huge new *semi*-juvenile book by the [author of the] *Heir of*

Redclyffe, The Daisy Chain, which seems promising. By the way, I forgot last term to advise you to read Shirley Brooks' *Aspen Court,* if you see it. Thinking of it afterwards, I don't like it as I did at first, but it deserves reading. George Meredyth's (*sic*) *Shaving of Shagpat* is a prose imitation of the *Arabian Nights,* which I had not patience to get through. It seems clever, but quite unworthy of him.

To his Mother

CAMBRIDGE, *May 3rd,* 1856.

. . . Your questions about lecturing, etc., I had already anticipated in writing to my father, and I do not know that there is any further answer to add now. You ask, by the way, about hesitation. Now and then for a few seconds the words do not come out freely, but that is only occasionally, and never to a serious degree. I do not think it ever occurs when I get into full swing. It has this moment occurred to me that perhaps you may be thinking rather about fluency than freedom of articulation; but the fact is, the word 'lecturing' is rather deceptive. What I have to do consists in hearing six or eight of the lecture-room read and translate a few lines of Latin each, correct their blunders, give any comments or cautions which the words of the passage suggest, and finally retranslate it myself; so that it is not at all like a continuous harangue, and nearly every sentence is directly suggested by the book before me. I have chiefly directed their attention to peculiarities of words or phrases, the exact force of particular expressions, the history of important words, and matters of that kind, which it would be difficult, if not impossible, for them to scrape together entirely for themselves out of books. For more purely historical matter I have referred them generally to accessible English books, occasionally translating to them passages of German books which seemed of particular value. I find myself quite unable to overtake the amount of preparation for lectures which I should like to accomplish, but I find the same complaint by all conscientious lecturers at Trinity.

We are very well satisfied with our new organist, who made his debut a week ago. Every stranger finds our organ difficult at first, and accordingly on Saturday Hopkins[1] blundered and struggled a good deal, though every now and then came a difficult passage so well played as to show that he was not wanting in skill. On Sunday he was quite successful, though, of course, not equal to poor Walmisley. He fails most in accompanying the chanted Psalms, into which Walmisley used to throw an extraordinary variety and flexibility without changing a note, but in the anthems he plays the brilliant and delicate parts equally well.

I have mislaid your last note, and cannot recollect whether there was anything in it that required answering, except about the fungi. But I am very much obliged for them; they are certainly the true edible Morell (*Morchella esculenta*), which I have long wished to see. Berkeley calls them "esteemed anywhere as a valuable article of food." About the beautiful little red fungus which you sent me before I do not feel so sure. . . . The little 'critturs' in the wood I popped into your little bottle of spirits of wine, but have not looked at them since. In the vacation Mr. William Kingsley took hastily two waxed paper negatives with his oxyhydrogen light to show me how he applies photography to the microscope. The objects were the spiracle or breathing-hole of a caterpillar, and a *Chelifer* something like the one I found at Hardwick, but a different species. He gave me the negatives, and I have just taken some rather indifferent positives from them, of which I have sent one of each, thinking you may like to see them.

To THE REV. GERALD BLUNT

CAMBRIDGE, *May 14th and 18th*, 1856.

. . . I was much interested in your account of the strange heretics you are fallen among. At the same time I fear I should rave at them like a madman if I got in their company. —— no doubt rejects the common doctrine because it seems

---

[1] Successor to Walmisley, whose much regretted death occurred in this year. Hort always regarded him as the prince of organists.

to contradict morality, and yet those vague sweeping theories of salvation introduce a meaning of salvation which destroys the very possibility of morality. All depends on our maintaining the inviolability of the will; and for finite beings a will is no will which *cannot* choose evil. If he admits that, but says that the continued rebellion of any is irreconcilable with the triumph of God's will and love, then I say that the *present* rebellion of any is likewise inconsistent with the same. While that awful fact of sin is staring you in the face, you cannot weave theories for the future that will hold water, except by the German dodge of refining sin into a lesser kind of necessary good, which is the very devil. " I don't know " is at last the only possible answer. And I do most cordially say amen to Davies' assertion that nowadays it is much more essential to insist on God's justice than His love. The idea of justice is so utterly corrupted that people oppose it to love, and that blasphemy must be overthrown. I quite allow that Davies made too much of the alleged contradictions in Jowett; but after all he devotes very few pages to them. The purpose of the pamphlet is not to scoff at them, but to protest against the sentimental atheism which is Jowett's fundamental doctrine. Where he finds an essay that he likes, he does praise it, viz. the last.

To the Rev. John Ellerton

CAMBRIDGE, *June* 13*th*, 1856.

. . . I have not yet told you my plans for the summer. I am going for six or seven weeks of hard labour among the glaciers and highest peaks of the Alps, eschewing the vallies and ordinary Swiss lions. Lightfoot and I have agreed to rendezvous at Luzern July 19th, spend a week in training among the peaks of Uri, etc., ending at the Grimsel, and a fortnight in the snow region of the Bernese Oberland (the ascent of the Jungfrau and Finsteraarhorn being dreamed of); and then make all haste to St. Gervais at the foot of Mt. Blanc, where we expect to find Hawkins and perhaps Ames or Watson, and thence ascend Mt. Blanc himself (this is a dead secret) by the new route, thereby avoiding the extortions of Chamonix. Lightfoot has not made up his mind how much farther he will accompany us before diverging to Germany, but at all events Hawkins and myself talk of moving eastward, crossing and recrossing the main chain till we reach Zermatt, and then spend some two or three weeks in that region, going up M. Rosa and as many other of the highest points (mostly unexplored hitherto) as we can manage, and then return home. I hope we shall find it an expedition to be remembered.

TO HIS SISTER, MRS. GARNONS WILLIAMS

ÆGGISCHHORN, *August 1st and 3rd*, 1856.

. . . My last letter was posted at Lauterbrunnen last Saturday. That day we did nothing particular. Next morning we read prayers to a party of present and old Rugbeians. . . . On Monday we started for Grindelwald by the Wengern Alp and Little Scheideck. The day was superb, and we had the best possible views of the mountains in a semicircle from the Jungfrau to the Blümlis Alp and Doldenhorn, then the Jungfrau herself, and finally the Mönch, Eiger, Mettenberg, and Wetterhorn. We reached Grindelwald at 12, dined and rested, and at a quarter to 5 set off on our first really great expedition, the Pass of the Strahleck.

At Lauterbrunnen we had engaged a good guide, Fitz von Almer, and at his suggestion we took another (the best) from Grindelwald, Peter Bohren. We had a very steep climb by the ordinary path to the level of what is called the Mer de Glace de Grindelwald. The precipices then closed in on the ice for some way, and after winding along their face we got upon the glacier for a few hundred yards, after which the precipices retired, leaving a rugged triangular slope, in the upper corner of which was perched the little chalet of Stiereck, which was to be our night's lodging.

August 3rd.—Lightfoot and I have just had evening service, and now I must try to tell a little more of my story before going to bed. While coffee was preparing, we strolled

about, and felt ourselves to be in a most amusing situation.
A number of goats crowded about us, with rather too pressing
familiarity, though we could not help admiring the pretty
creatures perched about in all manner of odd places, and as
inquisitive as cats; likewise there were some aristocratic but
decidedly stupid calves and three or four pigs. Presently
supper was ready, and a funny meal it was, but by no means
to be despised. We had to cut our bread and meat with our
pocket-knives, and I stirred my coffee with a smaller one that
I had. The coffee and milk were in two great pots, and
served out with a wooden ladle. Of course we had taken our
provisions with us. After supper we went 'to bed.' The
chalet consisted, first of a little closet or scullery, where the
fire was; next, of a little bit of a room with a table and two
short benches (our dining-room); and next, of a slightly larger
room or barn, with no furniture but shelves on shelves of
cheeses, the floor being strewed with plenty of hay. In one
corner lay two mattresses, or flat bags loosely stuffed with hay,
and between these we gentry reposed. The guides occupied
the loose hay. In our evening stroll we had meditated much
on fleas—in fact they were the one dark background to our
present amusement and pleasure—but happily the hay was
clean as well as dry, and we escaped unscathed, though the
heat and excitement kept me from getting to sleep. In the
morning I climbed over the rocks to a little stream and
washed my face, and after a breakfast closely resembling
supper we set off again at 4.15. We ascended the glacier for
some way to the other side, and then had a series of walkings
and scramblings up rugged banks and climbings over difficult
rocks, till at 6.30 we stood on the level of the upper end of
the glacier. Nothing could be grander than the views the
whole way, but especially at starting, when the range of snowy
peaks of the Wetterhorn stood before us in the clear starlight,
with a faint tinge of white twilight. We crossed the Grindelwald glacier a second time with great ease, and then had a
laborious ascent of the steep tributary Strahleck glacier on
our left. At 8 we breakfasted again, and again began
climbing over ice, snow, and rocks, till at 10.15 we reached
the top of the pass, and stopped again to eat, photographize,

and look about. The Schreckhorn was magnificent, close above our heads. The Finsteraarhorn had been hidden from us five miles before, but the loss was made up by the other peaks of the Aar glaciers, especially the beautiful Oberaarhorn, often confounded with the rather inferior Lauteraarhorn. By and bye we set out to descend the other side, having first been tied together with a rope. We first had to scramble down a literally almost perpendicular precipice called the Wand (or Wall), but the very rugged and broken nature of the rocks, with ordinary care, obviated all danger. The lower part, which, being coated with ice, *is* sometimes more dangerous, was made comparatively easy to us from the quantity of snow on the ice. We slid down the lower slopes on our guides' backs at a great pace. Just as we reached the bottom, we met an Englishman with two guides, coming up the pass. We then had a long and tedious trudge, with magnificent views, down the 'firn' of this arm of the glacier. This 'firn' is the upper end of all the greater glaciers, consisting of crusty, powdery snow rather than ice. Presently the Finsteraarhorn poured in its tributary stream of ice. The *firn* began to change, and we reached the Abschwang, where the Lauter and Finsteraar glaciers unite to form the great Lauteraar glacier. We had a singular walk for miles upon the united stream till near its end, where it became quite covered with lumps of rock, over which we clambered to the granite banks at the side. Tell my mother that the glacier stereoscopic photograph is of the Schreckhorn and Lauteraarhorn range of mountains. We must as nearly as possible have passed the spot where it was taken. Once more on level ground in the valley of the infant Aar, we set off at full speed, and reached the Grimsel at 7.23 P.M., having been on foot $15\frac{1}{2}$ hours. We ought not to have been so long, but we sometimes went very slowly, and there were some needless halts.

As we approached the hospice, we saw two figures watching us, whom I soon recognised to be Mr. Mathison and Mr. Ingram ! We had expected to meet them before, but in vain. We had a delightful chat before going to bed, but they were off early next morning. Though not more than very slightly tired, we thought it best to rest next day, merely taking a walk

of twelve or fourteen miles down to the Falls at Handeck and
back, and my old impressions of the wonderful grandeur of
the Grimsel scenery were more strengthened. We had fully
intended going next day up the whole length of the Upper
Aar glacier, over the Oberaarjoch, and down the whole
length of the Viesch glacier to our present quarters, but that
evening the charges for guides proved to be so exorbitant,
that we gave up the plan, and resolved to follow the Rhone
instead.   Accordingly at 5.15 we set off up the pass,
having transferred our luggage to a porter, and then had
a most thoroughly enjoyable walk over moor and moss
and down through forest straight to Obergestelen, getting
infinitely grander views than I had at all expected. We
reached Münster by the valley road at 9.30, had a famous
déjeuner à la fourchette, and rested two hours at the little inn,
and then tramped for three weary hours along a broil of airless
road to Viesch, getting no shade except from some dozen
chalets in each village. At Viesch we dined, and rested
about four hours, and then climbed the steep mountain side
to this half-finished but most comfortable little hotel. Next
afternoon (Friday) at 3.41, after making extensive preparations,
we set out for a great expedition, no less than the ascent of
the Jungfrau, with two guides, two porters, and for a part of
the way with a Mr. Bradshaw Smith, with his guide and porter.
We had a stiff climb over a shoulder of the mountain, and
down to the curious little lake of Märjelen, with little bergs of
the purest ice floating upon it, and bounded on one side by
high cliffs of glacier, passing from snowy white into the
deepest blue.   An easy scramble of a few minutes brought us
upon the astonishing Aletsch glacier, said to be the largest in
the world, a vast highway of ice from a mile to a mile and a
half wide and many miles long, leading into the very heart of
the greatest mountains in the Bernese Oberland. After walking along it with thorough pleasure for two hours we reached
our stranger night-quarters at a little before 8, but these, and
also our successful ascent of the Jungfrau next day (which,
as we have reason to believe, has been ascended by *but
two* Englishmen before ourselves), must stand over for my
next letter.

To his Mother

HOTEL DE L'OURS, KANDERSTEG,
August 8th, 1856.

My dearest Mother—My letter to Kate from the Æggisch-horn told you of no more than the fact of our having got up the Jungfrau, and you will naturally be wanting to hear more. One great difficulty about the Jungfrau is the distance of its only accessible side from any good resting-place. The route from Grindelwald is extremely bad, and it is question-able whether it has ever been accomplished before this year. Professor Forbes, Agassiz, Désor, etc., made their great classical ascent from the wretched chalets below Märjelen Lake. But this year an excellent little hotel has been opened on the Æggischhorn, not much farther off, and the moment I heard of its existence from Ames at Interlaken, I made up my mind that that must be our starting-point. We found the hotel still unfinished ; indeed, when we arrived, there was no glass to the windows, but it was put in roughly every night, and we enjoyed our quarters extremely. I should mention that the Jungfrau had been on our list before leaving England as one of the things to be done, if reasonable means could be found on the spot. We both were well acquainted with the ascent from Forbes' account. If you can get hold of his *Norway and its Glaciers,* you will find it in the appendix ; it is very accurate and good, but he must have found more difficulties from the width of the *bergschrunds* and from a comparative want of snow on the ice of the upper part. I had also read Désor's French account of the same ascent, and Studer's German account of his own. Thus we knew perfectly well what we had before us. Porters were sent on in good time on Friday to take fuel and a blanket or two to our night's quarters, and prepare them generally. We set out at 3.45 P.M. with our two guides carrying provisions and our plaids, and Mr. Brad-shaw Smith and his guide, who had not made up his mind whether he would go on with us or turn in the morning over the Lötschsattel. We had a rough scramble over two shoulders of the Æggischhorn and down to the wonderful little lake of Märjelen, which lies between it and the Viescherhörner. But

I forgot till this moment that I had told Kate of our journey
up to the night's resting-place.   This was in a triangular recess
of the Faulberg, sloping rapidly down to the glacier.   Climbing up some steep rocks on one side of it, we found a place
where the slanting strata had left a kind of little cave pene-
trating a few feet into the mountain.   We perched as best we
could about the entrance and proceeded to supper.   Finding
before starting that the landlord had provided only cold drinks,
we had got some tea from him, and, having now lighted a fire,
proceeded to *boil* it in a small stew-pan, our only cooking
vessel, and delicious it was, though without milk.   After supper
we prepared for sleep.   I forgot to mention that on the glacier
we met a young Austrian and his guide.   Chapman, an Etonian
and Trinity man of Calthorpe's [1] year (I think also a friend of
his), a capital mountaineer, had the week before made his way
from Grindelwald to the top of the Jungfrau after considerable
hardships; and this had stimulated the German to do the
same with a strong body of guides and porters.   At last he
had succeeded, but had now dismissed all the guides, etc., but
one to return to Grindelwald, and was proceeding with the
best to Viesch; but, night coming on, and his guide being
ignorant of the Aletsch glacier, he begged to be allowed to
encamp near us for the night.   Of course we gave him the
benefit of our shelter and some of our provisions, and he
joined us three gentlemen in occupying the inmost recess of
the cave, where there was scarcely room for the four to lie
packed as closely as possible side by side, with the rock 3
inches from Lightfoot's nose.   I do not think any one slept
well except the Austrian; I could not sleep at all, and had to
get up just as I felt symptoms of it coming on.   In the middle
of the night, to our dismay, we heard the pattering of heavy
rain above the noise of the torrent which supplied us with
water, and presently for an hour or two a drop descended
every minute on our helpless upturned cheeks from the not
too watertight rocks close above them.   I had made my light
little macintosh into a pillow; and with great difficulty I
unwedged myself so as to sit partly up and put it on after a
fashion; but it kept me dry, and the leather case made still

[1] Calthorpe Blofield, a cousin.

something of a pillow. We were up soon after 3, drove off
our cares with a good breakfast, and set off once more at five
minutes to 4. The rain had long ceased, and the clouds had
nearly vanished except from the Jungfrau. Mr. Smith had at
first decided on going with us, but after breakfast called off,
his guide having, as it afterwards; turned out, privately assured
him that we were quite certain not to reach the top, and that
the clouds would rest there all day. The Austrian, a silly,
chattering coxcomb, but obviously a good walker, told us we
should not have been able to get up if he had not gone
before, but that his track would now show us the way, and the
500 steps which his guides had hewed in the ice would save
us the trouble of doing the same. In reality the printed
accounts are so accurate that *we* could scarcely have missed
the way; but doubtless our guides were saved some trouble
by the tracks for some part of the lower ascent; as for the
steps, they were too much melted and filled up to be of any
use to us. Our course lay along the glacier nearly to its head.
It was now no longer glacier proper, but what is called *firn*
or *névé*, consisting of waves and hillocks of very dry, crusty,
powdery snow, with extremely few and insignificant crevasses ;
the ascent was very gradual, but steadily increasing. The
glacier ends in a col between the Jungfrau and the Mönch,
the former being at the left-hand corner, the latter at the right,
each sending out a ridge parallel to the glacier. When we
had passed all the lateral spurs but one of the left-hand ridge
(called the Kranzberg), we struck off to the left up a constant
succession of slopes of snow of all degrees of steepness up to
42°, sometimes going straight up, sometimes crossing them
obliquely up or down or horizontally, and passing in part of
the way over some rather troublesome rocks. At last at a
quarter to 11 we stood on the Col du Roththal, a high depression
in the great ridge which separates the Vallais from the Canton
of Bern, and looked down (or should have done, if the clouds
had allowed us) into the upper part of the valley of Lauterbrunnen ; as it was, we only saw gigantic ghosts of mountains,
which must have been the Blümlis Alp and its neighbours.
Now began the real ascent. The highest peak of the Jungfrau is a cone or pyramid of rock, sheathed in ice except on

part of the N. and nearly the whole S. side, where the precipices will not allow snow or ice to hang. We went up from
the W. or S.W. side nearly in a straight line, with a precipice
a few feet (not inches, as Forbes seems to have done) on our
right, and a smooth round surface of snow-covered ice sloping
steeply away on our left. After 200 or 300 yards every step
had to be cut with the axe. Of course we had been tied
together all day, and our progress was slow, partly from the
cutting and partly from the extreme care which we took in
planting our feet. Forbes says that he once found the inclination $48°$; the highest I obtained was $46\frac{1}{2}°$, but I believe there
were steeper parts. A great deal was from $40°$ to $45°$, and
still more from $35°$ to $40°$. At last we reached the top of
the slope, not more than 3 or 4 feet below the actual top of
the mountain, which was separated from us by a ridge of snow
much steeper than any church roof I have ever seen, even
abroad, and not an inch wide at the top. As the snow was
soft, however, we were able to walk along (for about 15 feet),
pressing our feet deeply in on one side and our alpenstocks
on the other, and so we stood on the top just before 1.
The view was unluckily obstructed in many directions by
clouds, so that it was difficult to recognize the mountains
which we did see; still the sight was a very wonderful one.
During no part of the day were we actually in cloud ourselves.
The descent required still more caution than the ascent, and
for the most part we stepped down backwards; but as there
was little cutting to do, it took us only $1\frac{3}{4}$ hour to reach the
Col du Roththal. Our great difficulty all along was from the
guides, who did not relish the business, but refused to advise
us to return, though they used absurd tricks to induce us to
do so. Had they given us reason to put confidence in them,
it would have been very wrong to have persevered; as it was,
we both feel perfectly assured that we were right in going on.
We had a rapid and mostly easy descent to the glacier; but
there Lightfoot was seized with a quite sudden fit of exhaus-
tion and sickness (arising, I have no doubt, from the thunder),
and, instead of reaching the Æggischhorn, or Märjelen, or
even our former cave, we had to drag him a long way to the
nearest rocks at the foot of the Grünhorn, and there spend a

wretched night in cold and wet with very little shelter. Of course I surrendered my macintosh and slippers to Lightfoot, and he got some sleep. I got very little rest, and no sleep : and unluckily there was not a square yard approximately level on which to walk up and down and keep oneself warm ; but providentially the heavy thunder which came on at dark brought hardly any rain. At 4 next morning we set off very leisurely, and after several rests got home about 11 A.M., and our good beds soon put us all to rights. I felt scarcely any fatigue at all at the time or afterwards. On Monday we merely ascended to the top of the Æggischhorn for its magnificent view, and on Tuesday walked to Viesch, and charred to Brieg. Wednesday we charred to Susten, bussed up to Leukerbad, and walked over the Gemmi to Schwarenbach ; whence yesterday we ascended the Great Altels, a mountain of great height and very rarely ascended, but called easy. It happened that there was very little snow on the ice ; so that in reality we found it worse than the Jungfrau (though nowhere so steep as that very upright young lady is occasionally), and had to cut an immense number of steps ; but we were amply repaid by the superb view on every side, the clouds being below the mountains till just as we were leaving. In the evening we walked down to this place, where we mean to stay, if the weather is fine, till Monday, and then cross the glaciers of the Wild Strubel to Sierre, reaching Martigny on Tuesday. . . . I hope to be able to write from St. Gervais or Chamonix about Sunday week.

It is very curious that our ascent of the Jungfrau was one of three in one week (the others neither producing nor in any way connected with ours), whereas it is believed that no other has taken place for many years.

To his Father

MONT ROSSET, HOTEL DU MONT JOLI, ST. GERVAIS,
August 15th and 17th, 1856.

. . . Our work for Monday was a glacier pass almost, if not quite, unknown to Englishmen, and as far as we could learn, hardly ever traversed by others, although it has no serious difficulties. Starting about 4.30, we continued above an hour nearly along the ordinary Gemmi route, leaving it just where the precipice descent upon Leukerbad strikes off to the left, and went straight on or slightly verging to the right over easy rocks and along the bed of the stream till we reached the terminal moraine of the Lämmern glacier, which we climbed. A few minutes brought us on the glacier itself, which was easy at first, but soon became harder from its steepness and slipperiness. A little higher up its crevasses became much wider and more complicated, and we had a good deal of cutting with the axe and leaping. But the skill and activity of one of our two guides (Melchior Anderegg) enabled us to get along with perfect ease and safety. When the glacier became level again, we breakfasted, and I took a photograph of the pass before us. The next rise in the glacier took nothing but labour up the steep slopes of snow, and then after another short level we had a succession of similar slopes to the top of the pass, a snowy saddle between the two great humps of Wild Strubel. After dining, our guides thought we should find it easier to try a lower pass a little to the left, which we reached in a very short time. The view from it was very extraordinary : 300 or 400 feet below us was stretched an enormous plain or very flat basin of dazzling *firn*, two or three miles wide, the rim being sometimes backed with masses of mountain or smaller rocks and sometimes merely snow. Three passes were discernible on the S. side ; the farthest, or most western, was the one by which Anderegg had descended before, three years ago, but he said it was difficult, and wished to try whether the others might not be easier. It was at first proposed to make first for the nearest, and then, if that should prove ugly on a near inspection, to go on to the next, which Anderegg agreed with me in thinking the most promising; but at last we decided to go straight to this one at once. Just before starting we saw a herd of six chamois crossing the plain as fast as the snow would let them. At that distance they looked to the naked eye more like the pictures one sees of ostriches running than anything else. We had a tedious and laborious tramp across the *firn* for about 1¼ hour, and then crossing a bank of shale, found ourselves at the steep head of a valley, down which we got with great ease on a bit of imperfect glacier, some snow-slopes, and screes. Presently we were baffled by finding ourselves several times on the top of unmanageable precipices, but at last we lit on a practicable passage by the side of the main stream, and soon reached the upper pastures of the valley, from which there was a magnificent view of the Weisshorn, the imaginary 'M. Rosa' of most Swiss guides and tourists who do not go to Zermatt. I forgot to mention that in ascending the glacier and from the first upper pass we had extremely beautiful and interesting views from Mt. Blanc to the Mt. Leone beyond the Simplon. After a while we left our valley, and struck off to the right down awfully hot and dusty zig-zags, ending at last among vines, till we reached Sierre at about 5. As we wanted a night's rest after our walk of 12¾ hours, and the diligence was to start cruelly early, we charred next day to Martigny, and spent the afternoon there. When the rain ceased next morning, we set off up the Col de Trient, but had our view of the Rhone Valley much spoiled by a thick mist in the distance; but from the top the S.W. looked so clear that we decided to go up the Col de Balme, and were amply repaid by a magnificent view of Mt. Blanc. While my camera and I were struggling with the difficulties caused by the wind, Mathison suddenly appeared. He had come up from Chamonix with a party of ladies, and was going on to St. Gervais in the morning. We therefore gave up our idea of proceeding beyond Chamonix that night. . . . That evening we had a most extraordinary thunderstorm at Chamonix. None of us had ever seen anything at all like it : large masses of pale but brilliant orange cloud, throwing the most gorgeous golden blaze upon parts of the Glacier des Bossons and its clear pinnacles of ice, and on the snowy bases of the three great Aiguilles de Chamonix; while the sharp peaks themselves above were quite cold with a ghastly lilac blue. Next day Mathison, Lightfoot, and I took a return carriage to the *Baths* of St. Gervais, left it at Ouches to continue its route with the luggage, and walked over the Col de Vosa to St. Gervais *le village*, getting magnificent views of the Glacier de Bionassai and its peaks by the way.

When I began this letter I was alone, Lightfoot having gone up the Val de Montjoie to cross the Col du Bonhomme and see the view from the Col de la Seigne (which I had two years ago). But two or three hours after his departure the truant Hawkins appeared, along with Davies and Watson. They had all ascended the Aiguille du Goûté, sleeping two nights at the Pavillon on the Col de Vosa, by way of exploration for our further proceedings. We are, however, much bothered by the weather in spite of its fineness. For its sultriness and other still plainer symptoms threaten stormy weather, and it will not do to go among the glaciers again till that has blown over. Lightfoot arrived last night (I am now writing on Sunday the 17th), so that we make up a strong party of five, all fellows of Trinity. This is a very delightful spot in spite of its present heat. We are just on the acclivity where the mouth of the Val de Montjoie begins to break away down into the plain of Sallenches, St. Gervais-les-bains lying at the foot of a ravine some hundreds of feet below us. The people at the Baths breakfast at 11, but we are going to have a second service for their benefit ; and, as Davies has brought a carpet-bag, and a white tie and black clothes therein, we shall carry with us some shadow of respectability.

To HIS MOTHER

HOTEL DU MONT JOLI, ST. GERVAIS,
September 1st, 1856.

My dearest Mother—Still at St. Gervais, and perhaps for some days more. . . . This week has not been idle, but it has hardly been satisfactory. One great object of our expedition this year was to ascend Mt. Blanc from this side. I did not tell you before starting, fearing that the name might make you uneasy. But we had the best reason to know that in reality the ascent does not stand very high on the list of glacier excursions for either difficulty or danger. Lightfoot and I had all along believed that the Strahleck would be a very good test of our powers ; and in May I was told by Mr.

Kennedy, one of those who last year for the first time made the ascent from this side, that it was child's play compared with the Strahleck. The Chamonix regulations, and all the charlatanry which reigns there supreme, have made the ascent much dreaded. No one is allowed to ascend thence without four guides for each person at 100 francs each, besides a whole army of porters, all of whom have to be fed (at mountain appetites) for two days, so that the expense is said never to fall below £25 for each traveller, and sometimes to be higher still. To crown the absurdity, you are obliged to take guides exactly as they stand on the list without power of choice, so that they may happen to be all bad ones. Last year a party of Englishmen, not relishing these prices and regulations, got some guides at Cormayeur, and for the first time on record ascended the mountain from that side. Another party, Kennedy, Hudson, etc., resolved to follow their example, but found that meanwhile a *corps de guides* had been formed, who demanded *le prix de Chamonix*, and intimidated some hunters who were otherwise willing to accompany them. Accordingly, being stout and practised mountaineers, they resolved to go themselves without guides, merely taking porters as far as the top of the Col du Géant. They ultimately reached a point within two hours of the top with great difficulty, and then were driven back by cloudy weather. Having descended to Cormayeur, they came round to St. Gervais, secured three *chasseurs* and some porters, and took them as guides to the top of the Dome du Goûté. There, the view of the way before them being clear, and the *chasseurs* preferring to receive half pay for that part of the ascent to whole pay for the whole, they dismissed them, and went their way alone. They wished much to try a passage by a ridge to the right past the Bosse du Dromadaire, but not having time for experiments, pushed down into the Grand Plateau, thereby joining the Chamonix route two or three hours from the top, reached the top with ease, and then returned by the Chamonix route. Later in the season two Irishmen, Darby[1] and Reeves, came here and determined to follow their example, but with guides. Darby was taken ill almost as soon as they had started, but Reeves made a most

[1] Darley : name indistinct.

successful ascent, returning to St. Gervais. Our plan was to
follow their example, pursuing the same route likewise with
guides. While, however, I was studying the geography
of Mt. Blanc at Cambridge, I came to the conclusion that
there was still untried one probably practicable route to the
summit by ascending the Glacier du Miage (probably from
Contamines) to the Col du Miage, and then joining the ridge
thought of by Kennedy's party near the Bosse du Dromadaire.
My idea was that, if we succeeded by Kennedy's route of the
Aiguille du Goûté, we might *try* the other (with guides) afterwards. Curiously enough, on arriving here, I found that some
of the *chasseurs* were already full of the idea, having talked to
Hudson about it last year; he had promised to come and try
in 1857, but they had thoughts of trying alone *this* year. As
Hawkins, Davies, and Watson had already been up the Aiguille
du Goûté, the whole party were therefore fully disposed to try
a passage by the Col du Miage *first*. Accordingly, on the
afternoon of this day week we set out with four guides and
three porters, and slept at a chalet high up on the Mont
Morasset over the valley of Miage. Our bed was hay, and
one of the guides assured us that we need not be afraid of
cold, *parce que les vaches sont en dessous, et vous en aurez la
chaleur.* There were, in fact, not only *vaches* but *cochons;*
but we should probably have got to sleep before midnight
had it not been for one pertinacious *vache* who carried a bell,
which she thought it necessary to ring in a vicious manner at
intervals of a quarter of an hour; and though, as Davies said,
the true hero would have been he who should have *un*belled
the cow, no one was found willing to undertake the feat.
At 3 we started in the dark, at least with only stars and a
nearly new moon, which last was soon hid by the mountain
side. For three hours we scrambled incessantly round ridges
over rocks, constantly ascending by a very broken but not
really difficult route, then crossed a piece of glacier, and then
got on rocks again. At 7 we stopped to breakfast and put
on our gaiters, descended upon the snow, crossed the head of
the chief arm of the Glacier du Miage, and began to climb up
one of the long ridges of rock which reach from the bottom
nearly to the top. There was not much difficulty, except from

the fresh snow intermingled with the rocks. We all carried, instead of alpenstocks, the *haches* or *piolets* of the country, consisting of ash-poles 4 to 5 feet long, shod at one end with a strong iron point, and at the other with a double iron head, a large axe on one side and a long narrow pick on the other. These we found very useful whenever there was a tolerably large slope of snow, as we could hold on by the pick without cutting steps except occasionally. We were getting on famously, when the weather changed and a severe snowstorm came on, the wind blowing small hail in our faces. It was in vain to persevere in the teeth of such an enemy, and about 10 we most unwillingly turned round, being then but ten minutes (the guides said ; *I* should have said half an hour) from the top of the coL Our only satisfaction was that we had had thus far a very interesting excursion on ground never before trodden by any but the natives. Having got off the ridge, we returned by an easier route straight down the Glacier du Miage, all carefully roped together in case of unseen crevasses, but without accident. On Thursday Watson set off for England, and we were all rather inclined to follow his example, when on Wednesday evening a sudden resolution was come to, to try again by the Aiguille du Goûté (a route already known to our not too courageous guides), and not be frightened by merely slightly unfavourable weather. Early in the morning Octenier, the chief guide, was sent for ; he approved, and went in search of the rest, but it was 1 P.M. before we were off. We dined at the Pavillon on the Col de Vosa, climbed along the Mont Lachat by a tolerable path, and reached the base of the Tête Rousse just at dusk ; but here we were able to take to the snow of the Glacier de Bionassai, and so easily ascended to a little hut of stones perched among the rocks at the foot of the Aiguille du Goûté, reaching it at 8.30. A quantity of snow had to be cleared out of the inside, but, in trying to remove what lay on the scanty roof, the roof itself fell in. However, the shelter was good from the wind, and we had taken up firewood and blankets, so that after some tea we lay down in tolerable comfort, and I got some sleep. At 5 A.M. we started, crossed some snow and rocks, and a *couloir* or very steep gully lined with smooth ice (now fortunately covered with

snow), and climbed a ridge of rocks like that on the Col du
Miage, but steeper. We got on unusually well, and reached
the top at 7.20. Here we breakfasted and roped ourselves,
reached the snowy top of the Aiguille immediately, and then
made for the Dome du Goûté, a huge round hump of snow-
covered ice, getting peculiarly interesting views on each side
by the way. As, however, we mounted the Dome, a thick dry
cloud came on, and then a most keen piercing wind. We
crossed the shoulder near the top (being not above 500 or 600
feet below the height of the top of Mt. Blanc), and kept
moving on to the right for nearly an hour, till the guides told
us they could not tell where we were for the cloud, and dared
not descend, not only on account of the crevasses, but because
there might be danger of having to spend the night in the
midst of the snow; nor could we stand still to wait for the
cloud to melt, lest our hands and feet should be frozen. As
it was we looked absurd enough, with fringes of icicles hanging
from our beards and the back of our hair. We had no alternative; so about a quarter to 11 A.M. we turned and retraced
our steps all the way. It was now a slower business to descend
the Aiguille, as the snow had become soft, but we reached the
bottom at last in broad sunshine, and had the annoyance of
seeing the top clear above us, and so it has remained ever
since.

To the Rev. John Ellerton

4 Victoria Buildings, Weston-super-Mare,
September 19th, 1856.

My dear Ellerton—I think I wrote to you last Monday
fortnight, after we had twice failed to conquer Mt. Blanc, and
Hawkins and I were waiting, a sadly reduced company, in
grim expectance to see what better hopes a change of weather
might bring. Two or three days restored our eyes from their
inflamed state; but Tuesday was all rain, and Wednesday
rather threatening. That day Hawkins went over to Chamonix and back, while I scrambled about the forest with no
particular object. On Thursday we were much tempted to

send for Octenier, our chief guide, and arrange for an immediate start, but forbore when we saw the glass low, and set
out for a moderate climb up the Prarion between the Cols de
Forclaz and Vosa, and then down to the Pavillon on the latter
pass.   Here we were surprised to find Octenier with some
Chamonix guides.   They were going up Mt. Blanc on our
side with an Englishman, and urged us to join him.   This we
agreed to do, and at once sent down Octenier to St. Gervais
to fetch more men and some things which we should want on
the mountain, while we remained at the Pavillon for the rest
of the day and slept there.   At 9 next morning we all set out,
and had an extremely pleasant day.   The rocky ribs of the
Aiguille de Goûté were tolerably free from snow, and we got
up with great ease, only incommoded by a cold wind.   We
reached the top of the Aiguille at 6.15 P.M., meaning to sleep
there ; but found the wind on the top so violent and freezing,
and the only shelter in the rocks so unsheltering, that all
declared it would be death to lie down for the night.   A proposal to push on over the Dome down to the Grand Plateau,
and so to the hut on the Grands Mulets, where we might pass
the night and reascend next morning, after a rapid start, was
abandoned by the guides for sufficient reasons, and most reluctantly we once more set our faces northwards, and proceeded to scramble down the Aiguille as hard as we could.
Night was upon us, however, by the time we were two-thirds
down, and then came the rather ticklish work of traversing
the great icy *couloir* (inclined at an angle of 47°) and snow
slopes leading down to it with no light but that of one lantern.
We were very cautious and took plenty of time, thereby elimi-
nating nearly all the danger.   It was past 10 when we reached
the half-ruinous *cabane* at the foot of the Aiguille where we
had slept a week before.   It was tempting to pass the night
there and try our luck again next day ; but the overcast sky
soon caused a general vote for an immediate return to the
Pavillon at all risks.   We despatched a good quantity of
supper, and then at near 11.30 set out down the Glacier de
Bionassai, mostly in pairs.   The ice was very steep, and we
were not inclined to waste time on needless caution ; so we
got down in a very short time by a mixture of all possible in-

tentional and unintentional motions, of which sliding (of both
categories) was perhaps the chief.   Then came a scrambling,
stumbling walk, almost run, down the Pierre Ronde, happily
without injury to ankle or shin.   After a little exploratory
climbing, we struck the path of the Mt. Lachat.   Here a
candle encompassed with paper made believe to give us a little
more light, as a good part of the winding path lay along the
edge of rough crags and craggy slopes ; but we did not relax
our pace.   Suddenly we felt a sharp shower of snow and hail ;
and then pitiless rain, which never ceased.   When we had
left the Mt. Lachat, but one mass of mountain remained, of
steep sloping grass without rock.   Here we failed to find the
thin path which runs along the side.   In the hope of crossing it we made a long traverse nearly vertically downwards for
a great way, and then another upward ; and then one guide
after another rushed off in various directions with the lantern
(the rain had long conquered the candle), while we stood in
the rain leaning on our axes against the steep incline of the
hill in such utter darkness that one might have touched the
other without being seen.   But even the rain failed to drown
the excitement and enjoyment of so novel an expedition,
though it certainly did somewhat damp the high spirits in
which we had floundered down the glacier.   At last, in despair
of finding the path, we climbed to the top of the ridge, knowing that it must take us right at last, and pursued it till it
ended in a rough incline of wet juniper, down and through
which we flopped with some discomfort.   At last at a quarter to
4 A.M. we reached the Pavillon, and after comforting the outer
and inner man tumbled into bed and slept till a late hour, when
we rose, breakfasted, and descended ingloriously to St. Gervais
through the close spungy air. . . .   In the afternoon [of Sunday]
I read prayers in my sole attire, shooting jacket, flannel shirt,
black tie, beard, etc., and ⸺ 'said a few words,' looking
terribly respectable.   These 'words' by their coherence, sense,
adhesion to the text, and charity, reminded me not a little of
Carus.   On Monday we dillied to Geneva, and slept there.
On Tuesday we steamed to Morges, railed to Chavornay,
dillied to Dole, and railed to Paris. . . . I was able to reach
home on Friday evening.

I have tried to develop four of the photographs with but partial success; and am going to leave the rest to be done at Cambridge under William Kingsley's advice; but I fear few of them had sufficiently long exposure.

To THE REV. JOHN ELLERTON

HARDWICK, *January* 1*st and* 8*th*, 1857.

My dear Ellerton—You are a bad bad boy to leave me without a letter from July to January, and accordingly my first letter for the New Year shall be devoted to stirring you up. Last term seems to have melted away unawares. Though I read incessantly for Coleridge from the day of my return to England, very little was actually on paper when I reached Cambridge, and so I had hard work for weeks, and at last sent off to press without any revision. My allotted space was 30 pages, but I could not squeeze into less than 60, and so shall have to pay for the paper and printing of the last two sheets. This is rather a hard case, but I made the offer, preferring that amount of loss to the mutilation of my essay, which is already frightfully condensed, little more than written in shorthand. Indeed, I had to leave out dozens of things that I wished to say, and nearly everything which lies on the surface of Coleridge's writings, patent to the whole world. However, I hope I have done something towards making Coleridge's life intelligible, and putting any thoughtful man seriously and honestly troubled with such questions in the way of receiving benefit from the workings of Coleridge's mind, and that is all that need be wished for. I have not written for the public, and shall doubtless be castigated accordingly. I hope you have not neglected the other papers in the volume. Grote's, Maine's, and Francis' are especially worth reading. Altogether the company is good, and likely to become better, for Trench writes on English Dictionaries in our next volume, and Gladstone on Homer and his use in education in the next Oxford volume.

A good piece of the rest of term was taken up in editorial work for the *Journal of Philology*, and preparing a longish lexico-

graphical article on *limes*.[1]   There is nothing in the number
that would interest you, I fear, except an excellent paper of
Lightfoot's on the Galatians.   I was absent for some days at
Oxford, having gone there to the first anniversary meeting of
their Working Men's College or rather ' Educational Institution.'
Its founder, Maskelyne, the Reader in Mineralogy, was in
Cambridge a little while before on a visit to Vansittart, and he
was anxious that Cambridge should not be unrepresented,
especially as Maurice was going down from London.   It seemed
that no one could go but Roby and myself, and so we went.
I picked up Maurice on the way and had some pleasant talk
with him in the Great Western.   He had been seriously ill, but
was much better and in good spirits. . . . In the evening the
dinner passed off very well.   Maurice's speech was very fairly
given (from the *Morning Post*, I think) in the *Guardian*.
Mine happily was spared, unless it has got into some Oxford
paper; I have seldom felt more uncomfortable than when I
sat down.   The best speeches, except Maurice's, were Dr.
Acland's [2] and Spottiswoode's, one of the Queen's printers ; he
seems to have organized much such institutions among his
men as the Wilsons have done in their candle factory.   It was
on the whole a severe proceeding—five hours and eighteen
speeches ; poor —— could not have survived it if he had
been there, for we had only two small mugs of beer for
dinner and speeches too.   The Oxford institution is much
more democratic than ours, being got up and managed by the
men themselves, and five only of the teachers University men,
and they nothing but teachers ; but apparently no other
constitution could have succeeded in Oxford ; and, by con-
ciliating the whims of the Mayor and Aldermen, they have
obtained the use of the Guildhall and accompanying rooms
gratis, which is an enormous advantage.   As far as I was able
to discover, they have hardly ventured to turn rhetorical
lectures into honest plodding catechetical lessons.   That night

---

[1] *Journal of Classical and Sacred Philology*, No. ix. p. 350.   The
article is an exhaustive and satisfactory account of the connexion between
the various meanings of this difficult Latin word, and is interesting for
personal reasons, because little remains of Hort's work on purely
' classical ' subjects.

[2] Now Sir Henry Acland.

Dr. Acland came in to Maskelyne's to see Maurice, and we had a most delightful midnight chat. There are few men whom I have more wished to know, and few seemingly better worth knowing. Next day I went to see the new Museums now building from the plans of a new architect, Woodward, who seems to be a true genius. I remember the plans being spoken of in the *Guardian*, when they were chosen ; and at that time they were called 'Rhenish Gothic,' to me a most unaccountable name. I should call it nearly pure Veronese Gothic of the best and manliest type, in a new and striking combination. It can hardly be judged fairly for some months to come, but I shall be much surprised if it does not prove to be nearly the finest building in England, incomparably the finest modern building. The inner quadrangle is surrounded with two arcades one over the other, each consisting of a series of pairs of arches surrounded with alternate slabs of (I think) oolite and very pale old red flagstone ; the arches of each pair separated by a polished shaft of marble or serpentine, all of different colours, all British, and all presented by friends. Between each pair of arches is to be a niche containing a statue of some hero of science. Monro is now at work at Galileo, etc., and Thomas is to do some others. That day I lunched with the George Butlers, and had a delightful talk with Mrs. Butler. Goldwin Smith came in, and looked as if he could be a good companion, if he chose. I dined at Wadham with Maskelyne, and in the evening he had a small party, which was not equal to what I had hoped. My old friend Shirley was too busy examining to be able to appear, and William Thomson of Queen's and his Greek bride were engaged. I received a note from Pinder of Trinity entreating me to stay till Thursday, as our mutual friend Curtler [1] was coming up next day, and he wanted me to meet him at dinner. This was a potent temptation. I breakfasted next day at Oriel with Arthur Butler, and had a very pleasant morning, walking away afterwards with Conington to his rooms, and getting a capital talk with him. He is really a thoroughly great and wise man. In the afternoon I had a walk with

[1] Mr. W. H. Curtler was in Hort's year at Rugby, and had a brilliant career there.

Shirley, who likewise showed that he had lost none of his old good sense. At dinner at Trinity I met several old Rugby contemporaries, besides Pinder and Curtler, and also Frederick Meyrick (author of *The Working of the Church in Spain*), whom I was very glad to know; he has a singularly beautiful face, and seemingly a corresponding mind. It was altogether a most delightful evening. Curtler, Shirley, and myself had sat next to each other without interruption for three years and a half before we left Rugby, we were exhibitioners together, and I had not seen either of them from that time to this. They are now both heads of families, but are not a whit changed. So that you can imagine what a pleasant evening I had. Next morning I breakfasted with Conington. Mark Pattison was there, but did not speak at all; he is a thoughtful-looking man, with the thinnest lips I ever saw. After breakfast I went with Maskelyne to the Convocation House and took an *ad eundem.* I was very near taking a very ambiguous degree, for, as I entered the Convocation House, I heard the V. C. reading out my name as belonging to Trinity College *juxta Dublinam ;* however the mistake was rectified before the more serious part of the ceremony was performed. In the middle of the day I set off for Cambridge. I should not forget to say that Oxford is improving architecturally in various ways. G. G. Scott has done a great deal for Exeter, and is building a very beautiful chapel for Balliol. Jowett I was sorry not to see, but Conington told me it is impossible to get him out.

I stayed at Cambridge till a couple of days before Christmas, and then went down into Devonshire on a visit to the Bullers, whom I met at Venice two years ago. . . . One day I walked over (three miles) to Ottery St. Mary, which was very interesting to me both as Coleridge's birthplace and for its own sake. His odd old father's monument is in the church, and there are three families of Coleridges in the neighbourhood, including the Justice's. The church itself is a very singular, nearly perfect Early English abbey, with one Tudor aisle, and an extremely elaborate reredos and other internal work of very late frivolous and extravagant Decorated character. The church has been excellently restored, chiefly by the Coleridges, and has many beautiful points about it, but does not rise above English commonplace. In a curious upper vestry we found the damp and mouldering remains of what must once have been a valuable library, beginning with Erasmus and other publications of the early Basle press, and seemingly rich in the theology of the Restoration. . . .

I am just now chiefly occupied about a proposed Cambridge translation [1] of the whole of Plato. Revised editions of Davies and Vaughan's *Republic*, and Wright's *Phædrus*, *Lysis*, and *Protagoras* are to be included ; and the rest will be divided between six translators, who are pretty certain to be Lightfoot, Joe Mayor, Benson, Montagu Butler, Hawkins, and myself. We are getting to work immediately, but shall probably not begin to print till all or nearly all the MSS. (including short introductions and a few necessary notes) are ready ; and then publish in eight successive octavo volumes. My share (as at present arranged) includes some of the stiffest dialogues of all ; being the *Timæus, Sophista, Parmenides, Menexenus, Io,* and the spurious *Timæus Locrus, Sisyphus, Cleitophon,* and *Definitions.* We mean to keep the matter quiet just at present, and not to tell even our Cambridge friends : when we have made good progress a full prospectus is likely to appear.

Another scheme likely to be carried out, if a publisher can be found, is a Cambridge Shakspere, containing the text only (at least in the first instance), with all the various readings of the quartos and folios, and the chief conjectures of critics, on the same page, like a well-edited classical work. This has been a favourite idea [2] of mine for several years, and so it has been (independently) of Clark ; and he is likely to have the main direction of the edition, if it ever comes into existence. . . .

Vansittart is a pretty constant resident, to the great satisfaction of us all, and, I think, of himself ; he acts as a kind

[1] W. H. Thompson (afterwards Master of Trinity) was to be asked to edit the ‘ Cambridge Plato.’ Hort worked steadily for some years at his share of the scheme ; the *Timæus* interested him most. The project, however, languished, was revived in 1860, and at last reluctantly given up.
[2] The idea was realised in the famous ‘ Cambridge Shakspere ’ of Mr. W. G. Clark and Mr. Aldis Wright.

of Cambridge πρόξενος of Oxford men. For a wonder he is gone this winter to Nice, but returns by the end of the month. I shall be curious to know what you think of Bradshaw's devotion of his life to the University Library. *It* is very lucky to get him ; but I cannot help thinking that so affectionate and genial a creature is thrown away on mere dry bibliography and yet more mechanical work. But he seems at present to like it.

One great pleasure this term has been Trench's visits, required by his being University Preacher for November. The matter of the sermons was in the main solid and good. The first, on John i. 1, 8, was peculiarly grand and deep, as well as courageous ; but I found no one except Lightfoot to enter into it, and it was generally abused and derided as un-intelligible mysticism. The other sermons, which were much more commonplace, were very popular, and restored the confidence of many foolish alarmists. But it was in con-versation that I liked Trench best, especially at Thompson's, with whom he was twice staying. He took great pains to dispel the notion that his decanal dignity was going to make him more of a don, and seemed vastly amused at finding himself among what he called 'the shovelry of England.' Sometimes, however, he was very grave and silent ; and he seems (like Maurice, though partly on different grounds) to be oppressed with a fearful foreboding of coming evils, especially of an outburst of rampant and aggressive atheism throughout Europe. . . .

I suppose you have seen Maurice's two new books. The *Mediæval Philosophy* is a treat indeed : he improves wonder-fully as he advances by more and more allowing his authors to speak for themselves, and keeping separate his own comments, where any are needed. The accounts of St. Anselm, Joannes Erigena, Abelard, Duns Scotus, and Roger Bacon are, I think, singularly profound and beautiful. The wit and elasticity quite remind one of his earliest writings. The *St. John* I have just finished. It is not exactly a striking book, but I do not think I have learned so much from any book for many years, and that almost solely from its merits as inter-preting the life of Christ, not as expounding hard sayings of the discourses. In this latter respect it is not very successful,

and there is throughout a painful swallowing up and oblitera-
tion of subordinate truths that will, I fear, make the book
repulsive and unintelligible to many who might otherwise
profit from it : for instance, the language about the Eucharist
is very unsubstantial and far inferior to what he has said in his
letter in *Fraser*. On the other hand, it is a great relief to
find that his views about resurrection and judgment do not
lead him to reject a future general Resurrection and Judgment.
But I feel ashamed of saying a word against a book which
seems to me of such transcendent value, one that we shall
read and re-read years after he has gone as at once the most
helpful of lesson books for daily life and the most pregnant of
prophecies. . . .

Now I have written you a tolerably long letter [1] (though I
might go on for ever), especially considering that you are in
my debt. I want to hear from you about all manner of
things, *inter alia* about ——, who by inanity and stateliness
seemed to me at Cambridge cut out for a Belgrave Square
head footman. But I did not hear him speak. About public
matters of all kinds one can say only *kismet*. It seems to
me that 1855 opened more cheerfully than 1857. However,
bona verba. Do write soon and long.—Ever yours affectionately,   FENTON J. A. HORT.

To THE REV. J. B. LIGHTFOOT

HARDWICK, CHEPSTOW, *January 5th*, 1857.

. . . I like your recommending me to read the *Plurality
of Worlds*.[2] It robs me of the fancied distinction of having
been the last man in Trinity to read it, as I did somewhere about a year ago. We shall not differ about its
merits and interest, though he does pat planets condescend-
ingly, as if they were Newton's head. But I did not need
'conversion,' never having been a pluralist, I believe ; at
least, not as long as I can recollect. When the subject
was proposed for the Seatonian a year or two ago, I was

---

[1] Nine sheets of letter paper.   [2] By W. Whewell.

much tempted to try, for the sake of taking a motto from the beginning of ' Peter Bell,'—"Such company, I like it not," or some of the following stanzas.

My only doubt about your writing on νόμος and ὁ νόμος would arise from the question whether it is wise to treat the matter as an isolated phenomenon of a single writer, the usage being, as I believe, strictly accurate and grammatical. It is really one particular case of the theory of articles and their omission, on which I have often thought of writing, especially in connexion with the logical question of the quantification of the predicate. But more of this when we meet. You have been so long about *Our Lord's Brethren* that you ought to produce something soon. Why apologize for writing about yourself? Never be ashamed of doing your duty. In the present un-developed state of clairvoyance how otherwise is it possible to tell what one's friends are doing? *I* have been doing scarce anything beyond reading some *Timæus.*

To Mr. A. Macmillan

Hardwick, *January 6th,* 1857.

. . . I am very glad to hear that the *St. John*[1] has sold so well. I have still two sermons to read. . . . The book disappointed me at first, perhaps because I had a wrong craving for rhetoric; but I still think he does not sufficiently get the steam up in the earlier sermons : they hang heavily, and want the fire of the *Prophets and Kings.* But below the surface there are deeper and more enduring (?) qualities, which give a peculiar value to the book. I do not think it very successful with the body of the discourses, or with most of the hard sayings contained in them ; but nothing comes near it in its power of showing their relation to the narrative, and inter-preting the narrative itself. Such a Life of Christ has never been written. I cannot tell the number of deep matters, not at all directly theological, on which it has incidentally given me the truest help. It is at the same time a singular and perhaps unconscious justification of Maurice's own method and the purpose of his life.

[1] Maurice's edition.

The year 1856 proved to be the last complete year of Hort's Cambridge residence till his return thither in 1872. In February 1857 he became engaged to Miss Fanny Dyson Holland, daughter of Mr. Thomas Dyson Holland of Heighington, near Lincoln. Miss Holland's family were intimate at Cheltenham with Hort's friends the Blunts. A few days after his engagement he was presented to the college living of St. Ippolyts-cum-Great Wymondley, near Hitchin, and there he settled in June with his wife, and entered on a new chapter of life.

Of his marriage it is difficult to speak ; the whole subject of marriage had been much in his thoughts for some time past ; he had studied it, not in relation to himself, but as a social problem of supreme importance. " For many years," to quote from one of his letters, " this particular question has filled a larger place in my thoughts than any other, and I have anxiously watched everything going on around me which might throw light upon it." A series of most careful letters too private for publication shows that he had attacked the question from all sides with characteristic thoroughness and fearlessness. He had reached the conclusion that no life of man or woman attains its full purpose in the single condition. The highest language in the Bible on marriage, as illustrated by the union of Christ and His Church, expressed for him the most living reality. To him personally, apart from the conclusions to which reason seemed to point, it was a necessity of his nature to have one nearest to him with whom to share his every thought. It is no paradox to say that this necessity was the natural outcome of his reserve ; reserved and sensitive as he was to the highest degree, he had always even in college days opened his whole mind to his one or two intimate friends, and marriage afforded him now full satisfaction of the craving which had driven him to communicate his thoughts and feelings to Blunt and Ellerton. Without marriage the full humanity which endeared him to so many would have been incomplete. He deprecated vehemently the idea that books were his life ; he preferred to call them his 'tools.' "I have never," he once said, "cared much for books, except in so far as they might help to quicken our sense of the reality of life, and enable us to enter into its right and wrong"; or again, "Such entities as scholar, author, clergyman, and the like, are worthless and worse for all else except so far as they are rooted in the entire *man*, first of all, and last of all."

Moreover, his sense of the meaning of home was very strong ; he had never forgotten Leopardstown, and now, looking forward to his marriage, he speaks of "being about to carry on the old home life, the heavenly calm of which seems so strangely distant across the restlessness of intervening years." His college rooms, he said, had been "the best substitute for a home, but nothing in any wise like a home." The interest which he showed in the smallest details of preparation was illustrative of the feeling attached to the change, in which nothing was too small to be important.

The parting from Cambridge was, however, doubtless a severe wrench ; his interests in the place had grown every year, and he was taking an important part in the graduate life of the University. He was consulted by all sorts of men on a great variety of subjects, and his correspondents had lately come to be very numerous. "Your letter," wrote one of them, "confirms me in the impression which I had formed, that it would be difficult to consult you on any subject that you would not throw light upon." Yet marriage and parish work caused no cessation of his many-sided activity. Throwing himself with entire devotion into every task which his new work laid upon him, he still pursued the aims, which as a scholar and thinker at Cambridge he had set before himself, with vigour and hopefulness quickened by the sympathy with which his life had been newly blessed.

To the Rev. B. F. Westcott

CHETTON RECTORY, BRIDGENORTH,
February 23rd, 1857.

My dear Westcott—In spite of the vagueness of my last note you will perhaps have been looking for me before this time. I may therefore as well say at once that the 'business' which has detained me has been of a tolerably engrossing character. The result of it is that I am going to be married.

All particulars I must reserve till we meet; but it seems as if all the perfectness of the one great blessing were coming upon me.

You must not suppose that this change of condition will alter my literary plans. On the contrary, I hope to go on with the New Testament text more unremittingly at St. Ippollits (*sic*) (which living, near Hitchin, I forgot to say that I have taken) than at Cambridge.

CHAPTER V

THE village of St. Ippolyts is about two miles from
Hitchin, lying a little way off the road from Hitchin
to London.   The vicarage has a large garden, and is
an almost ideal country parsonage.   Fortunately a
careful description of the place and its people by Hort
himself is extant in a letter[1] to Mr. Gerald Blunt.

Of society, of course, there was not much, but
several neighbours became before long intimate friends.
A few yards from the vicarage lived Mrs. Amos, at a
house called St. Ibbs, a still further abbreviated form
of St. Hippolytus' name ; she was the kindly squireen
of the village, and her son, Sheldon Amos, author of
many works on constitutional and international law,
was Hort's companion in many afternoon walks, in the
course of which they discussed at large political and
philosophical questions.   The vicar of Hitchin was
another ex-fellow of Trinity, the Rev. Lewis Hensley,
and the rural dean, the Rev. G. Blomfield, became a
close ally.   At Hitchin were Mr. J. H. Tuke, author of
Irish Distress and its Remedies, and other pamphlets on
similar subjects, and Mr. Frederick Seebohm, author

[1] See pp. 388-90.

of *The Oxford Reformers*, *The English Village Community*, etc. Some other neighbours, who, like a
considerable number of prominent Hitchin people,
belonged to the Society of Friends, came frequently
to St. Ippolyts' Church to hear Hort preach. When
the Ladies' College was founded at Hitchin, some of the
students used now and then to come over on Sundays ;
one of these, Miss Welsh, now Principal of Girton
College, thus gives her recollections :—

Mr. Hort was still at St. Ippolyts when I entered as a
student in 1871, and I well remember how, attracted by what
we heard of him from his former pupils (see vol. ii. p. 57), some
other students of my own year and myself walked over one
Sunday in our first term to morning service at St. Ippolyts to
hear him preach. I can still recall the pleasant walk through
the Hertfordshire lanes, hung with bramble and wild clematis,
and the pretty village at the end with its quaint old church,
and, above all, the delight with which we listened to the first
of the many sermons we heard within its walls. I cannot
analyse the characteristics in those sermons which produced
such an effect, but what I remember best is the impression of
extraordinary breadth which his treatment of the text always
conveyed, and the earnestness of delivery which lent weight
to every word. It was marvellous to find such a wealth of
thought, such manifest carefulness of preparation in addresses
to a village audience.

At Hitchin and afterwards at Welwyn, six miles
from St. Ippolyts, lived Mr. C. W. Wilshere, a genial
and generous neighbour, himself a student of ecclesiastical history and antiquities.

Very soon after his coming into residence two of
Hort's chief Cambridge friends, George Brimley and
Daniel Macmillan, were removed by death. The
memoir of the latter, by Mr. Thomas Hughes, published
in 1882, bears witness to a noble and affectionate nature.

He left to his friend as a parting gift among other interesting *Mauriciana*, John Sterling's copy of the first volume of the first edition of the *Kingdom of Christ*, containing many notes in Sterling's hand.

The story of Hort's country life is uneventful enough. At first it was most peacefully happy, it was only by degrees that he became conscious that this was not the work for which he was best fitted ; in 1861 he expressed to Mr. Westcott his doubts on the subject. But he never came to feel that it was in any sense unworthy of his powers. When, after fifteen years of parochial ministry, he returned to Cambridge and very different tasks, he was always distressed if any one spoke with the feeling that he had been wasted on a country village. The care of his humble parishioners was in his eyes a work second in dignity to no other. He took up the charge with enthusiasm, and his interest in it never abated. The work itself was one for which he had definitely been preparing himself for years past ; it was that which from his earliest days he had made his deliberate choice. His recreations also were just what he would have chosen ; he loved the country and the simple living ; the garden was his constant delight ; it was wild and overgrown when he came, and many afternoons were given to felling and pruning, the planning of beds, or the stocking of his Swiss corner. It had been carefully laid out by his predecessor, Mr. Steel, and planted with rare and beautiful trees. But Mr. Steel, who was a Harrow master, was often non-resident, and the place had fallen into neglect. It was Hort's great delight to reduce it to order, and preserve what he could of the original planting.

He could not but bring new life with him wherever he came ; nothing to him was dull even in the routine of vestries, schools, and clubs ; he taught in both week-day and Sunday schools ; the Church services under his direction began to revive ; the music was among his earliest cares, and he took great pains in his preaching to bring home to the people the distinctive services of the Christian year. To all the details of a country clergyman's life he brought a spirit for which 'conscientiousness' is too cold a word. The fact remains, however, that in the course of years the conviction grew on him that this was not his true sphere. His extreme sensitiveness and shyness were real hindrances, and he was well aware of the fact ; valuing reticence as he did, he lamented that freer intercourse was not possible for him. Again, his sense of responsibility was almost morbidly acute, the delinquencies of the villagers weighed on his mind as though caused by negligence of his own. In the parochial visits, which he paid to church people and Dissenters alike, his manner was most humble and tender, but he felt all along unable to speak to the people as he longed to do. He was and is regarded by them with reverent affection, but they must have felt, as he did, the barrier of his reserve. It would be most unjust to them to say that they did not appreciate him ; if words were few, there was no mistaking the man's life. It was long after his departure before he revisited the parish, though he was frequently asked to do so ; he shrank from going, from an ever-present feeling that he had failed there, that he had not done all that he aspired to do for his flock. When at length, after many years, he appeared one day in the church for a wedding, it was touching to see the hands of the villagers outstretched from every pew, and to hear the frequent appeal, " Don't you remember me, sir ? I was so-and-so," greet him as he passed down the aisle.

It was in the production of sermons that the difficulty of finding expression for his thoughts was most felt. It seemed as though the message which he longed to give lay too deep in his own heart to be uttered abroad. The difficulty was also doubtless of physical origin. The subject of a sermon was generally chosen early in the week. It was thought over perpetually, and towards the end of the week he began to write ; but he had hardly ever finished before the early hours of Sunday morning, and he would often sit hour after hour, pen in hand, but apparently dumb, till the words came at last, sometimes in a rush. Extreme fastidiousness was in part the cause of this remarkable *aphasia*, a habit of mind which, while it secured that nothing from his hand should see the light which he might afterwards wish to recall, yet deprived his hearers of much which they would have welcomed, even in what he considered an imperfect shape, since the perfection at which he aimed was always indefinitely beyond his present achievement. But it would be easy to exaggerate the importance of this fastidiousness ; at all events the peculiarity was more moral than intellectual, the sense of responsibility was almost crushing. Nor did the difficulty decrease with time ; he had always felt it, and he came to feel it not less but more as time went on, and the greater the occasion the more terrible became the struggle to put his thought into words. A notable instance of this was a sermon which he preached at Cambridge after Maurice's death ; this nearly caused a serious illness. His last and most painful effort of the kind was the sermon preached in Westminster Abbey at the consecration of Dr. Westcott as Bishop of Durham.[1] In the case of village sermons there was the added

[1] See vol. ii. pp. 371-4.

difficulty of making himself plain enough for his congregation ; this, however, he undoubtedly in great
measure overcame. His village sermons show the
same depth and concentration of thought which mark
all his writings ; yet the style is wonderfully simple,
and there is no trace of the terrible strain of composition. The simplicity of these discourses is the
more remarkable for the absence of any visible attempt
at 'talking down' to an uneducated audience. But it
is the simplest writing which taxes most severely the
writer who has something to say, and one to whom all
expression was difficult found this, which to many is
hardly an effort, the most exacting work of a clergyman's life ; the writing of sermons was to him at St.
Ippolyts and elsewhere accomplished only at a cost
ruinous to nerve and brain.

The principal literary work of these years was the
revision of the Greek text of the New Testament. All
spare hours of every day were devoted to it; occasionally
Mr. Westcott came down for a few days' visit in the
intervals between Harrow terms, when the two worked
together for several hours continuously every day. A
welcome variety of work was afforded by the 'Cambridge Plato' (see p. 349).

Hort had left Cambridge at an exciting time ; the
revision of college statutes had begun, and University
Reform was in the air. At Trinity among the most
earnest reformers was Hort's friend the Rev. J. Ll.
Davies ; the views upheld by the party of which Mr.
Davies, Mr. Westlake, and Mr. Vaughan were the chief
spokesmen were vigorously assailed by Hort in a
privately-printed letter, which is interesting in many
ways, not least because this attempt to state the case of
the opponents of change comes from a rather unexpected

quarter, from one who described himself as a man
" whom his worst enemy cannot accuse of aversion to
reform." The arguments, however, as might be
imagined, were hardly such as were current among the
majority of University Conservatives. In University
politics Hort was always reckoned a Liberal; to what
extent the opinions maintained in this pamphlet remained part of his maturer convictions I am unable to
say, but, when the new *régime* was established, he
certainly gave it his loyal support. This, however, was
not the only occasion on which he found himself hostile
to reformers in the interests of what he considered true
reform.

Towards University reform he once fairly defined
his attitude as follows : " I cannot wonder that the
prospect is alarming even to high-minded and open-
minded Churchmen. They see this University movement
caught up by the passion for trying exciting 'experiments' on the largest scale which has lately seized upon
our sport-loving people. Aware that old and respectable abuses need rough handling, and acknowledging
the timely wisdom of heroic medicine, they cannot
welcome violence which gives no better account of itself
than the necessity of doing something strong."

The title of the pamphlet is, ' A Letter to the Rev.
J. Ll. Davies on the Tenure of Fellowships, and on
Church Patronage in Trinity College'; it is twenty-
eight octavo pages long, and is divided into three
sections, headed 'The Condition of Celibacy,' 'The
Condition of Holy Orders,' and 'College Livings.'
On the marriage question one of the chief contentions
of the advocates of the proposed change was the
difficulty under celibate conditions of retaining competent lecturers ; to this Hort replied " that the loss of

good experienced lecturers was compensated by the
freshness of young lecturers " (" routine," he said, " is
a much worse evil than the possible awkwardness of a
novice "), and by "the teaching and influence of many
private tutors " : if, however, more was required, an
inducement to residence might be provided " by dividing
the tutorships in Trinity." But the greatest strength
of his attack lay in his recognition of the value
of 'temporary celibacy'; for permanent celibacy, or
perpetual vows of any kind, he had nothing to say;
recognising, as he had good reason to do, marriage as
the "greatest of human blessings," he yet believed that
between boyhood and marriage a period of temporary
and voluntarily imposed celibacy was of the greatest
advantage, at least to University men ; and he could
see no reason why a small percentage of the community
should not be made to defer marriage to an age which,
after all, would in most cases not be very late, earlier
probably than that fixed by Aristotle (thirty-seven) as
the best for entering on the marriage state. " I have
in view," he said, " a body of fellows, some of whom are
tutors and assistant-tutors, shading off imperceptibly
through the Bachelor scholars downwards to the
youngest freshman, carrying on a manifold work of
education on themselves and on undergraduates, partly
by instruction, partly by society." He had a very
great belief in 'college feeling,' and thought that it
was on the increase in Trinity rather than the reverse ;
in fact he valued the informal unofficial part of the education obtained by residence in a college above the routine
of lectures and examinations. And he thought that by
the abolition of the requirement of 'temporary celibacy'
the younger fellows would inevitably desert college life
for family life ; nor could he persuade himself that the

society of ladies was, as was sometimes argued, a necessary humanising influence to the undergraduates ; even under existing conditions the latter were debarred from ladies' society for only a small part of the year. He had himself experienced the good of graduate residence, and was disposed to be rather angry with those who did not seize such an opportunity of useful- ness to themselves and the college ; he could hardly believe such persons competent to judge the present question on its merits ; " those who leave the University at an early stage soon lose their youthful prejudices touching life in general, but have little or nothing to correct their prejudices about college matters ; nay, perhaps the new prejudices which they may acquire become impediments to a truer view.   There is such a thing as hardening in inexperience."   It is perhaps right to add that Mr. Davies did not consider his party's views fairly stated by Hort.

The controversy has long been settled, and it is of little use to revive ancient polemics for their own sake ; but these reflections on the ideal of collegiate life seem to have lasting value.   Even more valuable are some of the thoughts expressed in this forgotten brochure on the ideal of the ministry of the English Church. Though not opposed to a slight increase in the number of lay fellows, Hort defended the principle of the old ' clerical' system on the ground that the education of the sons of English gentlemen ought mainly to be in the hands of clergymen.   The common sense of the English laity would, he felt sure, be strong enough to prevent such a system from ever acquiring a ' Jesuitical' character.   As to the evil effects of the change on the clergy themselves he felt still more strongly.   The most emphatic part of the pamphlet is an eloquent

protest against the doctrine that the 'cure of souls' is
the distinctive and exclusive work of a clergyman.
His declaration on this subject powerfully emphasises
truths which are at least as liable to be forgotten in
1896 as in 1857, and must be quoted entire.

. . . In all periods of English history a clergyman has
been felt to be *ex officio* a teacher or educator. This feeling
is now called secular, and we are required to believe that the
routine of parochial work is the only employment worthy of
one called to holy orders. By implication every master of a
school or tutor of a college is accused of violation of his
ordination vows. The doctrine has grown up parallel with,
and partly in consequence of the wider and more zealous view
taken of parochial ministrations, for which we must all be
thankful. But it is at least equally due to another dictum of
'the public conscience,' of the most pestilent kind, that it is
the clergyman's exclusive business to prepare men for the
future life, as the schoolmaster's for the present life. Such
an interpretation of 'the cure for souls' follows naturally from
the degradation of theology. That intelligent laymen should
support it is a strange and mournful fact, since the next or
next but one step is to 'direction,' and all that 'the public
conscience' associates with Jesuitry. Against every such
heresy every devout and conscientious clergyman engaged in
tuition, especially college tuition, is a standing protest, and the
maintenance of a large body of such clergymen reacts upon
the whole English clergy with an influence which, if not great,
is at least greater than we can afford to lose. Further, breadth
of teaching implies breadth of study. The existence of a
clerical body at the University, drinking freely of all divine
and human learning, is a standing and not unneeded encouragement to every hard-working curate who rescues a few
hours for science, or history, or poetry, or philosophy as well
as theology, to believe that he is not robbing his flock of their
due, or breaking his vow to "be diligent in such studies as
help to the knowledge of the Holy Scriptures," since practical
knowledge of the Scriptures implies knowledge of the creatures
and circumstances to which they have to be applied.

Theology itself is no less indebted to the residence of clergymen at college, and that in two superficially opposite ways. Perhaps the greatest enemy to theology just now is popular zeal for its supposed purity. Nothing can be more contemptible or more injurious to sound faith than the behaviour of the religious world to criticism and science, now shunning and denouncing them, now caressing and patronising them, always trembling in vague apprehension of some unknown destruction of which they may some time be the agents. The Universities are looked upon with a suspicion which may soon become bitter hatred, because they are felt to be asylums where the utmost freedom of criticism and science finds a refuge and even a welcome, and where the engines of the modern style of persecution are comparatively powerless. I am too warmly interested on behalf of both criticism and science to be indifferent to the valuable standing-ground which they thus obtain, but I rejoice still more in the benefits to theology. In such a neighbourhood theological thought is compelled to increased depth and truthfulness. The science of the most universal and eternal verities is driven back from its tendency to become a science of names and *entia rationis*. I do not mean that all the clergymen in the University are free from the popular terror, though it is remarkable to see how little—and yearly less—hold it has upon men who elsewhere would certainly have yielded to it entirely. But it is worth notice that, when a timid theological vote of the senate is desired, its friends are obliged to summon their faithful followers from the neighbouring parsonages.

Will these advantages be less, you may ask, if the resident body consists chiefly of laymen? As regards the interests of science and perhaps criticism, I hardly know. Much in the ecclesiastical history of the last few years suggests an impression that a section of the laity are greater enemies to freedom of thought than the clergy or any section of them. At all events science can go its way elsewhere, without heeding what may be said of it. But theology will certainly suffer by being deprived of the wholesome association of which I have already spoken. The extent of the injury can by no means be rightly measured by the amount of theology actually proceeding from residents. Salutary influences received at Cambridge cannot altogether lose their power when residence has ceased. In this and in other indirect ways the Universities act upon the whole Church.

But there is another equally important benefit conferred on theology by clerical residence. Anxiety to secure complete freedom for both theology and other studies acting, or supposed to act upon it, leads rightly to an equal anxiety for its soundness and security. There are many who hate the existence of science and criticism chiefly as means of shattering our supposed cloudy fabric. By all means let them try; we shall be the better, not the worse, for the attempt. But in abandoning the negative and now suicidal method of repelling heresy by means of anathemas, suspensions, and the like, we are bound all the more to labour for the positive strength and fulness of orthodoxy. In this respect the clerical residents are surely of the greatest service. Every influence of the place counteracts the tendency to make popular opinion the standard of orthodoxy. At Cambridge those who have sworn, as we have done, to "set theology before us as the end of our studies," and to "prefer things true to things accustomed, things written to things unwritten in matters of religion," soon learn to find their best protection against theological tyranny in our sacred books and creeds, and in the genuine harmony of the voice of the Church in all ages. Above all, the lovers of antiquity and the lovers of speculation or criticism come to a better understanding of each other, and are led to recognise the mutual need of true permanence and true progress.

The same liberal spirit is shown in his words on the " invisible pre-eminence of theology at Cambridge under the old system." It was, he said, "an omnipresent element felt rather than seen." In passing he criticises severely recent legislation of a specialising tendency, such as the establishment of a Theological Tripos, by which theology " is exposed to the danger of assuming a narrow and technical character." " A body of fellows," he continues, " bound to the study of theology is needed

as a counterpoise to the influence of the Theological
Tripos as much as for other purposes."

Finally, he boldly defends the existing system of
college patronage of livings as the "best possible"; in
spite of occasional anomalies and evils arising therefrom,
"nothing can outweigh the benefit of keeping up a
multiformity of types among English clergymen, and
thus helping to save them from the curse of becoming
a separate caste."

The writer himself acknowledges at the end of his
pamphlet that "the picture here sketched . . . cannot
be taken to represent the actual state of things without
considerable qualification"; he was conscious that such
a system requires a high standard of duty among those
who are to work it; but he thought that even this
consideration was in its favour, since his desire was to
rely on men rather than on machinery. The pamphlet
concludes with a protest against subservience to public
opinion in questions of University reform : " A college
like ours is then exercising its most proper function
when it is counteracting the prevalent fallacies of the
day. We ought to be the refuge for forgotten and
unpopular aspects of truth."

It could not be expected that this letter would be
received with much favour among Hort's Liberal friends.
He was, however, gratified to receive from the Master of
Trinity (Dr. Whewell) a hearty and pleasant letter of
thanks for it; and at Oxford it was welcomed by
Conington : Mr. Westlake wrote a rejoinder.

Among the *parochialia* which engrossed a principal
share of attention during the early years at St. Ippolyts,
Church music was specially prominent. Hort had had
no formal musical education, but his ear was good, and
he had very decided preferences in music ; he went

occasionally to concerts in London (and afterwards at
Cambridge) as a rare treat, and most enjoyed classical
music of a not very modern type. The barrel-organ in
St. Ippolyts Church was an offence which he could not
long tolerate, and he took endless trouble in the selection
of chants and hymn-tunes, to say nothing of the hymns
themselves, at a time when the materials for selection
were scanty and inaccessible : both chants and hymns
were daring innovations. He introduced the *Church
Hymnal*, a book little known at the time. His work
in this field entailed a great deal of correspondence with
Ellerton, who about this time began to make hymnology
his special province : his *Hymns for Schools and Bible-
Classes* appeared in 1859, and contained four translations from Hort's pen, of the ancient 'Candle-light
Hymn' of the Alexandrian Church, of a Latin Epiphany hymn ('The Lord of heaven hath stooped to
earth'), of Martin Ruickart's 'Nun danket' ('All
praise to God alone, Heart, voice and hands shall
render'), and the Easter hymn beginning, 'Now
dawning glows the day of days.' Hort also gave
substantial help to Ellerton and the other compilers of
Church Hymns, to which collection he contributed the
translation beginning, 'Thou Glory of Thy chosen
race,' and the Easter hymn above mentioned.[1]

At the end of 1857 the Alpine Club was started.
A sketch of its beginnings was given by Mr. W. Long-
man in the *Alpine Journal* for February 1878, which
sketch was completed by a paper of Hort's in the
August number of that year, the only number to which
he contributed. From this paper it appears that the
idea of the Club was first mooted in a letter from Mr.
W. Mathews to Hort, written February 1st, 1857 : " I

[1] See Appendix I.

want you to consider," he says, "whether it would not
be possible to establish an Alpine Club, the members of
which might dine together once a year, say in London,
and give each other what information they could.   Each
member, at the close of any Alpine tour in Switzerland
or elsewhere, should be required to furnish to the
President a short account of all the undescribed excursions he had made, with a view to the publication of
an annual or bi-annual volume.   We should thus get a
good deal of useful information in a form available to
the members.   Alpine tourists now want to know the
particulars of the following *courses*, which I believe have
been recently made, Finsteraarhorn, Jungfrau from
Grindelwald, Altels, Galenstock, Dom, Weishorn, Zinal
Pass, Crête à Collon, and many others."   The formation
of a Club was resolved on at an informal meeting of
Cambridge men, held November 6th, 1857, and Mr.
E. S. Kennedy undertook the necessary correspondence.
In answer to his invitation Hort wrote on December
1st, criticising some of the proposed rules and suggesting
names.   He was anxious to minimise the expenses,
especially those of dining ; his criticisms were the outcome of a conversation with Mr. Vaughan Hawkins ;
he also conferred shortly afterwards with Lightfoot.
It is interesting to note that he suggested Mr. John
Ball as a likely member.   The first dinner of the Club
was held on February 2nd, 1858 : Hort was, to his
regret, unable to be present ; his name occurs on the
back of the circular of invitation in the list of original
members, which also included his friends Messrs. Lightfoot, Vaughan Hawkins, J. Ll. Davies, and H. W.
Watson.   He remained a member all his life, but
never held any official position in the Club.   Another
of the original members, Mr. G. V. Yool, wrote an

obituary notice of Hort in the *Alpine Journal* for February 1893.

After about two years of parish work it became painfully obvious that some extra effort must be made to relieve the *res angusta domi* which, in spite of rigid economy, began to be a serious anxiety. It was not a time when additional labour could be welcome; the overstrain of Cambridge years had already begun to tell, though the breakdown did not come at once. But, in spite of difficulties, some fresh work was inevitable; the literary projects already in hand could not be expected to bring grist to the mill for a long time to come; meanwhile he determined to put his hand to something which, it might reasonably be hoped, would bring in quick profits. Thus it came about that more writing was undertaken in the shape of some original work in English History. But Hort required too much of himself: after considerable research in what proved to be a most interesting field, the only visible result was a fragment on the *Last Days of Simon de Montfort*, which appeared in *Macmillan's Magazine* for June 1864. The unused materials were handed over to Dr. Luard and to Mr. G. W. Prothero. *Simon de Montfort* was to have been one of a series of historical biographies for boys, but the work grew to larger proportions under the historian's hand. Mr. Macmillan soon observed that Hort's contribution to the series was likely "to grow into a man's book." Besides de Montfort he was to have written on Grossetête, and perhaps Wycliffe; he consulted an immense number of authorities, causing his publisher some alarm by the length of his disquisitions on minute points.

Another piece of literary work alluded to in the letters of these years was a share in the Biblical Commentary projected by Dr. William Smith; Hort's portion was to be the Gospels, Wisdom, and Ecclesiasticus. The project was eventually dropped, and its place for Hort was taken by a new scheme for a Commentary, to be divided between himself, Mr. Westcott, and Lightfoot. This, though abandoned as a formally common work, was never lost sight of, and out of it grew various subordinate undertakings. Hort worked at his own share year after year, and dreamed of the completion for which many others hoped; but, strangely enough, it is only now after his death that the world has an opportunity of judging what he had produced to set alongside of the masterpieces of his collaborators, the two successive Bishops of Durham. A letter to Lightfoot, dated April 29th, 1860, suggests the following apportionment: Lightfoot, the Pauline writings and Epistle to the Hebrews; Westcott, the Johannine writings; Hort, the historico-Judaic writings (the Synoptists, St. James, St. Peter, and St. Jude).

A passing mention must be given to yet another unfulfilled project, a non-party quarterly review, to which Hort promised to contribute, as well as Mr. Thomas Hughes and others whose names were closely associated with the firm of Messrs. Macmillan. Mr. Hughes was to have been the editor. The articles were to be signed. Maurice gave the scheme the following characteristic encouragement: " The ruling idea should be the idea of civilisation, and all that tends to it, the idea which informed Plato when he wrote the *Republic*, and which was in St. Paul's mind when he said ' we seek a city.' " This idea was to be indicated by the title *The Citizen*. *The Citizen* never reached even its first number; publication was at first deferred for a time, and then for good.

Mr. Alexander Macmillan also suggested to Hort an English version of Winer's *New Testament Grammar*, at which he could work, without much extra labour, along with the Greek Testament text. He gladly welcomed the suggestion, and intended to make the book more than a translation. It occupied him for a considerable time, but was given up finally when Dr. Moulton's book [1] appeared.

Yet another book must be added to the list of unfinished designs; it does not appear, however, that it was ever seriously begun. This was " a short but very readable and, if possible, vivid Church History of the Ante-Nicene centuries (including a life of Christ), using as far as possible the works of the original records." Six popular and comparatively slight lectures on the Ante-Nicene Fathers, delivered many years later at Cambridge, were the only fulfilment of this scheme.

It is sad work cataloguing books which never were written, especially when the failure was due to no falling off in their author's vigour and enthusiasm. Yet the labour so bestowed was not lost; it survives, where the worker was well content that it should, in the finished works which others have been able to accomplish. Nor is the record after all one only of half-accomplishment. While various other tasks invited, they never distracted him from that which was to prove the chief complete work of his life, the revision of the text of the Greek Testament. At one time he thought of adding to it a translation; in this he intended to insert " many notes of interrogation, or other marks of uncertainty of interpretation as well as of reading." This purpose was, of course, superseded by the work of the Revision Committee formed in 1870.

[1] See vol. ii. pp. 134-5.

The Greek Text itself had proved a much slower work than had been anticipated ; but this was not a matter for regret, as the delay gave opportunity for using the fresh light supplied by the work of Tregelles and of Tischendorf. Hort had been for some time in correspondence with the former. He had communicated to him his own and Mr. Westcott's scheme in 1857, and had received from him hearty approval and promises of help. Dr. Tregelles' own First Part appeared in July of that year, and was reviewed by Hort, along with part of Tischendorf's seventh edition in the *Journal of Classical and Sacred Philology*, vol. iv. No. xi. This and other reviews by Hort in the same Journal (1855-1860) of the work of Tregelles, Tischendorf, and Scrivener are important as showing how the principles of his own edition were developing in his mind. The readings of the *Codex Sinaiticus* became accessible in 1863. It was in 1859 that Hort and his collaborator adopted the plan of doing their work by correspondence, each working out separately his own results, and then submitting them to the other's judgment.

For one who like Hort combined with his devotion to theology an ever-fresh enthusiasm for science and criticism, the year 1860, in which fell the controversies aroused by the publication of the *Origin of Species* and of *Essays and Reviews*, was to a very high degree exciting. Discussion of these two books fills a large part of his letters for some months, and on the subjects of both he burned to speak openly; yet here again eventually speech failed him. He had been invited to co-operate in *Essays and Reviews*, but declined in a very interesting letter to Dr. Rowland Williams. He contributed four years later to the *Record*[1] a vigorous

[1] *Record*, April 27th, 1864.

answer to an attack on Dr. Jowett's Greek scholarship,
which he believed would never have been assailed
"by any scholar worthy of the name in the absence
of theological causes of difference." The immediate
occasion of the attack was the controversy at Oxford
over the endowment of the Greek Professorship, in
which Professor Jowett's contribution to *Essays and
Reviews* was brought up against him, and his opponents found fault with his scholarship, quoting in
support of their criticisms some remarks by Lightfoot
and Hort in the *Journal of Philology;* the former
directly, in a review of Stanley's and Jowett's editions
of *St. Paul's Epistles*, the latter in an answer to a
contributor's defence of a lax rendering of Greek tenses,
had criticised the Oxford Professor's methods of translation. But, when his authority was quoted against
Jowett, Hort, with Lightfoot's full concurrence, explained that they had been criticising, not 'ignorance,'
but what seemed to them 'erroneous opinions'; and
that in fact these opinions as to the rendering of New
Testament Greek were not peculiar to Professor Jowett,
but belonged to the interpretative method which was
'generally in use in England till very lately, while
the stricter method now coming into vogue was due
almost entirely to Germany.' Otherwise Hort took
no public part in the controversies which arose directly
or indirectly out of *Essays and Reviews*. All that he
actually wrote on the subject apparently was a criticism
of Mark Pattison's essay, which the latter declared to
be very valuable, regretting that he had not seen it
before the publication of the volume. Hort considered the tracts on *Essays and Reviews* issued by
Maurice and Mr. T. Hughes inadequate, and he
deplored the 'smartness' of Stanley's famous *Edin-*

burgh Review article. A joint volume of essays in reply to the book was meditated by Hort, Lightfoot, and Mr. Westcott, but came to nothing. When it was abandoned, Hort contemplated writing himself an essay called 'Doctrine, Human and Divine,' but this too remained an unaccomplished task. Such an essay, however, he continued to think about for a long time. His Hulsean Lectures delivered in 1871, and published at length in 1893, were in some sense a realisation of this long-cherished hope.

At the end of 1859 he had been obliged to leave his parish by a breakdown in health. A water-cure at Malvern was the partially successful remedy; but it was necessary for the next two years to take a long summer outing. He was abroad with his wife from May to October 1860, gradually rising from sub-alpine places such as Les Avants and Villard to the highest accessible habitation. A whole month was spent at the little Riffelberg Hotel, now superseded for most English visitors by the more luxurious Riffelalp. After this they crossed the main chain by the S. Théodule Pass, and made a tour of the south side of Monte Rosa, following in the steps of Mr. and Mrs. King of the *Italian Valleys of the Alps.* Unluckily it was a wet season, and an otherwise most enjoyable tour was somewhat spoiled. The last perch of this season was the Æggischhorn. He pursued the botany of these regions with keen delight, and a very large Swiss *hortus siccus* was the result of the rambles of this and subsequent Alpine summers, when hard walking was out of the question. In planning such tours he always endeavoured, if possible, to get to some almost unknown spot, which at that time was still feasible. His know-ledge of the topography of most of the Alps was very

minute. In 1861 he was again abroad with his wife
from June to September, first in the Engadine, at Pontresina, then little known, and over the Bernina to the
Baths of S. Catarina, so sympathetically described in
Mr. Leslie Stephen's *The Playground of Europe;* then
to the top of the Stelvio for a fortnight in the very
roughest of inns, and finally in the Dolomite region
near Botzen, where a rich harvest of new plants was
found.

Mr. Yool's obituary notice in the *Alpine Journal* for
February 1893 mentions that Hort "was one of the
first to recognise the value of the mountain hotels, then
very primitive, as health resorts." In this connexion
it is curious at this date to read some of his notes, *e.g.*
" Pontresina, Hotel Krone ; homely, but very clean and
comfortable ; . . . beer excellent."

" Bormio, Hotel Poste ; did not seem bad, but we
did not sleep there.

" S. Maria, near top of Stelvio ; floors dirty, and
food monotonous ; not otherwise bad."

Botany was of course a great resource in these years,
when mountaineering was no longer possible. He also
amused himself with making careful pen - and - ink
sketches, which had at least a scientific value ; his
drawings of the Ortler group, done in 1861, were found
extremely useful by Mr. F. F. Tuckett in his preparation of a paper for the *Alpine Journal* on the topography of that region.

Both of these summers did immense good, but they
were not sufficient to restore his exhausted powers.

The effect on his nerves of glacier air was always
very remarkable ; in 1860, when he was thoroughly
exhausted, and a breakdown was imminent, an excursion up the Cima di Jazzi from the Riffelberg had

almost miraculous results. He even had the hardihood
to bathe frequently in glacier streams. While staying
at the Riffelberg, he had taken some observations with
thermometers in the Zermatt region for Mr. John Ball,
to whose *Alpine Guide* he contributed botanical and
other notes; many of these were inserted over the
initials F. J. H. Hort was one of the very few who
helped in all three of Mr. Ball's volumes (*Western
Alps*, 1863 ; *Central Alps*, 1864 ; *Eastern Alps*, 1868).
The best known of these notes is his description in
Central Alps of his passage of the Lämmerenjoch in
1856.

From the letters written in this period one would
hardly guess that there had been any failure. Keen
talk on his various literary ventures, the New Testament Commentary, Plato, Darwin, *Essays and Reviews*,
fills many sheets. In 1860 his duty was taken by
Mark Pattison. He returned to work in the autumn
of 1861, but was not fit for it, and the next year
the collapse was complete. He now for the first
time realised the gravity of his condition. He put
himself under a London physician, Mr. Seymour
Haden, who advised him to give up parish work for
three years ; meanwhile he was to live quietly with
his parents (who in 1862 moved from Chepstow to
Eckington House, Cheltenham), and a long summer in
each year was to be spent in the high Alps. The
medical verdict was a severe blow, yet it was hoped
that complete recovery was possible, and that without
medicine, by a carefully regulated life. There was no
organic disease, but a thorough enfeeblement of brain
and spine, from which came other secondary disorders
connected with circulation. The principal cause he
believed to be the late hours which he had kept at

Cambridge. At first an attempt was made to do with less complete immunity from parish work than the doctor had enjoined. In June 1862 he so far obeyed orders as to leave St. Ippolyts for five months. He went to his parents' new home at Cheltenham, where his eldest child, a daughter, was born, and after this event he went alone to the Bernese Oberland. The next year his mother's precarious state of health brought things to a crisis. He now definitely gave up the parish, and went first with his parents, eldest sister, wife and child, to Vichy, Mont Dore, and then to the Bel Alp. In the autumn he took up his abode at his father's house at Cheltenham, where his eldest son was born in January 1864.

Before Hort left home, a serious interruption to regular work had been caused by the composition of a pamphlet on the Revised Code of Education, " its purpose and probable effects." These criticisms were originally intended for a magazine article, but eventually appeared in the form of a pamphlet which was widely circulated. It sums up the tendencies of the proposals of the Committee of Council as " a reduction in our funds which will make it impossible for most of us to maintain a good school ; and a sordid type of teaching, above which we must not dare to rise for fear of losing the means of existence." On this text he enlarges for thirty-eight pages, of which the following is his own summary :—

(1) The Code desires to save public money, and on the whole does so. The money withdrawn is not now wasted, and will not be replaced ; so that the saving represents an equivalent loss of education.

(2) The Code desires to correct a supposed neglect of reading, writing, and arithmetic not wholly imaginary but very

limited in extent. It secures the naked arts of reading, writing, and summing, at the cost of discouraging all other elementary and all higher instruction, and debasing the tone of education in schools generally.

(3) The Code desires to extend the area of government aid. The advantages offered barely exceed those already within reach. The classes of teachers created are not of a kind to improve education in their own schools, while their influence may lower the character of better neighbouring schools.

(4) The Code desires to simplify office business, but re-creates in one quarter the complication which it abolishes in another. It destroys the position of teachers and apprentices, and relaxes the control over the private hobbies or incompetence of managers.

The combined effect of all the regulations is to discourage excellence of education, and enfeeble all the energies hitherto accumulated to secure its excellence, especially the Training Colleges.

It may still be of interest to refer to some of Hort's well-weighed declarations on the first two of these heads, since they show what thought he had given to these difficult practical questions; nor can the problems of National Education be said to have yet reached a final solution.

(1) Against the financial scheme of the Code he protested on behalf of the country schools, which would in future have to look for their support to increase of the children's payments, or to private subscriptions; in neither case, he contended, would the burden fall on the shoulders best able to bear it. Incidentally he criticises adversely the alternative plans of 'local rates' suggested, *e.g.* in Dr. Temple's article in the *Oxford Essays* of 1856; to local rating he objects first, " because it means handing over the education of the poor to the lower middle class of their neighbourhood,

nearly all indifferent, many of them secretly or even
openly opposed to the education of labourers' children ;
secondly, because no way has yet been found of making
local rating compatible with the ' Denominational '
character of English education, in other words the connexion of all, or nearly all, assisted schools with some
one religious body ; and no other method than the
denominational has been suggested either expedient or
practicable. The show of unanimity obtained by excluding from the regular school-teaching either religious
instruction altogether, or all except a residuum supposed
to be common to nearly all Christians, would not remove the danger ; a system administered by ratepayers
would still be in the greatest danger of falling to pieces
through religious squabbles. The teachers are, and
would soon be felt to be, of more importance than the
subjects taught ; and there is no subject not purely
mechanical, whether called ' secular ' or not, in which
the character of a master's teaching may not be deeply
affected either by his own creed, or by what is equally
important, the circumstances of his own education as
determined by his creed. Further, in the ' combined '
system, the separation of ' religious ' and ' secular ' subjects is injurious by tending to deaden and debase the
instruction which is always being reminded that it is
only ' secular,' and in like manner by imparting a needlessly dogmatic character to the ' religion.' "

Besides reducing the grant to schools, the new
regulations proposed to save money by crippling the
resources of the Training Colleges, abolishing the
salaries to lecturers, reducing the number of Queen's
Scholars which each College might receive, and discouraging the continuance of their training for more
than one year. This proposal Hort assailed as another

attempt to secure economy by lowering the standard of
education ; and he defended the Colleges on the ground
that they were now becoming promoters of national
education with a zeal which was learning not to be
exclusively religious.   "Training Colleges," he said,
"founded not many years ago to resist the theological
tendencies of each other, are now working together for
their better common purpose in perfect amity and
goodwill " ; and he protested loudly against the notion
that the prevailing tendency of the Colleges was to
'over-educate' the teachers.

It should be added that, coupled with Hort's
criticism of the proposed measures of financial reform,
were some positive suggestions of legitimate methods
of economising.

(2) The evils of 'payment for results' have perhaps
become sufficiently patent since 1862 ; they are forcibly
catalogued in this pamphlet with the remark that "they
would be evil still if the whole duty of man consisted in
learning to read, write, and cypher."   The desire of the
promoters of the scheme was for palpable results, while,
as Hort says, "'Education' cannot be weighed and
measured."   His position was that (*a*) examination in
the 'three R's' cannot be satisfactory ; and that (*b*)
even if it could, the limitation of 'elementary' education to such instruction is evidence of a very low educational ideal.   For instance, the only 'reading' which
can be tested is reading *aloud*, while "the really valuable 'reading,' that which opens the Bible and every
English book to its possessor, is silent reading " ; the
value of reading aloud is that it is "a means of giving
others the benefit of proper or silent reading," but the
former is a rare accomplishment, while the latter is
within the reach of all : according to the New Code, all

the pains spent on teaching children the more essential
kind of reading "will count for nothing, because they
are still bunglers at an accomplishment which a very
large majority of the educated classes have never learnt
to practise decently."

The above strictures fall on what, comparatively
speaking, may be called details of management or
organisation ; the most trenchant part of Hort's attack
is reserved for the low view of all the possibilities of
national education which seem to him to be implied in
all the provisions of the New Code. " It is a coarse and
petty view of national education which would lead us
to think chiefly of bestowing the means of success in
life with or without the addition of 'religion.' It may
be true that the poor for the most part desire nothing
more for their children ; if it be so, it is only the more
incumbent on us to provide correctives to a spirit which,
if unchecked, must destroy the well-being of the nation.
We ought by this time to understand clearly that the
same great purposes should be kept in view in the
education of all classes alike, however the methods
appropriate to each may differ. We need not be too
anxious to give the poor, though we do not grudge
them, a 'professional' education ; they will for the most
part contrive to pick that up in one way or another,
whether we give it them or not. But they have the
greatest need of a 'liberal' education ; not a feeble or
mutilated copy of what passes under that name for the
rich, but one capable of producing corresponding
effects by different means. No theoretical scheme of
subjects is required, nothing of an ambitious or
doctrinaire character. Doubtless all that can be done
is already being done in innumerable schools throughout the country. Whatever gives an interest not

connected with personal gain or advancement is in fact a piece of liberal education. The general effect of all such acquisition is to supply a counterpoise to the various absorbing influences of society, whatever their precise nature may be. . . . The fault of the new legislation is one which a moderately rational positivist might join hands with a bishop in condemning. Whatever of an informing, expanding, ennobling nature, whatever faculties of learning, thought, or feeling it is in the power of education to bestow or call forth, are ruthlessly ignored, and thereby sacrificed."

To Mr. A. Macmillan

CAPEL CURIG, LLANRWST, CONWAY,
N. WALES, *May 26th*, 1857.

. . . It was the 'pikters' that attracted me in the Scott; but then I wanted the 'pomes' too, some one having (rather to my relief) made away with the very scrubby and imperfect little edition that I had.

If ed. 2 of *Tom Brown* is to come out in but a few weeks, I think it might fairly be of the same size and price, so long as the edition is not a very large one. I am rejoiced to hear it is so well received.

The sooner Maurice's *St. John's Epistles* come out, the better. I want especially to see him at work on the Apocalypse and the Warburtonian subjects thereto appertaining. I was thinking a day or two ago that he ought to be spirited up to carrying on the *Prophets and Kings* through and past the Captivity; he would write grandly about those latter times, and at present there is an ugly gap in his series on the O. T. in consequence.

To the Rev. John Ellerton

ST. IPPOLYTS, *June 27th*, 1857.

. . . I write now in haste, to ask you to send me at once —if possible, by return of post—either Mercer's *Church*

Psalter (which I saw at Crewe, and which seems tolerably good), or some other good book with the music of the better-known old psalm tunes, such as 'Rockingham,' 'St. Ann's,' etc. Dear Daniel Macmillan is dying, if not dead; so that I cannot write to his brother. . . . You will perhaps wonder at my speaking especially of such tunes; but both churches have barrel-organs only, with ten such like doleful ditties. We heard the one at Wymondley yesterday play at the rate of about 10 to 20 seconds to a syllable.

N.B.—This is probably only No. 1 of a series of questions and requests parochial that I shall be compelled to address to you. But I will write again very soon less professionally.

We got here on Tuesday, and found things in tolerable order. I was inducted yesterday, and read myself in to-morrow. *Ecce* postman.—Affectionately yours ever,

FENTON J. A. HORT.

TO MR. A. MACMILLAN

ST. IPPOLYTS, *August* 12*th*, 1857.

My dear Macmillan—I have kept ——[1] to the latest day allowed, and yet have not had time to read more than a small part, three or four chapters at the beginning, and two dips elsewhere. I don't know what to say. The man (or woman??) annoys me extremely. The language is abominable, saturated with the worst form of the deadliest of literary sins, fine writing. I have not seen one of his prettinesses which is not absolutely worthless. It is not fair to judge of the people without reading more; but they seem to me poor and char-acterless. In short, as a work of art or literature, I should condemn the book without mercy. Whatever value it has, must be in the ideas of which it is the vehicle, and a very bad one too. Of course many are true and important; but. very well known, much canted about, and very cantingly pro-pounded here. There is a surprising ignorance of common facts (the would-be philosophy of the introduction is purely

[1] A novel sent by Macmillan for criticism.

ridiculous), and the way in which in practice one principle works on another. I don't think the author has ever *thought out* a single point. He has seen difficulties or rather evils, and something of the questions which must be asked (though not a bit better than scores of other people), but his answers are of the crudest, sometimes very decidedly false. The cardinal heresies are (1)—throughout, I believe—the aiming at teachership and lordship as the true goal of man, and (2) what —— justly charges against the better sort of the rising generation, a desire to 'do good,' *i.e.* produce good results, instead of doing right and leaving the results to God; in short, practically assuming that we have got to work instead of Him, instead of under and with Him. Nevertheless my two dips have shown considerable force in the man, and given me a feeling that there must be stuff in him; but he wants a tremendously long apprenticeship before he begins to write. I should say, Reject the book, but try to get some intercourse with the man. Excuse my writing so shortly, but I have no time.

To the Rev. John Ellerton

St. Ippolyts, *August* 14*th*, 1857.

. . . I have got and read Ruskin's book. It must be mainly good, but is surely too short and sketchy, and yet too rambling for its purpose. One is by this time pretty well used to his impertinent custom of delivering his opinion of things in general *à propos* of nothing. To read his talk of that kind is ruffling to the temper, but one soon says, "Oh! it's only Ruskin," and passes on. I suppose there are people who form their opinion of books by his dicta; but would they be better off by going to some one else? Among literary popes he is surely not the silliest or sickliest.

. . . Is it to be inferred that you are about to learn to draw? I have had some such thoughts; but time is wanting at present. I have not yet seen the illustrated Tennyson, nor the two books that you mention. I do not believe it possible to illustrate much of Tennyson. Few of his pictures are more than slightly visual, and you must not fill up but add, and that largely, to express them on paper. Still he may give good hints for good drawings.

To Mr. A. Macmillan

St. Ippolyts, *September 22nd*, 1857.

. . . I have in my drawer a letter to you begun nearly a month ago about ——. But it was then too late to be of much use, and quite so now. I really do not know a single book to recommend thoroughly on any of the matters. On the genealogies Mill is very valuable, and, I thought when I read him, satisfactory on all the critical points but one; but his tone as towards sceptics is dreadful. —— I have only looked at. He is sure to be honest and tolerably learned, but not sure to be strong. The question of the inspiration of the Gospels is, I think, pretty well put in the last four sections of the first chapter of Alford's introduction. . . . Nothing I have ever heard or read agrees so well with my own ideas as an University sermon that I once (not *more than* two or three years ago) heard H. Goodwin preach; I believe it is in one of his published volumes, whether Hulsean or not I don't re- member. But I hope —— won't read that horrid *Restoration of Belief.*[1] That and the *Eclipse of Faith* I look upon as about the two most damaging books to Christianity ever published in this country. As regards the Chronology of the Gospels, I like Browne's *Ordo Sæculorum* (as far as I have looked into that part of it) above any other. I am nearly sure he is right in returning to the ancient belief of our Lord's ministry being not much more than a year long. I am now at inter- vals working a little at the subject myself. The only material obstacle, I believe, lies in the words 'the passover,' in John vi. 4, which he shows pretty conclusively cannot have been in the text used by several of the Fathers.

Please always send any fresh piece of Tischendorf by post as soon as it comes, without waiting for a parcel. I am getting more and more convinced of the necessity of West- cott's and my work. Tregelles is very good, but he does not go to the bottom.

[1] Published in 1852.

To the Rev. Gerald Blunt

St. Ippolyts, *November* 17*th*, 1857.

. . . We are flourishing well enough as to health. I don't think it is a very bracing place, but otherwise it is healthy (gravel atop of chalk), and being perched on a hill, we have the luxury of beholding our neighbours swaddled in fog, we being dry and clear. The house is good and convenient. The garden is very pretty, and has some pleasant flowers in it, specially roses ; but will take a good deal of arranging and stocking. I have been pruning roses by the light of nature like mad, when I could get a spare hour, and flatter myself that I have done considerable execution upon them, and improved them for next year ; but they have been so neglected that every tree is a quickset hedge. We are soon going to make some walks in our plantation, and then I shall have to do some woodcutting. We have had a beautiful, and as amusing as beautiful, cat ; but she died only the other day after a week's illness, brought on, we fancy, from jealousy of Miss Loraine's dog. Another is, we hope, coming from the same family. There is also a second cat, a domestic nigger, fat, greedy, and stupid. But what will make you happy above all things is the news that we are actually going to have a dog ; nay, it may be here before I finish this letter. . . . There is also a small green creature like a miniature cockatoo, called a Budgeragar, which was brought from Australia. He is quaint and now and then noisy, but not on the whole a demonstrative being. Also there are squirrels in our plantation, though they don't often let themselves be seen, and lots of birds, and therefore by no means lots of currants, and hardly any gooseberries.

The people we like much. They are mostly very friendly . . . decidedly above the average of parishioners, I should think. Nor is there much real poverty. Practically we have five villages, St. Ippolyts, Gosmore, and Little Almshoe in the parish of St. Ippolyts, and Great Wymondley and a series of Greens in the parish of Great Wymondley. Gosmore, the largest of them, is chiefly given over to Dissent. Each parish has a (mixed) school, neither very flourishing at present. Great Wymondley school is not very old, and has great disadvantages. Still it seems to have done great good. St. Ippolyts school has been successful enough. . . . We have had some low fever in the village (a rare thing), and that has frightened away many children. The first note I received on the evening of our arrival in June was the resignation of the mistress. However, by great good luck we got at Michaelmas one whom we like much better, and I think she will get the school up. There is Sunday school at both schools every Sunday. F. and I teach at the St. Ippolyts one, which precedes the service, and F. at the Great Wymondley one corresponding. Those held when there is no service are taken by the mistresses. They are not at present very full or lively, but still hopeful, and at all events useful as giving us some dealings with those who have left the day school. This they do dreadfully early, being much addicted to straw-plaiting, a practice which does both good and harm. But the increase in the number of plaiters is bringing down the prices, and one does not see what will happen soon. The churches are both rather good-looking and tidy, having been done up by Steel. Of course there is only one service each Sunday at each church. The morning attendance is but so-so; the afternoon has much increased, and is now extremely good, especially in labouring men; the women don't come much. Hardly anybody comes to the Communion. We have a doleful barrel organ at each church, on which we grind out Tate and Brady to 'Bedford,' 'Rockingham,' and such like. But we hope a good time is coming. F. has had a singing class in the drawing-room every Saturday evening, which is well attended even by grown or growing-up girls. Yesterday (this is November 23rd) we had arranged to make our first public rush into chants; and, as luck would have it, the grinder of our barrel was laid up with a bad leg. So we boldly had both chants and psalms without organ with agreeable success. Next Sunday we are going to make a still bolder move. We are going to start a hymn-book and hymn tunes. For weeks I have been surrounded with all manner of collections, and have at last settled on a really good High Church one, published by Bell and Daldy, and rather pretentiously called *The Church Hymnal.* The selection of tunes is no easy matter; but we have got several books, including your wife's Mercer.

Our neighbours are many and very friendly. The clergy are really a very nice set, none 'rageous in any direction. Gentlemanliness has done a good deal for them, and this is an undeniably gentlemanly county. Almost everybody has a beautiful garden, and takes an interest in it. We are very lucky as to country, being not much more than a mile within the genuine Hertfordshire region, wooded, rather broken, and undeniably pretty for the east of England.

All this strange Indian drama has been being acted since we have had any real letters from each other. I believe I take it with a kind of Islamite composure, hardly knowing what is most dreadful. All that has happened does seem to me a most just and needed lesson to England, and to the English in India; but it is horrible enough, God knows. The great satisfaction is the masterly wisdom, energy, and courage of nearly all who have had to act in India, from Lord Canning to the units of the English regiments. The Indian authorities (not society) do seem to set justice before them in earnest. But it is shocking to see the increasing spirit of injustice (equally lax and unmerciful) which the crisis brings to light in England and in Indian society. All that has happened might be of great use to India, and perhaps may be in the end of ends; but meanwhile the warning seems almost wholly lost at home. It is the old dismal wickedness of the time of the Crimean war revived. And the religious talk is the most sickening of all. It almost makes one wish one were a Hindoo or a Mussulman. But one must try not to croak. There must be something at home worthily represented by Outram and Havelock abroad.

To Mr. E. S. Kennedy.   (On the proposed Alpine Club)

St. Ippolyts, Hitchin, *December 1st*, 1857.

. . . The chief point which raises doubt is the expense : on what do you propose to expend guinea subscriptions and guinea entrance fees? Surely there is nothing to be gained by having 'rooms,' 'curator,' and that style of thing? William Mathews wrote to me about such a club for *one* dinner nearly a year ago; and I then told him I thought it would be an excellent thing, provided care were taken that the dinner bills were kept within reasonable dimensions. When he was here a few weeks ago, he quite concurred; he was then going to write to you on the subject, but I have heard no more from him. Is it not rather much to ask a guinea a year, besides *two* dinners and (for all except Londoners) two double journeys to town? Granting that it is desirable to make the club select, we cannot see that a money standard is a desirable one. It may be well to have a few books and maps, though most of us would be likely to possess the best maps of districts which we meant to visit; but their annual cost ought to be something very small. Circulars would also cost something. But these are the only necessary expenses we can think of (except in connexion with dinners, which will, as you propose, be divided among the diners); and they might be annually divided among the whole Club without a large fixed subscription. What idea lurks under 'geographical explorers' and 'other guests of celebrity'? Surely we do not want speeches from Dr. Livingstone or Sir Roderick Murchison? The introduction of such elements seems likely to impair the genuineness of the whole affair.

Hawkins rather demurs to that qualification [Rule VII.] of altitude as uncertain, because, *e.g.*, the ascent of the Cima di Jazi is no test of Alpine prowess; but I cannot myself see how any standard can be fixed not liable to exception; and yours seems fair enough.

You must forgive my writing so freely on behalf of two outsiders, but I suppose the Club is not yet absolutely born; and there may be still time to think over possible modifications. Might not the final determination of rules be left to a meeting of all such 'Original Members' as should be able and willing to attend—say, at the February dinner,—when their number shall be considered as complete?—Believe me very truly yours,   FENTON J. A. HORT.

To Mr. E. S. Kennedy

St. Ippolyts, Hitchin, *December* 21*st*, 1857.

. . . I hope you will plead the cause of us rural members or would-be members, remembering that journeys to town add materially to the expenses of dinners, and thus to the practical annual cost of membership. Indeed two dinners *plus* a guinea a year are alone rather frightening to those who, like myself, have not a long purse. I do not mean that any favour should be extended to us, but that the guinea subscription should be reconsidered, as possibly showy rather than needful.

Lightfoot, who left me this morning, begs me to say the same on his behalf.

To his Mother

St. Ippolyts, *December* 30*th*, 1857.

. . . We have had no great Christmas festivities. The time here for the school festival is June. So we only gave away the club tickets along with big slices of cake. We were too busy to do anything to either of the churches ; and indeed we rather wished to see how the people themselves did them, not wishing to break in rudely upon them. St. Ippolyts looked very well ; but I think we shall next year put a little finger in the pie.

To Mr. A. Macmillan

St. Ippolyts, *January* 4*th*, 1858.

. . . First touching the Greek Testament. . . . Westcott has long done St. Matthew and St. John and part of St. Mark, but nothing lately. I have been working very hard, and have really given much time to it, but some weeks I have had much other business to do ; and I could not have done more. I work more slowly than he does, and examine more authorities, and find it answer ; for I have obtained much very valuable evidence unused before.

. . . Many points of N. T. grammar come unavoidably before me in working at the text, and I want to note down more regularly than I have done corrections of or additions to Winer; and before long I may be able to do something for you in that way.

To HIS MOTHER

ST. IPPOLYTS, *January* 12*th*, 1858.

. . . I read *Tom Brown's School Days* in April, when it first came out. The author, Tom Hughes, has been an acquaintance of mine a great many years, but I had not got to know him well till the last year or so. When I went up to town in the spring, I slept one night at his house . at Wimbledon. Curiously enough I had taken the book as a travelling companion, and finished it a few minutes before reaching his house. His brother married a niece and adopted daughter of Lady Salusbury, who lives at Offley, three or four miles hence, and Tom Hughes and his wife were over there in the summer for a few days. He and his brother appeared in church one afternoon; I did not see them till the middle of a sentence in the sermon, and was nearly upset. After church they came up and had tea. Next day Lady Salusbury drove them over with Mrs. Hughes, and on the Thursday we dined at Offley. The book I like much; only I wish he would not defile the true Rugby slang with foreign additions.

To MR. A. MACMILLAN

ST. IPPOLYTS, *January* 21*st*, 1858.

. . . I am in earnest in wishing and hoping to do the Grammar, *i.e.* a revised and improved translation of Winer. In the last few days I have jotted down by the way a lot of things useful for it. I only wish I had kept it in view from the beginning of Matthew.

The Church History may be only one of my many castles in the air. But what I meant would have been preliminary to the big thing, covering only 325 years instead of—how many? It would also be shorter, more popular, and less thorough; probably not more than one octavo volume, possibly two; the object being to give a lively picture of those centuries as bearing on the Church for the general reader, and to make people see the huge interest and importance of Church History.

My notion of the N. T. translation was to put into English in the shape of a translation the results of our Greek work, retaining all, or nearly all, the doubtfulnesses of text, and adding to these the doubtfulnesses of the meaning of text. Some notes would probably be required; and also pretty full discussions as to the exact meaning of the more important Greek words, and (since no translation from one language to another can be perfect, even when the meaning of the original is perfectly ascertained) as to the balance of advantages in using this or that English word. It would thus practically contain (what I have sometimes dreamed of trying to write) a 'Prolegomena to all future translations of the N. T.,' along with an actual translation, conveying the meaning of the Greek so far as I am able to ascertain what the Greek is and what is its meaning.

To the Rev. John Ellerton

St. Ippolyts, *January* 23rd, 1858.

. . . I don't think I have written since Christmas. We had 'Hark the herald' to your tune ('Ulverston' provisionally), and it went off very well. The singing goes on with fair success; F.'s class amounts to nearly forty. We have *some* idea of moving as many as possible into the chancel.

Joseph Mayor sent us the other day Walker's Rugby book. I was glad to get the music of two old school favourites of mine, 'Gethsemane,' by Rogers ('Go to dark Gethsemane'), and one by Pleyal for 'Glorious things of Thee are spoken,' not equal to Haydn, of course, and faulty in some points, but a fine tune. We like the Parish Choir book better and better.

At odd moments I am working into Milman's first volume. It is interesting and good, but less really impartial than I expected, and thoroughly Oxonian—liberal. Theology seems to him a mere chimera,—in fact, one might say, all truth.

And, in spite of the honest pains he has taken to read the documents presented to him by text-books, and by rival parties, with his own eyes, his learning strikes me as nowhere profound. But he may be better farther on, when he has quite warmed into Western politics, his real field of interest. . . .

No time or space for India, the recovery of which may under present auspices be a greater curse to England than its loss would have been. But Inglis' story, and Havelock and his death, and Sir C. Campbell's deeds — silence is best. One noble and deep word has been said about Havelock's death in Maurice's sermon two Sundays ago.— Ever most affectionately yours, FENTON J. Λ. HORT.

To MR. A. MACMILLAN

ST. IPPOLYTS, *January 26th*, 1858.

. . . I am glad Kingsley is fastidious about his volume of poems; if so, they will be right good ones to a certainty. Silence also is not a bad thing for him; unless he did something more in the *Heroes* line, whether Greek or Teutonic or anything else. He has done nothing so flawless of late : I am very stubborn in my prejudice that *Two Years Ago* was, taken as a whole, a step backwards.

To MR. A. MACMILLAN

ST. IPPOLYTS, *February 3rd*, 1858.

My dear Macmillan—I am ashamed that *T. B.* is still here. The preface is good ; for hath not Tom Brown written it ? but unsatisfying. The long letter ought to have been partly answered. I was five years in a house of fifty boys constantly changing, one of the roughest (perhaps *the* roughest) and most lawless house at Rugby ; and I do not believe that one nervous or sensitive boy was blighted. I don't doubt that much of that kind of *petty* ill-usage went on, though I *saw* but little, being myself in a præpostor's bedroom all the time. But I doubt the evil *effects*. The evil itself is clear, and should be put down if possible; but how? Every remedy hitherto proposed is worse than the disease. Increased supervision by masters is the very devil. . . . The most successful antagonist of bullying hitherto has been the præpostorial system which enlightened public opinion wants to put down. Possibly *its* supervision of bedrooms may be improved. Much also may be done by a wise master, putting little or delicate boys in rooms where there is a præpostor. Every boy in my room (there were five) knelt down night and morning during those five years. But indeed I suspect Hughes' correspondent's letter is a good deal out of date. Things became more civilised in my memory, and have, I believe, since become more civilised still. If the master of a house deals wisely with his præpostors, a great deal may be done in that way.

Dr. Tregelles has most kindly promised to let me have the sheets of his *St. Luke*, etc., as they are printed off; this is a very great help. Poor old fellow; he seems sadly lonely down at Plymouth, all his friends and neighbours thinking him only a madman; and then to have to bear a savage attack from Tischendorf.

TO THE REV. JOHN ELLERTON

HARDWICK, CHEPSTOW, *March 4th*, 1858.

. . . I have just been rash enough to undertake to join the affair of which I enclose a prospectus (which please return). I have undertaken the Gospels, Wisdom, and Ecclesiasticus. Dr. Smith (he of the Dictionaries) is the speculator. Westcott takes Daniel and most of the Apocrypha; Temple (of Rugby), Romans; Lightfoot, the Acts; Ellicott, some Epistles; Barry is also to take part, and perhaps Scott; so one will be in good company. Printing will not begin for nearly two years. But I shall have enough to do in making up my mind about the Gospels, and reading all manner of books besides the commentary itself. It is rather a weight upon one's mind to have undertaken so much; but it was a great opportunity, and tempting to rescue the Gospels from some unknown Philistine. This leaving home has sadly interrupted Greek Testament, at which I was able to get on famously in Influenza time. Westcott will, I hope, come to us at Easter, that we may go over St. Matthew and Mark together, and send them at once to press. I have just corrected and sent back a long notice of Tregelles and Tischendorf which I have been writing for the forthcoming number of our Journal.[1]

To Mr. A. Macmillan

St. Ippolyts, *March 30th*, 1858.

. . . I have just run through Kingsley,[2] and am only sorry that there is not more. Except ' Andromeda ' and ' St. Maura,' there is little *new* worth much. But they *are* great, ' St. Maura ' in particular.

To Mr. A. Macmillan

St. Ippolyts, *April 15th*, 1858.

. . . Tregelles wants to know if any Cambridge publisher would take the risk of a quarto tract of about two sheets, with a complete facsimile of the important Muratorian fragment on the Canon at Milan. There are curious discrepancies in the collations. But last August Tregelles made an exact facsimile. . . . The thing will hardly sell *much* in England, unless trouble is taken about it ; more probably in Germany. It is of much consequence ; so much that Lightfoot was talking not long ago of going to Milan for the express purpose of thoroughly overhauling it.

To Mr. A. Macmillan

St. Ippolyts, *April 28th*, 1858.

My dear Macmillan—I don't know what you will say to the purport of this letter. Westcott came here the evening after

1 See *Journal of Classical and Sacred Philology*, vol. iv. No. xi.
2 Viz. the *Poems*.

you left us, and went away last evening. We worked without intermission all day long every day except my confirmation classes, some time on Saturday for sermon, and about three-quarters of an hour of exercise. Yet we got done only $20\frac{1}{2}$ chapters of St. Matthew. . . . We now find that final revision is a slow process as well as preparation. Further, although it is very unlikely that we shall see occasion to change any of our present results, there is a *possibility* of making use of new discoveries of MSS., etc. (should such arise), which would be sacrificed by printing at once. . . . These reasons have occurred to us against printing at once. . . . In any case, you may be assured that we both shall go on steadily and without intermission at our work of separate preparation. We are thoroughly satisfied with our work up to this point. There were at first many superficial differences, which mostly vanished on thorough discussion. We each surrendered about equal quantities of first impressions ; and without any compromise or sacrifice, are now both quite content with our text, though we have been obliged to put many readings in the margin. We have inserted none which had not strong direct or indirect external evidence, referring to an Appendix for private suspicions of our own, as also for interesting but improbable ancient readings.

TO THE REV. JOHN ELLERTON

ST. IPPOLYTS, *May 1st*, 1858.

. . . I know nothing about Mansel's lectures save from the *Guardian*. But he holds the doctrine of universal nescience more consciously and clearly than I suppose any other Englishman ; a just Nemesis on Butler's probabilities ! So perish all halfway houses !

TO HIS MOTHER

ST. IPPOLYTS, *May 17th*, 1858.

. . . F. told you that I had been trying extempore preaching. I get on better than I expected as to fluency, but find, as I expected, great difficulty in expressing myself simply enough. I am often obliged to use words which I am conscious will probably not be understood, simply because I have not time to find out better ones; and the same kind of difficulty meets me in other ways. But practice may do something.

I wish you could have seen the garden about a fortnight ago. We have a great quantity of *Ribes sanguinea*, some of the bushes 8 or 10 feet high, and they were covered with blossom. The foreign *Berberis* was in perfection at the same time. The lilacs are now coming out, and in two or three days we shall have the *laburnums* and *Wistaria*. . . . The seeds that we sowed are coming up nicely, but we were late with *them*. In the cooler weather I cut down many of our laurels, thereby spoiling for the time our walk at the bottom of the garden; but they were getting very bad below, besides throttling ever so many other shrubs and monopolising the border. Plenty more have the same fate awaiting them; and a great deal has still to be done in clearing spruces and other trees too much crowded in several places.

Like you, I never had so much enjoyment as this year in watching the green things coming out.

TO THE REV. DR. ROWLAND WILLIAMS

ST. IPPOLYTS, HITCHIN, *October* 21st, 1858.

My dear Sir—I owe you many apologies for my remiss-ness in writing to you about the invitation[1] conveyed to me through our mutual friend Mr. Roby. He has, I hope, pre-vented any actual inconvenience by informing you of my un-willingness to contribute to the proposed volume of *Essays*. But I feel bound, both in courtesy and on my own account, to explain why I must decline so high an honour, for as such I sincerely regard it.

The chief impediment is a wide difference of principles and opinions from the body of your coadjutors. I can go all lengths with them in maintaining absolute freedom of criti-cism, science, and speculation; in appealing to experience as

[1] To take part in the projected volume of *Essays and Reviews*.

a test of mere *a priori* dogma; and in upholding the supremacy of spirit over letter in all possible applications.   Further I agree with them in condemning many leading specific doctrines of the popular theology as, to say the least, containing much superstition and immorality of a very pernicious kind. But I fear that in our own positive theology we should diverge widely.   I have a deeply-rooted agreement with High Churchmen as to the Church, Ministry, Sacraments, and, above all, Creeds, though by no means acquiescing in their unhistorical and unphilosophical treatment of theology, or their fears and antipathies generally.   The positive doctrines even of the Evangelicals seem to me perverted rather than untrue.   There are, I fear, still more serious differences between us on the subject of authority, and especially the authority of the Bible; and this alone would make my position among you sufficiently false in respect to the great questions which you will be chiefly anxious to discuss.

If this primary objection were removed, and I could feel our differences to be only of degree, I should still hesitate to take part in the proposed scheme.   It is surely likely to bring on a crisis; and that I cannot think desirable on any account. The errors and prejudices, which we agree in wishing to remove, can surely be more wholesomely and also more effectually reached by individual efforts of an indirect kind than by combined open assault.   At present very many orthodox but rational men are being unawares acted on by influences which will assuredly bear good fruit in due time, if the process is allowed to go on quietly; but I cannot help fearing that a premature crisis would frighten back many into the merest traditionalism.   And as a mere matter of prudence, it seems to me questionable to set up a single broad conspicuous target for the Philistines to shoot at, unless there is some very decided advantage to be gained.   Moreover I must confess a strong repugnance to any measure likely to promote anything like a party organisation, even supposing the principles to be my own.

Mr. Roby mentioned a suggestion of yours that I should write on Justin Martyr; that is, doubtless, his theology.   But the truth is, I do not feel at all competent for such a task as yet. The growth of the early theology requires such careful study that I wish not to be tempted into printing mere crudities. Indeed at present my hands are full. Just now I have enough to do with the text of the N. T.; and, when that is done, I have other engagements in N. T. criticism which must occupy me a considerable time.

I cannot conclude without expressing my very great regret at being obliged to decline so inviting an opportunity for association with men, several of whom I respect very highly, and with whom I feel that I have in many respects a common cause. I must also ask you to pardon the (perhaps unavoidably) egotistical tone of this letter.—Believe me, my dear sir, very truly yours,   FENTON J. A. HORT.

TO THE REV. JOHN ELLERTON

ST. IPPOLYTS, *All Saints Day* (*past post*), 1858.

. . . I send the Epiphany Hymn and *Aurora Lucis*.[1] . . . I am going on with Carlyle,[2] which is thoroughly good and interesting. There is a very strange (not readable) chapter on an extraordinary incident which introduced poor Frederick to the premature debauchery which destroyed his health and the finer parts of his character, and at its close the dear old prophet takes up his parable with terrible quiet force and solemnity against the whole 'wild oats' theory. I am also reading Mansel, who is less unfair than I expected, but he must be very chuffy food to his orthodox admirers. — Ever yours affectionately,   FENTON J. A. HORT.

TO THE REV. GERALD BLUNT

ST. IPPOLYTS, *November 5th*, 1858.

. . . In a (financially) evil hour I put my name down for Carlyle's *Frederick* years ago, when I expected such a sized book as the *Cromwell;* and now I have got the first half in the shape of two ponderous octavos. But

[1] See Appendix I.   [2] *Frederick the Great.*

they are uncommonly interesting, and tell me a world of things I wanted to know, besides the never-ending charm of Carlyle himself. I am also getting on with Mansel's book,[1] comforting myself with the thought of what a very juiceless and indigestible morsel it must be to its orthodox admirers. Otherwise it is clear, vigorous, and not often unfair; only a big lie from beginning to end. Our love to you and your wife.—Ever yours affectionately,   FENTON J. A. HORT.

To the Rev. Gerald Blunt

St. Ippolyts, *December* 17*th*, 1858.

. . . I will begin with church decorations. The great principle is to follow and not contradict the lines of the architecture, and generally to keep the character of the architecture of your building; *e.g.* on no account to admit festoons into a Gothic building, though they ought to be bearable in ball-room or pump-room Renaissance. You need not always merely ornament the exact existing lines; but if you make new lines, they ought to harmonise with the old ones, and in fact to represent in general character what a good architect might insert if he wished to extend the existing ornament of your church.[2]

To Mr. A. Macmillan

St. Ippolyts, Hitchin, *January* 4*th*, 1859.

. . . You may judge of my state of work when I tell you I have read only half the *White Horse*,[3] entirely delicious as it is.

Westcott's four days dwindled, alas! to three, but we worked incessantly Wednesday, Thursday, and Friday. Alas! we only finished St. Matthew and three chapters of St. Mark. We

---

[1] *Bampton Lectures,* delivered and published in 1858; see Maurice's *Life,* vol. ii. chap. x.
[2] On the same subject Hort wrote also a letter of three sheets, with coloured architectural drawings.
[3] *The Scouring of the White Horse,* by T. Hughes.

are doing it *well* while we are about it, and *could* not hurry it. St. Mark is frightfully slow to get through, nearly every word wanting rigid scrutiny. St. Luke will, I hope, be decidedly easier, and the rest quite another thing. It is really very lucky that we did not do it a year or two ago, so much fresh light comes from Tregelles and the new Tischendorf. Tregelles has lately rooted out a MS. of part of St. Luke belonging to the Bible Society, which is as good as any except the Vatican. They have had it ever so many years! Now for our future doings. . . . The plan of *correspondence* answered so well in Romans that we are going to try it for the easier parts, reserving only single points for personal discussion.

To THE REV. J. B. LIGHTFOOT

ST. IPPOLYTS, *February 18th*, 1859.

My dear Lightfoot—Thank you very much for your kind present,[1] which has duly arrived. Only you must not go doing that sort of thing again, if ever I ask you to give an order on my behalf. If in the autumn it shall turn out that the College in its brewing capacity deserves censure, I will take care to forward to you a complaint to go before the Master and Seniors.

But why did you send beer instead of coming yourself? You promised to come on your return from winter meditations on S. Paulus, and it is too bad to slip by in this manner. I expected to see divers friends, but no one has appeared except Luard, who dropped in after dark one evening in a praiseworthy manner,—not praiseworthy only in this, that he went on by the next train.

I have another question to ask about a proposed publication of Dr. Tregelles. He has, as I daresay you know, found in the possession of the Bible Society some extremely important palimpsest fragments of the first eleven chapters of St. Luke. The writing is almost invisible, and it is only by the labour of months that he has been able to read the text. The marginal *catena* (chiefly from Cyril and Origen) he has

[1] Of some Trinity 'Audit' ale.

not touched.   There is not much chance of the Bible Society
allowing chemicals to be used.   Dr. Tregelles wants to publish
the text, but can't afford the risk ; and hints about the
University Press.   Is there any chance of their consenting to
do it ?   Or, that failing, do you think it could be done by
subscription ?   Of course he uses the MS. in his edition.   He
has kindly allowed me to use the proof-sheets, which now
reach to Luke ix. 1, and I can testify to the high value of the
MS.   It is inferior to B, but scarcely, if at all, inferior to C
and L.   Dr. Tregelles calls it ≡.[1]—Ever yours affectionately,

FENTON J. A. HORT.

TO THE REV. B. F. WESTCOTT

ST. IPPOLYTS, *March* 31*st*, 1859.

[*A Postscript.*]

The postman came yesterday before I had finished, and
now your note and sheet have arrived.   I am sending the
latter on to Cambridge (though I should still hardly likely
to subscribe exactly to what you have written), because you
have removed what seemed to me to be *needlessly* open to
objection.   You could not go further without suppressing
your own convictions.

The change on p. 65 [2] opens a door for the admission of
my view by the side of your own, but leaves your own untouched.   I am far from saying it is wrong (Matt. xiii. 58,
Mark vi. 5 certainly suggest that it may be true, at least under
an important modification implied by both passages) ; but I
think you arrive at it by a wrong road, viz. by considering
miracles solely with reference to the present needs of men,
and as conditioned solely by men's capacity for them at the
time.'   I think they are at least as much connected with
crises of God's eternal plans of revelation, education, and
government, which cannot be set aside by men's unbelief.
Surely you would shrink from saying that B.C. 50-1 was an age

---

[1] See Westcott and Hort's *Introduction*, p. 153.
[2] The criticisms which follow are on Mr. Westcott's *Gospel Miracles*.

of unbelief, and A.D. 1-50 an age of faith, and therefore the latter had miracles, and not the former. Again, in p. 67 'limited philanthropy' is less offensive to me than "natural charity"; but I have the strongest objection to helping in degrading the meanings of 'charity,' 'philanthropy,' 'humanity,' or any such words. Etymology, association, and meaning all, I think, require us to hallow them, and rescue them if possible from popular debasement; and that because the 'spirit of the age' is in nothing so evil as in its deification of good-nature, and estimation of outward as more vital than inward needs. My objection to your tone on this point is twofold; first, that it introduces a confusion as to the word 'spiritual' by assuming that the character of a feeling is determined by the nature of its objects, *e.g.* that a care for man's bodies *cannot* be spiritual, and that a care for their spirits *must* be spiritual; secondly, that it actually does assume one, if not both, of these propositions. It seems to me that the spurious and unspiritual feeling of the day, which I agree with you in denouncing, is directed to spiritual even more frequently than to material objects; and above all, that to divorce from each other a care for men's bodies and for their spirits, or under any pretence whatever to cast a slight upon the former, or even upon those who exclusively (at least as they fancy) devote themselves to the former, is to set at naught the first and last lessons of the Gospels. It would be utterly shocking to me to doubt that the plainest and most literal meaning of such passages as Matt. xv. 32, Mark viii. 2, 3 is also the most important, whatever other meanings may likewise be contained within them.

To THE REV. B. F. WESTCOTT

ST. IPPOLYTS, *Easter Monday*, 1859.

. . . Seeing only the *Guardian* and *Saturday Review*, we have not been able to watch so well the different steps of the frightful crisis, of which I do not think you speak at all too strongly. There seems to be no gleam of satisfaction or hope in the war looked at from any side.

Its miseries for Europe must be immediate, and one knows not what it may bring—destruction perhaps—upon us presently. Austria is indeed very irritating, but still, I think, almost innocent in the matter. I mean, its present state is the growth of centuries. Has it taken a single unnecessary step? Doubtless the root of all is the anomaly of its presence in Italy; but that is poor comfort. Better a German than a French Italy, and I fear there are but the two alternatives for a long time to come. Indeed has *Italy ever*, in ancient or modern times, been a free or united country? The present struggle of France and Austria in Italy seems merely the continuation of their old struggle for the same ground, which was interrupted by the consequences of the Reformation, now renewed with fearful aggravation in an age of emperors and prætorians. But there is and has for generations been a tone about the Austrian Government (I hope and half believe not the Austrian people) which is repellent to the last degree, and keeps down all hopes which otherwise might arise of a regeneration of all Europe from that quarter. I confess I have very little feeling for Sardinia. It has made a good stand against military despotism and Mazzini-ism, and that is all. Perhaps every one of its *internal* acts has been necessary, and even good; but the spirit seems to me little better than one of unbelief and prudentially economised anarchy. The late foreign policy has some excuses, but none that will justify its insane wickedness.

Then, as you say, what a Government at home! Only surely better than one under Lord Palmerston can ever be, or even under Lord John Russell. But the growing cowardice and dishonesty of public men is the worst of all. But I suppose the root of all this and much more is the deadness and unbelief among ourselves, the clergy more than any, which every one of us must best know by what he finds in himself. Certainly you need not fear my being 'angry' at your confessing what I, at least, for one, feel I ought to confess every day. But I suppose no outward or inward discipline can be too severe, if it is to plant and maintain in us the practical belief that God Himself, and not men's faith in Him, is that on which all things rest, and that truth is true though all denied it. It cannot be a bad thing to be driven back to the Psalms and the Creed. They, at least, take us out of ourselves into the very heart of the kingdom which cannot be moved.

To the Rev. B. F. Westcott

ST. IPPOLYTS, *April 7th*, 1859.

My dear Westcott—I am quite willing to believe that our difference is rather verbal than material, though I fear the choice of words betrays *some* latent difference. The word 'ideal' is used in so many dissolving senses that it is difficult to tell what is meant by it in any particular case, unless clearly defined by the context. No use of it is so common, however, as in cases such as that in which you employed it, viz. when the actually existing state of things as a matter of fact is contrasted either with a perfect theoretical standard or exemplar, or with the view supposed to be taken of the actual state of things under some peculiar conditions by which its evils and effects are eliminated from sight and ignored. The former of these senses is much the more common of the two, and most persons reading your language would, I think, take it accordingly, even if they were puzzled by the seeming contradiction of your references; it is to this sense that I entirely object. In the latter sense I could admit your language as true, though expressing by no means the whole truth.

It seems to me that the Bible teaches us that such truths as that of the death to sin are by no means to be considered as true only under conditions and limitations, only by a tacit suppression of existing facts; nay, that such truths express just the most absolutely true and fundamental facts, and that any other facts which are apparently at variance with them are themselves only conditionally and secondarily true.

St. Paul acknowledges the deflexion of men's acts from the state in which he believes them actually as a matter of fact to stand, just as much as any modern religionist could do; but he does not make the deflexion itself to be the true characteristic of men. He says, "You *are* in a right and true state, I beseech you to *walk* accordingly." This is his standard formula. He refers men's irregular acts to their *walk*, not to what they *are*.

There is of course a question behind, on which language must needs be contradictory,—In virtue of what are men dead to sin? and further, Who then are dead to sin?

The first question is of course answered by St. Paul,—in virtue of Christ's death on the cross. But, though this really contains the answer to the second question, it is not usually understood to do so. The answer must be, All who bear the same flesh and blood which Christ bore. It is therefore strictly true that every Jew, heathen, or outcast from the true fold of any kind is, in St. Paul's words, already " dead to sin." But it is not the less needful that this eternal and invisible truth should have a temporal and outward embodiment and attestation; and that can be only by baptism. Therefore St. Paul connects the state with a past completed act, by which it was formally taken possession of. The outward temporal act of passing from the world into the Church was the true symbol of the transition (if so it may be called) from ' nature ' to ' grace,' from the life of sin and death of man (Rom. vii. 9, 10) to the death to sin and life of man, which in reality does not belong to time at all, at least only in so far as evil and sin themselves are only temporal.

Hence we have the necessity for such phrases as that in Gal. v. 24, which represent the man himself as the agent in the crucifixion of the flesh; and which would convey a deadly falsehood, if they were not based on the deeper and more universal truth that Christ Himself nailed the flesh to His cross.

I did not mean to have run on into this long lecture. But I wanted to explain what seems to me the truth, and one of the most essential of all truths. I confess your language seemed to me by implication to deny it; certainly to obscure it; though your references went the other way, if taken, as of course I wish to take them, in the strictest letter. But I shall be delighted to find that I was mistaken. I must, however, think that the word 'ideal' is likely, through its ordinary associations, to mislead most readers. — Ever affectionately yours,   FENTON J. A. HORT.

To Mr. A. Macmillan

St. Ippolyts, *April 25th*, 1859.

My dear Macmillan — Your plan,[1] under one form or another, is very tempting, and ought to produce good fruit. . . . I confess I think a Biographical History altogether a mistake. There is a great inclination in the present day (Stanley being a principal offender) to resolve history into biography *plus* geography, which seems to me almost purely mischievous. It not only destroys all essential continuity, but leads people to think of men as heroes on their own account rather than as doing a particular appointed work for the nation (and also the generation) of which they are members. Doubtless we want biographies; and we want also that they should not stand alone as units, but be felt to be links in one great chain. Boys and men want history as well as biographies; but you will never be able to make history by stringing biographies together in a row, let them fit on to each other ever so closely. You must have the history a separate and substantial thing. Then the biographies will be expansions of particular figures in it. I don't mean to say that *you* are or are not called on to provide a history by way of thread to your biographies. Doubtless the history of England for either boys or men yet remains to be written; but I doubt our being ripe for it yet. Anyhow the main facts of English History can be and are learned in series by boys and men from existing books; and the impression given by them is quite thread enough for your biographies. . . . The historical Arthur (if he ever existed, as I suppose he did) is very far as yet from being at all interpreted. No one should attempt it who is not a good Welsh scholar to begin with. In a few years perhaps we may know something, but not yet. The Arthur whom we do know is a mediæval, whom it is the grossest anachronism to stuff in before the Saxons. He again is quite worth knowing on his [own] account, but on the same footing as Perseus or Jason.

As regards myself, the whole thing is very inviting, though

---

[1] See p. 371. The allusion is to a projected English History in the form of a series of biographies.

I don't know that I have any special 'eager 'ness, beyond a preference for working at the earlier times. Of your present volumes, I should prefer the third (Edward I. to Richard III.), though I don't in the least know how I shall ever be able to get sufficient knowledge of such a lot of people. I confess I should like to strike out Chaucer and Froissart (who of course would be in a history) as not having enough of a life, though, perhaps, this is fanciful; and Wallace and Bruce (who also belong to English *History*), just as I would not put Hannibal among Roman heroes. But I still hope you will go back to the independent lives. In that case I think I should like to go in for Roger Bacon,—or Wycliffe, if you prefer it; or Edward I. or Edward III.

To the Rev. John Ellerton

St. Ippolyts, *June 6th*, 1859.

. . . Thanks many for your hymn-book.[1] I sent one to Vesey the other day, and have just given the other to Mayor. I ordered a supply through our Hitchin bookseller. It seems to me very greatly improved since I saw it in MS. There are now, I think, only two or three very trifling things at which I should stumble, and almost everything I like very decidedly; especially your own funeral hymn.[2] . . .

Tischendorf's new discovery may delay our N. T. greatly, as Westcott wishes (not I) to wait for it; but there can be little doubt of its importance.—Ever yours affectionately,

.   Fenton J. A. Hort.

To Mr. A. Macmillan

St. Ippolyts, *June 29th*, 1859.

My dear Macmillan—If you can get out the books at once, so much the better, but I daresay I shall have enough for my holiday with digesting Pauli, Eccleston, Adam Marsh, and

---

[1] *Hymns for Schools and Bible Classes.*
[2] The hymn beginning, 'God of the living, to whose eye All things Thou madest open lie.'

Roger Wendover. . . . Certainly my wish and endeavour will be strictly to keep to a boy's book. I have not time for anything more at present, though of course the subject may prove tempting hereafter. But I must get a pretty full and clear account of the men into my own head before I can write *anything;* only I shall let alone as far as possible all special subjects of study, though they could not be let alone if one were taking at present a more ambitious flight.

To the Rev. B. F. Westcott

ILFRACOMBE, *July 27th,* 1859.

. . . My English History work is a life of S. de Montfort, R. Grostete, and Roger Bacon. By this time I am getting to know almost as much about Henry III.'s reign as, I suppose, Mrs. Markham may contain. It is very interesting, but takes time. It is meant as pure narrative, chiefly but not solely for boys : purpose, if any beyond the facts, to counteract the Dickens and Punch view of deceased Englishmen and deceased (?) ages generally.

I have had nothing the matter beyond what I said ; but I have been long and may long continue much below my natural health. Unfortunately it is my 'routine' that wears me most, with its never-pausing frets and anxieties. *Extra* work is to me luxury and repose.

To the Rev. B. F. Westcott

HARDWICK, CHEPSTOW, *August 12th,* 1859.

. . . I get on slowly with the historical work. I am now reading Adam Marsh's *Epistles,* published only last year, and full of interest, though I have never had to wade through more intolerable verbiage. Then I shall have Grostete's own epistles. There are a good many Chronicles to be read, and I fear I shall have to spend some time in the MSS. of the British Museum and Tower.—Ever affectionately yours,

FENTON J. A. HORT.

P.S.—Since writing this we have decided to try Malvern,[1] under Dr. Johnson, formerly of Umberslade, where I was when we met and determined on the N. T. text.

TO THE REV. JOHN ELLERTON

OSBORNE HOUSE, MALVERN,
September 7th, 1859.

. . . I suppose the existing standard of idyls is Theocritus (and Bion and Moschus if we had them); but I can hardly think that Goethe and Voss have done wrong in giving them a more human centre, or that they have so made them less idyllic. It is the singleness and as it were privateness of the action, I suppose, that makes them[2] idyllic. Together they form a whole, of which Arthur is in a manner the centre, as he might be of various other similar wholes; but they do not make an epic, an Arthuriad, and I suspect that one reason for the title is to warn people that they must not expect such a thing.

We have not yet plunged into Mudie; but I have just read one volume of *Adam Bede*, and am waiting to get hold of the second. It is very delightful. I am still sceptical as to the authorship; what good authority is there? What strikes me most is a spirit of criticism and scientific analysis of everything into its elements: the humour is delicious; but perhaps there is too much consciousness of good writing, especially in the descriptions.

TO MR. A. MACMILLAN

CLEVE COTTAGE, CLEVE, BRISTOL,
February 17th, 1860.

My dear Macmillan—By this post you will receive a specimen[3] of Simon and Co., namely the last few months of Simon's own life. To make it intelligible, you must remember thus much. After years of vain attempts to keep

---

[1] *i.e.* the Hydropathic Establishment.   [2] *The Idylls of the King.*
[3] *The Last Days of Simon de Montfort*, subsequently published in *Macmillan's Magazine*, 1864.

Henry III. from misgovernment, the barons, headed by Simon, had come to blows with him. At the battle of Lewes in May of the year before, they had defeated and taken him prisoner, his son Prince Edward (afterwards Edward I.) surrendering himself as a hostage. The following February there had been a Parliament. Soon after this my fragment opens. The Earl of Gloucester had co-operated with Simon, but was now jealous of him, and inclined to separate from him.

Of course very little of the earlier part of the story will be told with anything like the same amount of detail. Not many years will cover as much space as months do here. I ought also to say that this is somewhat of a plum; I cannot expect to have much to tell of equally stirring interest. But still I hope you may be able to judge from it whether the thing is likely to do ; and I shall be glad to have your honest opinion about its readableness. As a piece of research, I am tolerably well satisfied with it so far ; and I have reason to suspect that the events of these months have never been thoroughly worked out before. It is likely enough that I may make alterations in it presently, as I get more matter. There are only two more original printed authorities that I care much to see, *Robert of Gloucester* and the *Continuation of Florence of Worcester.* But there are several modern books which I must examine before printing, and I quite expect to glean additions from MSS. at Oxford and in London.

I don't think I can do without the references ; as the book, being one of research as well as a story book, must be able to justify itself for any unfamiliar statements. I have put the references in a very short form ; and, if printed small, they will seldom occupy more than one or two lines at the foot of the page. I hope to eschew all notes, except probably a few in small type at the end of the volume, not for boys. I have sent one of these as a specimen.

You will want to know whereabouts this fragment will come in the book. Rather towards the end. The early part will be the most troublesome, and I don't yet see my way clearly about it. There will be, in some shape or other, I hope, Simon's early life ; a rapid sketch of the reign before his appearance on the stage ; Grosseteste's early life (? A sketch of Oxford

and Paris in the thirteenth century); the early days of the
Friars, chiefly Franciscans, in England; Grosseteste's Episcopate
to his death in 1253; Simon's parallel history; Simon's
history after Grosseteste's death till his own death in 1265,
ending with this fragment; that chapter being wound up with
a very short sketch of subsequent political events; then Roger
Bacon, the great year of whose 'literary activity' is just after
Simon's death.   This is my present notion.   The middle will
probably be written first; then the beginning and end.

To Mr. A. Macmillan

CLEVE COTTAGE, CLEVE, BRISTOL,
February 26th, 1860.

My dear Macmillan—I am going to send the MS. to
Westcott for his opinion on the points in dispute between us.
He is almost the only man not of my own family who knows that
I am writing, and is greatly interested, often asking me about it.
He also takes particular pains to find out his boys'[1] tastes in
reading.

To the Rev. B. F. Westcott

CLEVE COTTAGE, CLEVE, BRISTOL,
March 1st, 1860.

. . . I am quite thankful that we have not been able to go
to press yet.   Almost every day I see reason to shrink from
accepting or rejecting readings of slender but very early
authority in *any* of the Gospels without a connected examination of all such readings together, as well as on their individual
merits.

To the Rev. B. F. Westcott

HARDWICK, CHEPSTOW, *March 10th*, 1860.

[*A Postscript.*]

. . . Have you read Darwin?[2]   How I should like a talk
with you about it!   In spite of difficulties, I am inclined to
think it unanswerable.   In any case it is a treat to read such
a book.

[1] Viz. at Harrow.   [2] The *Origin of Species.*

To Mr. A. Macmillan

HARDWICK, CHEPSTOW, *March* 10th, 1860.

I shall be glad to know whether an article on Darwin, if I can manage one, would do for your *Magazine*. I can't now promise; but for some reasons I should like to write, only I would not spend time on it unless I were pretty sure that it would serve your purpose. It would probably be mainly a clear popular statement of the various facts of the argument, put in a different form and order, and partly criticisms and additional illustrations of particular chapters.—Very truly yours,

FENTON J. A. HORT.

To Mr. A. Macmillan

HARDWICK, CHEPSTOW, *March* 16th, 1860.

. . . I am glad to be able to infer from what you say that you have not spoken to Masson[1] about Darwin. Since I wrote I have more than half repented mentioning the subject, I am so overwhelmed with other reading and writing. But I was carried away by the appetite for speech on such a subject, and also glad to gratify your wish for an article on something. But anyhow you must not keep the subject open for me. If any one else at all competent wants to write, pray let him : only let me know as soon as you do, that I may waste no more [time], and then I shall be only too thankful. Pray bear this in mind. For really I cannot promise to write. I will make the experiment, and that is all I can say. It is very bothering to write without having a single natural history book to refer to. . . . So again, if I write, I will make no rash promises about the 'moral' bearings of the subject : it is a ticklish matter, and one wants months and months to think and read about it, or one will be driven to utter only brief and cloudy oracles. My first idea had been to have it thus : 'Mr. Darwin's Theory of Species and its Results. Part I. The Theory. Part II. The Results,' each part in a separate number ; but at present I shrink from having a whole article of ' Results.'

[1] The editor of *Macmillan's Magazine*.

To the Rev. J. B. Lightfoot

HARDWICK, CHEPSTOW, *March* 16*th*, 1860.

. . . I had two long and interesting talks with Mark
Pattison at Malvern in October.   He told me distinctly that
Jowett is going to bring out an edition of all Plato, by himself
and his pupil-friends, but he did not know for certain whether
it would include a translation.   I thought it on the whole best
to mention our scheme,[1] but told him we did not wish it talked
about.   He seemed much interested, and asked leave to
mention it to Jowett, to which, of course, I assented ; at the
same time adding that, while I did not see why the two
schemes should clash, we certainly could claim no priority,
having *done* little or nothing.

. . . I shall also be glad to hear what Sedgwick, and indeed
Cambridge in general, says to Darwin.   I suppose you have
read it ; if not, do.

To the Rev. John Ellerton

HARDWICK, *April* 3*rd*, 1860.

. . . Have you seen H. Lushington's republished articles
on the Italian war of 1848-9 ?   Read them if you can.   They
more than ever make one feel the *prophetic* nature of his
mind.   Venables' memoir of him is also very beautiful in
its way, as well as curious as an inlet into the true self of
an out-and-out Saturday Reviewer.   We have also been reading the Shelley *Memorials* with great pleasure.   Mrs. Shelley
in particular comes out wonderfully, and one only wishes
that the editress (Lady Shelley) had given more of her letters
and diaries.   But *the* book which has most engaged me is
Darwin.   Whatever may be thought of it, it is a book that
one is proud to be contemporary with.   I must work out and
examine the argument more in detail, but at present my feeling
is strong that the theory is unanswerable.   If so, it opens up
a new period in—I know not what not.

[1] See p. 349.

To the Rev. John Ellerton

HARDWICK, *April 20th*, 1860.

. . . You should read the *Essays and Reviews*. Temple's is at least powerful and interesting. Mark Pattison's is, I think, very good, and likely to be of use to you. He almost ignores Clarke, W. Law, and the Cambridge Platonists; but as to the general current of religious thought he seems to me quite right. Jowett is provoking as usual. I suppose he will do good to some in forcing honesty of criticism upon them, though there is perhaps not a single thought new to you or me; but his blindness to a providential ordering of the accidents of history is very vexatious. It is curious to see how completely he is leavened with J. H. Newman. R. Williams on Bunsen is R. Williams all over, and quite worth reading. I have not yet touched Wilson and Baden Powell. C. W. Goodwin, as far as I have read, is poor enough. I read about three-quarters of Masson, and mean to finish him some day. He is, as you say, a very odd sort of a good sort of man; perhaps as interesting as a man can be without one spark of genius. His discovery of an 'inward affinity' between Puritanism and the literary calling is delicious.

I hope I shall know more of Edward I. presently. I am quite disposed to like him, and his ability is transcendent; but I fear the popular feeling of his deep-rooted falsity, at least in his youth, was well founded.

To the Rev. J. B. Lightfoot

2 WELLINGTON SQUARE, E., CHELTENHAM,
April 29th, 1860.

. . . Smith[1] failing, might not we three venture to make a partition of the whole N. T. among ourselves? It falls into three portions, which *contain* your and Westcott's suggested arrangements; viz. the Pauline writings (including Hebrews) for you, the Johannine for him, and the historico-Judaic for me. They might be brought out by degrees,

[1] Viz. Dr. William Smith's scheme for a joint commentary. See pp. 371-2.

according to the following scheme. Numerically Westcott
would have much the smallest share, and I much the largest ;
but his is very compressed matter, and in the Synoptists
allowance must be made for repetitions.

I hope something will be quickly settled, for it is now
probable that I shall have to leave England in about three
weeks ; and I want to know about books some little time
before.

	Westcott.	*Lightfoot.*	*Hort.*
1st Issue.	St. John's Gospel.	Rom. Cor. Gal. Thess.	Synoptic Gospels.
2nd Issue.	Apocalypse.	Eph. Phil. Col. Pastoral Epp.	Acts.
3rd Issue.	St. John's Epp.	Hebrews.	Jac. Pet. Jud.

A similar letter, with a copy of the above scheme,
was sent to Mr. Westcott the same day.

To THE REV. J. B. LIGHTFOOT

2 WELLINGTON SQUARE, E., CHELTENHAM,
May 1st, 1860.

. . . I am extremely obliged to you for expressing plainly
your doubt about my taking the Synoptic Gospels. Westcott
gave me no hint of it at Harrow, and it is clearly essential
that there should be no misunderstandings at starting. I will
therefore say my say with equal plainness.

My first feeling on reading your letter was that it might be
better for me to withdraw at once. The scheme in its present
form is yours. It takes up and meets an old scheme of
Westcott's, long in abeyance but never relinquished. If I
take part in it, it will be by your permission, not as an independent projector. If your idea is, to have an uniform com-

mentary, which shall demonstrate that the final results of accurate and honest criticism do not disturb 'orthodox' assumptions, you are quite right not to admit a coadjutor who cannot feel certain of having equal good luck. The integrity of your plan must take precedence of all personal considerations, and I should not have any reason to complain. At the same time, as far as I can see at present, I should shrink from transferring myself to other books of the N. T. in your scheme on the ground that you could not trust me with the Gospels. The difference between us, if difference there is, can hardly be confined to a single theory; and I could not work freely at any book of the N. T., if I were under an obligation to produce results of a predetermined colour.

On second thoughts, however, it seems rash to call off without ascertaining distinctly whether we really are at variance.

First as to the special point you mention. It would be hardly too much to say that I have as yet *no* theories about the Gospels. I remember the conversation to which you refer. The opinion I expressed,—by no means a mature conviction, but merely and avowedly a tentative *prima facie* impression,—related to one isolated question. Agreeing to the best of my belief with Westcott as to the oral or traditional narrative which was the common foundation of the Synoptic Gospels, I demurred to his explanation of the cause of its local limitation. I found it difficult to believe that the events and discourses belonging to Jerusalem were deliberately excluded by the Apostles (or others concerned) as unfitted for the then circumstances of the Church; and I thought it a more natural explanation of the admitted fact to suppose that the first form of the narrative was a local Galilean tradition, which the Apostles (and others), finding ready to their hand, variously modified and corrected, supplying, *perhaps*, beginnings and endings, but did not go out of their way to supplement with matter belonging to a different cycle of events. This view I now hold neither more strongly nor more weakly than before. I have seen nothing to make me think it untenable; but I have undertaken as yet no such careful investigations as would alone justify my setting it forth in print. In any case it is surely in substance by no means novel. I am convinced that *any* view of the Gospels, which distinctly and consistently recognises for them a natural and historical origin (whether under a special Divine super-intendence or not), and assumes that they did not drop down ready-made from heaven, must and will be 'startling' to an immense proportion of educated English people. But so far, at least, Westcott and I are perfectly agreed, and I confess I had hoped that you too would assent. And, if thus much be conceded, I cannot see that my supposed view is a whit more 'startling'[1] than Westcott's.

But I now feel that I must say a word about more general principles. If you make a decided conviction of the absolute infallibility of the N. T. practically a *sine qua non* for co-opera-tion, I fear I could not join you, even if you were willing to forget your fears about the origin of the Gospels. I am most anxious to find the N. T. infallible, and have a strong sense of the Divine purpose guiding all its parts; but I cannot see how the exact limits of such guidance can be ascertained except by unbiassed *a posteriori* criticism. Westcott—and, I suppose, you—would say that any apparent errors discovered by criticism are only apparent, and that owing to the imperfection of our knowledge. I fully believe that this is true of a large pro-portion of what the rasher critics peremptorily pronounce to be errors; and I think it *possible* that it may be true of all, but, as far as my present knowledge goes, hardly *probable*. And if, as I expect, there are cases where there appears to be just a thin loophole for the possibility of admitting imperfect know-ledge as the sole cause of an apparent error, but where the circumstances are such as to suggest a natural explanation of the origin of a real error, such as would be at once accepted in any other book, I should feel bound to state *both* facts, expressing at the same time my own feeling that it is *more* reasonable to suppose an error. I do not think there is a real difference of principle between (at least) Westcott and myself, but only a (perhaps hypothetical) difference of opinion as to facts. But you must judge whether the difference is such as to disqualify me for your commentary. I believe I am imprudent in sometimes uttering in conversation rude and

[1] See the next letter, p. 422.

premature conjectures and suspicions, which I have not yet had time to test and work out, and which persons of a more guarded temperament would probably under such circumstances keep to themselves. But I do not think that I should be rash in deliberate print, least of all in a commentary on the Bible. At the same time it would be mere working in fetters to me to attempt an apologetic commentary as such, though I have not the smallest doubt that most of the results would be to that effect. Also forgive my saying that it seems to me the truest wisdom to think as little as possible about disarming suspicion. Depend on it, whatever either you or I may say in an extended commentary, if only we speak our mind, we shall not be able to avoid giving grave offence to both Jowett's friends and the miscalled orthodoxy of the day. It has been not altogether to my taste to go into all these details; but you will see the necessity of my doing so, and form your judgment on what I have said.

Other points must wait. Your textual suggestions I should like to think about. But I do not quite see how they go with Westcott's plan of notes, without either Greek or English text, intelligible almost throughout to persons ignorant of Greek. It is plain that we have, at present, not all the same thing in view.—Always most truly yours, FENTON J. A. HORT.

As I was writing the last words a note came from Westcott. He too mentions having had fears, which he now pronounces "groundless," on the strength of our last conversation, in which he discovered that I did "recognise" 'Providence' in Biblical writings. Most strongly I recognise it; but I am not prepared to say that it necessarily involves absolute infallibility. So I still await judgment.

TO THE REV. B. F. WESTCOTT

2 WELLINGTON SQUARE, E., CHELTENHAM,
May 2nd, 1860.

My dear Westcott—Your note came just as I was finishing a long letter to Lightfoot. He too had written expressing "a little hesitation about the Synoptic Gospels," in consequence of our former talk at Harrow, which led him to fear my propounding "startling theories." The tenour of your present note makes it needless for me to write to you in equal detail, though he will doubtless show you the letter, if you care to see it. But, as doubts have been entertained, perhaps I had better say a word on one matter.

I do most fully recognise the special 'Providence' which controuled the formation of the canonical books : my only difficulty is to understand how you can have had any doubt about the matter, considering how often we have talked over subjects in which such a belief was implied if not expressed. Certainly the unlucky suggestion, which gave rise to your doubts, seems to me quite consistent with it. But I am not able to go as far as you in asserting the absolute infallibility of a canonical writing. I may see a certain fitness and probability in such a view, but I cannot set up an *a priori* assumption against the (supposed) results of criticism. So perhaps you would say—in terms, at least—but you would deny that the fair results of criticism, making allowance for our imperfect knowledge, prove the existence of any errors. I am as yet prepared neither to deny nor to assert it. I shall rejoice on fuller investigation to find that imperfect knowledge is a sufficient explanation of *all* apparent errors, but I do not expect to be so fortunate. If I am ultimately driven to admit occasional errors, I shall be sorry ; but it will not shake my conviction of the providential ordering of human elements in the Bible. It is perhaps possible that these words might be used in various senses ; but I am sure that, saving my doubts about infallibility, you and I mean precisely the same thing by them. I shall be glad to know whether, after this express explanation, you still are *perfectly* content to take me as a coadjutor in the commentary. The difference does not seem to me essential ; but you may think otherwise, and will, I am sure, speak freely.

I fear that day in town left its mark on me for the rest of the week, and I am not very well now ; but I hardly expect much amendment till we get to the Alps.—Ever affectionately yours,

FENTON J. A. HORT.

Lightfoot wants you to take the 'Hebrews,' if it does not go to Benson. Of course I can have no objection.

To the Rev. B. F. Westcott

2 Wellington Square, E., Cheltenham,
May 4th, 1860.

My dear Westcott—I am greatly obliged by your letter, which removes all my fears. Lightfoot asks me to send you the accompanying answer to one of mine which he was sending to you. You will see that I misunderstood the words and still more the tone of his previous letter. It is, however, needless to go into the particulars now, as the upshot of the correspondence is to leave all clear, and, I hope, make us all understand each other better. My letter to you was perhaps too brief; but you will see that, though you "had not contemplated me as not being a coadjutor," *I* had felt that, *under my then impression* as to Lightfoot's, and perhaps your, view of the work I could hardly be a coadjutor.

I quite agree that it is most essential to study each Synoptist by himself as a single whole. Only I should add that such a study soon leads one to the fact of their having all largely used at least one common source, and that fact becomes an *additional* element in their criticism. Their independent treatment is most striking; but it is not identical with the independence of three absolutely original writers.

I certainly regard Dr. Smith's letter as for all practical purposes a release, and I shall write to him to say that I accept it as such as regards the Gospels, but that if he goes on with the scheme I shall probably be glad to take Wisdom and Sirach,[1] if he will let me know in good time. I hope you will do the same as to the rest of the Apocrypha.

I need hardly add that I shall take out the Synoptists to Switzerland. But what say you as to the rest of the tripartite arrangement?—Ever affectionately yours,

Fenton J. A. Hort.

We three must meet and discuss *details* in the autumn. I return to Hardwick on Monday.

[1] *i.e.* Ecclesiasticus.

To the Rev. J. B. Lightfoot

2 Wellington Square, E., Cheltenham,
May 4th, 1860.

My dear Lightfoot—I can hardly say how much I am obliged to you for your letter. You will see that my last was written under a great misapprehension, which could hardly have arisen if we had not been (unintentionally) somewhat reserved even to each other. So pray don't be angry, even in the most subdued and harmless degree.

I entirely agree with your justification of your own supposed doubt. . . . I am also glad that you take the same provisional ground as to infallibility that I do.

To the Rev. J. B. Lightfoot

2 Wellington Square, E., Cheltenham,
May 5th, 1860.

In our rapid correspondence about the N. T. I have been forgetting Plato. But I should be very glad if you could come to *some* conclusions in the next week. Westcott protests against our undertaking such fresh and heterogeneous work, but I think we must not listen to him, even though we *may* hear some inward echo of his warnings. The first thing, I suppose, is to ascertain whether the Oxford plan will really stand in our way. So I hope that you will very soon write to Jowett, as you proposed.

To Mr. A. Macmillan

Hardwick, Chepstow, *May 10th and 11th*, 1860.

. . . About Darwin, I have been reading and thinking a good deal, and am getting to see my way comparatively clearly, and to be also more desirous to say something. It would in purport be not unlike the *Saturday Review* article last week, but touch on many other points. But it is utterly impossible to do anything before I go abroad, and there I can do little or nothing for want of books of reference, which would be much too heavy to carry. I think it is likely enough that I should be glad to write after I return; but, as I said before, don't consider the subject occupied, but let anybody else have his say, if it be worth saying. If I *am* so inclined on my return, and you are willing to accept, I shall ask you again for some of the books, and start afresh. The subject will be none the worse for churning in my mind through the summer. Except some Greek Testament (and perhaps Plato), I am going to give myself up in the Alps to botany and geology. The article, if written at all, will be grave, and, I venture to hope, telling.— Most truly yours,   FENTON J. A. HORT.

TO THE REV. J. B. LIGHTFOOT

BRIGHTON, *May* 18*th*, 1860.

. . . I confess I am very doubtful about the various readings. They must of course be occasionally referred to, and even discussed. But I believe the knowledge of authorities which a person would gain from even a large number of select passages, as distinguished from a continuous apparatus like Tischendorf's, to be positively false and misleading. In a great number of cases it is impossible to estimate rightly the value, absolute or relative, of many single authorities without such a knowledge of their peculiar affinities and 'tendencies' as can only be gained safely by observing their behaviour in various classes of readings, in which there is no real doubt as to the text of the N. T.[1] It sounds an arrogant thing to say, but there are very many cases in which I would not admit the competence of any one to judge a decision of mine on a textual matter, who was only an amateur, and had not had some considerable experience in *forming* a text. And it seems to me worse than delusive to appear to submit our decisions to the verdict of persons whose jurisdiction we challenge. The very few really competent judges will not need such selections of readings.

[1] See the treatment of 'Internal Evidence of Documents' in Westcott and Hort's *Introduction*, pp. 30 foll. It is interesting to note that the principles there formulated were already developed at this date.

To the Rev. B. F. Westcott

Riffelberg, *August 14th and 16th*, 1860.

. . . We have been here since Saturday three weeks, and have had, according to every one's testimony, very much more than a reasonable share of bad weather of most kinds, and yet find the place very tolerable. I have every reason to be glad that we came here. At first I seemed to gain little or nothing, but a concurrence of circumstances induced us to attempt a little expedition over the snow nearly a fortnight ago, and I have since then been quite wonderfully better. I have, unfortunately, I scarcely know how, been able to do hardly anything but dry plants. It is very difficult to manage Gk. Test. here, and I have not touched it for some weeks, but I think I must try. We have now quite made up our minds to stay in the Alps as long as weather will permit. On the one hand, it seems pretty clear that they are more likely to benefit me than anything else ; and, on the other, I have a great deal still to regain, to say nothing of confirming what I have already gained.

. . . I do hope some day to see Rouen in rather less hot haste. S. Laurent I did not see. I quite agree with your enjoyment of the "rich picturesqueness of foreign Gothic" as opposed to English flatness and meagreness, but I was disappointed in not seeing nobler leading lines and more complete subordination and (free) purpose.

Now about other matters. I have not seen (perhaps not heard of) Mr. Hebert's answer to Davies.[1] Davies' own sermons he gave me, and I read them hastily just before leaving England, but have, I fear, no distinct impression of them. I have never been *satisfied* with anything of his that I have seen on the Atonement. I have quite agreed with his main purpose and doctrine, but hesitated as to some of his arguments, and above all felt that he left out of sight important elements which must be retained, however hard it may be to apprehend them rightly. If I understand you rightly, you would confine your own positive statements to these, that

[1] The Rev. J. Ll. Davies.

we are saved by our Lord's death, and that we could not have
been saved without it. This is the doctrine of Coleridge,
Thomson (*Bampton Lectures*), and (I suppose, though I once
understood him in a more destructive sense) Jowett. Sometimes I feel disposed to say the same, but on the whole I
believe we may say much more. Certainly such a mere statement of results seems to me very preferable to the popular
attempts at explanation, but still it seems to me a mere pro-
duct of despairing (but not unbelieving) speculation opposed
to the actual revelations made to us in the Bible. To me the
necessity being Divine does not appear sufficient reason for
our not being able to apprehend its nature, as I do not admit
your (?) axiom that man cannot know God as He is. It is of
course true that we can only know God through human forms,
but then I think the whole Bible echoes the language of
Gen. i. 27, and so assures us that human forms *are* Divine
forms. In this respect I quite hold with Davies. Again, I
quite agree in your low estimate of current notions of justice,
but I think they are just as inapplicable to man as to God. I
think them inadequate, not because they are human, but
because they are derived from one part only, and that the
most accidental and least universal part, of man. The imperfect notions of human justice into which we are prone to
fall need to be corrected by what we can discern of the
Divine justice. I do not pretend to be able to explain many
perplexing facts any better than other people, but I think that
many of the current difficulties arise from taking jural rather
than moral justice as a standard, and that we have much to
learn respecting moral justice. *E.g.* the *facts* recorded in the
Bible seem to me to show that it is not unjust (1) that the
innocent should suffer, and (2) that the suffering of the innocent should be the benefit of the guilty; and the experience
of human life seems to me to confirm the same. But this is
a very different thing from taking a human *explanation* or *interpretation* of the facts (as the 'forensic' 'plan of salvation') as itself a criterion of justice. That suffering may be a
necessary consequence of sin, "quite apart from free forgiveness," I most fully believe, and so I think does Davies. But
surely the essence of the Atonement must consist in the for-

giveness itself, and not in the abolition of such suffering; whether it involves at all any such abolition, I cannot yet make up my mind.   Perhaps we may be too hasty in assuming an absolute necessity of absolutely proportional suffering. I confess I have no repugnance to the primitive doctrine of a ransom paid to Satan, though neither am I prepared to give full assent to it.   But I can see no other possible form in which the doctrine of a ransom is at all tenable; anything is better than the notion of a ransom paid *to the Father.*

You will probably gather from this what answer I must give to your question about the Essays.   To anything doctrinal of which —— is at all representative, I can give only the most decided refusal.   I know him and in some respects like him; but I feel orthodox unbelief to be worse than heretical unbelief.   A sermon which he preached and printed against Jowett annoyed me almost as much as anything I ever read.   But, putting him aside, I could not consent to join in any volume of essays which could be plausibly regarded as simply an orthodox protest against the *Essays and Reviews.*   Probably I should agree with you in all essential points as to their shortcomings and positive errors, and perhaps also as to the amount of truth which they contain; but I do not know whether you feel as strongly as I do as to the extreme importance of that side of truth which they exhibit.   It is familiar enough to us, but there are very many to whom it is new, and to whom it will be valuable.   You will say that they will receive injury by taking truth and error mixed, and I feel the same, and therefore think that we ought to try to set forth the simple or rather twofold truth. But such a volume as you speak of would be accepted by both sides as simply polemical against the *E. and R.*, and to this I could not consent.   The *E. and R.* seem to me to *believe* very much more of truth than their (so-called) orthodox opponents, and to be incomparably greater lovers of truth, and a triumph given to the latter seems to me by no means a triumph to what we both hold to be precious truth.   This objection need not perhaps apply to a volume written entirely by ourselves and a few who agree with us, and, if *such* a scheme is persevered in, I should at least like to hear what is proposed. But—unless you use E. and R. merely as a symbolical expression—there is scarcely anything to grapple with in the whole volume except principles of Biblical interpretation, which are, I think, better dealt with by the way than in a controversial volume. You have had your say in your *Introduction to the Gospels*, I hope to have mine (which will differ considerably in form though not much, I think, in substance) in the 'Preface to the Synoptists.' Do we need anything more, as far as we ourselves are concerned? Jowett surely set a good example in first exhibiting his principles as applied to an actual commentary. If, on the other hand, you are thinking of dealing with such questions as are discussed in Jowett's Essays generally, I do not say that it may not be well for us to write upon them (though here also I am rather in favour of indirect dealing with them); but I should be still more anxious that the volume should be obviously as much sympathetic with Jowett and his friends as antagonistic to them. They reject much which we know we can ill afford to lose, but it is from a misdirected zeal for truth and for God's Name.

To the Rev. B. F. Westcott

CHELSEA RECTORY, *October 9th*, 1860.

Here we are once more in England, to our great satisfaction. After consulting with my doctor, I have resolved to try returning to St. Ippolyts (probably in about a month) under strict orders not to try myself overmuch. I am a great deal better than when I left England, but I must still be very careful.

To the Rev. B. F. Westcott

HARDWICK, *October 11th*, 1860.

. . . Unfortunately I do not know any of the country which you have been visiting. If I understand your meaning right, I believe I should quite agree with you: that is, it seems to me hardly a paradox to say that *all* formations whatever are local.   But I do not think this class of phenomena has been neglected by Lyell and his school, whatever the earlier generalizers may have done.   You must tell me more about it, however, when we meet.   I fear further thought through the summer has only deepened my impressions as to the origin of species by some sort of development; an extremely interesting conversation which I had with Owen walking down from Breuil to Châtillon tended greatly in the same direction.

To the Rev. B. F. Westcott

Hardwick, *October* 15*th*, 1860.

My dear Westcott—I protest that I do understand the eloquence of silence, when it is a speaking silence; nor was I forgetful of your preference for the golden over the silver mode of communication.   But I have, I confess, no gift of interpreting a silence which will bear four or five different meanings equally well.

. . . To-day's post brought also your letter to the Eggischhorn, which I should have been very sorry to have missed.   I entirely agree—correcting one word—with what you there say on the Atonement, having for many years believed that "the absolute union of the Christian (or rather, of man) with Christ Himself" is the spiritual truth of which the popular doctrine of substitution is an immoral and material counterfeit.   But I doubt whether that answers the question as to the nature of the satisfaction.   Certainly nothing can be more unscriptural than the modern limiting of Christ's bearing our sins and sufferings to His death; but indeed that is only one aspect of an almost universal heresy.

I do not see why the inconceivableness of a beginning is any argument against any theory of development.   The contrary theory is simply a harsh and contradictory attempt to conceive a beginning.   That we are in doubt about the early history of organic life arises not from an impotence of conception, but from the mere fact that we were not there to see what, if it were taking place now, we certainly could see.

The beginning of an individual is precisely as inconceivable as the beginning of a species, yet up to a certain point we can go confessedly as to the growth of the individual : that is, we know something of the individuals that gave it birth, and also of itself soon after its birth. The same conditions essentially hold good of species, the only difference being that the evidence is dead, partly decayed, and partly capable of different interpretations. It certainly startles me to find you saying that you have seen no facts which support such a view as Darwin's. But I do see immense difficulties in his theory, some of which might by this time have been removed, if he had understood more clearly the conditions of his problem, and made experiments accordingly. But it seems to me the most probable *manner* of development, and the reflexions suggested by his book drove me to the conclusion that some kind of development must be supposed. Owen's view I found to be precisely the same, except that he prefers the *Vestiges* [1] to Darwin without having any certainty as to either. He has no doubt in his own mind of the upward development of all species, though he thinks it not yet capable of being scientifically proved, and is very angry with Darwin for rushing prematurely in the face of the bigoted and unprepared public. This was what I had suspected from some enigmatical phrases in his last books, and still more in his article in the *Edinburgh*, and asked him the question point-blank, so that he could not evade it. It was very difficult to ascertain precisely what he thought of *Natural Selection :* my total impression was that he saw great difficulties in its application to the extent of Darwin's theory, and regarded it as *at present* little more than a deeply interesting *guess*, which Darwin had as yet done little or nothing to test, but which deserved a thorough investigation. He also admitted spontaneous generation as morally certain, though hardly yet sufficiently proved ; and, sneering much at Darwin's single miraculous primæval cell, he expressed a conviction that cells capable of endless upward development are constantly being produced, so that the sum total of organic nature has not one initial point but innumerable. Indeed one could hardly read Darwin's book without being struck with

[1] *Vestiges of Creation.*

the arbitrariness of his contrary assumption. It was a deeply interesting conversation. . . . I have rarely met any one who so impressed me with his simple greatness : the entire absence of pretence or oracularness and the natural and thorough enjoyment of whatever came before him were also very striking. He seemed to me to have genuine and original religious convictions ; but the tone of his random allusions to Genesis did not please me ; it was, however, I think, chiefly the annoyance of a man who had been much bored with silly attempts at ' reconciliation.'

I am afraid Owen is not so sceptical[1] as you seem at present inclined to wish ; but his reserve in print is so great that you might very naturally claim him.

P.S.—Perhaps my *wishes* for the Italians go farther than yours ; nor do I quite see my way as to what is or is not lawful for Italians under such anomalous circumstances. But I fear I must in the main agree with you. Cavour seems— not now only but always—to have a genuine Napoleonic dis- belief in anything but lies and bayonets, and not to know what morality means. In England what is said and done in Italian matters follows naturally from the general subordination of right to vague feeling, which is gaining ground so rapidly : the fruits will some day no doubt be bitter enough, though just now in regard to Italy they are to me, I confess, chiefly amusing.

To Mr. A. Macmillan

Hardwick, Chepstow, October 18th, 1860.

. . . I have not done so much *observing* on Darwin this summer as I hoped, but I have thought about it a good deal, though I do not yet see my way clearly on some important points. As far as I know, nothing comprehensive has been written as yet really to the point, for or against, but I don't think I shall attempt it for your Magazine. One thing is want of time, as my leisure will be fully taken up with Greek Testa- ment and Grosseteste and Co. The mere writing would take much time ; but the fact is, writing on that subject, as I must

---

[1] Viz. as to Darwin's theory.

do if I write at all, will be a very serious matter and must give great offence, so that I ought not to put pen to paper without a great deal more of actual reading than I have yet managed. Another thing is, that I can't and won't gossip in print about the matter; it is far too serious, and I can only write seriously about it; in other words, I can only, in discussing the theory, go into it on pure grounds of science with minute scientific details, and in discussing the results go regularly in for theology. All this would make it both too heavy and too long for your Magazine.

To Mr. A. Macmillan

St. Ippolyts, *November 9th*, 1860.

. . . I wish I could take a hopeful view of the roughness of manners which struck us so much this year abroad. Part of it is, no doubt, mere manners; but over and over again we were compelled to see it to be the expression of utter selfishness and disregard of others. There was no mistaking the fact that good manners are not only originally the conventional exponent of consideration for others or, as Kingsley truly interprets St. Paul, 'charity,' but also in their turn conservative of it. We had rare opportunities for observation, remaining quietly fixed at the Riffel for a month and watching the daily stream of travellers of all nations. It is but right to say that I thought there was an improvement in the manners of English people, at least of the less educated and refined of them.

Another last word on Darwin. It is not 'statistics' that are wanted, but the scientific question is a very complicated one—far more complicated than Darwin seems to have any idea—and cannot be discussed to the least profit without much scientific detail, such as your readers would not stand. The difficulty about the theological part is different. Yours is not a theological magazine, though you admit a sort of allusive treatment of theology. But, to discuss this matter properly, one must go in for a thorough theological discussion, less popular even than the *Essays and Reviews*. However, I shall not let the subject drop in a hurry, or, to speak more correctly,

it will not let me drop.   It has completely flung me back into
Natural Science.   Not that I had ever abandoned it either in
intention or altogether in practice.   But now there is no
getting rid of it any more than of a part of oneself.

TO THE REV. B. F. WESTCOTT

ST. IPPOLYTS, *December* 11*th*, 1860.

. . . Do not think me wholly devoted to textual criticism.
I am apt to be engrossed with what is at the time in hand,
and I am deliberately anxious to get the text done in order to
be more free for other work.   But I am also engaged on
Simon de Montfort, and never lay aside more serious matters,
though it may be only in a desultory way that I deal with
them.   I think it will be necessary to lay down a fixed division
of time.

Once more, I am quite ready to believe that you are right
in thinking that we ought to gird ourselves at once to definite
thought and writing in behalf of the truth ; though, if left to
myself, I might drift along for some time to come without
immediate action.

Nevertheless your note raises doubts, which I will try to
state candidly, trusting to you not to misunderstand me.   The
doubts refer to your proposal for a joint publication of
preliminary essays separate from the Commentary.   The
more I have thought over my own part in the Commentary,
the more impossible I have felt it to make myself intelligible
without a very full, though if possible very condensed,
introduction, containing more than is usually found in such
a place.   Some topics would be general, some critical and
special ; but few of them could be treated satisfactorily
without being both one and the other.   I will put down some
that have occurred to me, without attempting any order.   The
origin of the Gospels—Their common traditional basis and
their distinctive modifications and additions—The lesson of
the exact historical and chronological fact when it can be
ascertained, and the lessons of the several representations of
it and associations connected with it in the several Gospels

—The quotations from the O. T., involving the nature of prophecy—The doctrine of Messiah, not only among contemporary Jews, but much more (to this I attribute special importance) as traced progressively through the O. T. —The critical problem presented by the Gospels as an historical phenomenon, and the various ways of attempting it, *e.g.* given the impossibility of a miracle, to explain the existence of our records, or, given their literal truth, to discover what they do and do not say, and deduce the consequences, or various intermediate ways of putting the question, involving a discussion of how much weight 'external' evidence to a miraculous record can possibly bear—The nature of miracles in general, and the relation of those in the N. T. to those in the O. T. in particular—Demoniacal possession—The order of events in our Lord's life—The necessity of not limiting the Incarnation in interpreting the Gospels (*e.g.* in Mark xiii. 32, Luke ii. 52)—The principles of N. T. lexicography, especially the deduction of theological terms from O. T. usage, usually through the medium of the LXX.—Generally the principle that the N. T. is written in terms of the O. T., etc.

These and probably other like topics I feel that I should have to assume and merely illustrate in the Commentary itself, and therefore must lay down concisely but clearly and methodically beforehand. Now there is scarcely any question raised by Jowett and Co. which would not necessarily be discussed under these heads. And to make such an introduction satisfactory for my purpose, I think it must be in my own language throughout. I hope and believe we should agree in a large majority of at least the most essential points, but every one has his own habits of mind, and I should not feel that, *e.g.*, your published book would represent what I should wish to say in my own person; it is difficult to go into particulars, but, *e.g.*, its tone is what for want of a better word I must call too 'apologetic' for my own purpose. It is an obvious objection to this wish of mine that owing to the accident of the first books falling to my share, I am virtually supposed to write an introduction for all three of us. I feel this objection very strongly, and therefore shall be thankful for your and Lightfoot's honest wishes on the matter. On the other hand, you have already in a great measure said your say in your *Introduction;* and I do not know whether Lightfoot would wish to have a separate exposition. If he does, he would still have an opportunity, as beginning the Epistles. I should in any case submit any introduction of mine to you both, and endeavour to remove any non-essentials which either of you might object to, besides of course stating that no one but myself was responsible for what I wrote. Further, the Synoptists *do* involve a far greater number of points for discussion than any other book, and weighty questions are brought there to a more direct issue. Thus it seems to me that a good deal may be urged in favour of what is *prima facie* an unfair arrangement; but neither you nor Lightfoot must scruple to express freely any contrary feeling. It does not seem to me that it would be well first to publish a separate volume of introductory essays, and then to *repeat* introductory matter of the same kind before the Commentary itself; but this particular point, I confess, I am not so clear about. Also, waiving the doubt whether it would be satisfactory to refer back to what would partly be the writing of others, I think it would be very awkward in the Commentary to have to refer to a separate book published some time before, which would probably not be in the hands of many readers, for three will buy a Commentary to one who will buy essays. Lastly, I cannot but think that Jowett's plan was a good one, of exemplifying his principles *at once* in an actual Commentary.

These are my doubts, which I do not at all wish you to take as final. For I am quite open to conviction, and you may be able to suggest some plan not open to similar objections. It would be a good thing if we could have some conversation : is it quite impossible, text apart? I have off and on much annual parish business till Christmas, and Butler comes, I hope, for about ten days at the beginning of the year ; for the rest I have no engagement, and this would be a good middle point for you and Lightfoot. In fact we ought to meet, if it were only to settle the plan of the Commentary. I quite feel with you that we are in a very critical state of things. The *Essays and Reviews* have, I think, flung back into mere orthodox assertion many who were feeling their way onwards, and such views will on the other hand be accepted widely as the utmost now tenable. Our own position is becoming more unpopular, but also, I think, more important. And yet, as you say, it is a fearful thing to have to write on subjects in which every fresh thought only reveals to us our own ignorance. But that, I suppose, after a time ceases to be an argument for silence.

To Mr. A. Macmillan

St. Ippolyts, *December* 13*th*, 1860.

. . . Jowett, at least, has no right to accuse us of inaction, considering how much older a man he was before he put pen to paper. Also Westcott ought to cover many shortcomings. . . . Those fellows don't know what work means, and they fancy that the weightiest questions of criticism can be dashed off without work.

To the Rev. B. F. Westcott

St. Ippolyts, *December* 14*th*, 1860.

Pray look at my letter again and see that you misunderstood what I said about our position becoming unpopular and suspected. I gave it as a reason for writing, not for silence. I think it very necessary to keep constantly in mind that popularity is no measure of usefulness, and very often a hindrance to it.

Will you let me ask you, without cavilling at words, whether the phrase "a true mean" accurately represents your own present wish? I am sure we are substantially agreed on this head, and yet I could not use this language. Surely there is no mean between reason and authority. Does not the mischief consist in their separation rather than the excess of either? The distinction seems to me important not only in itself but in reference to the conviction of others, especially young men. It would be a pity needlessly to alienate just the most sincere and earnest seekers after truth by introducing

the notion of a compromise in matters of belief. Surely the
via media belongs rightly to practice, not to speculation.

Now that you have explained your plan more distinctly, I
feel that my doubts are scarcely applicable, though on the
whole I am glad that I sent them to you. The division of
subjects which you suggest had not occurred to me for our
present purpose, and I doubt whether it could be improved.
I agree with you that they are distinct from a commentary,
but I think also they must be explicitly presupposed in one ;
and, as far as I see at present, I could not with satisfaction to
myself write notes on the Gospels without a preliminary statement in my own words. This difficulty may, however, be
met by the distribution of parts. I have little doubt that you
would like yourself to take the middle division, 'miracle and
history,' and Lightfoot would probably agree with me in
wishing you to take it. Certainly I should shrink from undertaking to write in a few months on some of the most essential
points of that subject. The first and third divisions belong,
in a manner, to the Synoptists and St. Paul respectively. But
it would meet my difficulty best, and be otherwise advantageous, if Lightfoot and I were to change parts in the essays.
We could then each have his respective say in the Commentary without repetition ; and I think increased good might
be done by the same subject being treated independently
by two different minds agreeing in the same general principles,
the principles themselves might thus be seen to be independent of idiosyncrasy. Further, overwhelming as it is to have
to write upon any of these subjects, ever so roughly and
tentatively, within a few months, I think I could undertake
the third with rather less preparation than the first. But this
is a point for further consideration, and above all for consulting Lightfoot. I should like the first division to include *all*
the preparation for the Gospel, heathen as well as Jewish, the
'prerogative' position of Israel being of course clearly maintained, indeed the one is, I think, necessary for the exhibition
of the other.

You will see that I am prepared to take up the plan as
decidedly as you can wish. But I think it essential that we
should very emphatically preface the essays with a statement

that we do not intend them as the best approximations to a full
and satisfactory exposition of the truth that we can make, believing that longer and more careful study is needed for that purpose, but as a rough though careful declaration of so much as
we have thus far been enabled to see, which the critical state
of theological opinion induces us to publish thus prematurely.

To the Rev. B. F. Westcott

ST. IPPOLYTS, *February 12th*, 1861.

. . . It was a great satisfaction to get your question about
E. and R. It has been much on my mind of late, though,
not feeling hopeful about it, I have said and done nothing.
But the matter is very serious, and I am quite disposed to
think it is worth making an effort, even if not so successful as
we could wish. . . .

[*A Suggested Declaration.*]

We, the undersigned clergymen of the Church of England,
desire to protest publicly against the violent and indiscriminate
agitation now being directed against a book called *Essays and
Reviews*, and against the authors of it. Believing that the
suppression of free criticism must ultimately be injurious to
the cause of truth and religion, we especially regret the adop-
tion of a harsh and intolerant policy, which tends to deter
men of thought and learning from entering the ministry of the
Church, and to impel generous minds into antagonism to the
Christian faith.

To the Rev. B. F. Westcott

ST. IPPOLYTS, *February 15th*, 1861.

. . . It is perhaps true that I feel the errors of the *E.
and R.* less keenly than you do. It appears to me tolerably
certain that I have a stronger sense of their truths.

Also—a distinct matter—I am probably less able than you
to condemn decidedly the course they have adopted in pre-
cipitating a crisis. That is, while I should myself (even if I

had shared their opinions) probably have thought it on the whole wisest to refrain,[1] I still feel they have very strong grounds for their conduct, and I do not altogether trust my own caution.

Both these considerations, however—their truths or errors and their policy—are surely beside the present question. I think we need not discuss the comparative 'guilt' of themselves and their accusers. They happen at this moment to represent the cause of freedom of thought and criticism, and that fact constitutes the greater part of their claim on our sympathy and help. A league is forming between the Evangelicals and the High Churchmen to crush all belief not founded solely on tradition, and, if possible, to drive from the Church all who, whether orthodox or not, value truth above orthodoxy. The danger seems to me great and immediate. Perhaps there is no way of meeting it. But even a weakly signed protest, if it either had some prominent names at the head or were taken from a well-selected area, might be of some avail. I wish it were possible to have an Oxford and Cambridge Conference. Surely in maintaining a purely defensive position it is not needful to give prominence to our differences from *E. and R.*

I quite think that *E. and R.* did write (not exactly appeal) *ad populum ;* they give [as] reason for doing so the uneasy scepticism among the *populus*, which threatens to destroy their Christian faith altogether. But that means the readers of such books in libraries. The present agitation is forcing it before others. However, that I think a light evil beside the conspiracy of *clerus* and *populus* to destroy whatever threatens their repose.

To the Rev. John Ellerton

St. Ippolyts, *February* 15*th*, 1861.

. . . I see I wrote to you from Villard. . . . On July 20th we reached Zermatt, and the 21st, the Riffel,

---

[1] See pp. 399-401.

where we at once resolved to stay, and there we did stay
till August 20th. A strange time it was, very pleasant
in the rare intervals of fine weather, but not at all so
within doors. The house is small and badly built, the *salle*
wretchedly small, not large enough to accommodate even the
twenty-eight occupants of beds, and the bedrooms narrow
wooden cells. The cold we did not find extreme ; but the
noise, confusion, and want of comfort were a good lesson in
patience ; some of our worst annoyances came from the bad
manners of tourists, chiefly Germans, German Swiss, and
Americans : the English, even of the vulgar majority, behaved
surprisingly well. It was a curious study of 'mankind' to
be fixed there for a month while the stream of travellers
flowed by. One great pleasure was the number of friends
we saw, and others we made. Some of the best of the latter
were W. E. Forster of Burley, and his wife, Arnold's eldest
daughter Jane. We had a very happy visit from Frederick
and Arthur Blunt, with James of Cheltenham and the Bodleys
(one of them the architect). Frederick Blunt stayed behind
after the rest, and, though temporarily lame, was most anxious
to do something. So it was settled that we three should
attempt the Cima di Jazzi, the easiest of the real snow
mountains, some 12,000 feet high, but commanding a splendid
view of M. Rosa and down into Italy. After leaving the
Riffel we slept one night at Zermatt, and then crossed the
main chain of the Alps by the Col de S. Théodule. We
stayed at Breuil, at the head of the Val Tournanche. . . .
The last two days we had there Mr. and Mrs. Cole (the 'Lady
who toured round M. Rosa'), and with them Owen, and on
the Monday we all descended the Val Tournanche together
to Châtillon in the Val d'Aosta. You may imagine what a
treat it was to have a good talk (or, as he called it, a
'Platonic Dialogue') with Owen under such circumstances.
I was able to catechise him to my heart's content, and fully
verified my belief that he could not possibly differ from
Darwin either in the manner or to the extent that the sapient
public supposes. As I feared, it is but too plain that he is
wanting in more than one respect ; but still he is a magnificent
man, as truly a king as old Sedgwick.

. . . I have been induced to begin a fresh undertaking, about which, however, you must keep dead silence. *Essays and Reviews* are producing apparently such rapid effects in opposite directions, leading some to give up revelation, and driving others back to the merest traditionalism, that, at Westcott's suggestion, he, Lightfoot, and I have resolved to attempt a mediating volume. It will not be at all controversial, but simply try to state what we believe to be the truth on both sides. It is to be called *Revelation and History.* Lightfoot takes 'the preparation for the Gospel,' *i.e.* the stages of Jewish history, the work of the different nations of antiquity, and the special calling of Israel. Westcott takes 'the witness of God in His Son,' in short, the Incarnation as an historical revelation of God, especially with reference to miracles. I am to take the development of doctrine out of revelation, including the progress within the N. T. and going on to the epochs of Church History since the close of the Canon, especially showing the growth of a Scripture and of its use. When at Harrow, we also settled more definitely about our Commentary. It is to have a Greek (and *perhaps* English) text, with but one set of notes. They are to be very full, but in most cases exclude the discussion of other people's opinions. They will unavoidably contain much Greek, but be framed as far as possible for English readers. We have agreed to defer the Gospels till last. We are not without hopes of publishing each a part next year, I, St. James, St. Peter, and St. Jude; Westcott, St. John's Epistles; and Lightfoot his Prolegomena to all St. Paul and his Commentary on .Thessalonians and perhaps Corinthians.

There is another way in which these *Essays and Reviews* are troubling one just now. The agitation against them seems growing to a most dangerous height, and may do untold mischief. I wish I could see what is to be done to stop it. Westcott also is anxious. He thinks it would not be possible to get enough signatures to any protest against the agitation; but I am still hoping something may be done. Altogether times are getting very critical.

Then, to keep us warm, there is the prospect of a French invasion of Prussia, and, for our part in the affair, prize essays from Lord John till Prussia is exhausted and the little states have left her in the lurch, and then perhaps we may discover that we are somewhat concerned.

To the Rev. John Ellerton

St. Ippolyts, *February* 28*th*, 1861.

. . . What an unreal and absolutely unsatisfactory debate it was in Convocation on *Essays and Reviews* / Who would have supposed, from reading the report of it, that any of the questions started were capable of any answer but one, or that the speakers were anything b"t the representatives of an unanimous Christendom? Surely this wretched paltering with great questions must soon come to an end, or else the Church itself.

To the Rev. B. F. Westcott

St. Ippolyts, *March* 1*st*, 1861.

. . . I, too, have come to feel that just now we must acquiesce in silence as to *E. and R.*, though I am prepared for its becoming necessary to stand forward.

To the Rev. J. B. Lightfoot

St. Ippolyts, *April* 1*st*, 1861.

My dear Lightfoot—I delayed answering your note till I should hear from Westcott, which I have not done till this morning. I cannot say what a disappointment it has been to receive such an announcement.[1] After what has already passed it seems hopeless to ask you to reconsider your decision. All that you say of yourself is precisely my own experience ; but I force myself to forget it in the face of the great urgency,—increased, I fear, rather than diminished, by the prospect of *Aids to Faith*. I wrote a hasty line to Westcott on Saturday suggesting his taking your part with his own ; though I think a third person would be preferable,

[1] *i.e.* of Lightfoot's withdrawal from the proposed ' mediating volume.'

if such an one could be found; but a line from him this morning implies the probable abandonment of the whole scheme; and I confess I think it must come to that.

Up to this time my results consist of some half-dozen beginnings, not one of which can stand. But I am sure that, unprepared as we all are, we could all say something that would be of use to quiet readers, though it would have no effect on the controversy, except perhaps to draw down fresh fury.

To the Rev. John Ellerton

St. Ippolyts, *April 9th*, 1861.

. . . Our joint essay scheme falls to the ground, as Lightfoot declines his share, solely as beyond his time and present powers. Whether Westcott and I do anything with our parts, each separately, remains in doubt; but, indeed, Haden's advice [1] makes havoc among all my plans for books.

I have just finished Maine's book on *Ancient Law*. It looks technical, and requires some elementary knowledge of legal terms and history; but it is not really difficult, except by its condensation. As might be expected, it bears deeply on several weighty matters, and, though the public are hardly likely to find it out, is, I think, quite as important as *Essays and Reviews*.

To the Rev. B. F. Westcott

St. Ippolyts, *April 12th*, 1861.

. . . As touching the essays, I should much like to know your own intention as soon as you have formed it; whether you mean to publish a separate essay. If so, whether it will be of the same range as before. Independently of change of mode of life, I feel less courage than before. Doubts recur whether I have a distinct call to write. It was quite otherwise while the joint scheme lasted. The responsibility was divided, and the call seemed strong, if not clear. It is a serious matter to take one's first plunge into separate publication by means of such a subject, above all when I know

[1] See p. 378.

how meagre and inadequate the result will be. Also—but this may be cowardice—I have a sort of craving that our text should be cast upon the world before we deal with matters likely to brand us with suspicion. I mean, a text, issued by men already known for what will undoubtedly be treated as dangerous heresy, will have great difficulties in finding its way to regions which it might otherwise hope to reach, and whence it would not be easily banished by subsequent alarms. Of course I felt this doubt all along, but made it give way to the necessities of our joint plan of essays; now, however, it returns upon me. On the other hand, the desire to write does not abate. Perhaps we had better act quite independently; though if we should both write, it would seem desirable to publish, if possible, at the same time and in the same form. Please comment.

To Mr. A. Macmillan

St. Ippolyts, *May* 16*th*, 1861.

. . . I quite feel the importance of something being said on the scientific matter, and have a strong craving to write myself. But it is too ticklish a matter to write on in a hurry, for fear one should say what will not stand testing, and I want much more time and thought. Also a tract would not at all serve my purpose. What I should dream of would be a book, half of it pure science, and the other half theological discussion. I want both, first because I care for the scientific question only less than for the theological; and secondly, because I should be glad, if I could, to gain the ear of scientific people for the theology. Tracts few of them will read or attend to. Even were it otherwise, I could promise nothing now. I am going abroad for five months, when I could at best write only a rough draft, such as nothing would tempt me to send to the press without an amount of reading which would require some months more at home. However, if I know myself, I am silent now only in order to be able to speak with more effect hereafter.—Very truly yours,   Fenton J. A. Hort.

To the Rev. John Ellerton

BAGNI DI S. CATARINA,
VAL FURVA, NEAR BORMIO, *July* 13*th*, 1861.

. . . While I think of it, let me say that I left at Chelsea for you a packet of Alpine plants. We dried last year for our friends a few sets of the plants, at once small, best to look at, and best retaining their colours; and this is one of them. . . .

On Friday June 7th we started from London Bridge. . . . About 36 hours carried us from London to Chur. I forgot to mention that on our way to town we were lucky enough to meet John Ball, our late Alpine president, and got various useful hints from him. Also we travelled from Basle to Olten with Tuckett, another great Alpine man, who is specially great in minimum thermometers. He was a sight to see, being hung from head to foot with 'notions' in the strictest sense of the word, several of them being inventions of his own. Besides such commonplace things as a great axe-head and a huge rope and thermometers, he had two barometers, a sympiesometer, and a wonderful apparatus, pot within pot, for boiling water at great heights, first for scientific and then for culinary purposes. Let us hope the apparatus will have produced some results by the end of the summer. The journey was in several parts new to me. . . . Chur itself is a pleasant old city (a small one enough) at the mouth of a ravine, and a little raised above the Rhine valley. There was much less to see architecturally than I expected. The cathedral is not striking; but there are many curious things in and about it, dating from very early times, some parts probably Roman, and much early Lombard.

To the Rev. B. F. Westcott

CLIFTON, *October* 16*th*, 1861.

. . . I have only dipped into Zeller,[1] but have liked what I have seen of it; it seemed less 'viewy' than any other German

---

[1] Zeller's *Philosophie der Griechen.*

book on the subject. I should quite think you are right about the absence of any such book as you speak of. For many years it has been with me not only a dream, but perhaps my most constant and prominent dream, to deal with the course of Greek thought, as a necessary introduction to the history of the Church.

To the Rev. John Ellerton

St. Ippolyts, *November 25th*, 1861.

. . . Seriously, my dear Ellerton, I know not what to say to what you report of yourself in your long letter, except that I know it all exactly, and entirely feel with you. Only I must say, just as you know yourself, don't give in to it. That money trouble is perhaps the worst of all; but it does not mend matters brooding over it. I am obliged to spend much time at parts of the year at getting accounts clearly and fully made out, which is the most essential thing both for economy and for peace of mind. But when that is done, it is worse than useless going over the same thing again, pottering over figures, in a dim [hope] that somehow or other 2 and 3 can be induced not to make 5. Comfort should begin when one has once realized the existence of the brazen wall that hems one in : one can't get on without a little Islamism. As touching the cry of 'literary work,' that is all true too; it is just what I always find with sermons. The brain won't secrete to order. The only remedy I know is to take some definite material and *study* that. Research is possible when invention and composition are not. It is worth while to remember Fynes Clinton, whose work began as a sedative on his first wife's death. He needed the sedative all his life through; but research did give him calm and steadiness, and the *Fasti*[1] are the result for the world. . . .

I must say the Hughesian Tracts[2] do not satisfy me at all. They go about it and about it, anywhere but where their antagonists are. The tone of Chretien's is very beautiful, and there are many to whom it might be useful, though it leaves

[1] *Fasti Hellenici* and *F. Romani.*   [2] On *Essays and Reviews.*

everything unsolved. Ludlow is always interesting, if sometimes provoking. But one gets very weary of the fainter and fainter echoes of Maurice all through the series. The most really pertinent saying of the whole, I think, is Maurice's own, that much current error comes merely from recognising the fact of Law and ignoring the fact of Will. The notice in the *Guardian* gave me a pleasant impression of Garbett's book. I confess I have at present no wish to see any more of the replies. For Jowett himself, much as he vexes me with his lazy taking on trust of objections, and general deference to the sceptical section of public opinion, I find I have an increasing love. There are things in his essays (not in *E. and R.*) which meet the real *ultimate* difficulties better than anything I know. It is at once Maurice's strength and his weakness that he can approach nothing except from the purely theological side : all other aspects he tolerates and even approves in words, but they remain outside of him. This is an unlucky defect for just the present state of controversy.

I hope you saw Lightfoot's election to the new Hulsean Professorship vacated by Ellicott. It was really a critical thing for Cambridge. . . . He talks of beginning with some of St. Paul's Epistles, but eventually making the history of the fourth and fifth centuries his main subject.

While I think of it, let me remind you that Luard is standing for the Registraryship. He is about the best man in the University for it, from his extraordinary knowledge of University biography.

To the Rev. B. F. Westcott

St. Ippolyts, *December 4th*, 1861.

. . . It would not be easy to say how much I felt about Lightfoot's election. I am afraid any other result would have greatly estranged me from Cambridge. Curiously enough, I was within a few minutes of hearing the news first from himself. . . .

Now about the 'Philosophy,'[1] on which I have followed

---

[1] The allusion is to an article on 'Philosophy' contributed by Mr. Westcott to the *Dictionary of the Bible*.

your injunctions. My chief impression is a strong feeling of incapacity to criticize, partly from want of knowledge, and still more from not having fully thought out cardinal questions, such as the relation of 'philosophy' and 'faith.' *E.g.* you seem to me to make (Greek) philosophy worthless for those who have received the Christian revelation. To me, though in a hazy way, it seems full of precious truth of which I find nothing, and should be very much astonished and perplexed to find anything, in revelation.

. . . The account of the early schools does not satisfy me, though I could not rewrite it. My own feeling is that the pure Ionics sought a philosophy, the Atomists a science, and that Anaxagoras' work was a most deeply interesting attempt to harmonize the two.

Is τὸ ἄπειρον of Anaximander 'the infinite' of modern, or even late Greek, philosophy? Is it not almost 'the formless,' 'limit' being a simpler and less developed state of the notion of 'form.'

. . . Without condemning anything you have said on the Stoics, I yet feel you have not done them justice. The spiritual need which supported, if it did not originate, their doctrine is, I think, profoundly interesting, above all in the present day. It is the attempt to keep alive among men that which distinguishes them from the brutes, by means partly of an unknown and unknowable and yet not unreal 'God,' and partly by the order manifested in the world, itself the standard or centre both of being and knowledge. Much—by no means all—of the apparent self-sufficiency arose not from pride but from the necessity of dwelling on man as the highest thing in the world, that is, in the circle of knowable things. We must remember that the old religions were for all good purposes gone ; and Stoicism was surely an attempt to provide a good working substitute for religion for the common man as well as the philosopher. . . .

P.S.—I forgot to say that the paper which used to hurt your eyes so much on the walls of my study is now superseded. Will not that tempt you to come ?

To the Rev. B. F. Westcott

St. Ippolyts, *December 7th*, 1861.

. . . My objection was that you seemed to make philosophy *only* propædeutic, and therefore of interest chiefly as an historical curiosity. 'First principles' I also think cannot be *established* by philosophy; but I should hesitate to say that they are established by revelation either. I doubt whether the truth can be expressed so neatly and antithetically as your theory seems to require. Whether the fact be true or not, you have not attempted to prove that the successive abandonments from Plato onwards were intrinsically necessary, and not 'accidentally' arising from the character of the men and the times.

To Mr. A. Macmillan

St. Ippolyts, *December 19th*, 1861.

. . . As touching Simonides, I want to examine it carefully for myself. If you can get me the loan of a copy, so much the better; if not, I must buy it. One never knows where to have that fellow. He undoubtedly has found genuine and valuable MSS. as well as forgeries. To make the thing more complete, he says he forged Tischendorf's Sinai MS., which is the biggest lie of all.

A good deal of my work has gone into Luard's[1] book just out. For the part before printed (about half) I gave him a complete index, analysis, and the dates of a good many letters. I am *hoping* to get steadily to work at Simon and Co. now and try to get it done. It is a big job, but I like it much.

To the Rev. John Ellerton

St. Ippolyts, *January 8th*, 1862.

My dear Ellerton—No time to-day for other matters; but I must send one word on a pamphlet, which you will, I hope, get by this or the next post against the Revised Code.[2] It is

---

[1] 'Grosseteste' in the Rolls Series.
[2] Viz. of Elementary Education.

an enlarged and altered copy of what I sent to Macmillan. It now appears by the wish of, and with some improvements suggested by, our good inspector, D. J. Stewart. The expense is borne by a friend of his. Copies are gone to all M.P.'s, bishops, and peers ; also all leading or clerical managers in some districts, especially our own five E. counties; also London, and, I believe, Brighton. But centres of distribution are wanted much in the W. of England. Can you suggest any people who would take charge of distribution, or at least supply lists of people to whom it would be worth while to send copies over a large district, say one, two, or three counties ? Copies in any reasonable numbers will be supplied gratis.

I had four such days in Cambridge early last week for the revision and correcting proofs of the pamphlet ; and—will you believe it ?—I did not *see* Trinity, being all the while at Stewart's house in Bene't Place. He is a wonderfully fine fellow, and I greatly enjoyed the talks and consultations.

To THE REV. B. F. WESTCOTT

ST. IPPOLYTS, *January 20th*, 1862.

My dear Westcott—I am greatly vexed to hear that you are a friend to the Revised Code. My own feelings on the subject are very strong and decided. In the preservation and extension of precisely those features of education which R. C. cuts away, lies, I believe, the only hope of counteracting the terrible worldliness which is now taking hold of the lower orders, and of saving the mass of the clergy from being worse than contemptible. I cannot allow that 'popular clamour' is on my side. I am constantly annoyed with the small appreciation of what we really owe to Sir J. K. Shuttleworth by those who grumble after a manner at the change. But there is also, I think, a considerable amount of—not noisy—disapprobation from those who have given their lives to the work. I cannot help hoping that you will yet change your mind ; more especially when you find out how very much larger and more reckless a section of public opinion supports the *Times* and Mr. Lowe against us.

To the Rev. B. F. Westcott

St. Ippolyts, *February 21st*, 1862.

. . . I forgot at Cambridge to ask you whether you had seen Simonides' papyrus fragments. They are extremely satisfactory from the incredible grossness and yet elaborateness of the forgery. The clumsiness and ignorance of the text are quite enough by themselves to dispose of the notion that א[1] could be his handiwork, if it were not incredible already.

To Mr. A. Macmillan

St. Ippolyts, *April 15th*, 1862.

. . . You must have misunderstood Lightfoot as to his part of the New Testament. It is only the 'Galatians' that he hopes to get out this year, and that only because he wants to feel that something is actually out. I want to get on with a volume containing St. James, St. Peter, and St. Jude, and I am not without hopes of getting to press before the end of next year. But it is very doubtful. Independently of the Commentary, which will cost much labour, there will have to be copious Prolegomena, including in point of fact a discussion of nearly all the great questions of German criticism for the last ten years. Everything turns on, or at least is involved in, what St. Peter's real position was, with reference to St. James on the one side and St. Paul on the other.[2] I shall also probably have to append some theological essays after the manner of Jowett.

To the Rev. John Ellerton

St. Ippolyts, *April 30th, May 1st*, 1862.

. . . By the way, in speaking of 'doings,' I forgot that I have been up twice to Blunt's. Once I went with him and Haden to Denmark Hill to see Ruskin's pictures.

[1] Tischendorf's Sinai MS.
[2] This question was treated in some of the latest of Hort's Cambridge Lectures, those on 'Judaistic Christianity,' published after his death.

Ruskin unluckily was obliged to be out, so that we did not see him. The pictures, almost all Turner's, we did see, to our great enjoyment. Blunt has twice had him at Chelsea, and speaks of him in the highest terms. He seems to have been wonderfully taken with Blunt's children. Altogether Blunt has fallen on his legs as to that sort of society. You know Carlyle lives not fifty yards from his garden door, and they have become great friends. Of Mrs. Carlyle they see a great deal. She is quite an oddity, but very genuine and good. After seeing her and hearing about her, one can quite understand John Sterling's love for that household. Dear old Carlyle himself seems to be terribly bitter, that being the form taken by his increasing sadness and despair of the world.

Many thanks for the chants. They are, however, above us at present. I am indeed degenerate enough to be backing out of having Benedicite more than three times a year. In passing, I may as well mention that we have had for the last few weeks a Tonic Sol-fa class for the parish taught by a man at Stevenage. It takes very well, and will, I hope, be useful.

I really don't know what to write about the Revised Code. I am simply disgusted at everything. Mr. Lowe is only like a sulky child, who, finding its own toy damaged, stamps on whatever lies in its way. What on earth will turn up out of the present hopeless medley, no one, I should think, can prophesy.

I have not yet seen De Tocqueville or many other books that I want to read. We could not afford Mudie this winter; and indeed had more than enough to read without him. Wilshere has lent me vol. i. of Hook's *Archbishops*. As far as I have read, it is very amusing as a picture of Hook. It is quite whimsically commonplace,—such solemn truisms announced, not without humour, as philosophical discoveries. It seems a useful and honest book of reference, but, as far as I have read, quite wanting in historical power. I am greatly afraid he will get out his third volume before mine,[1] and spoil the freshness of my subject.

I am now working through Maurice's thick new volume of his philosophy. It has hardly so much life as its predecessors, but is full of matter.

[1] The volume on Simon de Montfort, etc.

Macmillan has sent me a life of one Robert Story, which is well worth reading. He was a great friend of M'Leod Campbell, Irving, etc., and the first patient in the prophetic movements out of which Irvingism arose was a parishioner of his. He does not strike me as a great man, but a vigorous, wise, and very good one. The latter part of the book contains a very strong attack on the Free Kirk movement.

I have got but only glanced at Stephen's defence of R. Williams. It looks very different from the newspaper reports and much longer. Altogether I shall not be surprised if it becomes an important document in the Church history of the century. It seems to be clearly and broadly directed to maintaining that the English clergy are not compelled to maintain the absolute infallibility of the Bible. And, whatever the truth may be, this seems just the liberty required to be openly claimed and secured at the present moment, if any living belief is to survive in the land. And, when the issue is thus broadly raised, I do not see how the civil courts, with a library of English theology before them, can refuse the claim. If they do, there will be a pretty mess. Unfortunately the laity take things abominably coolly, and are far too much disposed to let the clergy fight it out. The best hope is in the traditional tolerance of English law.—Ever affectionately yours,   FENTON J. A. HORT.

TO THE REV. B. F. WESTCOTT

ST. IPPOLYTS, *May 3rd*, 1862.

. . . I envy you your wandering by the Wye. This has perhaps been *the* week of the year for Tintern, though I cannot but think autumn the best time for most of the Wye, and especially for the Bowder Stone and Symond's Yat views. You could not attribute 'uniformity' to some autumn evening views I have seen from the Bowder Stone. Such subtle variety of atmospheres I have never seen elsewhere. By the way, I hope you do not join C. B. Scott in blaspheming Tintern as a building, though it is undeniably limited, and may have been so even before it was systematically stripped.

To the Rev. B. F. Westcott

St. Ippolyts, *May 6th*, 1862.

. . . You have taken a weight off my mind about Tintern. When Luard agreed with Scott, I began to distrust my own impressions, but every time I have seen the ruin since, it has vindicated its rights.

To the Rev. B. F. Westcott

St. Ippolyts, *May 9th*, 1862.

. . . I quite enter into your feeling about revision. It comes over me now and then, especially after doing such a piece of text as Colossians. But I am quite sure it would be wrong to give way to it. The work has to be done, and never can be done satisfactorily—relatively, I mean, to our present materials—without vast labour, a fact of which hardly anybody in Europe except ourselves seems conscious. For a great mass of the readings, if we separate them in thought from the rest, the labour is wholly disproportionate. But believing it to be absolutely impossible to draw a line between important and unimportant readings, I should hesitate to say that the entire labour is disproportionate to the worth of fixing the entire text to the utmost extent now practicable. It would, I think, be utterly unpardonable for us to give up our task, and, if so, every reason conspires to urge us to finish it as quickly as possible, if only to get the burden off our necks. Every right-minded person, I suppose, has a relative contempt for orthographic details. Their dignity comes from their being essential to complete treatment. And I confess, when once at work upon them, I find a certain tepid interest as in any research depending on evidence and involving laws.

To his Wife

Mürren, *August 22nd*, 1862.

. . . I am in luck at present as to people. Besides the old folk, another couple have turned up. At first I looked at them only with curiosity, and we wondered who they could be. . . . To-day at dinner they had a budget of letters, from which I found it was Dr. and Mrs. Acland of Oxford. He is about the first doctor there, very highly cultivated and scientific, and especially known as one of the *best* men living, given to every kind of good work, a great friend of Ruskin and Maurice. I was introduced to him (which he had very naturally forgotten) six years ago at Oxford, but he knew my name well enough. This may tempt me to remain here a little longer; to-morrow is sure to be cloudy, but if Tuesday is fine we are to go up the Schilthorn together.

To his Wife

MÜRREN, *August 29th,* 1862.

. . . The Aclands started this morning, I fear for England, as it is so wet they are sure not to be going up to the Wengernalp. It has been such a very pleasant time with them both. . . . I have had a great deal of talk on several subjects, mostly scientific, university, or theological; and I have never seen a more perfect union of deep and fervent Christian feeling with unflinching love and desire of truth on all possible subjects than in him; and whatever she said was in complete keeping. Fancy a man having and retaining as dear and intimate friends Dr. Pusey, the Bishop of Oxford, Jowett, Stanley, Ruskin, Maurice, Owen, and the scientific people, and the artists.

To the Rev. John Ellerton

ENGSTLEN, *September 25th,* 1862.

. . . I wonder whether the new archbishop is appointed yet (my last paper was the *Journal de Génève* of Saturday), and among the possible candidates I hardly know whom to wish for, possibly the Archbishop of York or Lord Auckland. Chambers (whom I met the second day at the Little Scheideck returning from a four months' honeymoon with his very pretty young bride, a niece of Hare's) told me that Stanley had a

very fair chance; but that (without thinking him exactly a
model archbishop) is surely too good to be true.
- . . . My feeling about the famous judgment[1] is very mixed.
It leaves an impression of a scrupulous anxiety to be just, combined with strange ignorance of theology and helpless self-
surrender to the popular nineteenth century interpretations of
theological terms as the only possible ones. . . . As regards
the effect, it is a great thing to have the Bible almost wholly
unbound from its protecting chains, and some of the other
decisions are good so far as they go. But that on the Athanasian creed and punishment (which was not even argued (!)),
and some others, may be very mischievous; and above all,
Dr. Lushington has laid down two sweeping doctrines which
seem to me most unjust and fatal if allowed to stand: (1)
that 'precedent' (the holding of similar views by earlier
Anglican writers) cannot be pleaded for an opinion which
verbally contradicts a single sentence of *the Articles* (nor
indeed can other sentences of the Articles by themselves be
brought in justification), although the Gorham judgment was
based on such a pleading of 'precedent' as against the
words of *the Prayer-book;* (2) that a clergyman is legally
responsible for all doctrines contained in another man's book
which he in any way edits or reproduces, except for such as
he has separately and expressly repudiated. I suppose from
what you say that the defendants have already appealed on
the judgment itself; if so, I cannot help hoping that the
superior court will think itself justified in assuming a semi-
legislative power, and laying down the widest toleration for
the clergy as well as the laity.[2] I am convinced that now, and
for some time to come, mere naked freedom of opinion is the
great thing to strive for as the indispensable condition of
everything else. I wish St. Bartholomew's could have been
marked by a voluntary dropping of the Act of Uniformity;

[1] On the prosecution of Dr. Rowland Williams and Mr. Wilson, two
of the writers in *Essays and Reviews.* ᐟ See *Life of Dean Stanley,* vol. ii.
p. 157.
[2] Dr. Lushington's decision, which sentenced the two essayists to a
year's suspension, was in effect reversed by the Privy Council on February
8th, 1864. See *Life of Dean Stanley, ibid.*

and I have for some time felt the Athanasian Creed to be a most serious hindrance to the Church. It alienates many, obscures the meaning and worth of the real Creeds, and is out of harmony with the rest of the Prayer-book. Therefore I suppose it will be hopeless to get rid of it, though thousands of the clergy of all schools in their hearts wish it would quietly vanish in the night. I am disposed to think we should on the whole be better also without the Articles in spite of their great merits, but I suppose Protestantism will guard them jealously.

On things American I fear we do not agree. I do not defend the language of the English press and society, least of all their insane forgetfulness of the Southern character and policy in regard to slavery, behaviour towards England, and morality generally. Lincoln is, I think, almost free from the nearly universal dishonesty of American politicians (his letter to Greeley I know nothing about); I cannot see that he has shown any special virtues or statesmanlike capacities. I do not for a moment forget what slavery is, or the frightful effects which Olmsted has shown it to be producing on white society in the South; but I hate it much more for its influence on the whites than on the niggers themselves. The refusal of education to them is abominable; how far they are capable of being ennobled by it is not so clear. As yet *everywhere* (not in slavery only) they have surely shown themselves only as an immeasurably inferior race, just human and no more, their religion frothy and sensuous, their highest virtues those of a good Newfoundland dog. If enjoyment and comparative freedom from sorrow and care make up happiness, probably no set of men in Europe (unless it be the Irish) are so happy. Their real and most unquestionable degradation, if altered by slavery, is hardly aggravated; the sin of slavery to them is rather negative in hindering advance, yet what advance has there really been in the West Indies or Northern states? Nevertheless the thing is accursed most positively from its corrupting power over the dominant race. But, while agreeing with the advocates of the North that slavery is at the bottom of the whole conflict of South and North, as the chief though not sole cause of disunion, and also that the South separated simply because Lincoln's election was a signal that the North had decided not to allow Southern policy any longer to hold the helm of the whole Union, I hold that the South had a perfect right to separate themselves and go their own way, it having been clearly shown by experience that one or the other half *must* ride rough-shod over the other, and that no really *common* action is possible. Hence I think the North is trying to do just what the South did before the rupture, with this vast difference, that it uses force and conquest. I hold, therefore, that the war is at once entirely a war of independence, and not at all for and against slavery, though it sometimes suits the North (and still more its English supporters) to represent it as such. *While the war lasts*, therefore, I fully sympathize with the South. So much for the mutual rights and wrongs of the two contending parties. But that is only one part of the matter. I care more for England and for Europe than for America, how much more than for all the niggers in the world I and I contend that the highest morality requires me to do so. Some thirty years ago Niebuhr wrote to this effect: Whatever people may say to the contrary, the American empire is a standing menace to the whole civilization of Europe, and sooner or later one or the other must perish. Every year has, I think, brought fresh proof of the entire truth of these words. American doctrine (only too well echoed from Europe itself, though felt to be at variance with the institutions of Europe) destroys the root of everything vitally precious which man has by painful growth been learning from the earliest times till now, and tends only to reduce us to the gorilla state. The American empire seems to me mainly an embodiment of American doctrine, its leading principle being lawless force. Surely, if ever Babylon or Rome were rightly cursed, it cannot be wrong to desire and pray from the bottom of one's heart that the American Union may be shivered to pieces. This is not wishing ill to Americans, quite the reverse ; the breaking of their power as a nation (which has not brought, to the best of my knowledge, one single blessing on mankind) may, we may hope, be the first and a needful step towards their advancement in all higher and nobler respects. I am afraid you will think all this rank heresy, and I confess I should be puzzled to know how to speak wisely before the public, but thank God I am not a journalist; as to my own hopes and fears (the latter of which are still very considerable), I have no scruples.—Ever affectionately yours,   F. J. A. HORT.

To a Lady who meditated joining the Church of
Rome

St. John's Mount, Brecon, *October* 1862.

My dear —— I am much obliged to you for writing to me as you have done, though I could wish that your letter afforded more grounds for hope. You will forgive my saying that the points you dwell on leave the impression of being rather the most *tangible* and easily presentable grounds of 'attraction' than those which really have the greatest power over you. I do not in the least mean that you are insincere in putting these prominently and even exclusively forward. I can quite understand the very natural state of mind which makes it scarcely possible to do otherwise ; what is really most to oneself is often just what is least capable of being conveyed to any one else. Only the consequence for me is that I must write very much in the dark, though using the points you have mentioned as so many finger-posts, if nothing more.

One important exception must be made. You intimate pretty plainly—and it is an important fact—that what impels you in the first instance is weariness and dissatisfaction with the Church of England, and that Rome only comes in later, as it were, as possibly supplying that which you have sought for in vain here. This leads at once to what must in any case have been the burden of my letter, viz. that there are two entirely distinct questions for you to consider, the former and more important of which is commonly without any reason taken for granted. You ought to inquire whether you have a right to demand this or that as a necessary mark of a true Church, before you go on to ask whether the Roman Communion possesses these marks that you have prescribed. Unless you can clearly decide that such marks are *necessary*, to pass from

England to Rome merely because *you like* those marks, and because Rome has or seems to have them, would be only to act on the same principle as those Dissenters you speak of, who leave their church to follow a favourite preacher because he 'does them good.'

This is my text, and as I don't want to write you a sermon, I must ask you to consider the text dispassionately and repeatedly, in various lights. I know that if you come to my conclusion, it will involve, not merely your not stepping forward across the boundary, but also taking some steps back-wards in one sense, though more truly forward in another direction; I mean, you will have to give up some theories about the Church which are held by a great many English Churchmen. But we cannot too often remind ourselves that in all ages one of the commonest and most fatal snares has been our inbred fondness for making our own hopes and desires the standard of truth. For many most widely-spread opinions no other ground can be found than that it would be very pleasant to think so.

I do not mean to dispute your statements about the Church of England. You would yourself, I have no doubt, allow that there are other *opposite* facts in abundance; signs, I mean, of real unity in the midst of much difference, and of real guidance and instruction to the people at large. Nearly all that you say against us comes to this, that wide difference of opinion is tolerated within laity, clergy, and episcopate. There is no doubt about the fact, and I for one heartily rejoice at it, and am not in the least disposed merely to make apologies for it. The existence of differences of opinion among Churchmen may or may not be an evil; but that is not the question. The differences being there, such unity as you seem to desire could only be obtained by excluding from the Church or ministry all who did not hold, or at least profess, a certain minutely prescribed standard of doctrine. It would surely require very strong proofs indeed of the Divine necessity of such a proceed-ing to reconcile one to the flood of obvious evils that would certainly ensue. Some would answer that the *past* latitude of the Church of England is responsible for the *present* differences of opinion. But this I entirely deny. On the whole, it seems

to me that the guiding power and influence of the Church of
England has been enormously multiplied by its toleration ; and,
at all events, the differences of opinion are really due to a
number of powerful causes which nothing could have resisted,
and which may shortly be summed up as the political and
social state of England at the time of the Tudors, produced
by events during the Middle Ages, and to a great extent uncon-
nected with religious matters.   Whether we like it or no, the
fact is undoubted that the Church of a country is only one
out of many very different agents which bring about its religious condition.

No good would be gained by disputing whether the Prayer-
book, Catechism, and Articles do or do not in any points contradict each other.   On the one hand, it is quite certain that
they do spring from different ages of the Church, and therefore necessarily express different tones of mind.   On the other
hand I, at least, think it equally certain as an historical fact,
notwithstanding the existence of contending parties within the
English Church ever since the Reformation, that antiquity (in
the Creeds and Prayer-book) and the sixteenth century (in the
Articles) have harmoniously combined to produce in England
a very noble type of Christian belief and devotion, which has
powerfully affected for good even the extremes on either side.

I am quite aware of the many faults in what is called the
spirit of the English Church, and especially lament its *insular*
character.   But when disposed to find fault, I am once more
obliged to ask myself how it could have been otherwise.   The
history of European politics and religion in the sixteenth and
seventeenth centuries explains the unhappy necessity.   But I
cannot admit that this of itself shows the English Church not
to be Catholic in any legitimate sense of the word.   The word
is habitually used in three different senses besides its literal
original meaning 'universal.'   First, we speak of a catholic
spirit, meaning one of wide and far-reaching sympathies, willing
to hold converse with others very different from ourselves.
Secondly, there is the stricter theological sense of belonging
to the one historical undivided Church of different countries
and perhaps different times.   Thirdly, Romanists claim the
title exclusively for those Churches which obey the Roman

See, and for convenience sake they are often called merely
Catholics in ordinary conversation. Now, when you say that
the English Church "can scarcely be called Catholic when she
is not in communion with any portion of the Catholic world,"
you use the word first in the second and then in the third
sense, thereby allowing Romanists to beg the whole question.
Lord Shaftesbury might just as well ask, How can any one
live an evangelical life who does not belong to the Evangelical
Alliance? Doubtless catholicity, in the second, which is the
only legitimate theological sense (the sense of the Creeds
which we inherit from a time when any supremacy on the part
of the Roman See was all but unknown), is a somewhat vague
and indefinite thing; doubtless communion with the See of
Rome would supply a sharper and more easily applicable test;
but what of that, if it be a false and wrong one?

To go back to what I was saying just now, we may well
regret that the Church of England is in avowed communion
only with the Episcopal Church of Scotland and those of our
own colonies and of the United States. But, on the one
hand, our isolation from the ancient Churches of the East and
West has been far more their act than ours; and, on the
other, *every* existing communion is guilty of the same exclusiveness as ourselves. The undivided Christendom of the Roman
Empire has, under the changed circumstances of modern times,
split up into separate communions which most unhappily
think they strengthen their own ground by questioning the
legitimacy of the others. It is simply absurd that Anglican,
Roman, Greek, Armenian, or any other, should suppose himself to be the only true representative of the Church of the
Apostles. The fact is, the *absolute* and *perfect* catholicity,
which Rome claims for her own dependants, now exists *nowhere.*
To some this would seem a shocking denial of Christ's promises to His Church. But that is only because, in German
fashion, they have settled in their own minds beforehand what
the Church *must* be, without waiting to inquire what God has
actually made it.

After noticing the defects of the English Church, you contrast with them certain merits of the Roman Communion, most
of which are comprised under uniformity and identity, and this

you think likely to be a mark of Divine guidance. It is no satisfaction to me to spend time in pointing out Roman short-coming; but I must say one or two words.

First, I freely allow a very considerable uniformity in the Churches subject to Rome, while I entirely deny the inference. Such uniformity is the natural and necessary consequence of superior organization—that is, of compact and systematic co-operation devised by human heads, and carried out by human heads and hands. Such an organization is, of course, in itself a merit. But the Roman organization would be powerless without the Roman supremacy. That is the keystone of the whole fabric. So long as there is an opinion in men's minds that the judgments of individual Churchmen or individual Churches must bow to the decision of a single Italian bishop, there is a powerful engine for nipping in the bud the tenden-cies to diversity which are constantly arising. It is this human conviction, and the conduct which springs from it, which pro-duces the uniformity, and not any Divine inspiration; and the conviction will necessarily act in this way, whether it be true or false, which is quite a distinct question. I cannot see that the doctrine of the Roman supremacy has a shred of support from the Bible, or from the history of the early Church. The strongest point in its favour is the benefit which it rendered to society in the infancy of modern Europe before the great states had consolidated themselves. But then it seems to me equally clear that even during part, a considerable part, of the Middle Ages, and still more since the Reformation, its influence on society has been almost wholly mischievous. Its other great merit I have already mentioned, viz. its efficiency in pro-moting external and, to a certain extent, internal unity. But this efficiency is gained only at the expense of truth, freedom, and the like, which we Protestants think more precious still.

Secondly, The uniformity of which you speak is, after all, very imperfect. There have been and are still very violent oppositions of belief and practice within the Roman pale. No small proportion of the books prohibited in the lists of the *Index Expurgatorius* are written by zealous and able Romanists. Of course few would publicly assail distinctly recognised articles of the Roman Creed, but it is a delusion to suppose that you can be sure of everywhere hearing the same doctrine. The widest differences of tone and feeling undoubtedly prevail, and this is what really constitutes the doctrinal effect of preaching far more than the articles which receive verbal homage. More-over, the very attempt at absolute uniformity is of quite modern origin. Romanism, as a sharply-defined distinctive Creed, is still younger than Protestantism. The decrees of the Council of Trent, as well as the last new Roman dogma, involve the condemnation of some of the greatest Churchmen of the Middle Ages, to say nothing of the Fathers.

Thirdly, you say "a Roman Catholic is at home in his Church all over the world." I suppose most honest Protest-ants have felt something of this when travelling abroad, and wished that they could have the same feeling. Why can they not? Chiefly because there is so little communion between the different parts of Christendom, and for this Rome is even more responsible than any other body. It is a privation which Protestants have to endure; but it throws absolutely no light on the right or wrong of the Roman supremacy. And most assuredly the advantage is not all on one side. The real blessing of Roman universality, viz. that community of Christians in different countries, has, I think, been dearly bought by the comparative loss of sympathy with national aims and interests. Every devoted Romanist sits compara-tively loosely to the country to which he belongs, he cares far more for foreigners of his own communion. I do not deny that such a state of things may now and then be inevitable; but I do say it is always an evil. It is mischievous both to the country and to the Church. A religion which is not fed by home and local influences is always morbid and usually superstitious; a country with which its own Church does not identify itself, goes its own way very much without the bene-ficial influence of the Church, and regards it as something outside, often even as an enemy. A time, we may hope, will come when it will be found possible for a Church to be in real communion with other Churches without losing its proper and natural place among its own people. Till then, we may, I think, well console ourselves in our isolation by the thought that, in spite of its own defects and in spite of Dissent, the

Church of England is still on the whole a really national Church.

Thus much I wished to say about the arguments which stand in front of the more shadowy but more persuasive 'attractions' of Rome. The nature of these latter in your case I think I can in some degree conjecture by the help of one phrase that you use, viz. that your present state of mind is the result of the system in which you have been educated failing in your grasp like a dead branch.

It may be that, like thousands of others, you have found yourself in increasing difficulty and uncertainty in matters of belief. Possibly you are perplexed when you try to think important subjects out for yourself, or to understand clearly what the Bible has to say upon them ; and still more perplexed when, in despair of success, you turn to the various written documents of the Church of England, and yet more to its various living teachers. In such a state of mind there is necessarily a wonderful charm about a communion which professes to have an oracle able to pronounce with a single paramount infallible voice on all things in heaven and earth. This alone has drawn and will go on drawing innumerable people to Rome, enabling them to swallow the horror which they cannot help feeling at many Romish doctrines or practices. There is so strong a craving for such an oracular voice that the mere claim to possess it is eagerly accepted without question. But here, as in other cases, no foundation for the claim can be discovered except its convenience. Without going into the usual arguments about inconsistency, etc. (though I do not see how they can be answered), I would merely ask you to think over a few of the points on which the papal doctrines differ from those of other Christians, and then examine them by all possible tests of truth, such as harmony with the letter and spirit of the Bible (as distinguished from one or two isolated texts)—harmony with the best and purest experience of yourself and of others whose whole character you honour—tendency to promote a really noble and elevated thought of God—tendency to promote a wise and Christian character in all estates of life—and the like. The mere fact that men of singularly high character believe these doctrines proves just nothing; the same may be said for almost any imaginable doctrine. Nor, on the other hand, would I now lay much stress on considerations drawn from the moral state of Romish countries : other causes come into play there, and the whole question is too complicated for your purpose. · But your own thought and experience ought to make it possible for you to come to a sufficiently clear decision as to the natural effect of papal doctrines, without having to decide between theological arguments.

In saying just now that papal infallibility has only its own convenience in its favour, I used the word advisedly. I do not for a moment allow that it is a blessing denied to us, I believe it would be in reality a curse. In God's real teaching of us, asking and receiving, seeking and finding, are inextricably combined. No truth is vital and fruitful to us at which we have not laboured ourselves. There is no disguising the doubt and difficulty which beset our inquiries; but that is part of our appointed trial; to fly from them to a supposed oracle is only a cowardly shirking of the responsibilities which God has laid upon us.

Once more, it may be that you find life more vacant and insipid than it seemed a few years back. Perhaps you cannot easily find a purpose for your own life, or settle the footing on which you should stand towards others. And the Church of England seems to hold out no object to you, but to leave you very much to yourself. The Roman Communion promises better things. First and foremost, it puts you in the charge of a skilful and practised adviser, who will solve all practical doubts for you by telling you what to do and what to avoid. Then it supplies you with an object in the shape of a minutely prescribed life, consisting chiefly of observances which occupy the mind equally well whatever its own moods may be. By such helps as these, and by its whole spirit and system, the Roman Communion is very frequently successful in quieting and soothing those who have had much restlessness and trouble of mind before. Rome is therefore the natural refuge of those who think, or act as if they thought, that they were sent into the world to seek first their own comfort and ease of mind. The consolations, and even what are at first sight the

painful duties, of Romish religion are for the most part carefully contrived means of relieving us from the burden of
ourselves which I cannot help thinking we were intended to
carry.   In this case once more I would ask you to apply the
same test as before, and, putting aside thoughts of personal
inward comfort, consider whether the distinctive features of
Romish religious life agree with the letter and spirit of the
Bible, and whether they promote a higher communion with
God, and a worthier and more really useful life towards
others.

I do not go into the question whether the English Church
and clergy might not with advantage possess a greater guiding
power over the minds and lives of individual Christians, without injury to the personal liberty of spirit which seems to
me the first condition of a truly Divine life.   It is a question
with many sides, and not easily answered.   But I do say that
the one great instrument of guidance which the Church ot
England already possesses, viz. the Prayer-book, is, almost
without exception, of the best and most wholesome kind.   It
leaves us to the responsibility of choosing our own path in
life, and does not follow us minutely into its several changes
and conditions, but keeps steadily before us the image of an
ever-present God, and yet more steadily the unclouded image
of His character, which all systems of personal religion, Romish
and Protestant alike, are so prone to darken.   Its purpose (as
for instance in the two pairs of morning and evening Collects
and the Collect before the Commandments) is not, when the
work of life has lost its savour, to provide a consecrated substitute, but to remind us for Whom all work is done, and to
quicken life again at its very springs by pointing to Himself,
and not any earthly representatives of Him or homage offered
to Him, as the one permanent source of hope and peace.
Such help as this is far harder to use than what Rome
supplies, it requires the constant renewal of our whole selves;
but it is harder just because its purpose is so much higher
and nobler.

This letter is already much longer than I intended it to be
when I began, and the subject is endless; but I must stop
now.   I hope that nothing here said will give you pain.   On

the other hand my wish has been, not to conceal my own
very strong opinions on the subject, and I am sure this is
what you would wish yourself. I hope you will let me hear
from you again in a few days.

To THE REV. PROFESSOR LIGHTFOOT

CAVERSHAM GROVE, READING,
November 3rd, 1862.

. . . I have got and partly read Colenso's book. His
fussy wordiness is trying; but on the whole I feel less inclined
to blame him for publishing it than before, though the consequences are likely to be bad enough. I suppose we shall all
now be obliged to study the O. T. a little more, but I fear
it is nervous work for those of us who would rather *quieta non
movere* in that particular matter. I cannot help fearing that
we shall sooner or later be driven to take some such ground
as that of Ewald and Bunsen, however little satisfied with
their special criticisms. But at present I feel as if I knew
nothing either way.

To MR. A. MACMILLAN

ST. IPPOLYTS, *November 25th*, 1862.

. . . "Some one thing." Yes, so I say to myself (say)
twice a day; but which? Text must always go on till done.
Commentary ought to be being prepared for years beforehand; and Lightfoot will so soon be ready with something,
that I don't like to be much behindhand; also one wants
some theological work that is not all BLX. am., etc;[1]
also the three apostles will cover what I have to say on
divers things; at least I hope before printing to be able
to make up my mind what I have to say. Then I took up
the Simon and Co. as a rapid and remunerative job, and
have actually (a great fact) written a great deal, almost ready
for the press; so that can hardly be put in the cupboard.
Thus, like the youth in *Bleak House*, I take credit to myself

[1] Viz. symbols representing manuscripts.

for adjourning Winer and things in general; though the latter topic sometimes threatens to take precedence of everything. This is a lamentable state of things, I daresay; but how to mend it?

To Mr. A. Macmillan

St. Ippolyts, December 26th, 1862.

My dear Macmillan—I rather want to have a few words with you on book matters. One consequence of your conclave at Lightfoot's rooms the other night was a strict injunction to me from him and Westcott to give up everything else (except N. T. text) and work steadily at the notes on St. James, and then on my other epistles. Rebellious though I be, I must confess that it is good advice, and I am prepared to act on it. Said notes will certainly take me a long time; and, when they are done, there will remain a big piece of work in the shape of introduction and essays, critical and theological, to be done before going to press. All this and other thoughts of my own of the same kind have been leading me to suspect that I ought to shelve Simon de Montfort and Co. I do so very reluctantly, as I enjoy it thoroughly, and have written a great deal almost ready for the printer. But, even keeping the book within the narrowest limits, I have still a great deal before me. If I were to put everything else completely away, it would still take several, probably many, months. I should never in the first instance have undertaken it except as a means of rapidly getting some money, in which it has signally failed; and the series to which it was to belong has to all appearance dropped through. I shall still hope some day to go on with it, and it is a great vexation to me to let it alone now, but on the whole it seems wisest

In its place another small plan has arisen, which seems rational. The work upon St. James, which is now to occupy me chiefly, will necessarily involve minute study of the LXX., of Proverbs, and the kindred books of the O. T., and perhaps still more, Wisdom and Ecclesiasticus. You may remember that long ago I undertook to edit those two books for Dr. Smith; and, though his commentary is apparently shelved, I have still always hoped some time or other to complete the edition. For the last year or two, however, I have sometimes thought that, without waiting for that, I should like to print a revised *translation* of those two books separate from the rest of the Apocrypha. I fancy that a great many people would like to have them so, to whom they are now practically lost by being buried under Bel and the Dragon, Judith, etc. And the last day [or two?] it has occurred to me that they would form a good subject for a not unpopular volume of your Golden Treasury series, which would have the further advantage of being remunerative. I should entirely exclude all critical matter, which would require much labour, and for which all the materials are not yet published. It would be merely a revision of the Authorised Version from the Greek, with *perhaps* a very few short explanatory notes where absolutely necessary. In the case of Ecclesiasticus there are two different arrangements of the parts (with some differences of text), the Greek and the Latin. In a critical edition both must be taken into account. The Authorised Version follows the Latin arrangement; I should simply follow the Greek. My Greek text would be constructed almost entirely from the four great MSS.; of course it would not appear. Of course this little book would take *some* time from other things, but very little. Nearly all the *study* required for doing it is what I ought in any case to do with a view to St. James. It would be to me very enjoyable work, and I have little doubt that the volume would sell well. Write and tell me what you think.—Very truly yours,

FENTON J. A. HORT.

To MR. A. MACMILLAN

ST. IPPOLYTS, *January 4th*, 1863.

My dear Macmillan—I acquiesce in your verdict without a murmur, at all events for some time to come, and will try to gird myself resolutely to the commentary and the text. Of course you do not expect me to agree in your estimate of

Wisdom and Ecclesiasticus, which seem to me books of singular interest for their own sakes as well as historically. I do not indeed agree with Tom Hughes in wishing they replaced Proverbs and Ecclesiastes in the Canon, as there are divers good reasons for not making them Scripture ; and he obviously did not appreciate Proverbs and Ecclesiastes. But I do think they are very much more than echoes of the older wisdom, for, to mention only one point, they represent some of the most wholesome effects of Greek thought on the Jewish mind.

One thing that made me think of the plan is that they are the truest link between the O. T. proper and St. James, who is himself a 'flyleaf.'

I will now work hard at St. James, and try to get his commentary done. But I should greatly shrink from publishing him alone. I quite wish to combine with him all my epistles, viz. 1, 2 Peter and Jude. This will make, to say the least, a portly volume, as there will be an immense introduction, which will virtually have to include all the great N. T. critical questions discussed of late years in Germany, and even the Church history of a century and a half. There must also be some heavy theological essays in Jowett's manner. In some respects it would be a relief to have *something* printed, and so to separate James from the rest ; but practically this would be impossible in the historical part of the introduction.

I am very anxious to see the type, as I cannot make it out from Westcott's description. But I suspect that anyhow I am not likely to be ready for two or three years, even with unremitting work. If I had no parish and no nerves, it might be different.

To his Mother

St. Ippolyts, *January 5th*, 1863.

. . . I cannot let the 5th of January pass by without sending you one line just to tell you (what you know already) how precious you are to us all, and to send you all possible good wishes from us both. We do quite trust that with God's blessing your two doctors will between them set you on your legs again; but we have under present circumstances more faith in Dr. Kate than in any of them, and are so glad to know that she has really succeeded in putting you into a band-box and walking you off to Brecon. So now what you have got to do is to set hard to work to amuse yourself as much as you can; have Mudie (or some substitute) for part of the day, try to know every stone in the Priory by heart, see what mosses you can find in the Priory walks, or something of that sort.

To THE REV. B. F. WESTCOTT

ST. IPPOLYTS, *February 9th*, 1863.

. . . I have a piece of news which will perhaps surprise you. We have decided to leave St. Ippolyts for three years, and live chiefly with my father and mother at Cheltenham. There is a twofold reason for this : first (the immediate occasion), my mother's very low state of health and eyesight, which makes our presence almost a necessity; and, secondly, my own health, which has declined very much this winter, and requires a long rest from the worry of parish life. . . . I must still go to the Alps or some such place in the summers. Naturally botany and geology will occupy me a good deal, if only for medical reasons; as they will attract me to the Cotteswolds, and so supply both exercise and pure air. But I shall hope to get through a good deal of other work too.

I had a friend staying here not long ago, who helped me to explore the drift which covers this country, and interpreted its pebbles and fossils, which are tolerably numerous. He identified it clearly as chiefly composed of the waste of lias, Oxford clay, and Kalloway rock, besides flints, and some sandstone from the Old Red. The common fossil is the monstrous oyster of the Oxford clay, *Gryphœa dilatata*.

To THE REV. B. F. WESTCOTT

ST. IPPOLYTS, *February 17th*, 1863.

. . . I am wading wearily through Colenso's *Psalms*. Was there ever such a mess ? I hope you saw Mat. Arnold's (*second*) article in the February *Macmillan*.

Your scepticism amuses me much. Our drift is assuredly
not exclusively formed from the waste of our own immediate
neighbourhood (I suppose very little drift is); indeed the
number of flints is to me the most surprising fact about it.
Mr. Norwood told me that all the drift about which he knows
anything in the E. of England has come from the N. or
N.W., and the N.W. agrees well with the contents of our
drift. He has a minute and exact knowledge of the fossils and
rocks of the lias and inferior oolite of Gloucestershire and
Yorkshire, and a tolerable knowledge of those of higher formations. Some specimens he took to town to show to Woodward of the British Museum, and Etheridge the palæontologist
of Jermyn Street, both of whom he knows well; and they
(Etheridge in particular) came to the same conclusions. The
majority of species are from the lias, all the others, that can
be certainly identified, from Oxford clay, Kalloway rock, and
perhaps Oxford calcareous grit. There are also rolled pebbles
of quartz, which Norwood says can come from nowhere nearer
than Old Red, though doubtless not directly thence. They
make up, he says, what is called the Bredon (drift) gravel in
Worcestershire, and occur, as rounded as now, in beds in the
New Red, out of which they were probably washed. This
one drift includes remains from all the softer formations to the
N.W. except the Kimmeridge clay, which appears to be a very
narrow strip, and the gault, which there is some reason to
think not to be fossiliferous hereabouts. At all events there
are the two great soft formations, the lias and the Oxford
clay.

To the Rev. B. F. Westcott

ST. IPPOLYTS, *March* 19*th*, 1863.

. . . My mother has been ordered to Vichy, and we are
to accompany her. She is to be there for two visits of three
or four weeks each, with an equal interval probably somewhere
in the Auvergne mountains. We shall then, I hope, be able
to get some little way into the Alps, whence I shall probably
go alone for a few weeks into the higher regions.
. . . I had three-quarters of an hour at Jermyn Street, and

showed Etheridge some twenty-three species of minute shells, etc. (chiefly fry), which had come out of a single small piece of soft sandstone from one drift. He pronounced the forms to belong without question to the calcareous grit (lower coral rag).

. . . Huxley's recent books have been somewhat annoying me. Those people seem incapable of seeing beyond their scalpels and test-bottles. On the other hand, there are some slight signs, I think, that their friends among University men are becoming less one-sided. For one, M. Arnold's second paper on Colenso had surely the true ring of belief, with all its defects.

END OF VOL. I

Printed by R. & R. CLARK, LIMITED, *Edinburgh*